CW00557860

Contents

D. A. SMITH

The Blood of Outcasts

The Bane Sword Trilogy

09/02/2022

First edition

This book was professionally typeset on Reedsy.
Find out more at reedsy.com

Acknowledgement

To mum and dad, who always encouraged me to be whatever I wanted,
To Shannon, who supports me no matter what.

DRAMATIS PERSONAE

OF THE GREAT CLANS

DATTORI (ELIMINATED)

DATTORI HOJIMOTO	WARLORD OF THE DATTORI (RECORDED DECEASED)
DATTORI MASAKO	HIGH BANNERMAN (RECORDED DECEASED)
MURAKAMI ZAKI	VASSAL TO DATTORI (NOT KNOWN)
FENAKA DABURA	VASSAL/HIGH CAPTAIN (NOT KNOWN)
DATTORI EDAN	HIGH ADVISOR TO HOJIMOTO (NOT KNOWN)

YOKUSEI

YOKUSEI KARINARO	WARLORD OF THE YOKUSEI	
REMOVED	*REMOVED*	
YOKUSEI SATOSHI	HIGH BANNERMAN	*2ND SON*
YOKUSEI GORO	RETAINER	*3RD SON*

KITSUTANA

KITSUTANA BARINAI	WARLORD OF THE KITSUTANA
REMOVED	*REMOVED*

SIKARA

SIKARA OJI	UNKNOWN

OF THE SAMAKI HEATHEN CLANS

BY ORDER OF THE GODLORD, TO BE ELIMINATED ON SIGHT

SHUJI-TO

SHUJI HAYATO	WARLORD OF SHUJI-TO	
SHUJI KEN ICHI	HIGH BANNERMAN	*1ST SON*
SHUJI SADA	RETAINER	*2ND SON*
SHUJI YOSHI	RETAINER	*3RD SON*
SHUJI GOYA	HIGH ADVISOR	*WIFE*

MAKO-TO

| MAKO OTSUTAN | WARLORD OF MAKO-TO | |
| MAKO HISAO | HIGH BANNERMAN | *1ST SON* |

KASUKI-TO

KASUKI GIN	WARLORD OF KASUKI-TO	
KASUKI FINGAR	HIGH BANNERMAN	*1ST SON*
KASUKI TSUJO	RETAINER	*2ND SON*
KASUKI IMARI	HIGH ADVISOR	*WIFE*
KASUKI MOKA	DAUGHTER	

DAICHI-TO

DAICHI MAKI	WARLORD OF DAICHI-TO	
DAICHI TETSUYA	HIGH BANNERMAN	*1ST SON*
DAICHI HARU	RETAINER	*1ST DAUGHTER*
DAICHI AIMI	RETAINER	*2ND DAUGHTER*
DAICHI HIRA	RETAINER	*3RD DAUGHTER*

MURAKAMI (MISSING/UNRECORDED)

OF THE HONOURABLE GODLORD'S CLAN

AKUTO

AKUTO TAKAHASHI	FIFTH GODLORD UNDER THE HEAVENS OF BASHO
KITSUTANA KITA	HIGH CAPTAIN OF THE OKAMI GUARD
YOKUSEI KABUTOMARU	OKAMI WOLFGUARD
AKUTO BARAKI	OKAMI WOLFGUARD 3RD SON
MURAKAMI AINU	OKAMI WOLFGUARD
BARIBARI JIZU	HIGH ADVISOR

UNDER AKUTO EMPLOY

SOSHIST PO	BORDERING REPUBLIC OF TAOS RELATIONS
SOSHIST TI	BORDERING REPUBLIC OF TAOS RELATIONS

CAPTAIN WANRIN	WOLFPAD ARMY
CAPTAIN ILNA	WOLFPAD ARMY
CAPTAIN GIJU	WOLFPAD ARMY

OF THE MOST HEINOUS AND WANTED PERSONS

BY ORDER OF THE GODLORD, TO BE CAPTURED AND DISBANDED

THE AKATE MERCENARY GROUP

GENARO KEKKEI	LEADER – ALSO KNOWN AS THOUSAND HANDS KEKKEI
YOKU JINTO	MEMBER – DO NOT APPROACH
ROPI THE DART	MEMBER
BUNTA	MEMBER
OBORO	MEMBER
THE HAWK	MEMBER
DANZO	MEMBER

TO BE QUESTIONED IN CONNECTION WITH AKATE

DAISUKI HAYATO	BUSINESSMAN
TAMIKURA FENA	LORD OF THE CHISAI TOWNSHIP
TAMIKURA BOICHI	ADVISOR TO TAMIKURA
TAMIKURA MINOKA	WIFE
BUNTA	OF THE BORDER TRADING GROUP
YOKU HEBIKAWA	SHAMAN OF GREED
THE SISTERS OF AIBO	WORSHIPPERS OF FALSE GODS

A MAP OF BASHO

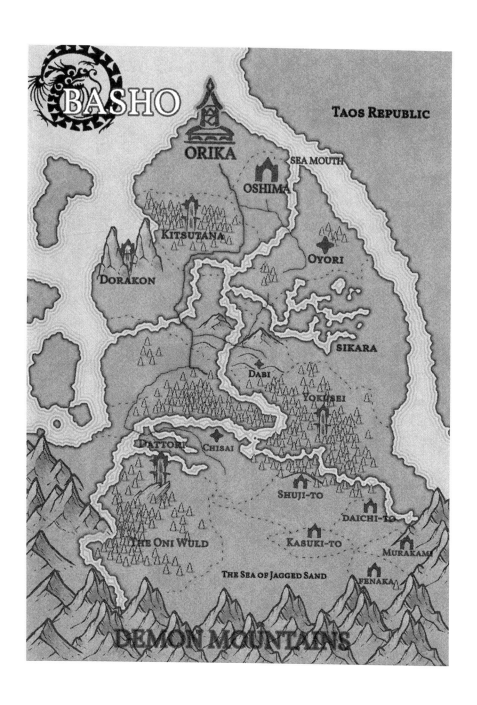

PART 1

"Every journey wearies the soul in the end. Give up, don't go on, what a waste this has been."

Source Unknown

Chapter 1

My wounds throb as I'm battered by the ferocity of the Kirisam's waters. Crying out in pain is futile. I gasp for air, swallowing more of the murk. Honour won't allow me to surrender to my wounds, not when I've got more blood to spill. My katana has not tasted its last.

The curs' souls will not climb to the heavens in smoke and ash, I'll send them to the mountains where the demons eat.

Agony.

Trying to grab anything, I spin through the waters. A spindly root reaches back. I clutch it. Softened by the waters but strong because that's the way it was made, it does not hold me back. I cling to it with the rest of the life that spills from my belly, that pours from my neck into the rush. I fight, like I always have, and force my other hand through the water, clutching the gnarled hand harder. I pull. Gods, I pull. A fire burns in both my lungs now. Not the kind that warms me, but the kind of fire that ignites the cool flames of the death god's servants around me, the flames of reckoning, of finality. But I pull once more and a bright light pierces through my eyes, the rush of the water louder now, I splutter. The dead flames recede and life, by its own small measure, floods back into me.

A gargle, air escaping through the gash in my neck, I'm not able to satisfy my bodily need. If only for the pain itself, I want to die. A tuft of grass between my fingers. Long grasses that Master loved, the reeds that sway as the gentle breeze caresses them.

He's gone.

I scramble up the bank, a pitiful beast. My stomach wound, and the unravelling organs, pull and tug. If I could, I'd scream like a horse-headed demon but I gargle again. Gnawing a hole in my cheek, I try to redirect my focus but it's useless.

I'm resolved to it. I must live. My blood spilling around me will be my salvation. With my last breaths, words on my tongue that I've somehow always known, I deny everything Master has taught me. What are the teachings of a dead man worth, anyway?

I slide my hand between the earth and me. I wince, but what is pain now? Freeing my hand, I chant the strange chant. Arm outstretched, my bloody palm imprinted into the ground eternal, I say, "Heangghnn. Ognh." My approximation of speech is but a garbled mess, I wish they'd know me now. The gods, anything. What use is my accursed blo...

–Impossible.

Something responds. I feel its wickedness through a gulf of distance. Worlds? Heavens? – stand between us. Damn it all. Come, take my life, drink it, I beseech thee. By the power of my accursed blood, pass into this realm, or end it all, I do not care.

No lightning strike, no great power, no burst of energy, nothing the Heavenists would have you believe. My skin crawls as if something walks over my grave. Stomach cramping, I wretch, but that might be the gaping hole sending a cascade of daggers throughout my body with every breath. A white blast. A pit of the worst black.

Something has come. Something does tread my resting place.

Are you...your senses, can you hear me? A chuckle, then a cacophony of familiar animalistic screeches overlaid into a voice crisp like the first frost, deep like the thunders. **Near death, but you opened this gate...though not as grand as you think, mortal. Not nearly.** It pauses, spits. **Stubborn. Trouble. A malleable puppet perhaps? Why should I not just let the life leak out of you? You've broken the first treaty...so you have my than–**

"L...lnghhh." I interrupt. "Hngh." What I want to say is lost to hacks and splutters. Yet, it is amused. I have its attention. It begins again, its voice raking through my mind. It knows what I cling to life for.

Funny creature. Let me help. Intriguing creature. Easily done, yes. But why?

"Mmggh." My throat warms; the scratchy grating subsides. I gulp. "Let me avenge mine. My honour. The peoples beneath the dragons…Hngh. Gods, the pain!" I stop as lights dance in my vision. My throat is the least of my worries. Not that I see anything, not that I even know this creature's form. But I feel it. Like an oni packed tightly into a cage, its presence is too much, too overbearing. A godsborne, it has to be. But one far beyond anything I've known. What have I done? "The dogs scurry under the dragons' watch. They yap and bark to their own tune. They forsake the gods and worship one man, but he is not a man of the gods. Let me at least strangle the cur an−"

SILENCE. Very well. But, human, you will be bound by that wish. You will not live a minute after you're done with this petty task. It chuckles and screeches. Excitement wells around me, pins pricking every pore. *Thump, thump*, it parades around. A foot grasps my face, picks me up by my head, peeling me off the ground in agony. It brings me up to face it. Blurry, I can't focus, can't take in its form. It's breath hot against my skin, its presence peeling away at my sanity.

I have but one other condition. You will not leave these lands without a leader. Do not presume to think you can do this in haste, mortal. You will shatter the lands and rebuild them in my stead. You will break apart the godless and depose their man. You will bring the crown of the gods back to this land, and as an apostle of the heavens, prepare the throne in my name. A godlord? No, that will be crushed. It will be an emperor that unites Basho's lands. You are the instrument who will bring the unity I need − rend it apart, open the gates once more.

"But…"

Die here and be done with it, but if you want to live, want to regain your foolish honour, you do it under my rule. The words wash the pain away, igniting the fire within me, burning death's grip away. **Entertain me, if you will. I'm bored waiting for my own to come back.**

The brightest light splits my vision, the blackest dark sucks me into its depths, and I fall, with nothing to hold, into the void of madness.

* * *

I open my eyes, dazed. Each finger, I flex in turn. The patter of some animal joins the rush of the waters behind me, but it is gentle now, more soothing than before. I open my eyes again; bright light floods my vision like a flash of the life I clung to. I am reborn, but into what? Into a world without anything I love. Into a world where only the anger Master tried to curb will reign supreme.

Did anger bring this upon us, Master? Did you blame me in the end? Did you wish that knife would cut me deep, deeper than I could survive? Those foolish words were not yours in the end, no. You were scared. You wouldn't wish that upon me, but I will live it nonetheless.

My eyes focus. I scan the area and see that I barely made it out of the reeds. Ahead of me, the earth is imprinted with the only evidence things are out of my control. The treaty was there to balance, was there to give humanity its due after the Victory, but now I've rent that asunder. I shiver wildly, shaking to the very core at the thought of a godsborne that could restore life. What have I wrought?

My accursed blood should never be drawn.

I squint as the sun sends its first tendrils through the land, lances of deep yellow split through the forest that looms further up the bank. Evergreen sentries guard my way forward. I rise, stagger, but pull through the haze as I right myself. Looking down at my body, my heart flutters and I stupidly grab at the tattered, white robes now dyed crimson; death was meant for me – maybe I will never truly live again.

The blood staining them is now the only evidence I have that Master existed.

Fingers run the rivets of my scars, across the line where my stomach was slashed open. Nothing. I follow it all the way from one side to another, it was as mortal as the katana stroke that tore open my neck, but that is no more. Gone, as if last night never happened. Fingers twitching over the thick, black, ungodly line. It shimmers with something not of this world. A sulphurous bite that snaps at me; magic beyond mortals – a godly bind.

4

I throw myself back down the bank, struggling to get my breathing under control, stumbling into the water. It engulfs me once more, sinking to the bottom. The yearning for air is painful but liberating. The *thump, thump* of my heart in my ears. Terrifying. I am alone now.

I have my honour. No, I need to regain my honour.

I am a warrior of the Dattori.

You will pay, Fox.

You will all pay.

Emerging from the waters, the droplets drip off me and so does the pity, the sadness I feel for myself, because now it is only anger. A wildness that won't give in until they are all gone.

Godsborne, whoever you were, I will do it. I am resolved to the war you wish to bring. But don't expect subservience. A leashed tiger is ferocious still, even with its reach shortened. Yet, it would have no trouble turning and devouring its captor. The leash only works one way.

As I drag myself from the waters, I turn back to look at my reflection, trying to piece itself together in the shimmering surface. Skin taut, unyielding on my neck in an ugly black scar – I flinch away. The same ethereal quality to it as the others, hair slicked around it blending in. Wishful thinking that I was named the Hawk for decisive, sharp, and ruthless command. I purse my lips, then spit at the reflection, laughing to myself. If my lips were thicker, fuller, maybe I would have been able to make my living as those that Aibo loves. A simpler life. I hack and wheeze as the laughter takes hold. A tear streaks down my face. Master always said he was glad he didn't have to chase the men away...no great family would waste a son on a hawkish woman who doesn't recognise that she is such herself. A warrior first, whose thighs were built for squeezing the life out of men, not for inviting them in. He was a son of a whore if I ever knew one. A smile tugs at the corners of my mouth. It'll be my last.

Tearing a strip from the ragged edges of the robe, I tie them close to me. For my honour may yet be hard won but I can at least have my dignity intact. I go to my side, grabbing desperately for a hilt, out of habit. It's second nature and I recoil when I don't find it there. The scar on my chest pulses and I grasp at it, sucking on my teeth as I fight back a sob. My head is a mess as I try to grasp the images of my death. I'm only here now because of this scar, the wound that Master gave me in his final moments. The path that he carved for me in my own blood.

Striding forward, the grasses rustle as if the wind is caressing them. I gust through with all the elegance of the elements. I have one job now. One measly job before I can rest. I'll cut them, the lords and their women, I'll crush the Lord Council piece by piece, and I'll break him, the godlord, the dog who started this. That greedy whoreson.

But first, those who were happy to be the impetus behind his wrath will know I live. The fieldclans thought my ire would end in a river? No. They will know I still walk this land. My body aches and it's because it's missing a limb. A vital organ. CrowKiller and HighWolf, my pair, my loves, my swords. I'm coming to get you; mother is coming home.

Chapter 2

I stand at the edge of the Takus wood, between the green of life and the yellow of it failing throughout the valley. My destination is even further beyond. I am thankful by Izenta's design the Kirisam runs away from the heart of Basho. The river carried me homeward in my first death. My clanlands lie in front of me. A step backward in preparation is needed before I can drive the blade forward, again.

The trudge is long and perilous, my feet calloused and cut. I have nothing but my dirtied robes and even they are more like a pauper's ragged cloth.

Purpose guides me through the wood for a day, it's void of other life.

I'm a hawk, so the hunt is easy and quick. A rabbit soon burns on my fire and it's not long before I'm picking salty, stringy bits of what is left from between my teeth. My tongue roams the gaps the godsborne didn't fill, the teeth lost over my life. Anger has been a source of great power, limitless energy, and poor choices. I scream, shout into the darkness, which responds with silence. How can I survive now? With nothing?

A low hanging branch is my quarry, picking off the needles as I go.

The swordforms of Earth first, Wind, then Fire, and Air. I go through them one by one; the branch does not even come close to CrowKiller, but it makes do. I dance with my fire. The air whips around me and sweat flings from my face. Finishing in the Guard of Heaven. Knees give way. Panting. My forms are weak, pathetic. What have I become?

"Oho, ya here alone, missy?"

My heart flutters. I freeze. I'm a fool.

"I'm out of practice it seems," I say to those behind me. "Enjoying my first meal of my new start, and I get complacent. The gods have certainly had their way with me." I turn as I speak; predators can't talk and bite at the same time, nor am I such a fearsome looking prey they would think me any bother.

"No gods, not out 'ere for you, missy."

I swivel to a kneel upon my log, facing the intruders. Three of them; their breaths betrayers. Maybe more, there's a numbness to everything I am.

"Everythin' ya got." A ghoulish man steps out of his own shadow to greet me. Gaunt, might be close to death with the amount of meat on him. I expect his brothers are the same. Not enough to put me down. Fools. Common brigands.

"Nothing." I sweep across myself. "Can you not see? I've nothing but this rob–"

"Shaddap."

Ears ring. World flashing white in throbs, pain explodes in the side of my head. Another has hit me. Again, I meet the earth, spitting a tooth. Whore's breath, I don't need to lose any more. "We'll do talkin'. Yous got plenty for us, woman. Come here!"

Skeletal hands go to grab my wrists, breath so rancid it stings my cheek, rakes its spineless fingers down my back before I dodge backward, stumbling – rabbit rises in my throat.

"What have we got 'ere then, eh, boys? Give us it everything ya' got!"

Nothing, you've nothing. I squint in the dull mix of fire and moonlight, sizing up my quarry. Rags, that's all they've got between them, and worse than mine. Not even worth the kill. I jerk my head away and glance down at my bare, blistered feet. Maybe those rope sandals are worth it.

They surge at me. A stone-strong grasp catching my face, a pinch that sends a searing pain through my cheek, blood trickles from it. I'm hit, again and again. Lurching forward, I headbutt one of the animals. Pain flashes in my eyes; the cold, sharp tongue of a blade rakes across my side as they miss me. But I'm a fighter, a wild beast that cannot be stopped. They've made a mistake. If I can't overcome a couple of bandits, what hope do I have of toppling the very foundations of the Lord Council?

They steal backward, creating room between us. I seethe in fury, the spittle leaks, froths from the corners of my mouth.

"Ya' idiot! Why'd we do this then?" A punch or the godless' estimation of one is a meaty slap against his kin's face.

The second ghoul leaps for his companion, and they break out into a brawl amongst themselves, almost forgetting I'm here. Lunacy, it has to be. "She's mine!" One of them shouts.

"No! Watch 'er" The third moves out of the shadows. "Not agen. Not now we've got summat! Ikihara! Her things. Mighta gold." The pound of bone on flesh beats away his plea as these imbeciles squabble over me. The hawkish, risen from the dead, washed up old hag. What kind of place have I ended up that I'm a prize? One of the ghoulish men falls over the other. This will not do.

"Look – at – me!" I say, thinking this rage was gone, lost in death, but the urge returns. Beckoning. The itching that crawls around my body, swirls and pumps through my chest, an insatiable burning in my blood. An anger that cannot be quenched.

I snarl and move into a crow stance, gritting my teeth.

One and two are still locked in a mortal, pathetic struggle, while the third watches. My eyes widen and a ripple of energy, of excitement takes over me. In the dull light, I catch the glint of a knife in the third's hand. A small blade. I lick my lips, tasting the fetid air.

Taking a deep breath, each muscle does what every battle, every duel and every hunt has taught it. I spring, with all the grace of a haggard, old lion. But it's enough for these.

My lead foot sure under me, he hasn't noticed yet. In one swift movement, I grab his knife-wielding wrist in my right and slam my free palm into his elbow. A crack splits through the wood. His elbow gives way, tendon and bones smashing and splintering into one and other. His grip loosens, the knife falls. I catch it and pirouette slashing out his throat before the pain even registers as a shout, a yelp. Just a gargle and he is gone.

I have the others' attention now.

They peel themselves away from each other and scramble to their feet. I face off against them. Lava burns seething tracks through my veins. Vision swimming, the rabbit rising to my throat again. I don't have the wherewithal to stop it now and hack up in front of them.

It's not right, this feeling. I falter in my stance, catching myself on a sapling that bends with my weight, almost losing my step while the enemies watch on. A snicker escapes a rancid mouth.

Swallowing, I taste something not right. I smack my lips and run my tongue along what's left of my teeth. Sour, off. Sulphur. I grimace, and the blood on my cheek cracks, the wound weeps. I put my finger in the wound and drag it to meet the corner of my mouth. Tasting my own blood, feeling the power, the magic that I'm cursed with, it becomes clear. Behind the rot, a sulphurous, sweet smell of the heavenly realm. This forest, it belongs to them. The godsborne. Minor, in comparison to the one who saved me, but dangerous all the same – the poor souls don't even know they're dead. Their pitiful lives bound to repeat themselves as food for ghosts.

I wanted to never use this again, but I settle myself; a light blood-fever takes ahold, my curse does its trick. Clawing at my wound, I smear blood across myself and scream at the spirits that lets them know their trickery is naught before me. Something in it freezes them, forcing their guises to fail. And I catch it for the first time, a wink in their eye, a ghostly purple flame that burns within each pupil.

And ghostly it is. The undying spirits of the vast Forest of Souls. Then, I'm not following the main branch of the Kirisam, just one of its larger fingers that rip through clanlands. Yokusei clanlands. A flutter in my chest as a swarm of butterflies gather there. I cannot be caught here, not in their territory. No. It's too soon to meet one of the lapdogs of the godlord, I can't be found alive. They are a Guardian clan, men in charge of one of the last places that the godsborne inhabit. A place where no man other than the sacred chosen should tread. Where only the heavenly beasts and creatures should live. But such a place was under my care. Is still under my care.

And I'm no man.

I look upon them. Oh, precious souls, I'm sorry for what I'm about to do. By my honour I shall avenge your departure from this land hundredfold in the weeks, months, and years to come.

The frozen Spirit-Bound aren't so for long. Possessed bodies of deadmen dash towards me; first, I'm attacked by putrid death. With the veil lifted, the full stench of bodies long dead is upon me. I turn. Letting the first past me, I paste a sliver of blood across the knife which flickers like a flame in the moonlight. I cut the second ghoul in two. If there's one thing I learnt in my death throes, it's my blood is sharp. Before the first can turn, I am upon it. A beast upon its prey. It is gone. Panting, I get up. The blood fever dulls and my body shouts in pain renewed. The black scars across my neck, chest, and belly burn. I take the rotted kimono from one and throw it over myself. My swollen feet welcome the sandals, no matter the smell.

The first spoils of this war.

With a sash fashioned from the last of my ruined robes, the knife is wrapped to my side. I track backward, but the night is clouded now, the forest grows quieter still. My heart beats in my throat. I can even hear it over the silence that engulfs me.

A snap. Something moves out there. Swift, quiet, but careless in my presence.

Shadows? More to my periphery, I'm surrounded.

A thud; my ears rings louder, my knees go weak.

Chapter 3

The carriage rattles and creaks beneath me. With each bump in the road, my wrists grow raw, bound with harshly wrought metal. I cannot make out my captors, but for the din of plate...soldiers, then. Fuck it all.

Rain drips down my neck, into my already sodden kimono, exciting the smell of rot that is buried deep within it. The skies have opened. The rain numbs the rest of my body, beating down memories upon me; the hushing house servants as we tried to stifle our laughter during morning meditation. Those younger, less disciplined days are lost to the husk of a warrior I am now.

"The she-devil lives," a throaty baritone says. "Which of the hells spat you out? Eh, I would move to get a better look at you, but they've done these shackles a bit tight. Not enough movement in them, can't even stretch."

I look up sharply. Head throbs as though I've been punched, reminding me of the days spent nursing steel-borne bruises, sparring with Zaki, Yoji and Hatamo. I wince, not from the wound this time, but from the memories I need to keep buried.

"Hey!" He says once more. "You alright?"

My vision doubles, Sukami's light scorching the back of my eyes until I focus on the man. Muscled, even in the tattered cloth he wears, I can tell he is of the warrior-class. Only those who've swung the sword thousands upon thousands of times have such a physique. But he's old, the bags under his narrowed eyes tell of someone who lives right at the centre of the upheaval.

"Warrior, why're you so incautious with your tongue?" I say. "Your shackles keep you alive. Come over here and I promise, by my honour, I'll slay you."

"You looked like the type." He turns to a bundle of rags, stretching his foot out and kicking, eliciting a groan from the pile. It too is shackled. "Told you, boy. This one's a fighter. A beast, maybe a warrior, too." The loose-tongued warrior looks me up and down and continues, "What household do you belong to?"

"What is it to you?"

"Why are you in a Yokusei prison cart?"

"Gods...damn it all."

"You didn't know?"

I hold my tongue, my heart flutters, this is bad. Damned to all the hells.

"You're a Yokusen prisoner," he smirks. "But so am I, Genaro Kekkei of the Akate. You're in good for–"

"Akate?" I know I'd heard that before. I know this man; his name earnt for the sheer number of men he could call upon, now lost to a past age. A thousand men sounds a bit...off for a mercenary. But rumours travel hard and fast. And for those thousands he controlled, he is but a shadow now, it seems. A time of war and warriors past. Of honour now lost to the annals of history. "Kekkei Thousand Hands. What's the leader of the largest mercenary group the Lord Council has ever suffered doing in a prison cart?" I chuckle, maybe it is good fortune. Two tigers in the same cage will either destroy each other or destroy the cage.

"–Answer this." Kekkei's eyes narrow, a smirk tugs at the corner of his mouth. "Why are you this far north, southern warrior? I don't quite think it's the twang of the mountains, and you haven't enough horns." He raises one eyebrow. "But that accent isn't midlandish. You're a warrior, right?"

"What does it matter?"

"Rōnin, am I wrong? No one looks like that with a master." He pauses, eyes-widening. "Southener, secretive and rōnin. Samaki? You're no–"

An anger-fuelled leap is stayed as the cart skits to a halt, throwing me sideways. Wrists flare red hot. Chains rattle a shriek. A horse whinnies as a rider pulls up next to us clad in a set of yellow and black acid-etched plate; his ghostly mask set into a grimace. The expression unchanged as he unclips the mask, hanging loose. "Quiet! You are prisoners of the Lord Council. You will not utter a single word unless it is under Yokusei order."

Damn it all.

"Vassal lords are really taking this serious these days." Kekkei has eyes only for me as he, no doubt, seeks to undermine this man's goodwill. A challenge to his honour. "Eh, Rōnin?"

I'm not sure what his game is, nor can I really be sure he knows more than my being master-less. Women warriors are few and far between in the north, where they bow to their sires. Southern women are different; the Samaki lands are harsh, and the Lord Council's grabbing claws cannot quite grasp the untamed beast. It's a place that builds women of my ilk, but warriors of my class are rarer still. Is that glower knowing?

My lip quivers, and I bite down on the lies. "Yokusei?" I growl and turn to the seated pretender. "Were there any such warriors who could command any respect among that household?" I don't question the rider, but play along with Thousand Hand's game, whatever he hopes to achieve with this nonsense.

Were the mercenary's name still worth the gold it was built upon, a troupe would have descended and sprung us from this godsforsaken processions already.

The Age of War is truly gone.

A twitch the rider can't hide ripples throughout his body, cracking the mask. Clipping the ghostly grimace back in place, his hand flies into the air in a flurry of signals. Sandals pound on dirt in response. Plate-on-plate scratches, shuffles over each other. Armour escorts surround us once more.

"Ten pikes. You must be a dangerous man, Thousand Hands." I stay my laugh as it makes my position better none. "Metsuku's ill-omen shines upon me." They may as well wave their cocks about for all the action they back it up with; spineless. Northern.

A shout and we're moving again, the warriors of the Yokusei march tighter to the carriage.

* * *

With a close eye on us, and over-eager pikes dancing above their warriors, day passes into night and the marching stops. To our insult, handfuls of rice are dropped onto the floor of the cart around us, doused in excrement that I've let go of in front of my fellow prisoners. They've made me a dog – I'll have them just for that. Our captor clan spits on their own code, revealing how widespread the godlord's folly is. Even as prisoners, a warrior commands respect; the immaturity of this clan, and its readiness to follow current rule to its own demise shines through the night like the roar of Sukami's inferno. The inside of my cheek is chewed into shreds to quell my rising anger. I've a coppery taste in my mouth, spitting out the blood as it pools. I wouldn't want a blood fever. Not here.

The night looms over me, a pest. A rushed camp is spread in pockets around our prison cart, marked by a few meagre campfires. Still on the track. It would seem their prisoners are too valuable to spare time enough to set up properly; only bedrolls, no coverings, and the light rattle of armour these men daren't take off. Embers of fires glow lethargically and a charred, fishy smoke hangs in the air. I lick my lips, the swines.

Turning to my companion, I want to tear his tongue from his mouth, "Stop it!" I say. "That infernal whistling. Stop."

"Grouchy after a nap?"

"I've not slept," I say, "not amongst enemies. Not with you around."

"I'm not your enemy." He pauses and leans closer with a slight jingle from his chains waking up. "Rōnin, how would you like to get out of here?"

Mercenaries, whether they were warriors to start off with, or just thugs, have a way of being that gets to me. A warrior, in this case, forgets his honour, his sensibility, and turns to pomp and machoism, lies and delusions. I scoff, "You're chained, as well as I. They've spared no metals in their production, my blacksmiths would jeer at the waste. We're done."

"Your blacksmiths, Rōnin?"

My damned loose fool's lips. I'm blunt as the smith's hammer. I quiet. He doesn't press the matter, and says, "Do you know why they call me Thousand Hands?"

"A miscount, perhaps?"

"Smart, huh, Rōnin." The forest deadens, holds its breath. Kekkei's eyes dart side to side and focus back on me. "I have more hands than just my own. They run to my tune."

Gaps between the trees writhe. Like an owl, my vision pierces the darkness, it's never overcome with the turn of day like my fellow people. But that's my secret. Only my master knew.

"I see."

"Quiet!" a shout near me pierces the silence. "The Lord Captain told you quiet!" He leans in close to the bars. Rapid, shallow breaths tell me more about the man than speaking to him would. Perhaps only a warrior by training, he's never seen a battle. None of those trained in this Time of Peace have, yet. Something stirs, and I'll be at the forefront of it. The glint of sweat on his brow tells me that this man isn't suited to the armour, let alone guarding such dangerous quarry.

"You hear it, boy?" Kekkei speaks to the guard.

"Quiet, dog!"

"The silence," I take my time. "You hear it don't you? The night's usual chatter is dead. What happens next?"

A whoosh of iron cutting air. A gargle. The guard is frantic, I feel it in him.

"Hito?" A pause. "HITO! CAPTAIN SATOSHI, WE'RE BESET UPON!"

Ah, a name to burn into memory.

The camp comes alive again with plate – it is why I prefer warrior robes. Grabbing his pike, the guard steps away from the cart and plunges it through an opening straight at Kekkei. A movement not even I follow, something erupts from the pile of groaning rags next to him.

"Impossible. Ho...HOW," the guard says. "Unhand it! Release it at once."

A young, gaunt looking boy, no. A change. He's more like a beast, a dirty and untamed amalgamation of sinewy muscle built for this. Intriguing.

Kekkei sits back against the bars, his eyes now closed, a slight smile drawn on his face. Gods, I hate mercenaries.

"Now! Unhand–"

Muscles brace. It's instantaneous, but I see it this time. The beast tugs on the pike, lashing out through the bars with a knife at the same time, punching a bloody hole in the guard; he's done, blood oozes from the mess that replaces face and helm. It pulls me in. My eyes are fixed on every tiny droplet. I'm entranced but I wrestle my senses back, looking again at the boy-made-monstrosity. The surface of his skin ripples like a lake with every minute movement of its powerful muscles. But again, it changes, the skin on his face bubbles. It multiplies in one patch, a growth out of control sags from his cheek; the crack of bones fills my ears as he transfigures in front of me. Teeth grow and protrude from his mouth, one arm breaks and twists of its own volition.

I know this filthy magic.

Kekkei hacks a cough from his reclined position, blood runs from either side of his mouth. He wasn't waiting, no. It was concentration, gathering godki for this barbaric ritual to the God of Greed, Don Yoku. "Meater? Thousand Hands?" My heart thumps. "He's a boy!" I reach my side to draw a sword but there isn't one there.

"No, it's not—" Kekkei coughs up more blood and lurches forward onto his still shackled hands. "You don't know!"

"I know enough!" Dangerous, he's a damned man.

The night now full of shouts, gargles, and disarray. I survey the camp and the armed men of the Yokusei run wild in every direction, unaware of friend or foe as they clash with each other, trip over their dead, and fall in ones and twos to flurries of arrows. I turn back to Kekkei, but the mutant is upon me. Its broken arm a claw that hangs in the air for a moment before it swipes down, a cataclysm of flesh. Sparks fly, steel peels away. My arms freed; it savages the cart, and I am out.

A glint catches the stillness of the moon on enamelled wood; I liberate the guard's katana, holding it out in front of me, drawing the blade. It sings an unpleasant song along the scabbard until it is free. It's not mine, the weight is off, and it's too clean, too unused, but still calm radiates through me with it. I am not whole, nowhere near, but it helps. Around me, no one notices our escape in the madness. The beast drops to the earth screaming as his body writhes again. The mutated masses retreat. Monstrous carnage replaced by the fragility of a boy. Open wounds instead of the horrific features, weeping with an aura of the gods only know what. Kekkei joins us, with the grace of a merc. He lands and winces while grabbing his side. I must be wrong as I notice sorrow in his eye as he looks upon the boy; mercenaries are missing compassion. Throwing the infant over his back, he starts a run, stops, and shouts, "Come!"

If he's done to the boy what I think he's done, Kekkei won't survive the night if I go with him. I'll make sure of it. There's no forgiveness for that. A child is no sacrifice to Don Yoku. "You're not the man I thought, Thousand Hands." I pause, thinking the Yokusei spot us, but they carry on in their search for whatever Kekkei brought with him out there.

"Come! If they regroup, you're caught," he says, "you won't get far in their lands."

Another arrow strikes true. Another body slaps the ground with a meaty thump. It almost seems funny, the night is the day's murky friend, to me, but I remind myself that it is an unforgiving void to them.

"No! My own journey lies ahead."

"I won't wait any longer, Hawk."

That name pierces right through me. Mouth hangs agape momentarily with surprise I hope the night swallows. He knows. I'm in trouble...the Lord Council cannot know me until I am upon them. If only I had Metsuku's shadow, I would disappear where I stand. "Don't utter that name. You risk everything!"

"Then, come, now!"

To our left the Yokusei have found their bearings. The archer has let up and they notice us. Three warriors, brandishing their katanas, let out cries in turn and run at us. The stolen sword still clasped in my hand, I meet their charge; one of them hesitates and that's where I start. A warrior's resolve is that of death: death of the enemy or death of the self. When you draw a sword there is nothing else. But this man, he doesn't know that, isn't sure of it. His footwork is sluggish. I cut him down, turning to his friends. The next takes the initiative, tries to use the opening my large, tired movements leave. I parry, knocking his blade to the side, severing his hand on the backswing. The last's courage is used up with the death of his friends and falls with them. Then, my knees buckle, breaths hard. The only thing I know is the pounding of blood in my ears, the tightening of my chest as my heart fights against its constraints. Kekkei shouts something but I can't hear, nor can I speak through heavy, laboured breaths.

I manage a scream and spit. Then I find my centre.

Standing up and sheathing the blade, I turn to Kekkei, who still awaits my answer. He knows it in my eyes. He breaks into a run, and I follow. I cannot let him go if he truly knows who I am.

More shouts signal an alarum, what's left of the Yokusei bear down on us. I'm caught in the winds of upheaval.

Chapter 4

As those same winds carried us further into the trees, so too did it carry the shouts of our pursuers, the screams of them picked off one by one. But not by us. Whatever trap Kekkei laid in our wake swallowed them up until they neither had the numbers, nor the courage to continue our trail. Foolish Yokusei. One pair of shackles is not enough to imprison a thousand hands.

His allies do not join us. Our flight through the wood hastened still by the night's events; my breaths sound like rasps of finality, but somehow, I continue in this sorry state. Before destroying the temple upon which this land is built, I need to repair the one within. It's a desolate ruin. Stone by stone, I will restore it.

On trees, scratched and hacked into bark, strange glyphs, or code. I don't know, but it's old. More signs mark the way. A hand here and there, without seemingly meaning anything, they lead our path straight and true until the mercenary stops. Placing his hand upon a pile of leaves, he yanks open a hidden wood panel, revealing a small store with food and supplies enough for emergency. Why here? How did he know our flight would – wait. This reeks of preparation. Thousand Hands, indeed. Conniving. From within, he pulls a gourd for each of us, and then spare. I open mine, drink deep without a heeded thought, before I hack and spew it all back up. I grit my teeth and swear to the gods about the man who would store wine in desperate reserve; I'd take rancid, stagnant waters over a foggy head, and dulled senses, but a beggar is not one with a choice. So, I drink it up slower.

Kekkei watches with a shallow grin, and I remember that this is no man I travel with. This is a mercenary leader and his child soldier. His monster.

The robe and hakama he hands me are far too big for my malnourished frame, damp and cold from the store, but they better suit me than the fetor I've draped upon myself. There's a sense of belonging that comes with warrior robes. A confidence in the self I wear. Strange though, the robes have two holes hacked out of them where the family insignias should sit. The merc has a shield up when I look to him, sweeping around for distraction. He worries over the boy now on a bedroll, offering him some wine. The boy takes it without flinching.

After helping him to some grain, Kekkei turns back to me, hearing my blade's awful moan from its sheath. I tap it to his neck. His eyes beg me to test him. His smile impetuous. A dark stain spreads into the fabric of his fresh, grey robes. It loosens my resolve; my katana drops from his neck. Sighing, his body sags, all the tension escaping.

"Go on then," he says. "Do me the honour of a quick death. But first, let me ask you to take the kid?"

A hiss through my teeth. The knot in my chest clamps down. Why did I allow him to speak? He's a Meater, and the worst kind. One that would use a small boy for his rites. Greed worshipping whoreson. "You ask a favour of me? OF ME?" I pause, slowing my breaths. "Why should I? You've sentenced the boy to a slow death. I'll leave you both here with your necks cut. Thousand Hands, I respected the name. Respected what a common man built, but he disappeared, his story silenced. And this is what he's become? Child soldiers? Child sacrifices? For what, so that you carry on in this guerrilla campaign against minor lords?" I raise my sword but don't utter any prayers in his name.

"Stop!" The boy croaks. "It's not as it looks." I'm taken aback by the authority that springs from the young mouth, the age that wraps around the innocent tone. "Greed. If there is an execution today, let it be mine." The boy winces. He's the dead reanimated as he stands, or his own approximation of standing, anyway. He can barely hold himself.

"Stop, Jinto!"

The boy rights his hunch, and with a lethargic tug, pulls open the mercenary's robes. Fingers loosening, legs fail. The sword drops. Never have I been brought to my knees by a picture before, but the one in front of me shakes my core.

"Those bites," my voice cracks.

"Yes, Rōnin," Kekkei says, "I'm no Shaman of Greed."

"I am," whispers the boy, as if too ashamed to admit it any louder.

I cannot speak still, a boy so young? "Kekkei, how could you give yourself to this! Your soul!"

"A tide of madness sweeps through Basho. I'll do all I can to keep my head above it." Pain streaks across his face. Tying his robes, he sits. The boy joining him. "We razed a Greed temple in the north, on the outskirts of Oyori. It cost many Hands; it cost me Akate. But I couldn't allow it. Not with the rumours."

"Rumours?"

"Children. The Greedborn are not as the name suggests."

"Then..."

"Yes, Jinto here is a child of those rumours."

"But the northern temples are sanctioned by–"

"It's why the waves of upheaval won't stop. The current rule of the Lord Council must end. Though, I've already burnt too many fingers in that fire, and now this." He gestures over the unearthed store. "Is amongst all I have left. Simple stores. But whispers cannot be contained, and many hands cannot be shackled. It all must end."

I'm lit in a tingle; the ache of age and war wash away from my being for a moment. I suppress the smile trying to turn my mouth, the gods look down upon me today. Excusing the current situation, we stand at the crossing of fate lines. For the sake of it, I chance the skies, hoping to see one of the sora dragons, to no avail. Eyes of the Gods, await my signal. I will use this kindling to start a fire that'll sweep through Basho.

*　*　*

Elation is always short-lived, Kekkei withdrew into himself for the duration

22

of our rest, and then we're off again.

The morning sends blades of light scattering through the trees, the sun a glowing goal on the horizon. I squeeze my eyes shut, the dull throb between them is back. My legs aren't my own anymore. The rumbling of my stomach seems to echo throughout my entire being. I ask the mercenary, and his Meater, what is next. They don't give me a straight answer. Where are the archers from the night before? Did the Yokusei all fall to them? My mind is a storm at sea; I still can't be caught.

What keeps me going is the direction we head. In the summer, the sun rises beyond the lands in which my household grew its roots. Butterflies swarm in my stomach at the thought of returning, but I have to. It's where this all starts. My duty was to the Oni Wuld, the vast expanse of trees deep in my clan's territories, where the heavens leak into this plane. Like the wood I passed through in Yokusen clanlands, it's a sacred place where the spirits of the otherworld are left to their own devices, warping, and twisting the human into something far removed from it: the godsborne. Guardian clans cull and control these places. They are the four points where the Four of Creation retreated to the heavens after they carved the lands, filled the seas, and birthed the living; exhausted, near-death and bored, they each tore a path to heaven. But without power enough in the mortal plane, they could not entirely close the gates behind them, nor could they open the path back from heaven. Ascension is one way. So, they made a treaty with the mortals, **Guard the points at which heaven and earth intercepts, and we shall never interfere with the machinations of man**. It is in this where my worries lay; with the end of my clan, the 'Wuld has lost its attendants.

"Back with us?" Kekkei's voice grounds me. We're on the edge of the wood now. Farmlands, rolling jade fields sweep off as far as the eye can see, rice paddies dot the landscape. Smoke rises from a settlement halfway to the horizon.

"You look like one of Metsuku's servants," he says, "and now you're shambling around aimlessly as one."

I don't think I'll ever get used to the casual, unimportant chatter mercs fill silences with. I nod at him, but I've no words for that remark. Nor for the

Meater boy who seems to share his time on this plane with Kekkei's shadow. Vile.

"Okay. Not talking today? And after I got you out of there, like I said I would."

On and on.

He doesn't give up and bars my way. Chest puffed. But he's unarmed, brutish as he may be, I could cut him in twain, just above the red Akate sash hidden beneath his robes, making it permanent. And I go for the hilt of my blade, snarling like the mutt I am.

"Woah. Come on."

"I don't talk unless it's productive, mercenary. I have no need to fill this journey with idle chatter. A warrior saves their breath."

"You want important. Okay. See that town ahead, walk towards it."

I sigh. He's got me caught. "Why there?"

"Oho, we're talking now."

The hilt of my blade is sick with my teasing now.

"Now, now. The lord there looks the other way for payment."

"Chisai?"

"Yes. Still Lord Tamikura's den."

"We've strayed from the river, the Kirisam knows my destination."

"And what is your destination?"

I push past him, and as I leave the treeline, mud squelches between my toes. Gods!

"Hawk?"

This again. I wheel around with murder grabbing at my hilt. "Wildboy, I'll have that tongue." I address Kekkei now. "I'm a merc, a servant, your whore, lover, or whatever you want to tell the town. I'm with you, for now. But if he, or you say that in front of anyone, I'll cut you both down, and don't think I can't." Jinto's eyes are older the longer I look, terrifying but I've decided on a threat anyway. "I've diced a Meater or two up before."

By midday, we're in the town, Chisai. I know it to be on the very edge of our household's concern back when I had one; the lord is a small, fat nuisance who should have started a family decades ago but is too busy breaking every law under the nose of the Gods' Senses who preside over them. It's folly for one who owns so much to have no one to pass it to.

This place is an abode of demons, men with nothing good in their hearts flock to the many hot baths, and wine, sake, and alcohol houses. Of which the town has too many, and of which I find myself knelt in as soon as we arrive. Kekkei has greeted half the town, and the knot tightens in my chest. For someone on the run from the Lord Council, he certainly is making himself known. Though, not as a name I know him by.

We sit down, and the merc orders for us. It's not long before we've two plates of a brown slop served; the shopservant assures us its rice, but not the kind I'm used to. Brown, unpolished. A mush before it enters my mouth. The sour taste and grainy chew turn my nose. The next plate is better, but fried tofu is harder to get wrong. Yet my stomach welcomes it. A warrior's meal for some, but not the fortunate, as I was. My clan Dattori had two fish meals a day. Grilled or boiled, an extravagance that I have to bury, forget, with the rest of it.

The shop is the centre of everything bad in this town. A paradise that welcomes the merc. Brigands, and petty thugs are clustered on sacks around tables long sticky with plum wine. Clouds of tobacco hang as an otherworldly miasma over the heads of these underworldly men. And the chatter has taken on a life of its own. Rumours circle this place like crows, swooping in flocks at every man and woman who enters. Black objects in the seas to the south. Dragons, heathen dragons, one of Kekkei's friends says as he joins us, feeding the flock of crows. Thousand Hands has his own...educated opinion.

"Boats – traders from across the sea, my good man. Nothing else."

"The likes I ent seen," the shifty-eyed man says, "no boat that large. That evil. Tis wrong."

Another crow squawks, invading gods. The Faith of the One. A mistress in the sea. Another man stops by our table and stays too long chanting tales from other lands, running on about something so alien to me I want to gut him where he stands.

Basho is changing, and as much as I hate to admit, it is not all the godlord and his Wolves. External forces are at work, one of which I bear the shame of bringing to life. But my lips are sealed with it, Kekkei already keeps one eye trained on my every move. Confrontation can always wait. I'll bring him into my cause or cut him away; it would be a denial if I said I didn't need help from Thousand Hands to get back to my clanlands, so I pray for the former. I excuse myself. The merc is reluctant to let me go, but I have other business to attend. Exciting the smog on the heels of probing glares, I emerge onto the street, spluttering, retching. The pipe smoke was better than the faecal waft of the town, and puddles of gods-know-what in the road; double-taxes have starved these lands, the black poppy defeated them, and the lord has more interest in cleaning a plate of rice and grilled fish than the town.

I pull up the hood of a cloak I requisitioned as we entered Chisai and blend into the heaving mass. A hubbub of jostling heads; one man pushes past, his arm wrapped around a woman, hand groping into her robes. Commoners, I spit. The low births know nothing of honour and crave shame at every opportunity. Along the road, bodies lay scattered, propped up against shops. Wheezing, oozing, their faces blotched in a black menace: Devil's Spittle. Addicts and heathens. The plague the Lord Council refuses to admit to. The plague that lines their chests, the plague put on my family's head. My hand itches for the comfort of a hilt under my cloak, I'd end their suffering. But I'm not a warrior here. I'm a Hand in one thousand, a lowly soldier. Only sanctioned warriors may carry a sword. I need to know of my late clan, of the scattered remains, if there are any. But information about a destroyed, forsaken and treasonous clan is not something braggarts entertain themselves with, nor stick their nose into. That's Lord Council-owned information only the warrior-class are privy to.

I snake through the crowd, dodging elbows and shoulders, slinking between gaps so as not to attract even a sigh or a grunt. Laughing, and cheering erupts to my side, and curiosity gets the better of me until I clear my way through the swathes of plain, dirtied kimonos. The street opens up here, and slopes down towards what seems to be a stage; stalls line the slope filled with greasy black heads, not a single topknot in sight. Some sort of commoner theatre carved into the mud. On stage, puppets dance, an unremarkable Painted Lady in a white kimono that defies the filth around her, plucks at a shamisen leading the proceedings. It's the puppets that get my blood pumping. Plated in shades of yellow, and gold – the paintwork is spoiling, an amateur job at best – and taller than the others, is what could only be an imitation of the godlord. The only plate etched with dragons belongs to the highest dog in the Lord Council. The serpentine lines a cheap approximation of those that reign in the skies.

It prances around, chest puffed out, waving its hands as laughs and cheers erupt from this crowd of common sycophants. The puppetmaster, alone, is as his name suggests. Fortunate, am I, that he is not Taosii. Warrior puppets raise their katanas, retainer puppets bow at his feet as the godlord is raised into the air. Behind him, lights dance and shoot from the stage. Star-like flashes find their way to the skies, popping and streaking into the air; I leap back, heart thumping. Lungs fighting for air, the surrounding fence holding me up.

It seems Taos' influence on our country has grown, where even a fool's show has access to their ungodly machinations. The shadow-country that borders our own was long kept at arm's length, but those currently in power find delight in their pyrotheurgy, allure in their Soshists; where my clan only found ruin. The flashes are brighter in the back of my mind. The heat more extreme, painful; the screams more real.

Composure comes slowly but I wrestle it back, only for the memory of anger to wash over me hot as a pyre at what unfolds on the stage.

The show reaches its climax: a puppet woman with a bird's beak for a nose sits below the heaven-sent godlord. Next to her an elderly puppet stands. I grit my teeth. Another bang, the plucking stops, red rags are thrown into the air by a stagehand and the elderly head rolls off stage. The beaked puppet draws a red sword, flaps around squawking, the crowd goes wild, monkeys thrashing in their seats, screeching, laughing.

"How – DARE YOU!" I shout as I pull myself away from it. Turning, I run and run and force my way through the crowd. The throb in my head is an oni's smashing blow; knees throb as the hit the road. A scream disturbs the hubbub, one of my own. I scream until my lungs are empty. Not one person has stopped, the throng continues by. Just another lost soul to Chisai. Despite the crowd, I'm alone. One woman against the flowing tide of all the Lord Council has built. I know of the koi's challenge now. But worst of all, I'm godsworn to an entity beyond me. That truth sends shivers down my spine as I put my hand into my robes and run fingers across the black on my stomach. My hairs stand on end. The damp scent of animal hide and spice as the residual godki around the scar comes alive to my touch, reminding me of what I'm at the whim of.

My cry out in blood was answered by Metsuku's blade, still poised at my neck ready to take it all in an instant. What that godsborne did to me, I try to push to the back of my mind. Seal it away. My fears aren't born from the memory of its inhuman, animalistic stare, but from the fact that I may never regain my household's status. Its honour. Its justice. If the godsborne wills it so, my life could be snuffed out. A feeble candle flame handed back to Metsuku.

That my master's demise has become a puppeteer's living is unforgivable. Under the Eyes of the Gods, I will add a final scene to that play. First, I will choose my puppetmaster, a thousand hands would put on a grand show.

* * *

Kekkei has chosen a rat's nest. I can't see the polished wood floor through the dust, reed and dirt; an expense surely has been spared. The only candle flickers dimly in a corner, wax dripping onto the floor, the open flame is a little too unnerving in a den that would invite the fire.

Jinto sleeps where the reed is concentrated to one corner and Kekkei pores over what must be a missive, for all the attention he gives it.

Here, at the bottom of the pit, I will set the world alight. I'm prepared to die once more, for the words that will roll off my tongue will be treasonous without measure. I say, "Kekkei, who am I?

He grunts, not really noticing I've said anything.

"WHO AM I?"

Kekkei throws the parchment into the air. Knife flashing in the low-light, eyes wide and startled.

I smirk and push further into the candlelight glow that surrounds the merc, a yellow bubble within the darkness. His hand goes to his heavily beating chest and he slams the weapon down on the floor again. Lips curled, he says, "Five hells and Metsuku's sweaty–"

"I've got your attention–"

"Couldn't you–"

"This needs to be done now." I eye Jinto, who's now sat rubbing his eyes just outside of the bubble. More feral in the dim-light, not helped by the long mane of unkempt, black hair. "Both of you. Who am I?"

"A rōnin."

"No, Jinto."

"You're lost, a warrior without a household." Kekkei touches his chin. "What else?"

I breathe in deep, finding my centre, slowing the beat of my heart before it runs wild. These two could drive one of the Monks of the Scales to anger. "Don't play with me! Kekkei, what did you call me?"

"A dead woman." Kekkei flashes a white grin.

"Hawk!" The feral beast dissolves as Jinto jumps up with childlike excitement.

"Yes."

"Dattori's Hawk?"

"I am she." I unsheathe the katana that loyally sits at my side. "What will you do?"

"Put that away," Kekkei says, "you're as stupid as they say, as angry as the demons themselves."

I'm caught off guard by this, poison wells in the back of my throat as I prepare to spit back at Kekkei but the facade breaks, amusement crooks the corners of his mouth. "Y-you're not alarmed? Surprised?" I pause. "Say something. You knew? You really did know?"

"Didn't pull that name out of the heavens," Kekkei says, "don't look that much like a hawk, do you? That nose thou–"

"Kekkei!"

"Get off, Jinto. Hands off!"

"It's nothing new." A heavy sigh and compose myself. "I am...was First Commander of Lord Dattori's household."

"Ah yes, the Hawk of Fenika, was it?" Kekkei says. "That was quite the battlefield."

I pause again, wondering what his game is, why he dances around it. He holds my stare, and then his eyes waver, searching for something, anything else but my gaze. He has his secrets. He shakes his head, laughs to himself and his stare is back. Strong now, unyielding. Warmth rushes to my cheeks. I try not to break it; I'm not sure whether he looks through me or into me, but from within my centre there's a flutter of something. I knock it away and continue, "I'm not proud of that. More than a name was earned that day, sleepless nights in abundance. But that is what befalls a household that doesn't fall in with the Lord Council. I know well, now, how fate turns in a circle. How everyone gets their due. My household was part of a great wrong and suffered in turn."

"Pah, right."

"What?"

"War is war." He raises an eyebrow. "There's nothing more to it."

War? That's the way he describes a slaughter; the household of Fenika was small, on the outskirts, like us. Led by a Samaki lord. Not the first to show disinterest in the new godlord's rule, but the first to act against the tax reforms. It wasn't open rebellion, no one dared. No one was stupid enough to then. But they would die before they cut their rice paddies in two, handing a slice over to the Lord Council. Our master tried to talk to them because he knew what was coming; he put aside his hate for the lord, and what he did to that babe. They refused. And that was it. Being in close proximity to the Demon Mountains, it was easy to brand them as heretics. It wasn't the godlord's own scythe he brought down upon them, but a blade that was poised nearby. One that – at the time – couldn't refuse. The Dattori. I was the Hawk that swooped down and broke their small army. Cut down the Old Oak.

I gulp, my throat is dry. Not sure why Kekkei mentions it. Is it an open challenge perhaps? I was part of it before, so I got what I deserved. Is he winding this up to say no? Whether I was right or wrong to start this, I continue. "The Akate formed after that age." It's a statement, there was no Akate when Fenika fell.

"A mercenary has more than one beginning." He folds his arms, shrinks back out of the light, sitting on the edge of the bubble. As the flame flickers the yellow tide ebbs back and forth over his eye line. "Anything for coin, eh?"

"Enough! This back and forth irritates me; I could grind my teeth down in one exchange with you. Mercenaries."

A silence sweeps through the room.

"You've heard, I presume. You know how it ended for me?" I stride across the room, my arms flailing in the air as I work into the rhythm of this, the anger. "My household was cut-off, destroyed, by the Lord Council. My master, and I, publicly executed. Of one, they were successful. Of the wrong one. Master was not as tenacious as me." I stop again, Jinto has crawled next to Kekkei, watching me in my madness. "For what? Policy and laws my master did not abide, crimes we did not commit. This plague the poppy has wrought is not ours. Our fields violated." Everything else is better left unspoken. "To be a Samaki lord, on the outskirts of Basho, was freedom the Lord Council could not toler—"

"Cut to it!" Kekkei interrupts, much to the disgusted look on Jinto's face. I bite my tongue and plant my feet as if to pounce, but he raises a hand, slowly bringing it down to the floor as if to pacify me. "We're in."

"What, but."

"You heard me. Things need to change."

I'm stunned. No debate, no objection, and he's onboard. Whatever it is he hides, I push the concern away, seal it. Now is not the time. I'm a fool to grasp at what he offers so wildly, but I'll fall into the snare to bite the Fox.

"Dattori clanlands, your lands, are occupied by the fieldclans, and I don't have the men, nor the resources to take it from them."

"Wha…" This is out of my control, already. Moving too fast. "How?"

"This town is built upon rumours, half-truths and news."

31

"Akate...You can't use."

"No!" Kekkei says, "for every Hand caught, tax relief for the town. Like I said, my resources are thin. But no matter." He scratches the back of his head, stands, and stretches. "I've got a plan. You're good with that katana, right, Rōnin?"

He strides from the room answered, the door issues a noise like the bray of a donkey, and he's gone.

"H-hawk." Jinto moves into the light. "Is it true?"

"What?" My heart misses a thud. The boy's eyes are wide, deep, black like the oblivion against the gentle warm glow that seems to dim with his presence.

"You worked blood?"

I retreat from his words, search for the door again, glancing back. "Stop it, Meater. You don't know what you heard. Don't know what you talk about!"

I fling the door open; the hinges cry out again and disappear. Away from the boy, away from the magic that surrounds him, away from the truth.

Chapter 5

The borrowed katana is out of kilter with my Way of the Sword. I couldn't use a side-arm in simultaneity. It's not made correctly; the steel is normal-forge and top-heavy. There's too much of it, not like my CrowKiller. Whore's breath, I miss that blade. But I make do, as it's not the blade that makes the warrior. It's not the smith's hammer, it's his knowledge of steel; it's not the seed, it's the farmer's care of the land; it's not the cut of the animal, it's the Meater's relationship with Greed.

I move my guard upwards, matching his; the warrior in front of me squints as he follows the slight movement, my changing guards eliciting a puzzled look from him. I bring my guard high to the heavens, then back down in front of me, the sun winking upon the steel showing the amateurish imperfections in the folds. The chips and scratches from previous exchanges. I sigh. This novice – where did he get the name Flashing Steel Against the Moon? Minor families are naming their Ways in such a grandiose manor these days it promises more than it gives. He's let me draw out the duel; he's lost control. His flanks heave like an old mule's would. Imbecile. An awkward stance, a step of hesitation. A bead of sweat trickles from his head. The corner of his eye weeps. The many-sworded Mistress watches my blade today, not his.

A mouse found itself in the lion's den.

Whatever his Way is it is too honourable too pure. He doesn't take advantage of his surroundings.

Use every advantage, Master said. The sun is behind me, Sukami's glare will win this in my favour. My forms are refined, Meganako loves me.

I step forward, blade held true.

He dashes to meet me, over-eager to finish this. A sand mist springs up in his wake; the livestock pen-now-arena is an arid husk on the edge of Chisai, farm-buildings in shambles, splintered tiles make up most of the debris. Feet moving in unison, he's watching my blade, not my being, not the minute tells I must give. He's a two-footed horse, his steps are singular, but I dance around it. Mine are simultaneous, free of thought. I swing my back-foot round and step forward with my left, pivoting away from his jab. Side-on from him now, I smack his sword upwards from my centred guard, so there's no hope of a riposte and let the return momentum carry my true strike across his belly. It bites deep. It's over.

Some boos, but mostly cheers erupt from the crowd around me. Anger bubbles, boils within but I swallow it. I'd rather gut the pigs that watch, than soil the sanctity of a duel, but we need it.

His blood seeps into my robes with a wipe of my borrowed blade, whispering my thanks to the old god of war and blades, who saw it fit for me to walk away.

Kekkei is on the side lines. Around him, people spit at his feet. They toss coinbags at him, through a jostling fence of smiles and cheers. The inner circle is full of people who're more than happy about this win. Thugs and brigands are now guards, assistants, hired bodies to further our joint cause. It's the lord's men, the shop owners, who take heavy losses, who misread the odds and have foolishly listened to cunning, misguided whispers.

My stomach turns and my surroundings merge and split again. I wipe the sweat from my brow, fighting against collapsing in front of these men. Deep breaths. I look for my centre, but it's hard. My grasp is an infant's grip on a katana. I'm not right still. Dragons above, what is wrong with me? My muscles are tight, unbending, they take more from the bamboo when they should be the waters that flow through it. I don't like this; I don't like it at all. What have I become? A hacky bag player for people to profit from.

A great plan, indeed. The merc's idea: *we need rice, silver, gold kobans. Lots of it.* I didn't like where it was going already. *It was child's play cutting those Yokusei guards down, I saw it in you. Warrior-bred, Hawk. A fine breed. Do it again. And again. They'll come from all over, this town is already a pit for such...*

sport. Currency is a resource of all kinds. Information, materials, and Hands, we need them all. We will take back Dattori lands one duel at a time.

One month I've been stuck in this hole and already every free man, woman and child is a Hand. It's hard to know whether I'm strengthening my own cause or rebuilding the Akate. The lines between both blur and my feet chill at the thought. I want to flee. To follow the Kirisam on my own, but I'm unsure of what awaits me at home, if I should call it that after my failings. Kekkei's intelligence says the fieldclans reside there, that it is Samaki no longer with the godlord's reach established there, but I don't see it. It was Samaki by location as much as it was by our blood. It can never not be. If the fieldclans have not grown, and the godlord not sparing any of his own, I could cleave them from our estate myself. But Kekkei holds us back. Kekkei warns it's too early. Kekkei says it's not the right time.

That the other Samaki lords sit idly irks me; this is not the way of our lands. They'd let their own fall with not so much as acknowledging it? Sama's blood grows weak.

I fear the dagger Kekkei holds at my back. I cannot be rash, must not strike without reason. But trusting a merc wholeheartedly is not something I can do. Trust is not something I can do.

I bow in greeting him, like the model champion.

There's a ruckus, more shouting and the surrounding crowd splits revealing a hidden palanquin. Four bound men carry it forth. Gold-painted, etched, a thing of wealth that only lords command. The palanquin stops and turns to face us; the curtains drawn.

Inside, a woman sits in silken robes that struggle to hold her grain sack-shaped figure. She doesn't look to us, but instead another man appears from within. Brushing his less-regal robes down, he pulls out an ornate fan. His lip curls as he surveys the crowd.

"Can I do for ya?" Bunta says, one of Kekkei's closest new hires. A balding, towering bulk of a man wrapped in brown; hair pulled in a tight bun on his head. A fluff beard. Trader extraordinaire of the Border Trading Group. Akate now. "That lordly miss the lord?"

The scrawny fan-wielder ignores him. His lip curls higher regarding my katana, not meeting my eyes, and then lands on Kekkei, before announcing, "Behold, Lord Tamikura graces you with her presence." He stops, tightening his glare. "Daisuki Hayato." Kekkei's guise. "I presume?"

"What dya want?"

"Bunta!" Kekkei reins in the trader before insult. "What of it, servant?"

The side of the man's face twitches behind the fan. Taking a moment to compose himself, and a cough from within the palanquin, he replies, "You bring new wealth and sport to my heavenly lord's Chisai, and for that she is humbled. Flattered that you would do so much." He pauses, letting his words hang. "However, you do so without the permission of the lord, under the nose of Heaven. The Four did not sleep so that commoners could profit away from the watchful eye of their chosen." One for theatrics, this lord. The True Heavenly Peace faithful always are.

Everyone is silent, as they wait for him to continue. Kekkei shows restraint. It's written on his face. The many missed insults, retorts, and comments. But he holds his tongue, for this is what we've been waiting for. *Let's draw the attention of the Heavens, let the fat cats descend from their snobbery, readying their paws for a feast in our name.*

"Humbled, you should be. Daisuki, my lord invites you to enjoy a Ceremony of Teas in her honour." He pauses, turning to the palanquin; his fan now hides a smirk as he looks back. "It is by my lord's graciousness that you are welcomed to discuss the payment she is owed for this, brutish, sport. And your *contribution* to Chisai, hereafter." He doesn't hide his smile now as he drops his fan. The palanquin chuckles, and Kekkei accepts.

The trap is laid. We have our invite.

I've discovered something. Kekkei had said. *The lord thinks she's so cunning.*

* * *

The entrance is unimposing, and quite frankly, I'm not impressed. An opening hacked into the curtain wall more than designed. I knew Chisai's lord was minor, but when you can't keep the grime from your own estate, you know you're the same ilk as it. Armed guards stand either side of a gate that whines in welcome; the guardsmen look of the same hire that Kekkei pulls from, the festering pit of thugs that call this place home. With no plate, the guards too are unimpressive in their spoiled-white robes and dust-covered hakama. I don't even need to see the blades of the katanas awkwardly stuck to their waists.

Through the gate, thug-guards line the way up to what I assume to be the main estate building; a squat, hunched over beggar of a structure – begging for restoration. Tiers of crumbling tiles lay over each other, rising into the night. The wooden paneling flaking, framing an amber-glowing entryway.

The dark hums, there's a buzz about me. This is where it all starts. I pluck my robes, ushering fresh air between the folds and my skin. It's hot. Uncomfortable. But Kekkei and Bunta seem fine, they crack jokes and laugh ahead of me, nodding to each guard, spouting nonsense to whatever servant the lord has sent ahead. Bravado. Luckily, the rodent that brought the summons isn't here. My blade itches to test his arrogance; hand lingering, then goes to rest on a hilt but I snatch it back, holding it as if I'm burnt by the fact that I'm not armed. That I had to come into the rat's nest without talons to claw my way out, sends a shiver down my spine.

"Okay?" Kekkei says, they've reached the entryway and wait for me to join them.

My gait reluctant.

"Yeah."

"But? But what?"

"That is all, *Master.*"

His eye twitches, this role not suiting him, perhaps wondering whether to react to the slight, but thinks better of it. It was only in front of a servant anyway, and I'm certainly no low-born; I wince at this charade every time I act upon it, sick to the whore's breath of it.

Kekkei stops. I near run into him. With a tilt of his head, he says, "Please. Focus. This is for us both." He lowers his voice. "This is the start of everything. For Basho." The speech trails off as we're ushered into a great, but not grand, hallway.

The canvas ahead glows yellow, flickers. It's slid open, and tendrils of smoky, incensed air reach out. Sappy, bitter notes refresh my airways. Juniper was always one of Master's favourites. I take a deep breath, and stride in behind the other two.

"Welcome!" The rat-servant beckons us further. Up on a dais, a woman spills out of the fool's throne, a bundle of silky, red robes. Her face is round; her neck is consumed by it. Snake-like, her eyes elongated by makeup. How fitting, for the secrets we've uncovered can only be coveted by serpents.

The minor-lord gestures, flicks her wrist, perhaps the only movement she is capable of unassisted. "Please, sit." The servant shows us to our seats. We kneel in front of a woman, who takes the same position before the dais, preparing the tea. The hostess is robed in pink, face-painted like the Ladies of Oshima. I bite my cheek, who does this pig think she is? Chisai is obsessed – a town in the shadow of the capital. A queen in her own queendom.

"Sit." The lord breaks the silence, patting her stomach. "Minoka, finish and go, wench. Your family is lucky I put up with you instead." There's more said in that sentence, but we'll never know the true depths of despicable Tamikura reaches. A deal with a demon, perhaps. It's necessary. As she laughs, the woman winces, picks up her bamboo and whisks the tea in the great pot. She stands with a tray of tea bowls, three, and places them in front of us. And then bows a full bow, exiting with both speed and grace, somehow.

"Common women, what use are they out of bed?" She eyes me with a hungry grin. "Now, serve me, *trader*."

The room holds its breath, a thin silence breaks over the room. I dig my fingers into my robe, squeezing my legs tight. My breaths are controlled, the wave of anger rolls over me.

But Kekkei grabs the tray without flinching and takes the hostess' seat. For that, my admiration of him grows. Remade as a trader, he's been elevated to the guest of a lord, then insulted beyond good measure. His status torn asunder. Put in place of a bought woman, the lord made sure we knew.

Kekkei ladles the tea into a bowl, climbs the dais and bows, hands held out, face dipped. The lord waits a moment as her station demands, then takes the bowl. Her bulbous hand emerging from a sea of robes. She drinks deep, slurping, rivers of tea drip down her cheeks. With a belch, she sends the tea bowl clattering across the room. An earthy baritone of a laugh breaks from her. Beetles race down my spine, and arms, raising hairs as they go. I add her to the list of people I want to see dead. But, alas, I do not have a blade fit for that weighty task. I smirk, probably snarl, at her but her eyes are fixed still on the merc.

"Apologies, gracious trader," Lord Tamikura says, "guests worth inviting to my grounds are few in these days of upheaval. You play a good host. From a respectable family, traditional family, I presume?"

Kekkei rises, and steps down from the dais without looking back. "Something like that. Now–"

"No, no." The high chair sighs and creaks as the bundle of robes rise from the seat, falling like an avalanche from the pig. I double-take. For a *peace-time* lord, she is imposing. Samaki blood seeps over the borders, she might be lucky to have such a lineage. With a great smile she draws my attention. I don't doubt she can hold the room even with her unremarkable face. "I do love tea, the art of it, and I'd like to see it out to the end."

The lord comes down from her high station, only in body, with the grace of an oni. And some of the danger. There's more to this woman and it isn't in her physical prowess. She's dangerous, but this is not the type of fight I can win; this is Kekkei's.

She ladles the tea, again going through the motions of ceremony. I grind my teeth as I wait for her to finish; she places a tea bowl in front of Bunta, who drinks, then she's in front of me. Still kneeling, I gaze up at the woman-mountain.

"You," she says, "will not drink what I serve. I do not serve warriors." My bowl lands with a clink at my knees. "Get it yourself, mongrel."

My heart beats a *thump-thump* in my ear, chest rising and falling. But I pay attention to the incense and everything I'm working towards. And the blood runs red again, and the laughter, the lords' barking rings in my ears, round, and round. The godlord. The blood. Uncontrollable, it boils. Mounting into an inferno, and...Tamikura walks away. Slowly, beastlike. The anger washes into the floor around me. I get up and pour my tea, for I do not deign to insult this gutter rat.

"Now, come, let me show you my estate." The canvas slides open, two armoured guards clink in, their plate onyx. The stories intrigued me; much are they the chatter of the town: the lord's Jet Black. Her bodyguard. A small army in their own right. They give nothing away. It's as though two silhouettes have entered the room. But as I pass them, I see deeper in, the demonic faces carved into the mask. We leave the main building, into the night now deep in its silence, only broken by far cries and the chirping of crickets. The incense clings to me, as do the two blots in the night. We enter another building, and the doors close behind me, my escorts gone.

We're led past treasures; bright orange and red pots of the Saman Era. Priceless. The fires caught in their making; hanging silks, vibrant, everlasting, Kakihira style, women warriors – pictures of the Second Reckoning; hanging armours the Terin Period made popular – for what more would a warrior of war want to see on their walls? Startling is this display of wealth, that a small-town lord could have such finery and still have the monies to run Chisai is unthinkable. The estate wears its disrepair in disguise. More paintings, weapons and jewels. The lord has a veritable hoard. At the end of the tour, we enter a grander room than the first. I'm awed by candles that line the four walls as they join the ceiling, wax drips into a lower gully, spilling over onto great murals and myriad scrolls piled high. The lord courts danger in many ways. An errant flame and it would all be gone. A strange woman indeed.

I step into history – from the show before, I wonder if even one of the Dying Scrolls might hide amongst them, but I doubt the Learned could be bought.

"Gods," Bunta says.

"My own design, I hired only the best to capture them. An expense, indeed." Both I and the merc know of the lord's spending, her dealings, and her trading; all of which bring us here, set this trap. "I dedicate my wealth to the histories of our land. Isn't it something quite captivating? A lot can be learned from its study, mistakes that were made before can be avoided again in the recount of the great battles before us, and in those who sought refuge in heretical practices, but were erased, locally, from this land." Tamikura sheds the skin of a giant oaf, and strides with energy I've only seen in battle-ready warriors. "Fenika. A shame, but they did not learn from Irahoto or the Yukis before them. Not that there's place for as many great houses today, but if only they'd turned to history. Lessons are to be learnt, Daisuki, lessons. But, what of those mistakes, those horrors that weren't recorded? How do we learn from them? I ask myself all the time, but you see, history loses nothing. Those dark, erased truths still live today, and we should do well in searching, studying for them, or they'll crawl out of the annals and rend all we know." With this, she rubs her belly, holding my gaze too long for comfort. I look to the painting we stop by as the beetles navigate my skin again. "Ah, our Lady Sukami, who saw it fit that we're blessed with warmth." Next to her, a giant rakes a mountain range, rivers springing from his staff.

"Izenta?" Bunta asks.

"Correct – I rather like the idea of him being a farmer; they had to learn it from somewhere. The pests." She chuckles.

We walk by a brutish woman, katanas spring from her hands; foolish is a warrior who wouldn't recognise Meganako. And a phantom with demons climbing from its seven maws – the hells.

"Enough. Please." Kekkei stops still, the smile sliding from the lord's face. "I'm honoured by this show of...wealth. But this is not new to me. The old gods live in the tales and teachings of every wet nurse and nanny in Basho. This is not why we're here, Tamikura."

"Follow me." The lord is abrupt and leads us swiftly out of the room, but before I leave my attention is drawn to a smaller painting, only just touched by the candlelight. There, a being painted in crimson, surrounded by skeletons. A bloody rain falls from the sky, the figure seems locked in a dance, a wicked smile drawn across its face. I pull myself away. The other three are already seated around a maple, lacquered desk. The room is deliberate, lacking the lavishness of the others – one for business.

The lord adjusts her robes, and readjusts, fumbling with them over and over. Kekkei chews on his lip, but Bunta seems unchanged. A pregnant

41

silence hangs in the air, as one waits for the other to make their first move; niceties have ended, Kekkei made sure that the transition was coarse, and jagged like fish scales. Where the lord was working her way towards this end, Thousand Hands changed the flow. Clever, really, how the change of pace has thrown our host out. I look to her as she wipes sweat from her finely plucked brow, resting on painted lips.

"You cannot tax me," Kekkei says, "duels and information are not commerce. You have no authority in the competition I run, it's barely Chisai lands." With all the grace of a lion, he crashes into the negotiation.

"What is it you want?"

"No taxes, my enterprise is just that."

"I look the other way." The lord sighs, seemingly fed-up with this exchange already. "Chisai is a safe haven for the wrong, the lawful-unlawful and the dog-eared. I cultivate it. I enjoy it. I keep my head above the waters, within the lawful reach of the Lord Council so my citizens, and visitors are free. All I ask, *the only thing I ask*, is a cut."

"I can't."

"Or won't? I've been nice. Very nice. Played your games when I didn't need to. I OWN Chisai!" She slams her fist down on the table which jumps in fright. "Do not anger me, Kekkei Thousand Hands."

If the merc was bothered by having his cover flipped, his disguise blown, he didn't show it. I'd even say his face grew more expressionless with the announcement that his cunning ruse had not been so. My own heart is fighting to compose itself again, and Bunta turns as pale as the milk-like ghosts of Upper Fangs.

Kekkei laughs, slapping his chest. There's a wink of a tear in his eye, and he says, "Exactly the woman I hoped I was dealing with."

"Humourous, am I?" Tamikura bellows, "Your fickle Hands–"

"Are your ears? Your eyes, your men?" Kekkei interrupts; he touches two fingers to his chin. A play is about to start. "Tamikura, you know who I am – so don't insult me! Drop that look! You sought to use me so why're you so disgusted that I don't cower to your *Heavenliness?*"

"My Jet Black will rip you limb from limb. How dare you!"

"Thousand Hands. Think on it, think on all you've heard and threaten that again." The problem, Kekkei, is that if her webs run deep enough, she'll know your bluff. She'll see that your core force amount to this room; I still myself, fight against the urge to fidget. This is not the kind of battle I feel comfort in. Kekkei continues, "Meater carts."

"A sharp tongue cuts your own mouth!" Tamikura is flustered, her wattle trembles and she plays the part of a floundering salmon.

"Chisai supplies the Demon Mountains. To what purpose, I do not know – despicable place."

"You're a damned fool!" The lord stands with a shout and a hurried *chink-chink* follows the twin Jet Blacks entering the room. They must have crawled from the door for me to have not noticed.

"At ease," Tamikura says, "back to the door! I didn't tell you to move." With that, the Jet Blacks disappear. Her mouth doesn't move, only her lips do as she says, "Now, mercenary, be very careful of the accusations you level at the Iruka household. I take every threat seriously, chew on it, and make good on my reprisal. You really want to do this?"

"It took me a while," Kekkei starts, "and, you do a fine job of hiding it. But you've allowed me to go unchecked. Knowing who I was, what you hide, that was foolish. My Hands multiply fast, I'm good at that. They worm their way in, fill gaps, seep into every nook and cranny I want them; cartsmen were a good investment." He pauses, almost comically inhales breath, and continues, the lord's face a plum fit to burst. "It could be nothing, but you remove the eyes. The livestock die from four wounds, facing the godki points. A farce, but you make sure of it. That is hard to pass off as anything but Greed Meat."

"So what? You've found my stores."

"No, not quite. I told you, cartsmen. Gods, you take no shortcuts. Following the Kirisam, east to Riba. A stopover in that town. A change of carts. Southeast to Tamas, and then far north, along the old trading roads, around Dattori lands then into the mountains." Kekkei seems to find this funny as he chuckles to himself, wiping a bead of sweat from his face. He glances sideways at me. I've no need to interrupt, no wish to enter this

43

battlefield. So, he finishes his show. "Do you know how difficult it was getting a Hand into each change of guard? I was worried they'd desert or give up halfway...it's a long journey I hear. Ever done it yourself, Tamikura?"

The lord is tense, uneasy, and less oni-like. I can see now, layers of thick robes shift over her untamed, untrained, body. She heaves a sigh, and the rest of her mass wobbles with it as she eases herself back down into her chair with a groan. From within the cluster of silks, she pulls a gourd, flicks the cap off and drinks deep. A theurgical, unnatural smell emanates from the bottle. Some alcoholic brew I assume. I don't like it, nor do the beetles. Her demeanour changes once more, a smirk draws slowly across her face. Her mouth then purses, and she lets out an "Ah." Sitting up again, she continues, "Fine. You got me. Well done, Thousand Hands, your reputation precedes you. Now, what do you want? Name it and let's be done with it."

"Jet Blacks. Trained and armed."

"In what quantity?"

"A unit or two."

"Not two, one. Thirty men. Done, they're yours. Uh-uh, no need to say it. Have them, no questions asked."

I can't help but feel utterly stunned. Bunta looks equally confused and Kekkei, well Kekkei is speechless. Look at him, he was in control, but that's been thrown out of the window. He scratches his chin, his face scrunching as he searches for the catch, but Tamikura doesn't leave him waiting.

"One condition."

The mercenary shifts, his form relaxing once more. I let out a breath I didn't know I was holding; we're forged from the same metal. Both of us more comfortable under threat than we are when things go our way. Born into unrest, brought up surrounded by ambition, war and death. Wrought out of the blood of others.

"Heh," Kekkei says, "good. What is it?"

"A strange man is Genaro Kekkei," the lord replies. "Lesser, or maybe more sane men – I haven't quite got the measure of you – would flinch at that. Well then." Tamikura bites her lips, trying to smother a smile but loses. "Kill my cousin."

A laugh escapes me. Absurd. "My pleasure," I speak out of turn, but I'm fed up of playing the kindly warrior-servant.

Both the lord and Kekkei shoot me daggers. But I'm a warrior, I slap them away like it's nothing and stretch a yawn, rolling my shoulders. Bored of this.

"Uncouth. But I'm glad you like the condition, warrior. Ah, but my lineage is a mess. I mean my first wife's cousin, once removed, *in the service of the Lord Council.*"

What is this nonsense. I scrunch my face, forcing the numbness from my mind to figure out where this is going, but my katana is not drawn, and the crows aren't home.

The silence in the room is fit to burst. But I'm startled once more, as Kekkei takes on the same ghostly white that Bunta did, and gods I'm annoyed that I've got no idea what is going on. I'm not going to reveal myself for a fool here, so I await the conclusion of the Lord's Game.

"Oh, don't make that face now, mercenary," the lord says. "You started this. You wanted this. I'll forget what you know, give you the men you need. But you take care of my dastardly cousin, won't you? Bitch-warrior, here, agrees. It is quite remarkable what you've done, but you're the second person to have found me out, and the first is quite the immovable object. You see, my cousin wanted such a large cut of my earnings that I'm much poorer for it. Men are cheaper than the knife he holds to my throat. You understand, I'm sure. Remove it, please."

"Your cousin is?" Bunta asks.

"Kabutomaru the Tanuki." She pauses for a moment. Her words don't register with me at first. I blink hard, the throb behind my eyes is a white-hot lance searing my vision; my master's head rolls, I can't escape it. They laugh at me like barking dogs. There, he stands, grouped in the safety of the godlord's numbers. One of the monsters. "Oh, are you okay? It seems you know my cousin. The Okami's reputation is far-reaching, I suppose. And he arrives here in one week. Do make sure it's quick and painless though, I wouldn't want my dearest cousin to suffer."

Chapter 6

"We've got ta' flee, Genaro sir," Bunta says to a Kekkei who clearly doesn't care for it as he readies a viper-quick rebuke. "No! I need this. I need Akate." Which adds to the tension on his face, the croak in his voice betrays something else. I thought only confidence suited him. "A coward or deserter can't raise Hands as quickly as I do. I'd be left with stumps."

"Stumps, sir?"

"Useless. Nothing."

Bunta is slow on the uptake today, he's a marionette to fear. But it wouldn't be a foolish idea. Everything the mercenary has built might just be ashes in the wind by this time next week, anyway.

Even with Akate's operations in Chisai growing, our base is still the same dilapidated room. Only now, we have a centre table with either a short leg or the reeds are bunched a bit thicker under one side of it. Upon the table, figurines slide around the map as pressure changes on it under Bunta's weight, devoid of hope.

Ropi readjusts the figurines over a map of this crooked town, she arrived a few days ago with a bow slung over her back and an empty quiver; I have an inkling about those arrows that put holes in our Yokusei captors now, but I can't be sure. She speaks in whispers to Thousand Hands. He confides in her, Jinto smiles warmly at her, but I don't much like the mouse of a woman. It's hard to trust someone with such tiny eyes. Unreadable.

"What?" Kekkei snaps, missing the mouse's quiet words the first time. "No. No. Well, your guess is as good as mine. Dead, I'd say. Wolves don't leave much to chance."

He pauses again, Bunta leans closer to them, trying to get the measure of what's been said, but I couldn't care less. There is but one simple solution to this, and I'm not sure this Yokusen blade of mine has the folds for it. Meganako and the Mistress of Swords, I envy your blade-born eyes. If I could see the path of every katana as I were you, would I see the Wolves dyed red, or would I see the carcass of the Hawk who forgot its wings?

"A waste. We can't."

"There's plenty goin' in alcohol houses. An' all this work, the gods'll notice. *Sleeper's bind'll* stop you."

"Bunta. You're a gods-be-damned fool with your superstitions." Kekkei spits. "We're talking an Okami and his Wolfpads. Trained soldiers. The finest."

"I just."

"Look, you're a great merchant, a friend, but this won't do."

Sick to death of this back and forth. A day's worth of pushing figurines around, ignoring the only solution – Kekkei pauses, as if they're going to jump at him with something other than the way he tries to go around.

"I said I'll do it," I say, but I don't believe my own words. With all the burning fury within me, I'll try. But I've felt the fangs of the Okami before. My body aches, it remembers. The black scars throb, they know the consequence. If I fall here, it all ends anyway. If Akate ruins, I do too. No choice.

"He won't duel you," Kekkei says, "you're a name only in Chisai, Nameless Swordswoman. Only in the towns and hamlets that surround. The wolves ignore the insect they can't see."

"I can be persuasive."

"You can't." Kekkei turns to me now. "Not now, they can't find out."

"It's my secret to tell!"

The merc doesn't reply, he flips the board, figurines sent flying to every inch of this pit, and the doors slams as he leaves. Bunta follows like a good dog, leaving me and the mouse. With one of the godlord's personal guard bearing down on Chisai, I feel their bloodlust; the full throb in my head, the flutter in my stomach, something is coming, but not even Kekkei knows the weight of my words. My choice was made for me by the godsborne that pried me from the hells. The fear that permeates every pore is not for the oncoming enemy, the fear that I will stray from the confines of whatever spell breathes life into my body, that I'll step one foot wrong and fall back into the arms of death.

"You're her?" A hushed question brings me from my rumination. Ropi doesn't know anything about personal etiquette as she's close enough that I feel her breaths on my face. But I don't move back, I level my gaze at her. "The one who failed to live in Orika?"

I grit my teeth. "I live! Don't I? What do you see here?" I don't even know the woman, yet she has a way of getting under my skin that I can't explain.

"Living," she says, "is that what you call this? A waste of good arrows."

"Ask your merc about living." I spit out each word. "Without this katana, he wouldn't be!"

"Hmm." She stares, still too close. "You do look like a hawk. What difference will you make this time, Hawk? Last time, you almost stepped into the pyre. Fascinating, though. How'd you do it? Survive, I mean."

She flits away before I can get my hands around her throat. I shoot to my feet, my breaths sounding like a laboured growl.

"Just don't die this time," she squeaks as she leaves, and I'm left alone.

I drop to my knees, clawing handfuls of reeds as I let her words sink in, repeating over and over. Tears fall but the hungry reeds consume them quickly. I need to swallow this. It's not the Way my master taught me, mine is to be a path of elegant efficiency, not this pitiful existence. Ropi's words cut true because she knew where to aim the knife; the Sword of the Dattori is *the tiger that always eats its fill.* That is, the blade that waits, the blade that uses every advantage, the blade bound to the honour of survival not the honour of the fight. I lost everything because I bound myself to redundant emotion. We forgot those words in the end. There was more to it, but no longer will I bathe in the sorrow of my household. That hasn't been for them, it was my own selfishness. Stop it.

Be the Hawk that soars high, the Hawk that sees all.

48

Master, why didn't you let me burn with the rest of my kin? The hells marked you that day.

I get up, grabbing the katana first and drawing it. I go through the forms of my house, acutely aware of the niggles and groans, creaks and winces that ricochet through my body. It's a mess. I need to start again, work the knots out, undo the folds, and reforge mind and body. I am not the Tanuki's equal, I know that. The Okami are comprised of the sword mistresses' favourites. The unequalled, peerless four warriors; their numbers stand as tribute, or mockery, to the gods.

The Tanuki, The Red Dog, The Fox, and The Slow Bear; each one a mountain to overcome.

Now, I'm aware of the beat of my heart in my ears, the dull throb in the back of my head, the blood that pumps life around my body, and the accursed thing that lies within it. I let my mind follow it for a moment, fly away, I'm soaring through the red sky. But I snap out of it and sheathe the blade. I can't. Not again. I have to rely on the Way of my household, not the curse of my bloodline.

* * *

The breeze's bite is a moment of relief from the beat of the sun overhead. Sukami's orb is at its zenith, and the wind's teeth are brittle; they do nothing to stifle my discomfort, but I work through it. Even though my robes are heavy with sweat, rubbing sores everywhere. A hundred, no, a thousand swings. I don't remember when I started, but this is the labour I was raised with. When the sword is unfamiliar, when the blade is distant, a thousand more swings you'll know it once more. A thousand more and you'll become it.

The farmer tends to his livestock at the edge of the arena; I catch him looking at me. Perhaps it's a longing for the land we forcibly turned into an arena, but he stays his gaze, pulling his lips inwards in an approximation of a smile that his eyes don't follow. He tips his head, what kind of a man respects thieves? I nod back and he finishes bringing his cattle into the shack he uses for cattle sheds, a horse stable, a sheep pen. He's no wealthy man, and we've taken half the land he has, not that he could graze them on such an arid dump. Hours he is gone in the morning, marching his living off into some distant grass, then hours back. All day it takes. And yet he still nods, still has a smile for the invader. Still seems more content than I'll ever be.

Swing and swing, burying frustration and thought in the pain. Learning the weight, the nuance of this foreign blade until my knees give way. Every muscle in my body is singing a different tune, and none of them I like. The sun winks above the farmer's shack, tendrils of orange whipping over the top, lashing my eyes with blue and purple strands. I can't stand it anymore. I wince as I try, my face taut, tight from sunburn.

The farmer appears again, he ambles towards me with resolve. In his hand a gourd, and the other a rice hat. There's something slung over his back, wrapped. Fool. What is he doing?

"Don't," I say, and he stops a few feet away.

"Is nothing." He winks. "Take it, warrior. Sunburn is no good for the likes of you." He winks with the hat outstretched. Rebuffed by his arrival, I heave myself up and snatch it. His smile is warm, orange like the sun; I don't like him. I don't like undeserved respect. Because I swing a sword I should stand above others? A lie I'd happily stamp out of Basho, I know many a dishonourable swordsman, many a scum that wielded the blade like a demi-god.

My robes are itchy, I'm tired, uncomfortable, but I'm of the Dattori, I still am. We survive with me and so do our duties. A stranger that presents himself as a friend is a friend until he proves himself a stranger.

Donning the hat, I tip it towards him. "What's on your back?"

He bows lower than me, handing over the gourd which I take and drain.

"Bokuto, eh!" He swings the bundle from his back and rolls them out onto the floor. I let a smirk tug at the side of my mouth as this strange little man has me perplexed. Training swords. He can't be... "And what do you plan to do with those?"

He picks one up, tests its weight and levels it at me in a loose, centred guard; I chuckle, for the first time in eternity, this picture is just too perfect. "I've not sparred in years," he says, "would you do me the honour?"

Fine. I sheath my blade and humour him. Picking up the bokuto is alien to me. It's light, the Mistress has never touched it. Lifeless, it's a wooden imposter.

A Dattori learns first that death awaits a drawn sword; to wield one means to be ready to kill, and to that end a bokuto is useless. No matter the age, or skill, we trained and lived, or trained and died, with a katana. Live, sharpened steel to break your teeth on. So, for what it's worth, I'm probably as out of practice as my opponent with it.

"Third's Peace, to the first hit," I say, marking the appropriate Samaki duelling etiquette, sure the old man wouldn't have it any other way. He agrees, we cross swords and then step away. I don't meet his eyes, nor do I follow the sword; both are too easy to be mesmerised by. I watch his posture, the small movements he has no control over, then I relax.

It isn't to the death, Masako. It's for fun.

His posture is intense, bright like a newly lit flame. He moves in quicker than I thought he could, jabbing straight at me. Predictable. I bat it aside and sweep into his guard, but I don't connect. Was he not committed to that strike? This...farmer has moved forward to meet me, ducking in close, his elbow strikes my forearm away. But now it is done, he's unable to stop himself falling to his knees as he drops his sword.

"Not out, not out. Heh."

"I think we're done." But I am intrigued. Up close, he is not small and weak like I thought; he's slender, yes, but beneath his leathery, sun-beaten skin, sinewy muscles writhe. There's little power in them now, but technique's beaten in. "Where did you learn that, Farmer? I'm warrior-trained, yet your riposte wasn't just luck. Meganako knows you."

"I studied the sword but have no house."

"Rōnin?!"

"No, you have to be a warrior first for that." He pauses, getting up from the ground, he dusts himself off and collects his bokuto. "As I said, I studied it. Oh, I tried and tried. But I never made warrior status, not the arms for it,

51

you see." This time his smile is thinner, his eyes dull and the candle seems to go out momentarily. "I tried to join a cla– oh, it doesn't matter. It's history now, not the kind worth a story."

"No, I'm intrigued," I say. "You got your duel."

"Win first."

He readies himself with the same loose guard.

I strike first, not like he did; I'm a viper springing from the many grasses of Weki, my forward thrust is perfect, if not for a bit painful on my lead foot. Something is still not right. I roar and spittle flies from my mouth as I feel my blade, my bokuto, turned. I let it stop me for a second, but my feet remember my trade better than me as they move together backpedalling away from the lacklustre riposte. The farmer's panting, so I don't let up. Between his heavy breaths I tread in, striking from my own Way's Fire Guard, a sidelong sweep. But he gets the tip of blade on it, narrowly saving himself from the flame – and there I see it, in that instant there's something different in his step. Unfamiliar. Perhaps one of those dead Steps, something old that his family have nurtured, kept secret too long.

His footwork is heavy but retreating – the nature of what he intends is at odds with the slippery way he moves, at odd with my own Step of the Foot; complimentary, hopping, moving with both feet always, the Crow Step. A way of keeping your feet about you, in a flow where they never meet but are always finding gaps – working together. It's the known way in Basho. The right way. We look to animals for their guidance for they move with nature where humans strive against it. The crow reigns above all as the thief who is never caught, so the warrior who becomes crow footed is the warrior the blade cannot touch. The Tiger Paw, too, borrows from its namesake. Though it's too committed, final for a prolonged duel. It's in the last moments where the tiger strikes heavy. When you need not worry about anything other than your opponent's end, when you are sure, that is when you move like the cat. Still, there are those useless and forgotten swords lost to generation or crumpled with their families – The First Godlord, Sama, died with a Step it is said, one light like the crow and vicious like the tiger. The stories of the Third tell of it but give no name.

It irks me so.

There are many once popular, outdated Ways – the last age saw the death of the Draw. A puritan duellist its main proponent, travelling the Three Coasts, Orika, Oshima, and Oyori, making famous the Single Draw Death. He met his end while missing his sheath amid duel. The fool. A slip-up that killed the Way itself.

The gods choose the sword they keep. Only those that close the duel, that win the fight in honour, still live on.

I don't claim to know them all, but a Step dangerous when wielded by an amateur that I don't know of is preposterous. The very thought of it heats my marrow, the scrape of my own teeth sends shivers down my spine. My chest is heaving now, I draw in a breath swilling the saliva and grit around and spit; we've worked the clay-tiled dust up around us. My sunburns sting. Beads of sweat tear lines through the grime on my skin.

Gods, why do you make me hate this man so? Damned Metsuku, damned it all. My eye twitches as I watch him, letting go with my offhand, flexing, knuckles pop and crack as I work the agitation through me. A side-arm is what I miss. Warriors are permitted two swords, so they bloody well should train in both.

I circle with him; his expressionless focus is a bother. It's all a bother. I want to run him through, unsheathe my katana and end this with the childlike spite that wells in my chest. The blade level with my eyes, I turn side-on, running my free hand along the blade and stopping at the end. The bokuto's point faces him.

"Study," I say, "you certainly know the technique."

I let fly for the last time, eyes on his feet; they are fluid, like currents flowing with each other, rivers that only know one route to take. But this is my own style now, the very torrent of the winds. His face is wrought with confusion as I dash by him quicker than he can change the mundane guard. I pass, I spin, letting my offhand take me, and lash out in the backspin. The farmer dodges, eliciting a gasp from me. But I've set him off balance. I regain mine as my free palm breaks my fall. Changing my grip in the same movement, I flip the sword, so the blade shoots away from the bottom of my hand, and strike him hard in the chest with the wooden hilt.

Eyes wide, with a gargle, he falls backward. Wheezing, unable to catch his breath, he lies prone.

I freeze now. Panic rushes through me as I realise, I've gone too far, got too serious with this man, until a laugh punches through the hacks.

"H-help me u...Get me up. Pl-lease."

Doing so, he brushes himself down again and bows. I mimic the depth for he has earned my respect tenfold. "Either I'm not the swordswomen I thought I was, or you were more the warrior that you let on."

"No," he says, coughing lightly into his hands. "I studied it. I studied hard, but never was that."

"Then tell me. I won."

"I'm a simple man. I always have been. My sword followed suit, as you can see. I'm at ease with the basics. I tried to join a clan, once, everything I lived and breathed for was that. I'm of low birth, you see, and it is only the way of the Samaki lords that gave me any hope."

I'd hoped he was being modest, but there really isn't anything to it. Though, he tells the story with the enthusiasm of blood spurting from a sword wound, and the look in his eyes remind me of Zaki, who coveted Dattori secrets, policies, and stories. Who I'm still shamed to remember with a heavy heart. But I'll face one thing at a time.

"And," I say, "that ended like this?"

"That ended at the feet of a fine, young commander. Now, I don't know where you're from, warrior. But you remind me of her." He pauses, taking the measure of me. His eyes widen, but he catches himself, dismissing whatever it was with a wave of his hand. The sudden urge to wrap my hands around myself takes hold but I'm still. "But, no. She was young, fierce. Patient. I couldn't hold my sword to her. You're...You would do well to learn that, patience. I'm not even half the swordsman you are, but you were too much in a hurry to prove that."

I feel my lips move into a snarl, ready for the attack, but I clench my fists and bury it. Patience? The Dattori words ring in my mind. I'm patient, I'm efficient. Why don't I just smash that warm grin off his face and run? Argh.

Is it so? I'm in a hurry, a hurry for revenge. To let master rest easy. But my sword, does it reflect that? "Impatient? That's your analysis of my sword?"

"Yes." I want to break his stare, but I hold it. The elderly look through into the soul, they don't have any time to waste on the physical. "I heard it. The town *cheep-cheeps* with your fate. I heard the provocation, clever, although I don't really get it. Are you stupid, swordswomen?"

"What?"

"I hear those stories too, of the warriors of the Okami. You'll die."

"What do you know?"

"I don't, I suppose. But please, remember my words, and the patience of my sword."

He turns to go, but I'm not finished with his story. "Tell me, what patience was it that you challenged a Samaki commander?"

"You're not an outlander, then. Basho has its rules, yes, northerner. But the South permit anyone. As long as you are unbound, swear your fealty and prove your blade. A Samaki clan may permit you." He sighs, and my heart flutters as I know the man is wrong. I realise it. Remember. "But I couldn't even prove my swing against that force of nature, that walking storm."

His words bother me as they're not quite correct, so I run. Run from the words, run from him, and I don't turn back. Don't head for the town, but away from it. Splashing through the rice paddies at Chisai's edge, then through grasses long enough to scratch at my sunburn until I can't anymore. What greets me is the tufty, scrappy bit of land that skirts between forest and fields. The trees stand as guards that urge me to not go any further and I collapse.

That isn't true, farmer, not the Samaki's rules. Only the Dattori lived by that Way; master was an orphan who rose to power. Anyone could in the harsh outskirts the Lord Council has always struggled to grasp. If you proved you had the mettle to, anyone could rise into the seat of a Samaki lord. Without a family, master recruited his own.

* * *

55

I awake to a yip, a growl off in the distance. But I take no notice of it.

The grass is dry, harsh against my cheek. I bring my hand up from underneath me, wiping the sleep from my eyes. Sitting up, my head swims, and it's a couple of seconds before I realise where I am. Annoyance is my friend these days. I don't seem to be able to escape it, stress and anger soon greet me. I tear a handful of grass, wincing as the sun-hardened blades slice my palm, and sling it into the wind only for the breeze to blow it back towards me. Pathetic; somehow, I fell asleep out here on the edge of the woodland. A short distance away Chisai hums. A dull glow emanates from it, making the night sway above like the drunk thugs that are probably out in its streets.

The moon hangs in full above me; it is not all that dark here, between the town and its glare. To my *heretical* vision, it's no duller than the hour before dusk. I stand up, and another bark punctuates the distant din of the town. But it's closer now, my heart grips my chest. Pivoting on my heel, it grabs my attention, begs I look into it.

The yips and growls are moving closer still. A little way into the wood there is movement. I take off not worried for myself, but more intrigued by this midnight disturbance. Perhaps, a pack of wild dogs. I check my blade on the run, the cool metal of the hilt charm suppresses any second thought. I draw closer to whatever lurks out here, stopping dead as soon as I see it, hand slipping from the katana.

Jinto is smiling, dancing around a pack of dogs, no. Wolves. Dragons above, I want to cry out, but I'm neither sure of the danger nor whether I'm going distract the Meater-boy as he holds them at bay. There's no time, the options tumble over each other in my mind. The wolves' ears prick to the whistle of my sword as I draw it.

They freeze, myriad yellow eyes fix me in their glare.

Unsure of my actions, I slow to a walk, ready to defend with a two-handed guard.

A chorus of growling starts.

"Jinto, go!" I shout.

"No."

I double-take, and whisper blasphemy at having discovered this mess. The boy looks as if he's overlaid with a dull, emerald ghost; dried blood splatters his face. A metallic tang greets my senses. The wildness subsides within me. "What is this?"

A wolf dashes to meet me, its gait is strange. It stands lopsided between us; veins pulsate and writhe around an overgrown leg. Mutated; a chunk of flesh has been bitten from its muzzle. I tear away from it and think twice about striking the boy. His company seizes my reaction. "Foolish!"

"Go, Hawk. Please, leave me here. We're not done."

I step forward, and the growling intensifies, yaps and barks breaking its monotony.

"This close to the town?" Strain laces my words. "What are you thinking?"

"Don Yoku can help, Hawk! The godlord is not the only one with wolves." The strange words are even more so coming from such a young, gaunt boy. "He can help, he always wants to help. It is in his nature; he reaches out to everyone. Strong. He is strong here."

"Not even the fat lord would turn her eyes to this if you're found."

"Greed." He ignores me. "Greed is plentiful here. In that town, Don Yoku plays. Why would they care? The whole place is a tribute to him."

My eyelids are heavy, feeling the tension between them. I'm tired. I don't need this now. "Gods, you Meaters are insufferable." I'm not half the warrior I was, and yet my foe rides closer as we speak; Kekkei is playing games I cannot even see, spinning webs too extensive for anyone to follow, and now Greed gatherings, rituals, I don't know. "Fine. Stay here."

"Don't tell Kekkei."

"Why not?"

"I-it's... it's for you."

"Don't you dare!" I shout. "What would I need this. This abomination for?"

He doesn't reply immediately, the growls subside and then he speaks, "So you don't die. Don Yoku doesn't want you to die."

"The gods are all gone or dead, only their curses remain! You speak with the tendrils of madness in your mind. Animal blood is crazed. Look at you!

Meatheurgy, curse magic, falls under *heavenly* sanction for this reason! Madness."

"Stop running." His voice echoes from the pack now, a mimicry of growled whispers. "You worked blood at the summit, is that not how you survived?"

"I. I don't know."

"Let me help," he says with just his own voice. "A drop of your blood?"

"No!"

I turn and leave, having had my fill of madness for one night.

Chapter 7

A few days pass and I see neither the Meater, nor the mercenary. A whiff of the mouse keeps my hackles up. Especially today when she brought a summons to me, from the great Thousand Hands. Did he climb so high he can't get off the horse to come fetch me himself?

The meeting place has changed, I'm promised. The Sinking Swan, *high-class plum winery, and fried rice balls,* it reads, not like the pig's trough we entered the town through; it's in the lord's own district, through checkpoints now manned by the Jet Blacks, mirroring the heightened tension that seethes through the town.

Wafts and waves of violence crash against the city with a drunken brawl, a pool of blood, or a stabbed denizen lying in every street. Okami visits are usually secret, restricted to the lord's estate. But, through my own doing, the cat roams free. Every man, woman, and child know of it. So, it's an official Lord Council visit, now. An honour for most towns, but not this one. Chisai, where the street vendor's headache prevents them from making the early morning cries of tofu, fresh vegetables, and fermented soybean. Whose court adjourned long ago, governors murdered or missing, replaced by Head Brigand of Trade. I smirk. Tamikura is the rhyme and rule of this place, and her concern is only herself; her cousin plays the part of blackmailer and protector, keeping Chisai under Okami veil.

Each one, a power unto themselves, answering only to the Lord Council when they are needed. They can do as they please. But one thing turns their stomach, and I should know, I'm no stranger to the Wolves. No stranger to their bent policies and criminal behaviour. One thing that makes them quake, and that's when the rest of the pack turns their focus on them.

I know these streets now. I know Chisai; I've spread word of my own, borrowed townsfolk for my picketing scheme. I spread but one message and now Basho looks upon this small town, the Okami's gaze is caught. I'm assured, by a little mouse, the Tanuki hurries to take care of the matter. To address the message from the grave.

* * *

At the entrance of the Sinking Swan, Bunta and Oboro meet me. An unfamiliar face in Kekkei's close ranks leads me to believe Hands of the Akate surface with the break of every day. Oboro is a slender, plain-looking man that has about as much presence as a whisper in a crowd. Nor could you pick him out of one. By design, perhaps. The daggers in his belt are not so subtle; catching the light, the inlaid hilt betrays him...sea gems. Anyone else might miss them, but I was commander, my eyes see it out of necessity.

As I'm ushered into the Swan, I'm met by a hot wall of incense, spices, and fried fats. They lead to a small private room. Servants part the doors, and Kekkei awaits, already seated at the table. It is not with warmth that he greets me. Was he always so grey? His short-cropped hair looks like snow against his oak skin. Without a smile for me, and only the shallowest of bows, he offers me a seat; it feels like years, not weeks, that separate our meeting in the prison cart from this moment. If Kekkei were a strong, unyielding tree of a man when I met him, now he's a withered old stump. The past weeks put the stress of the former on him.

"I've enough Hands now," he starts. "We can take what we...I've built and regroup in the Yata fields. Take what we have and nurture it." He's caught in his way, repeating himself, regurgitating old plans. I'm not here for this. It's not his cause I joined; it was meant to be mine. But I've become a source of income and, now that I've upset the course of things, a source of pain.

"No, I won't run," I snap, "this is what happens when you keep cowards close. Bunta is no advisor." There's noise from outside the door; the man in question doesn't like me being alone with his master.

The mercenary plays with the ties on his ornately clasped robe, silver veins spread across it in the shape of trees and leaves in a fashion befitting lords – *you forget yourself.* "We can't do this!"

"I've done it before."

"And died. You failed."

"I'm right here? Open your damned eyes."

"But not even Jinto knows how. Gods, Hawk, this is the Okami we're talking about."

So, the boy keeps secrets from him. Perhaps I should humour Jinto after this is done, see what he knows. It was never like we could uncover much anyway, Master Dattori and I. And then something hits me. Looking past the wildness in his eyes, he's fiddling with the ornate clasps still, that look is not wild with anger, there's fear in there; by now I should have heard what happened to the Akate. Kekkei was captured close to me, and yet there's no talk, no rumours of Akate, and we're in the very place rumours go to die. Most curious of all, the head of the largest mercenary company is acting more like the Lord of Thieves and Spies than he is a warlord for hire.

When the Lord Council wants to make an example of someone, you end up as a theatrical joke, but when you're linked to a secret they want to hide... Ah, and here it is. "Where is Akate, Kekkei?"

"Don't do this now!"

"This behaviour...What have you become? You promise change that would destroy the Lord Council, yet you cower hearing the name of the godlord's bodyguard. What was it? One or two? Did the entire Wolfpad army mobilise to wipe you out?"

He huffs, deflates into the cushions as he reclines back, "What does it matter? I told you we stumbled upon something they'd rather keep hidden. Hawk, you know better than most they don't." *Let it slide.*

I'm sorry for pushing him, but I don't stop. This won't end the way he wants it. "I died for my people, and I've risen again. The Fox put me in the grave, and I'll put him in his! The difference between me and you is that I will finish this."

"No, that difference is only one of us will make the same mistake again,

61

while the other will learn."

"And how do you suppose you'd do it then? You promised upheaval, promised change, Kekkei!"

"Take your hand off that. Why in the gods' name are you carrying that around with you now anyway?" I let go of my sword and adjust my robes back over it. I should have known. Mercenary honour is as valuable as the coin it is bought with, and his loyalty fades with every spent koban. He continues as I don't deign to answer him, "Yes, I agreed to take your estate back. With force, it was the easiest way, as long as we had the lord's men. It would be a seat of power, a place to grow, with your household name." I grimace at that, but he waves it off. "We could enter small town and Samaki courts, negotiate with minor lords, households, buy off officials, take the Lord Council down from Metsuku's shadow, reduce his power. Be smart!" Kekkei's worked up, face reddened, voice rising. "Less a single assassination, this is what I've been trying to do, but your ignorance leaves me in ruins, draws attention as only your spite could!" He slaps down a scrunched-up piece of parchment and slides it to me. "READ IT OUT."

"*To Chisai the Hawk flew.*

In Chisai, a swordswoman knows the Fox has seven tails, the eighth chewed off by the Hawk. In Chisai, a swordswoman knows the cowardice of Wolves who sit on the lap of the dog.

In Chisai, a swordswoman waits with sharpened talons, and a Fox-tail robe."

I can't hide my smirk. "A child's story."

"Do you know what you've done? I spent precious time and resources taking down these gods-forsaken notices, but for nothing! You've ruined it all. A childish story indeed, but the men we're dealing with mistake childish pride for honour. Regardless of its merit, your provocation is known. The Okami answer them all the same." He nods to himself. "Outriders from the Tanuki's retinue have already arrived in Chisai. Wolfpad guards are already here. I'm risking everything just having this meeting with the foolish, *Nameless Swordswoman.*"

I ran away with it, really thought after everything I'd been through, I found someone to trust again. Someone who cared about Basho, about honour, and knew what it meant to lose all of that. Clearing my thoughts, I swallow back my own self-pity, quash despair renewed, and look him right in the eye for what I feel is the final time. "What you plan to do just means giving another man the same power. Removing it from one and giving it to another. What I will do is break that cycle. THAT IS THE WAR I'M FIGHTING."

He touches his chin, eyes distant. Getting up, he stands over me, and says, "Ropi is already leading our operations away from your mess. You've been too self-absorbed to notice. We will rebuild from the Yata fields, and I'll do this my way. Now." His lips curls and twitches, like he doesn't want to say it. "Goodbye."

"You won't invite me?!"

"Would you come?"

* * *

Alone, I walk back to the inn.

I'm caught off-guard by the child-sized bundle in the corner where most of the bedding is bunched up. So, I sneak across the room. My silent footsteps send several things scurrying under the reed. I'm used to it now, so I don't waste a breath as I find space across from the wildboy. Why is he still here? After tomorrow, perhaps I'll try to understand him. For now, I remove my borrowed blade from the scabbard and take it to pieces, thinking back to the last time I did this with a katana. To the painful memories that I now feed from, the ones that will drive this clean blade through the blackened heart of the Tanuki.

Chapter 8

BEFORE MY FALL

Around the table, we stood over a great, tattered map of Basho. For a second, I'd imagined what it is to be one of the sora dragons, seeing our trifle lives scurrying, meeting, warring beneath them; not in known history had they bothered with us. A lost cause, perhaps. If only I, as one of them, could've soared above that petty nonsense.

My lip curled at the company Master kept. We shouldn't have entertained the same scum who would move in on our rice paddies. Our livelihood. The same cur that hailed from the pack of dogs that would see every gold, silver and bronze of our clan scattered to the wind. And why? Because we prospered, far from the reach of the godlord. At the end of the end. But they couldn't have had that. So, they imposed filth on us. The filth that stood in front of me boiled my blood. I could've just reached out...no. The thump of my blood in my ears was not a welcome sensation. Anger could take hold of me. It has always had a weird way with me.

With his finery, the dress robes were guilted in the bright greens, and yellows of the Lord Council's Inspection Service, he still looked like a mutt that'd taken too much pride in its owner's errands. His robe was a mural, a shrine to the prosperity of fields and lands of the Lord Council, but here he was treading all over it. Dishevelled whiskers, and the disappearance of his neck told of luxuries that made me hate him that little bit more; next to him, Lord Dattori wore age, strength and experience the younger man would never possess. His muscles were still full under the plain green robes, a Dattori clansman stayed as sharp as their katana, especially the lord. We followed by his example.

Despite Master's presence, the Inspector looked down his nose, as he fiddled with gemmed rings; he dared not inspect those close to the godlord, so he wished to make up for the loss there.

"Please, please, Inspector." Zaki, a favoured Dattori retainer, had patted the fat old man to my left shoulder. His battle plate sang a light chorus of metal as he did; never one to relax, the armour was as much a part of Zaki as were his eyes and ears. "Let me show you our fields," he continued. "We are but a humble establishment. On my honour, our common folk aren't many, and all give back to the lands. To tax us to the hells would do us no good. Do you wish to see this land fall into ruin? Surely, being so far out, it would not please the godlord to have to send his own men here."

"Hmm, I concur. You have a fine many peasants to me. And here." His chubby fingers encircled our small plot on the map. "There's a fine many paddies. I can see just well here. Plenty of rice, hmm, production. Plenty of profit hmm. Lord Dattori, you must be a wealthier man than you share." The dirty line that was his mouth stretched into a smirk and his eyes narrowed, so that the whites were barely visible. Rat.

Master, at the head of the table, took a deep inhalation of breath, stifling the grimace he let slip for a moment. He looked to me, warning, then to Inspector Origan. "Inspector, this is not comfortable. You must be weary from your travels. Even by carriage and palanquin, it must have been a testing journey. A party, in your honour—"

"No," Origan said. "I will not spend any longer than I have to at this shabby end of ends." He didn't try and hide his grimace. Nor respect the politeness of Master, and it grew thin with me. I clenched my fingers around the hilt of CrowKiller. Edan, our advisor to my right, jumped. Never a stomach for violence that one – but always an opinion to incite it. Nor his lackey in the fine silk robes beside him, who gestured to Master, who shot me a look as my plate scraped against itself slightly in the movement. He nodded, and I let my hand slip from the sword, from anger. Breathing in deeply, the smell of lilies, the incense always did soothe me. I half-thought that's why Master used it at those meetings; he couldn't tame the wildness inside me, so he tried to appease it. I don't even know why he had me there. No, not of high birth. But yes, the daughter he never had, the finest commander his men had ever seen, he said. But I would much rather CrowKiller had taken that man's head than let him walk out of there. Would that I could go back. That folly cost everything.

The fat plebeian flicked me a look as he noticed something amiss and raised his nose. "Is that all? Then we are done here. Hmm, two more gold kobans per yield should suffice, and one for the threat." He looked back to me and held the stare.

I shifted, and the room held its breath. But I didn't go for my blades and spat on the floor instead. He raised his eyebrow and his smirk shortened but did not disappear. Almost willing for him to give me a reason to take his life, I tensed. But he did not react.

I looked to Master, who closed his eyes slowly, and bowed his head. Only slightly. Honour would not demand more for such a man. And then he smiled. "Very well. Please forgive my commander, the young are too brash, too inexperienced sometimes for matters that concern the wise, and honourable like you." His words stoked my anger, the thump against my chestplate unbearably wild. But I breathed the scent in deep and slow. Finding my centre.

"Atrocity!" I didn't even need to react. Edan was tomato-red. "We can't, Lord Dattori. This is outrageous. Three kobans! What cause do you have, *impartial* Inspector?"

"Outrageous!" His assistant mimicked.

"Do not insult this good man." Master said. "He acts within the power granted to him by the Lord Council. It is but my fault alone that we have many taxable 'folk. Too many, but such is the way of the outer clans."

The only thing that was perhaps outrageous was that our humble advisors couldn't set aside enough coin for the finery they draped themselves in.

It was just Master, Zaki and I.

66

If he wasn't one of Dattori's sworn, perhaps Zaki would have been a good mate, one that could tame the beast that resides inside me. His long black hair was like mine but that's where the similarities ended, he was prettier than I. Zaki's oily locks swept down his back until it met the weather-beaten warrior's kimono; the faded old colour reminiscent of the moody sky that hung over our great household. It was a wonder to see him without a full plate on, but Master requested it. The time ahead was dire, we needed this before what was to come. Rest, time to relax.

Time to plot, and plan.

Zaki knelt, without a word, and poured Master, himself, and then me, tea.

Master's own quarters always smelled of lavender and orange. An incensed smog seemed to surround us once more, flecks of the unsubtle smell wafted through my nose. I coughed, not being able to bear the smell. But that was the way Master liked it. Less likely to be bothered for long, he had said, not that he minded it. The canvased walls around us dulled an inky blue on the moonless night beyond it, and a myriad of candles flickered. On my approach to the quarters, I saw movement in the heavens; the giant sora dragons above watched me that night, judging me as I went, I supposed. But then again, what interest is one little warrior to the gods' own?

Out of my reverie, and into the meeting, I knelt, as my honour required, and said, "Master, what great plan do you have to counter such an insult?" A growl in my speech I didn't intend. "The fieldclans are more the godlord's men that ours, and yet not only do they tax us for their paddies, but they raise it. Fieldclan fields are fieldclan run. Fieldclan problems. They tax us for their presence as if they are Dattori clanmen? An insult. Our fields suffer those scum. Reports say they've turned to the poppy, but we've not had the time, nor resources to ride out. The impartial inspector is but one of his *godliness'* dogs. An insult–"

"Masako, do not let the coals glow. Do not let that anger ruin you, burn away your senses," Master replied. "There is nothing to be done. Would you have me go to war against the Lord Council? I assure you that would present a direr situation than the one we find ourselves in."

I snarled, the spit in my mouth gathered almost on cue as the fires swirled within, but I did not spit, not there. Not in Master's quarters. "We would be undone, Master Dattori. It is not a simple request! Our fields produce a crop. A crop that is already heavily taxed, and that already yields a finite sum. A finite sum we live around. We are not a household of infinite wealth, we are no godlord's cur. My lord." I spoke to him as my all. The sole authority in my life, the one I would rend the heavens for, to implore him. To make him see sense. "They are trying to ruin us. My blood...let it be known."

"NO! absolutely not." Master's calm exterior broke and he panted heavily as he straightened himself, wiping the spit from his chin.

If Zaki knew what we were talking about, he didn't notice. Kneeling, he continued to sip the tea as if he were somewhere else, awaiting his arrival into the madness unfolding in front of him.

"The quickest way for a cat to die is to confront the pack of dogs who chase it. We will not be so foolish. To add, it is of utmost importance that we hold onto the hand the gods dealt us until the very end of the game. Masako, my card of death, do not rush into it. A carp becomes a dragon only after swimming against the stream." Master looked to Zaki and nodded. "For now, we have a way to keep afloat."

Zaki placed his cup gently on the table and turned to face me, not even the Painted could match his beauty. And he'd certainly make a more fetching one than I. "There is a way we can settle the sum." He began. "Among the clans, we are somewhat fortunate. You know of the godsborne forest that resides within our territory—"

Fury. "Those are to be left alone!" I snapped. "Honour to Sama's Third, under the sora dragons' gaze, they are sacred forests. Sacred beasts entrusted to us by the divine, no matter their nature. What business would we have with them? What could we want with the oni?"

"Our customer."

"Zaki! No, this is outrageous!"

"Listen first, Masako."

I got up and looked down on Zaki. Not happy still, I grabbed his robes and yanked him to his feet, pulling him close enough I could smell the garlic he'd eaten, letting him feel the anger in my breaths, see it in my eyes. "What do you mean LISTEN? I am all ears. Your idea reeks of death. Don't say it, you're asking me to do this?"

"We go together...with a unit."

"Certain death."

Zaki snatched himself free, and Master was there between us, forcing me back. "This is for the good of the clan. Hear him out or not, Commander Dattori. I've made the decision. It is by my command you will slay an oni."

His words hit my chest like the heavy strikes of bamboo we beat our bodies numb with, taking the breath from my lungs. Master hadn't consulted me. His strike leader. His sword. I regained my composure, not letting these men get the better of me, I said, "Go on!"

"Oni meat." As Zaki said it, I felt the warmth drain out of my body. "There are some Mea– Divine Greed Shamans that put out bounties for the godsborne in these...trying days. Some choose to break the treaty and use the fouled meats. For that, only the Gods' watchful Eyes may judge. A request came in, that I ignored until I found it prudent to share with Lord Dattori. And now, you." This formality irked me more than the task. Zaki, what is this? "They request a butchered adult. Twenty gold kobans in payment. Ten years of prosperity for the clan lay at our door, Masako. We must take it."

My jaw loosened at the price. Who could afford such a sum? I blinked hard and forgot my reservations for a moment, stepping back. Focusing on it again, I looked to Master and then to Zaki, my heart a dull patter in my ears. Even with my blessing, to slay such a being. Their eyes betrayed the same fear. "But," I started. "An adult oni. Under the great sora dragons, even if it were my wish to be a butcher in this ungodly hunt, to fell such a beast is not within my power." Master shot me a knowing look, but I doubted it myself. I couldn't.

He sighed and said, "A Shaman owes our clan a great favour." Master got up, pushing aside the tea, went to the desk behind him, and returned; he poured sake into a bowl and drank long, twice. Placing the cup back down, he gestured for Zaki and I to take our turn. I winced at the taste, never liking that bitter acidity anyway. He continued, "He will join you in this task. Willing to leave his volunteered exile, he will arrive in a few days. With

69

him, a chance presents itself. You will crush one of those ungodly beasts!" Master's voice trembled, with excitement or nervousness, I didn't know which.

I shook my head. That cretin... "Cat Food returns." I said, gritting my teeth. The last place in Basho I wanted to be was around that creep.

* * *

It was silent, only the beat of my heart, and the deep breaths I maintained to ensure absolute care was taken, disrupted my task.

CrowKiller, and HighWolf, my sibling swords, were balanced on stands in front of me. I took CrowKiller first, bringing her up in both hands, and bowing my head out of respect for the warriors she had helped deliver to the afterlife, to the scum that I've killed. To the innocents that fell for my family's purposes. For those she has yet to deliver to the otherworld, but that are written in the blade.

I took the hilt in one hand, and the hilt-peg in the other, enabling me to safely separate it from the blade. To gently free her from her hold. Holding the naked tang to my face, I marvelled at the workmanship once more, the infinite folds that produced this beautiful monster.

First, I patted the balm on one side, then the other. Taking a cloth, I freed CrowKiller from any impurity leftover by the lives she's taken since the last time, revitalising my partner. I took another cloth and carefully slid my hand along the blade. Silence. It must be perfect as I cleanse every evil she has helped me commit. Smoothing out the blemishes, I don't even allow my own body the care that I do my swords. I don't allow anyone as close to me as these two. Never. It is a weakness I can't afford.

Finally, so that she never leaves me, never rusts, and always remains strong, the treated clove oil was applied. I take the same care. The same careful movements. The same silence.

Like it was second nature, I put the sword back together in a flash, and repeated the process with my littlest, HighWolf.

Once done, I pulled open the canvas separating my quarters from our estates and let the dark night swallow me. Out there, I could hear the crickets chirping. The night was cold, and my nose was filled with the bitter freshness of it more than it could pick out any particular smells. It was just as well, the Oni Wuld carries a stench that you can't even burn out – so I should have revelled in the purity that night.

I sighed, working my body loose. The next day, a fight for survival started. That it was just a hunt, just a mission, just a request, was wrong. That was the start of something that has spiralled out of any control the gods would allow me; desecrating holy grounds was one thing and killing the godsborne that reside within was another. One that surely drew the attention of the sora dragons that fly in the skies above. My head thudded. I wasn't sure whether it was for excitement or nervousness. An evil part of me, the part that boils within, threatening to consume everything human, wanted that fight. It wanted to test its strength against those giant beasts.

I was peerless, in those clanlands. Only the Wolves made me look weak. Those warriors still stand in my path to make a change to these lands, to usher in something that is fair to all. To my master's memory. Hopeless. For I long to live in a world that isn't run by the godlord and his pack. But their warriors are many, and that many-bladed whoreson is the pinnacle of what I wish to defy.

The breeze caressed my cheeks, and I shivered a bit.

Pulling the canvas to, I turned, and placed the swords with my suit of plate armour. Praying to the sora dragons so they forgave me. That they wouldn't hold it against me. That my blades stayed strong.

A rustling. No, something disturbed the air. I couldn't quite put my finger on it. Not wanting to ruin this ritual, to worry my twins with the matter, I grabbed a small blade from under my kimono. Jumping back, I turned.

My eyes widened and Zaki didn't even flinch with the dagger millimetres from his neck, about to spill all that he was back into the earth if I wasn't so disciplined.

He said nothing. He knew that wasn't allowed but still he pulled me toward him.

Intertwined were our fates. That night, and the days after.

* * *

Now I sheath the dead man's katana, breathing deeply like my sword master taught. Centring, all the memories flood away from me, the stress and tensions spill out into this dank pit. The snake of anxiety coiled in my stomach unravels itself and slithers into the recess of my mind. None of this matters if I die. None of this matters while I wield my sword in the hope to find Master some peace. Some honour. While I face my first foe in a line of those who deserve to die for what the godlord orchestrated, I am just a warrior. A sworn sword of the Dattori; I repeat my path once more, *"The demons and gods crash against our walls, we hold fast, like the skerry. Strong like the stone. We will wait with swords sheathed for we are warriors of the Right Way. They breach the gates, we let them in, show them hospitality and patience. They dishonour us, mock us, hurt us, we show them war. We are unyielding, and the gods taste our blade. We are Dattori, not bent by the demon's trickeries.*

"For honour, our life is forfeit."

Chapter 9

The Tanuki is not at all that magnificent; his plate is dull, sandy, the yellow peeling off. Yet, it hides a wickedness. A sulphurous aftertaste pours from it – a crackle, a hint of something nasty. The armour is godsblessed, spell-forged, call it what you want. It's horrifying to behold. Barely am I able to make out the ghostly figures acid-etched deep into its surface. A seat for its power. His demonic mask hangs from his kabuto, at the side of his wide, bearded face. His eyes are round, foreign-looking. Not pure Bashoan, or perhaps his gene pool is weak. An oaf, if anyone asked me, is what I'd describe him as. Even his odachi doesn't look so great propped against his seat. Amateur is one who would wield anything other than the standard katana, it is not the Way of efficient killing to wield the unwieldy.

The Wolfpads, the Okami soldiers, skulk a ways behind him, worrying over their swords while they stare longingly at their master. Like caged dogs, they fidget along the edge of the arena, looking for a way out, a way in. Just one word from their master would do it, but it doesn't come. They whine and wait.

For the first time since my household was crushed, since I watched my master's head fall, the butterflies in my stomach are a storm; excited or desperate to flee their confines, my gut flips on itself. I grip tighter on the hilt of my sword to steady my hand. The other tucked into my robe. I came here, like every morning, to deepen my relationship with the sword-mistress, not expecting the town transformed overnight. Vendors cried tofu, and other foods like dawn-birds as soon as the sun broke the night. Ruined market stalls had been repaired, hammered together and, from the emerald colour of their robes, the lord's own servants served the usual rabble. The thuggish common folk of Chisai remained the same. But there was order. Jet Blacks dotted about saw to that.

My chest is taut; breath trapped in my throat refusing to go any further as I made my way to the farmer's field. I was not the first one here. Already, Tamikura's palanquin had been perched next to some makeshift throne, where she sits now, servants fanning her. In a similar chair was the Tanuki, surrounded by servants and guards; even here, vendors fried and boiled amongst their retinue. I've become a spectacle. It is as if a festival popped up in my honour, as if I am some kind of sport they waited to view.

It wasn't until the other player got out of his seat that it became real.

A guard almost trips over himself at the beckon of the Okami; he hands him the overlarge odachi.

I tumble through the depths of the Kirisam again, unable to push my head above the water.

The Tanuki unsheathes the blade. Chucking the scabbard to the side, he swings the sword up with one hand and rests the flat of it on his shoulder. He grins widely and says, "Where's Genaro Kekkei?" His voice is deep, gravelly. And I'm caught off guard already. Kekkei? So, he didn't come here because of my scheme. Not to see the swordswoman who knows a little too much about his brethren? He continues, "Oh. Why that look? I didn't come here to address ghost tales. I'm not interested in low-birth rōnin who seek to inflate their fame." He scoffs and the hyenas behind him cackle along. "Where is he?" Foolish was I to think that the Lord Council would move to crush stories from the crow's nest. Kekkei, is this why you fled? They're not done with you yet, but what do I care? You left me, and I've half a mind to walk away from this now, to let them go after you. But I hear the whine of teeth being ground together and realise it's my own. I can't tear my stare away from him. I hate him.

I draw my katana.

"Tanuki," I say, "a drawn sword is a question of its own. I'll answer only that. I don't care for anything else. Kekkei? I don't know the man."

It's as though I'm standing in front of a flock of birds as their wings flap about and the squawking rises a few octaves, the crowd is still trickling in from the town. Wolfpads jostle and push amongst revellers, drawing their weapons to mimic me. But the Okami swine raises his off-hand, and it goes silent. At least, his guard does anyway, frozen amongst the writhing denizens of Chisai.

"Pah," he scoffs, "duelling rights? I'm the godlord's Okami. This thing?" He swings his odachi in an arc in front of himself. "I like to carry it around. It breathes better outside its scabbard. Not a challenge. I wouldn't waste my time; I'd have you executed if I wanted." His jovial tone ends in a bite. This is a dog who truly believes in its own bark and thinks that's enough.

"SO. Where is Kekkei?"

The arena quietens, holds its breath while I level my sword at my opponent.

"Answer, whore!" Someone shouts.

I'd like to say that none of it affects me, that I brush it off but it's not easy. I refrain from snapping back, but I'm losing the fight against the boiling anger in my chest. My veins bubbling, something deep in my blood urging me on, begging that I cut off his head. It's easy to go with the voice, to flow with the tide but I stand against it.

He shakes his head and chuckles to himself before saying, "I didn't want it to go like this. I'm here." He gestures behind himself. "To visit my dear cousin. How I do love this hole and the…fine people that call it home. A holiday as such, from my heavenly duties. However, we border Yokusei lands here. My father's lands." In my haste, it was overlooked. But perhaps Kekkei knew of the Tanuki's former allegiances. The Okami are handpicked from the sons and daughters of the vassal families…save one, and laziness would have it that Kabutomaru polices his old family's borders in the name of the Lord Council. He wants his prisoner back.

"Ah. Loyalty," I snap. "And you'd be rewarded for murder in your household's name, but I was executed for it! While we're here, what did you think of my tale? You say it didn't bring you here, but then why do you stand with a curiously drawn sword, in front of a nameless, unimportant, warrior?"

"Woman, you're not a warrior. Under the watchful eye of the dragons, and the heavenly word of the godlord, blasphemy against the Lord Council will be met with force. I'd wanted to get more out of you before, but you test my patience much too much." He swings his giant blade up with speed and elegance I'm taken aback by, stopping in a high guard. "In the name of the godlord, whore, and Under the Eyes of the Gods, your rights to an honourable execution are nulled. I'll slay you like the common cur you are."

Repetitive swine. The talking is done. And I take my first step towards the godsborne's demand as I close the space between us in a couple of strides. Moving both feet in unison, my footwork always outshined my peers, I sweep around his side, dodging the first, predictable overhead swing. Dust kicks up around me as I move. Spitting grit and slashing across myself, I go for his outstretched strike. I have no pride as a swordswoman, so I don't mind taking his arms. I have pride in the win, so I look to finish it quickly.

Before I cut, he let's go of his two-handed grip, and slashes backwards wildly with his near hand, forcing me to pull out of my slash, and retreat. Inhuman. Impossible movement. The tang of magic oilier now. Sun glaring, I blink the blue and orange fires that dance across my eyes, circling with my guard up. I squint, tears run down my cheeks. This is bad. The bright flashes from his armour make the Tanuki almost invisible as he rights himself, the chatter of his plate revealing more than my eyes can see. Though, it is the height of summer and, magic or not, he's a fool to be fully plated. If not, I'd already be dead. He's sluggish as if he hasn't woken up and doesn't take the opportunity to press me while I'm blinded, that heavy armour will be the making of me.

I back-pedal as he tries to close in, not giving him an inch more than I mean to, working my feet like a good warrior should. When one moves the other follows. A resting foot is a dead body. With a dash, he strikes. I pivot on my lead foot and trace my blade along his as I guide him away from a killing blow. Still, he turns and follows. I'm in awe, but I shake it off. If it wasn't my duel, I'd be impressed. He dogs me with the speed and precision of a much smaller warrior, with a shorter blade. Savage and light. The pressure is too much. Before I'm forced into a mistake, I stop my retreat. Changing tact, I place all my weight into my back foot and switch into a crouch; from there, he's mine. I burst into a flurry of slashes and am left breathless as he turns them all. His ripostes are quick, relentless, as he gets into the swing of things. My body is a mess of cuts and bruises; only the uncountable times I've swung my blade help me avoid his blows. This is what I'm built for, but still, it isn't enough. Bones creak, old wounds tight and unyielding, slowing me. But not him.

I'm in trouble with his odachi's reach, he slashes in a large forward arc and clips the tip of my katana as I try to make space enough between us to work my Way. The force throws my blade aside and, in the opening, he erupts, a volcano spewing sand and dust in its wake. It's too late for me to avoid. I bring my blade, one-handed in a diagonal across me, and brace the back of the blade with my offhand. As his sword's wicked, immense slash reaches my blade, I fold up, pulling all my strength into my centre. I go to one knee against the volcanic tide.

Wincing, I bite my tongue, the back of the blade jars into my hand, my elbows and arms sing out in pain, the pressure sending white-hot lances through my old, broken joints.

His breaths beat down on me and I'm trapped between his blade and mine. Locked in a deadly embrace, my arms shake. Master said never to challenge a man's strength, in pure weight difference, it would mean my death. Skill and speed were my allies. Meganako would see to it that my blade is agile. But, the Tanuki is twice a man, younger and blessed by Taos' foreign gods, that allow such a cruel match up. My thoughts are broken. He bellows a laugh through laboured breaths. The rank, cabbagy smell of sweat surrounds me.

He hacks, and spits through the struggle, phlegm hits my cheek and I scream out in madness. The guard loosens. I'm relieved, but why?

My vision goes blank as something thumps my side with enough force to knock the air out of my lungs. Numb. And then a warm twitching, building into a furious hornet buzz as though one is trapped in my robes, attacking my side as it vies to escape. I lurch forward and the laughing is distant. A hot, fast trickle of something follows. Blinking my vision back, I smell it first, my blood. Scarlet red, and plentiful. I'm hurt. I feel my side and touch something that sends me cold. Looking down at a fletching, blood oozes from my robes. I cry out. The dishonour...these wretched northern dogs. Fumbling around the arrow that is now embedded in my side, it's just a flesh wound, I'm only just pierced through, but they don't know that. I'm lucky. The gods do have some hand in this, the mistress' blade turned the arrow so that it didn't pierce my gut.

I look up at the Tanuki, he wears the elation across his face in a yellow grin. A warrior? No, a coward. Five Wolfpad archers at the edge of the arena tell the tale, three of them notch their arrows loosely, while the other two hold an empty bow, bickering amongst themselves. Pushing and shoving, a fight breaks out. A few paces away from me, another arrow pierces the earth. Then, they argue over who stuck me. Swines.

Searching the crowd, I know now that I was destined to die like a dog, alone. Neither Kekkei nor Ropi stare back at me from the flock of onlookers. Whore's breath, I'd even be at peace if the weird, little Meater watched; he'd probably enjoy it, that strange god of his feeds off this kind of sport. Don Yoku takes delight in spilt blood, in open wounds and rent flesh. I glance one last time and sigh, slumping back. Anything to take my mind away from that gnawing, insatiable ache that comes with the spilling of my own blood. That urge, the voice that is both my own and alien at the same time, the excited bubbling that fills my veins as it leaves me. I know little of what I am, but I know the crimson river spilling from my wound would be my salvation; Meaters disgust me, scare me, because they know it, see the magic that lies within me. But none can explain the gates it opens, the insanity that lurks within. So, I steer away from it, bottle it away. A shiver runs down my spine at the thought of giving over to it again, even looking Kabutomaru in the face as he towers over me. He is a god of death who comes again, cheated the last time. Not now.

I roar and scream at him, and I'm punched in return. His giant fists are a bludgeon. Head cracking back, my world spinning. I lurch forward. Ears pulse a ring. I spit blood at him, but it doesn't go far, just dribbles down my robes.

He pulls me to my feet by my hair. I can't help but yelp, betray myself. My vision, blurred, returns slowly until I meet eyes with Lord Tamikura, who is still at the seat of the crowd. Her glare is cold, expressionless, but she tips her head slightly, in a bow or disgust I don't know.

"Now, whore," the Tanuki says, "hmm, no." He turns to the crowd. "This is no whore! You're wrong. Too old, a hag!" He bellows. And leans in close, his breath rasps in my eye. "Ugly, you, hmm." Pulling his head away, glancing over me, his eyes widen. "Gods damned, that's a beak. Familiar, that black scar too. Intriguing, maybe you are the ghost." He leans in so only I can hear. "You see, I don't remember hags, so I wouldn't know. And I don't really give Metsuku's rotten arse about the godlord's orders. Oh, you were so close. They didn't kill them all, you know. Some might still live. The fieldclans don't own just your land now but never mind, I'll put you–"

"L-let go!" Someone says. They're close. Familiar. "Let her go!"

I fall back onto my slump, and the warmth runs out of my face as I see him. "Foolish farmer, go away!" I croak. He stands there, not in his work rags, but in a grey, moth-eaten robe with warriors hakama; it has seen better days, haggard and tattered. He wears the stained rags with the pride of a lordling in their regalia. Not armed with a bokuto, he points a wakizashi, a small side-arm at best, at the Tanuki. "This is not your fight."

"Worm," Kabutomaru says, "you deign to challenge the godlord's authority?"

"There's sacred honour in duelling," the farmer says, "O-Okami, you should know that. There's no pride to be had in foul-play. End this!"

What the Tanuki does next, I don't quite follow as I grow lethargic from the loss of blood. He feints a slash of his odachi at me. I don't flinch, as I know it, there's not enough time. The old man is a fool, and he steps into the pyre as he moves forward to take what he considers an opening. Kabutomaru pulls out of the slash as the farmer moves, sliding his lead foot around in a blink, he pivots and thrusts his sword to meet the old fool; to the farmer's credit, he doesn't break from his guard and follows the path set by the fate lines. Reaching inside the Tanuki's slash, his blade glides along the odachi. He tries to do what he did to me, but there's too much power, the Okami eclipses his swordsmanship in every way.

79

Mid-thrust, Kabutomaru slashes downwards, ending the old man as the blade bites into his arms, severing them roughly at the elbows; they spin through the air.

I'm cold. Colder than death and sicker than the pit Kabutomaru has crawled from. I hear a screaming, thinking it's the farmer, but he collapses to his knees without a sound, as if the gods have muted him. It's my scream.

There're cheers and whistling from the crowd. Kabutomaru, the scum, stabs his sword into the earth next to the only friend who came for me, and bellows in laughter once more.

I'm no better than him. In my anger, I drag friends, innocent peoples and allies to their death. I'm nothing. Kekkei would be dead if he were here, and all for my own schemes; he's right, I should've run, the farmer would've lived if I'd just taken my time. But, instead, I rush in, just like when Master died. The farmer tried to teach me patience, and he dies in my impatience. "I'm sorry," I mutter. The Tanuki no longer pays attention. He plays to the crowd's jeering. Something is wrong, the air is punctuated by screams, but it's too delayed to be for the farmer.

I swallow, tasting something off. Rancid, meaty, and metallic. The air hums.

The Tanuki turns so sharp the dust fans out behind him, a veil of glittering debris falls back to the earth; his hard stare is fixed beyond me.

A chorus of growls split the air and I follow his eyes to the outer edge of the arena, to where the paddies meet the outskirts of the town, and the forest beyond. Where the crowd had thinned, they now run, rush towards the town and to the safety of the Wolfpad guards who stiffen at the sight; a pack of wolves has appeared out of thin air. They snap and snarl. Stranger, each of them fights against an invisible leash. It baffles the arena into silence. They thrash, desperate to go further than they seem to be allowed. All eyes focused on Kabutomaru, who looks grim.

Beyond the wolves, I see him, the boy. He, too, has traded his rags and wears a silk green robe. His greasy hair pulled tight into a ponytail, hands clasped together in prayer. He shuffles forward and the ghost that overlays him is visible once more. As he gets closer, so do the wolves. The invisible leash, Meater magic, that's what I taste. No warning is given; he severs one of the bindings.

The wolf is one of the hells' own arrows as it darts towards Kabutomaru.

In an instant, the Okami grabs the hilt of the odachi in both hands and slashes through the sword's earthly sheath in an arc as vicious as the wolf, rending it in two as it meets him in a spray of blood.

Both parts of the wolf hit the ground either side of the Tanuki, writhing, still growling and snapping with their half mouths, entrails are worms searching for each other as they knit back together. Kabutomaru slashes again, severing their attempt at unity.

Jinto is closer now, the smell of Greed curses thick and rich in my nose. As the sinewy tendrils try again once more to rejoin, the boy's face is awash with discomfort, the rest of the pack in a fury now. "Run!" he cries as he releases the rest of the shackles. A tide of spittle, fangs, and anger surges towards our foe. His archers' arrows do nothing to slow the beasts down, faces painted with anguish.

Kabutomaru gives no order to do anything else, so the rest of them stand greyly, running in to help would dishonour their Okami master.

My eyes struggle to follow the Tanuki, rushing in to face the pack. He meets them and I don't see every slash, I miss some of the footwork. The dust whips up around him, adding to the surreal effect things have frozen, when really now my eyes are only just keeping up; he isn't the oaf he would seem. It's his intimidating presence that makes him appear to be larger than life. He's big, yes, but his movement amongst the wolves betray a body void of anything wasteful. A body built for the hunt. Even the minute details in his swordsmanship are flawless. The perfect warrior, an army in his own right as he trades blows with a pack of Greed cursed wolves. Ripping welts and slashes into them, slowing the beasts down as Jinto pulls one and then two back to regenerate, his face shiny with sweat.

The boy's steps forward are careful, sluggish. The severed wolf no longer writhes behind the mass.

But it's not enough for the lone warrior, even flawless swordsmen give in to their greed; they get desperate hasty, greedy with the steps they need to take. With the patience needed to see the fight through. A rushed step, a slash meant for one, that he tries to end two with and he falters in the presence of wildness. Don Yoku waits, and so do his beasts. They're unpredictable. He only keeps his off-hand, when a wolf takes it in his maw, ripping and thrashing wildly, because of the spell-reinforced plate. He struggles to break free and the odachi, now too cumbersome in the other hand, leaves an opening. But before he is engulfed, his unit charges the arena.

The six wolves split. Madness ensues. The Wolfpads are too disorganised and it's as though two small armies clash here on the farmer's land, where his own blood spills. The farmer needs me. Not heeding Jinto's request, I drag myself his way. Heart *thuds.* Stop. *Thud.* His chest convulses. Surely Metsuku isn't cruel enough to let this man suffer any longer. Fire still lights up my side as I get up and stumble the last steps, falling to my knees at his side.

Opening his eyes seems a mammoth task. "Don't move! Don't waste this on me you fool!" Squeezing my eyes shut, my whole body laden with sadness; tears rolling, I chance another look, they drip onto the man who tries to smile. Why does this affect me so? I didn't cry when Master went, I didn't have the chance.

"Why?" I growl in whisper.

"T-take my s-sword." His wakizashi fell next to his feet, and I thank the gods that I don't have to pry it out of severed fingers. I sheath the sword in the scabbard at his belt, removing it. I'm no woman to quash a man's dying wish. I hold it to his chest and promise I'll look after it, but I'm not sure he hears me now, neither am I sure I believe myself.

His eyes glaze over, breathing slows and something about it maddens me. Desperate, another soul can't die for me. "Why?" I shout at him, but he's too gone to notice. His wakizashi throbs in my two-handed grip. Biting my lip, I don't know what I'm doing. Though, here, I see it. A strand of red in my mind's eye. So, I grab it as once I grabbed the chance at a second life. Slippery, it's difficult to hold but it's the old man, I know it, and I dig deep as I wrap the strands around me, around the sword.

In front of me, the scarlet pool of blood at his back bubbles and shoots towards the small sword in my hands.

What have I done?

The man is howling. Not the kind a man is capable of, but one akin to the beasts' behind me as they lose the fight. Tendrils of blood escape the man's mouth all searching for somewhere to go, to live on, finding the sword still. I can't stop it.

"Stop. STOP. Stop!" The farmer's voice echoes in the distant recesses of my mind. "Please, gods! No. Stop." Laced with agony, the body writhes before me, wilting. The life is sucked out of him, into his beloved sidearm. I can't break my hands away, nor can I stop this. What have I done? I scream, then it's over.

Shoulder clutched; I wheel on it with the scabbarded sword. It's Jinto, he's frantic, exhaustion steams from him. "We need to go!"

A glance back reveals three wolves still living. Still fighting. They back away from pikes and swords. The welts and slashes have mutated, leaving them as the twisted abomination I'd seen Jinto become.

I can't see the Tanuki and grit my teeth that I leave this here.

The boy urges me on again. I'm all over the place on my feet, a drunk. Ignoring the throbbing in my side, in every inch of my body, I run with the boy. Cries and shouts follow us but it seems Don Yoku will see us leave. Two horses await our flight out of the tall grasses he's led me through. There's a strange aura about the steeds, a tinge of green. I ignore it. Both are geared up with saddlebags, but I don't care if they're empty. We mount in a hurry and spur the horses on.

As we gallop across fields and into the treeline, I notice the wakizashi tied at my side, but don't remember tying it there. Worst of all, I don't notice it by sight, I feel it there. Feel it in the blood that courses through my veins. I hear something distant in there. I focus on it and hear the screams of the farmer.

Chapter 10

The next few days became a blur between the throbs of the arrowhead still lodged in my side.

Only after Chisai is an unrelenting ride behind us is Jinto finally happy to slow down; the revelation that some of my household may still yet live crawls across my skin in desperation. The hunger seethes within, boiling over when I rest, when my mind wanders from it, when I stop a second to check my pulse. A reminder that I'm still living. There's more to life than the existence I live right now. I have arms to wield my katana; I have legs to avoid the enemies' and I have a mind to remember the guards of my Way. The least number of steps it takes to kill lingers at the forefront of my mind still. There is hope...

...so far, I have failed in that. I will not fail a third time.

The warrior loses once, dishonour to him. The warrior loses twice, dishonour to his sword. The warrior loses thrice, dishonour in death.

A warrior's fallacy, really. Failure is death where I come from, should be final.

We stop twice a day after we leave the Chisai lordship and follow a path through the nameless hills on its outskirts. They're glum, greyed mounds; dried up welts on a corpse. Shrubbery is sporadic, concentrated in some places as if Izenta saw fit to dump his seed bags all in one place out of laziness, or by accident.

As we descend lower into the hills and meet the Fish Tail, a small offshoot of the Kirisam, anxiety drips away. Tall trees shade us from the beat of the sun and sprout up as far as the eye can see along the 'Tail. We go as far as the day will let us, and stop, making camp under a leafy canopy that stretches over the bank, fingers reaching across the river.

Jinto is in the water a few heartbeats before a wild hand pierces the surface, fish flapping in its powerful grasp.

We eat the fish raw. I run a small dagger along it and drop the guts out. Jinto does not. It misses the delicate cuts of an expert, but it does me. All throughout Basho fish is a luxury, for the upper echelons of the warrior caste, for the nobility, and those fat cats in Orika who make the laws, but not for the common folk. Even so, the fish is tough, not the silky, break apart in my mouth fish that Ozumi brought us up on; lovingly prepared, expertly dissected. Her warm salt broth would go well with this. My heart tightens and turns to lead in my chest as I wonder whether she is one who survived this, whether the fieldclan treat her well. The woman who brought up Zaki and I. We raised hell whenever we could but met the *mercy* of Meganako when we brought trouble to her. I still bring trouble to her. For if she is gone, dead or defiled, it is on my head. She wasn't my mother; I never knew that woman. Lord Dattori, Master, said she died in the fires with the rest of my small village of exile. A quick death, he proposed, but I don't doubt she suffered. The gods would have made sure of it.

"What is it?" Jinto breaks me free from my thoughts with his soft, musical tone.

"Nothing," I say, not needing Don Yoku's musings on my troubles. "I–"

I'm interrupted by the crack of a twig and the rustling of leaves. Something lurks behind me, and, not hindered by the dusk-light, I see them; three wolves return from the hunt, one with a rabbit in its mouth, the fur around the others' muzzle is blood-splattered and I wonder what they ate that they dare not bring back with them. Jinto would know, but I don't press him about what he can do with the Greed curse, for I don't want to stoke the burning questions his eyes betray he has about *mine.*

That these three survived, and caught us up, is a surprise. But now I know why Jinto urged us on, why he seemed to know that the Wolfpads didn't give up at Chisai.

"Your scouts," I start again, eager to change the conversation, "Why pull them back?"

"I grow tired." His voice is laden with it now. "Chisai is a greedy place. A dark place. Don Yoku is strong there."

"So you've said."

He pauses, then smiles, his eyes follow. "Yes, you remember." He doesn't get my tone. "Don Yoku weakens where people are not. He loves them, everyone. We only want a big family, the Shamans." His eyes settle downwards. "But the Lord Council limits us. Not in the mountains, though."

I'm fed-up with the riddles, the half sentences. It's as though he talks to someone else present that knows more than I do every time he speaks. "I've met Shamans of Greed before, and not a single one of them was a devout as you." I chuckle for the first time in days. "He's a close friend of yours? That curse-giver?"

"The Shaman at Yoku-Na thought the same," he says. "Jealous that I'm not limited as they were."

"You speak as it were the past?"

"Gone," he looks up. "Kekkei said so? Yoku-Na burnt to the ground." His eyes waver, watery. A smirk unseats the sadness. "But Master Yoku wasn't all that upset."

"S-sorry. I mean." He's only a boy, and he's brought me this far, so I need to give him a break, humour him. "Thank you."

"Why?" The wolves snap and snarl at each other next to where we sit on the bank, arguing over who gets the rabbit carcass.

"Because you stayed behind when Kekkei wanted you to flee."

"I told you before, Don Yoku doesn't want you to die." He considers me for a second, eyes seemingly drinking in all I am before continuing, "Your body is a mess."

I shudder as I run my fingers over the lodged arrowhead. "Can you free it?"

"Yes. But not that. There's more wrong."

What, how? "I know."

"I see it. It is the Shaman's duty to know the body. It helps with the experiments, the possession. Your body is one giant knot. It is not good for a swordswoman's centre to be tied into a lump like that. The wounds didn't heal well, your movement is limited. One side of your arm...wait. Does it lock up? Ache?"

"Y-yes," I say, wanting to shrivel up. To hide. To get away from those eyes. "My body...it feels like I've aged twenty years since be– since I was injured."

"I can fix it. Some of it – certainly the arrow wound." Jinto flinches away from me, scrabbling back like an animal discovering something it shouldn't. Cowering, he says, "Those scars. I cannot touch those scars. No, I can't touch it. That's a power that I can't bend." I shiver, the words chill me to the bone. And suddenly I wish we could start a fire, but it's dangerous. We can't risk being seen. By anyone. And I have greater fears of my own. I'm not taking the chances that the Tanuki doesn't have a Taosii Soshist among his ranks, hidden, our fire would be a weapon around one of those foreign sorcerers. Not that their magics stop there. There's a lot about this journey that gulfs my ability, but still, I must tread this path.

Burying it, I push the godsborne, the Soshists, to the back of my mind. Jinto shakes off the possessed look and climbs back into his human skin as he sits next to me again. "Fix it, fix me, please." I turn to him, the river shimmers beyond. A white flame in the moonlight. The desperation floods in. More than I knew, I need his help. "Do what you can. I need to be a sharper sword!"

One of the wolves yelps. I flick my eyes to where they play. Cuts and slashes appear on the wolf who just won the carcass, its body undoing itself. Blood and gruel slop out and it succumbs to the injuries it received at Chisai. It drops to the floor like a withered flower. Poor beast.

The other two don't stop, don't notice the third is gone, and continue the fight.

There's a hammer-beat in my chest. Jinto is ghostly, an ethereal glow snakes off him in tendrils that lick the night. He says, "I couldn't keep all three and help you. We chose to help you." He shifts and scuttles to the front of me, straddling my outstretched legs. "Don't scream. Please."

Before I can question it, he asks for my hand. No hesitation, my own greed is strong, and I strike a deal with his.

Jinto brings my palm up to his mouth and bites; his teeth are a rake across the heel of my palm. I snatch it back. A piece of my flesh is gone and the boy chews, swallows. He draws both of his palms into his chest, inhales, and thrusts them at my own.

I brace myself, the wind squashed out of me. And then something else. It's warm, then burns. His hands are hot irons that he forces slowly into my body, pushing, with phantom fingers, into my chest. Working, and massaging, tearing, and ripping. I bite down hard on my cheeks, trying to stifle the scream that fights to break free of my lips. Agony like I've never felt. There's a pinch and the clink of metal in my side...but I'm overcome. My world shrinks, the darkness closes in, and I blackout.

* * *

The song of some river bird wakes me abruptly. I want to reach for my sword, a rock or something, and dash its brains out. I try to sit up and the muscles in my abdomen fail, twitching uncontrollably as a warm throb reverberates throughout my torso and down the side of my sword arm. One side blooms in pain; they vibrate, hum a song that hurts. I hate this. A low fog hangs in my mind, I barely remember what Jinto did to me.

Spittle builds in my throat. I'm caught between the agony of the cough and stopping it. I swing my good arm across my body and roll to the side, hacking phlegm and blood into the dirt.

A soft crackle distracts me, a smoky scent nudges me with the gentle breeze and I crane my head around to Jinto, who sits in the warm morning glow worrying a bubbling clay pot over a fire I told him not to make. It takes everything I have, but I turn over and sit up. Still, he doesn't notice my gaze. I see something in his jovial unawareness, something kind and innocent masking what he truly is. A warm, unfamiliar feeling in my chest, something long forgotten. An antithesis to the pain I've long felt, but I shrug it off. Idiotic. Protecting him is one thing, but I've done little of that so far, and my body doesn't know what my mind does. I've never had a child, never wanted one. It doesn't befit a warrior's body. Never would I go through the ruinous process, but I'm confused, as despite my mind, my body yearns for it in that moment.

He turns and smiles knowingly; warmth flushes into my cheeks, snatching away from his eyes. He hands me a bowl of brown rice. As he finds a seat with his own bowl, next to the dozing wolves, the feeling evaporates.

Jinto's no child. I love him like a dagger to the throat; he keeps me alert, but fearful. I wouldn't let either too close.

"Fix me?" I croak. "I can barely move. Is this your idea of foolery?"

"Nothing is for free." A wolf groans and rolls onto its back. "I said I'd help, but there's a limit. Muscles woven, changed, stitched back together anew. New." He repeats and I feel some significance in it but my mind fogs over again. "They lack the experience of your sword. Lack the knowledge of ten thousand swings."

"They're weak, useless then. What good are they? I don't have the time–"

"Time. You don't need it." He says in the same incomplete, annoying manner. "You're more attuned to it, what you really are. Practice, train hard in these free moments. Don't rest. Don't let new muscles learn old mistakes."

I get up, force myself to my feet. I'm wobbly, my head light.

"An hour, when the sun climbs past the trees, we leave. Use the time. Be greedy with it."

The kid starts to make more sense and I wonder whether I'm just too far into this madness now, but I heed his words. First, I ask, "Where are we headed? I know where I want to go, where I'm going, rather. But what about you, kid? Are you going back to Kekkei or does Don Yoku have some other plan?" I can't resist the sarcastic tone in my voice.

"To Kekkei. Please, to Kekkei," he says, ignoring my other question. "I will not raid the Dattori estate with the two of us. It is folly."

"More than Chisai?"

"I told you, Chisa–"

"I know," I snap. "But what is a small fieldclan against wolves?"

"We have a bigger one on our tail, he lives." Jinto points to what's left of his pack. "They don't die easily, the Okami. You know this. These two tell of more worrying things, though. A Taosii has the leash, it always has."

A Soshist? I didn't want to think it true.

"You know of them, Hawk, your face tells me so." He smiles, but his eyes betray him. "If we move as I dictate, we will be fine. They wear the shadows for a reason."

"We'll go your way until Fish Sister, but I won't follow that river to Yata with you. I have to go."

"Okay." I'm surprised he doesn't argue. Instead, he walks off and the wolves follow.

Pulling on my robes, then my hakama, my nose turns at the stench. Too long on the road. A stale, dried sweat smell emanates from them. One thing Jinto didn't consider was comfort, but what would a wildboy know about that. I decide the training can wait as my body throbs and throbs. It can't hurt. Instead, I go down the bank and wring out my robes in the crystal waters before immersing myself. Underneath the waters, I panic, scramble up the bank on all fours, and lay panting, breathless.

I can't go back there. I can't let this happen again.

* * *

We follow the river for three days without trouble.

I haven't slept much, not while I still heal, while I can still mould my body into a temple for my katana. Every sunrise since is greeted with my swordforms; I go through everything Master taught me, so I can show my new muscles what they must do, how they must act. It isn't easy. My body will never be the same. In a two-handed grip, I overextend myself in a low-sweeping blow meant for dismembering horses, unseating mounted warriors or taking the lead leg from an assailant, my stomach tightens. Cramps ricochet throughout my abdominals, the dark, inhuman scar doesn't stretch. It won't move with my body, it hinders me. I curse the godsborne for the amateurish job it did at stitching me up.

Jinto steered away from the spiritual, kept his god at arm's reach, and didn't pry into the scars. Only that, he couldn't change them. The farmer's wakizashi was another taboo. I couldn't talk about it; couldn't begin to comprehend what I've done. The boy hissed last night when I unsheathed the blade, begged me to put it away; the wolves did too howl. The blade was a crusty, crimson shade now, flecked with a dirty brown and black that smeared the seemingly polished weapon.

I didn't sleep a wink after. As I closed my eyes, even now I hear his screams of anguish renewed.

Magic, accursed blood is all my master knew before he was sent to raze our village. A settlement of savages, cursed peoples, at the foot of the Bad Tooth, a mountain on the edge of the Demon Range. In the Lower Fangs. Only the sanctioned magics, those of the tamer gods, are permitted to be practiced in Basho: Meatheurgy and Elementheurgy. The practitioners of the latter only now appear in the foreign lands of Taos, and the Meaters do their bit to ensure the Lord Council has its fingers in all the illicit activities it can. They preach and protect in the name of Don Yoku, dressed as pious priests, but really, they're thugs for hire in the pocket of the godlord. A police for the underworld of Orika, and Oshima nearer to the Taosii border. Or were, Akate saw to that. But, my mind wanders, as it does when I consider my condition; Lord Dattori always knew more, I'm sure of it...he recorded the details from the Lord Council, of what he did for them. He wanted me to grow as a warrior, a loyalist, not one forged out of whatever he knew. Little good that did me.

As I near my clanlands with this wicked blade, I think on it again. I pray that Master's records still exist; before I can free myself of this task, I need to remove the weight that has always burdened my shoulders.

Now, as I sheathe my blade in the dull grey light, I pray to the Mistress, and to Meganako. Moody, purplish clouds roll overhead in the morning skies, blanketing the sunrise. It starts to spit. My breath mists in front of me. The soft chill of the rain soothes. I hate the summer. The auburn tinge to the leaves around me gives me hope for the quick approaching autumn, the rain promising cooler days.

Back at our camp, a single wolf sits by my horse. Jinto is gone. Even though he said he'd not journey home with me, I still held out hope. The wolf follows my horse and I. Not knowing what I do, chucking stones at it doesn't work, nor shouts to follow its master. No matter what, it follows. The boy has eyes on me, and I swallow the regret. Even now I'm a burden. I know what a Greed-sworn means to a Shaman, separation is a weakness, let alone sacrifice. And he's now given me two, but that's one more than those greedy magicians should be able to manage. Jinto is a mystery after my own heart, and I won't solve it in the dark.

After two days hard riding, I breach the thick shrubbery of the Saras Wood as I crest a hillock I know too well. The Dattori estate slumbers beneath me. A tendril of water, too small to be a named river, sweeps around the front of the estate. A wide horse bridge sprouts from the mouth of the chalky-white curtain wall, topped with black clay tiles. Within the wall, the compound buildings are the same white; they borrow their design from the capital. The roofs are reminiscent of a black lotus. Towards the back, at the foot of a giant jut of rock, where the curtain walls meet again and before the land dives down into a sea of trees, sits the main family building, a giant in full flower.

As I sweep my gaze across all that will be mine again, my heart flutters at the sight. The Eastern wall is still ruin. The nearby buildings torn apart by the foreign sorcery that clipped my wings the first time.

Chapter 11

E ven in the hours just before sunrise, it's as though the occupiers of my estate expect an attack; armed warriors, if you can call anyone in the fieldclans that, stalk the walls. Lord Dattori's power was understood, known in the Samaki, so there was little need for anything other than a couple of night guards at the estate entrance. Now, there's double, and just on the outside.

Despite that, an intruder cannot effectively guard a home from its owner. And my midnight incursion goes unnoticed as I emerge from the crisp, icy waters and scurry up, over the channel walls.

Torches lit on every corner of my compound wobble lethargically in the light breeze that must flood through the hole to the east. The shadows move with it, making my heart lurch every time as I wait for a guard to find me, raising the alarum. But they don't, it's just a shadow after all. I know these walls but I'm just one woman. The wolf would have fortified my position, but it didn't follow me through the small water inlet where the surrounding stream flows into the grounds. It's why Dattori built here. Grain and rice can be stored, fresh water cannot.

I shiver, teeth chattering, and I try to stifle it. I'm too heavy. There's nothing to be done, so I remove everything but my thin under-robe. I waste precious moments wondering what to do with the robes. I can't leave them here. I can't risk alert, so I go over to the inlet, lowering the sodden clothes slowly into the waters. Fingers slip as I'm caught unaware by the low mumble of speech. Not expecting the weight of my water-logged robes, they splash. For a moment, I freeze like a common thief caught in the act.

A mad dash follows the inlet walls as they curve towards the kitchens. Not too far, watching the movements of those who come. Pressing my back up against it, hoping the shadows hide me as I peek, the men rush around the corner.

Fieldclan. Scum, I'm glad it's them. The Imanta fieldclan; they don't follow the rest of Basho in attire, instead, they wear a hakama that grips the leg tight, and a tunic instead of robes. Dusty, uncouth. My lip curls as I notice the blue tinge to their garbs, the symbol of grass over their heart, in the torchlight. Nomin's men.

The weapons they hold are where they are most distinct. Most foolish. The length of their nagamakis' handle is equal to their blades; an uncivilised, ungraceful weapon befitting of savages. But I run my hand down my leg, and free the small dagger I brought with me. I'm not sure I'm up to the job.

They relax, finding nothing, scabbarding their weapons. They disappear back around the corner, chuckling to themselves. I spit at their nonchalance. The fieldclans never prosper and it is the fault of the Samaki lords? I concur. When you can only rely on your men for such a relaxed response to sounds in the night, you can never be safe. Never will your roots tap into the ground far enough to survive the storms of Basho.

Never will you see the sword before it cuts.

I let go of a breath I didn't realise I was holding and then struggle to catch it. My heart fights against its constraints, a surge of anger seethes from me. I hit my head backwards against the stone, biting my lip. Again, and again. My head a mess of emotions I can't decipher. It's too much. I'm home, but I cling to the shadows, scared of being found. I lurch forward onto my knees, and struggle to find the will to stand as my tears patter the ground. The flashes of Soshist sorcery light the darkness behind my eyelids; the last time I tread amongst these walls I fought for my life, alongside men who I'd give it for ten thousand times over.

It is the reason that I stand. Resolved to be a rat for now, if I must. I follow the paths I know, slipping by a lazy, dozing guard and scrabbling my way under the lotus leaves that tower around me, to the nanny's quarters. A candle flickers from within the doorway and I've cause to pause, checking my flank. It's foolish, ridiculous that I find myself here first. My beloved katanas slumber nearby, but I'm here. I must know if she lives.

I touch the door, press my ear to it before I enter. A yelp, a smash. My heart is loud again. It would be like me to run in, to swing the knife around to be rash, but I fight against it. For whoever lay behind the door, it is a normal night. I've not stumbled upon something rare, no. Not in these hours. These are the hours evil men work their wickedness into normality. Whoever lay behind the door needs my help, my calm, but they've needed it since I've left.

In one movement, I push open the door, it swings wide but doesn't make much of a noise. Before it swings back on me, I'm through the threshold, knife in hand. I stumble over something and break into a roll. Blasphemies roll off my tongue as I'm foolish enough to remember the nanny's quarters is divided by canvas walls. I listen with intent, there's a pregnant silence now. I run along the dimly lit corridor, hearing something towards the back. Ears pricked; I find it. Shadows writhe within and I slide the door aside, pulling it from its runs. A man, field-hakama around his ankles, fumbles for someone who clings to the corner of the room like it'll save them. I couldn't stop myself now if I tried, the fire has me. It's stoked within and I'm upon him before he registers anything. My knife flowing in and out of his neck quicker than even my eye can follow. His blood fuels me, the coppery smell driving me onwards.

A hand on my shoulder and I swing up in a savage arc that only stops when my eyes connect with hers. I'm the one who came here to free them of this, yet here she is delivering me, saving me from this madness with a look.

Blood splatters the walls, it's over the bedroll and seeping into the tatami flooring; just the scent threatens to trap me into a frenzy not even she could stop; the Imanta's blood seeps into my skin; I'm in a light blood fever without wanting to – this place has me on such a fine edge. This is bad.

"Mimi!" I whisper, croak. "How. I." I've no idea what to say to her, not in this state.

"Stupid child." Her hand whips up, cracks across my cheek and it numbs. Numbs my anger as I watch her face turn from surprise into a hard, grim

95

mask I wouldn't wish upon my enemies. Tears gather at the edge of her lightly wrinkled face. Despite the many years she has on me, she could be my sister. A beautiful one at that. I'm surprised still at how healthy, how unharmed she is. Not a scratch on her.

I touch my face where it pulsates from her slap, and snap, "Sort yourself out, *mother.* I don't want to see you like that. Not after this...monster has hands on you." I pause, can't stop my face from screwing. "Why didn't you scream louder? Even the fieldclan hang his sort."

She pulls her robes too, fastening the pegs at the front of the tired, floral nightwear. Her eyes bore into me. The godlord didn't show me such disdain. "Mother? What did I do to deserve that; Lord Dattori gave me no choice, I'm sure you remember that, *Lady Dattori?*" She's still as sharp as the sword you don't see coming, and I yearn to stick her with one. "This man was drunk, useless, but he passed the time. You always did see the worst in things. What that sick mind of yours wanted to show you."

My breath catches, I was sure... "No. Ozumi, how low?" I chuckle. The trickeries of Metsuku. I spit. "You let the Imanta inside of you. Gods, what did I rush back for, then? Lord Dattori may never have reached the pyre, but that's fine because the ruins of his household have wet cunnies over the enemy." She slaps me again, I deserve it.

"How are you here?" I hear a why buried in that sentence but ignore it. "The runners from Orika...The Imanta said..."

There's real uncertainty in her voice. "The godlord didn't dig a deep enough grave, so I pulled myself out of it. He forgets old traditions, you see. Pyres are most final."

She glances at my neck, the black scar throbs against her gaze. Mimi reaches out, brushes it and I snatch backwards

"What have you done to get here? Why bother, Masako? This isn't what Lord Dattori would want. We're tired, tired of your schemes. Of your feud with life. It was a tragedy what happened here, but it was a reprisal well-earned. You knew which viper's nest you poked."

"OUR MASTER!" I stop myself, grab my mouth with one hand. After a few deep breaths I try again. "My master. Lord Dattori built this. The Samaki do

96

not cede their lives to the beck and call of the northern mutts. This – is – not – over, until Master's honour is regained."

She sighs, and crumples to her knees. *Whose honour really?* She whispers. "Then, Lady Dattori." Her words are long and drawn out. "How should I serve?"

I crouch down beside her and notice how the blood pools around my feet, tendrils of it climb into the fabric of her robes. "First, change. Clean this mess. But leave the body, I won't need long." I consider my words. "Who else lives?" There's movement behind me, a whimper. I turn, dagger flashing out of my robes but there's no need. "Mina?" I'm not happy to see the youngest of our house staff alive, she's fickle. Always has been. And I'd hoped that was a burden that would have been buried by now. "How many?"

"All of us." Ozumi sighs.

"He said you'd come," Mina says. Ozumi hisses behind me. "The hells wouldn't suffer you for long."

"Who?" I'm intrigued, who deigns to know me enough to speculate of my return within the fieldclans?

"The prisoner."

I can't hide the surprise. Mina smirks and I'd wipe it off her face if she wasn't presenting herself as useful.

"Take me to him." I stand with the Imanta's *bedslave* at my back. "Ozumi, we're not done." I remind her. "Join us after you've taken care of this."

* * *

Mina is not light-footed, neither is she particularly fast. I agonise over the time it takes her to lead me to the estate jail. Looking over my shoulder every second, I'm waiting for my presence to be sprung, but it isn't. The only thing that watches is the moon, hanging like an icy sickle; a line snakes across it, highlighting one of our scaled watchers as it looks down upon me from the highest heavens. I pause for a second. It is never a good omen to sight one of the sora dragons when you're trying not to be seen; the gods tell me they're watching, they know what I do in these early hours, but I don't know why. I can never know the significance. It circles as if outlining the incomplete moon and disappears behind an oncoming cloud formation that seems to suck the moon and all of its light in.

Master was a student of moth-eaten, crumbling old scrolls, lusting after the Dying ones; of etched stone and of stories passed down only by the words of the families that still repeat them. The Eyes of the Gods, the twin sora dragons that inhabit our skies, have never once broke ground in Basho, not in the stretch of histories that he'd found. And why? Because of the first treaty, because the gods handed rule over to the pitiful humans. But, in the Last Teachings of the Creators, something intrigued him. Not in an old scroll, but in the fanatical swine muck the missionaries of True Heavenly Peace spout it in every unwanted sermon they delivered in these walls, there was but one line Lord Dattori mused over. One line that nags at me now: *if the heavenly throne shall be filled, united be the heavens and the earth, the dragons shall confirm it.* Master did love to speculate, to trifle with his own prophecy, to humour the Heavenists, perhaps.

And I think on that hard. For what is it that the godsborne tasked me with? Is it in mockery to what we've created here? Or is it perhaps something I should heed with careful consideration?

"Masako!" A sharp whisper in the night sets my chest into a frenzy, and I pull myself back from the heavens and into Mina's irritated gaze. "By the Gods, do you want to get caught now?" I'm a fool, but movement in the heavens is not something to ignore. I leave it, for now.

If the main house is a jewelled dagger amongst knives, the great stone it backs onto, and the Caverns of Penance within, are a stain on this plane. Without the torches that flicker from within the tunnel, I would pass it by. Only Master knows why our estate was in need of it. There's two ways we deal with crime in the Samaki: duel or death. For the former, it's up to the Mistress whether it becomes the latter. Though, I dishonoured that. There's no room for excuse, or pardons, in a land where first words are exchanged for sword forms.

I catch up with Mina, grab her arm, and pull her into the shadows cast by the great lotus leaves above. "Wait, woman. The guards," I whisper.

Something does not sit well with me, here. There's barely a blood family's worth of Imanta here. This place is a breeding ground for damp fiends, their preference of abandoned buildings would be well met. "Tell me the jail is guarded?"

She spins on me, one eyebrow raised, her eyes squinting; there's a homely beauty about her that annoys me. With a hushed growl, she whispers, "Quiet. I've told you. One, maybe two."

"Do as I say then!"

She crosses out of the shadow we stand in, walks in a yard-long diagonal line, into the flickering mouth of the jail.

Shouts muffled by the stone disrupt the night. My stomach clenches as I wonder whether a trap is sprung, whether the clan is larger, healthier than I expected, all lying in wait for me here.

I get low and dart across to the entrance, back pressed to the bleak, cold stone.

Dagger in hand.

Penance's mouth spews one guard, he clatters out of it in a huff of plate and sweat. I almost pity him as my dagger flashes out from the blackness, catching the moonlight as I stab him in the neck twice, where the cheap plate leaves him open. Before he falls, I get behind him, one hand over his mouth in case of a death rattle, the other wraps around him, and I drag him into the dark. Where I wait for a reprisal, for more to come charging out. A blunt silence falls over the night. The moment drags on longer than I'd like it but not before Mina returns. The way is clear, and my guest awaits me.

She leads me through a short tunnel until it opens into a dank, stony room with nothing but a wooden desk, piled with clay bowls flecked with leftover rice. A jug of sake pours out onto the floor, our stores have been ravaged. Beyond that, the cells. Each is a small hold dug out of the rock. The wooden doors for the unoccupied ones lay open lazily, and I shudder. I won't ever go back into one of those; this place is designed with Metsuku's hells in mind.

Mina stops at the last, pulls the bolt. She swings the door free and steps back. I pull up my robes, saving my nose as try not to retch from the smell; a mixture of urine and rotting vegetables greets me, with a tinge of something worse. Peering inside, the mess buckets are overflowing. Nothing more can be expected from the savages that ruin my home.

A familiar chuckle from the prisoner catches me unaware; Mina said a Shaman, and I expected this one. But what brought him here is beyond me. So, I intend to find out, maybe free him with the small cut under the chin he always deserved, "You. It had to be you." I don't try to hide the scorn. "Come out. Gods, I can't speak to you here. The smell offends every fibre of my being." I try to laugh but end up choking.

Out of the cell, he staggers, grabs the walls as he tries to right himself. His back is arched. He follows me back to the antechamber; it's not only his stench, it's the smoothness of his bald head, the smirk that never leaves his face, and the proudness he carries despite the situation. Despite now standing in robes browned with his own excrement. Yoku Hebikawa, another child of Greed. But that never suited him, so I have my own name for the man. "Cat Food, why're you here?"

He rolls his head, stretching side to side. It clicks and he sighs. Looking back at me, smirking, he waits. He always waits.

"Don't test me, I'd happily bury my dagger in your face, too. But I'm hoping you'll give me reason not to. A reason your here."

"Oho, always violence. You know that's what started this, wasn't it?"

"What?"

"A penchant for violence only breeds violence. You're good at that, Hawk."

My jaw aches as I bite down hard. I stop, focusing only on my breaths, then continue, "Why – are – you – here?"

"Your problem is thinking you're the only one who tries."

"Cat Food!"

"That night the Soshist dragged Lord Dattori, and you, off. What did you think the rest of us did? Did you even know I was there? My Keta was there, too."

A Shaman of Greed is never far from his Greed-sworn. "Where is the mutt?"

"Dead." I'm speechless for a moment as his smirk falls. "Gone. Don Yoku has him."

This again. I shake my head, "He died here?"

"No. He died in Orika. Died, most likely, the same night as you, as poor old Lord Dattori."

"Impossible!" The fire bubbles in my veins. "You weren't there!"

"Like I said, Masako, it's always about you. What you did. Not even noticing the people who try around you. Why am I here? Because they thought it humorous that I be locked up, forgotten about, on the grounds that I traded Don Yoku for. That my sweet Keta died for." His eyes are a deep quagmire of suffering as he retells this. "I was there in Orika, with many good men and woman of the Dattori. We came for our lord and for the witch that condemned him. And I'm the only one left of that resistance. You see, the disciples of Greed are less savage than the Lord Council. They only ask that I leave. Leave and never come back." Cat Food pulls both arms from within his robes, and I stumble backwards, sickened by the sacrifice before me. "Yes, they took my hands. Greed cursing requires malleable fingers, you know. And they took my 'sworn. So, don't – you – fucking – think for a second that you're the only one who tries."

Warmth flushes to my cheeks, and I struggle to match his glare. Am I really that blind? Does the madness in my blood cloud my vision so? I shake, can't stop myself as the trembles find their way to my feet. Instead, I bow my head slightly. "Thank you," I whisper.

Before he can say anymore, the tromp of feet is a cacophony against the stillness of this early morning trespass. I don't react quick enough. Mina cries out, a mousy alarum at the entrance, and scuttles into the room, before falling to her knees. Four, no, five men dressed in full plate follow her. Our family's plate.

I cry out, pulling my dagger free, go to charge but am stopped by a shout from behind.

"NO!" Cat Food cries. "Go with them. Talk to them. Enough of this!"

I drop my hands to my sides, and my dagger falls with them, as the men surround me, beating me to the floor. Arms bend out of sorts behind my back, I snap and growl. But give in as my muscles throb and ache against the strain. They're too new, too fragile from Jinto's work for me to do anything but submit.

Chapter 12

BEFORE MY FALL: ACT 2

The winds whipped up off the grasslands, miscanthus stalks swayed side to side, shambling like the undead, never getting anywhere. Wait, miscanthus? A smirk tugged at the corners of my mouth. I'd spent too much time with Master. That old fool liked complicating things. Grasses would do me.

The grasses rolled down the hills in front of me and then cut off abruptly by the Oni Wuld. Following a sheer line carved out by Izenta's rake, the forest was a walled barrier. I drew my hand across my body and found the hilts of CrowKiller and High Wolf. The kashira cool to the touch. Calming to me. Serenity were my swords. The wind carried rotten, sulphurous notes to my nose. But it was such a place that smelled like shit. Got that and its name from its inhabitants.

As I turned, my black and green armour plate clattered, and like a wave, my unit's plate mimicked it as they straightened at my attention. Twenty katanas and a Meater. Really enough for those godless giants? Master put too much faith in me, forgetting that I was no taller than him. Even with my blade pointed to heaven, I certainly didn't match up to the giant whoresons lurking amongst the trees behind me.

The Meater stepped forward. His shiba inu not quite as tall as the surrounding stalks, burrowed through the grass. It growled at me, wretched cur. It always growled near me. Tell you what, dog, I don't much like you or your master's type either, I thought. Your types get me into these missions.

"Ready, are we, Leader Hawk?" The Meater's pet snarled as he spoke. "The oni separate in the morning. Gathering, one might suggest. It would be foolish to tarry. One oni–"

"Spare me a lesson I know, Cat Food," I said. "One oni is a fight. Two and the underworld is the destination." I looked down at the ratty thing, still growling. "The dog up to it?"

"Why of course." He smirked as he held up a pack that smelled worse than an oni's hovel. "Cat meat aplenty. He's fed. Well-prepared."

Sickening beings, Meaters. But they carve up the godsborne good. "Swords!" I bellowed. "On me." And we sank down the hill, and into the forested depths.

Beyond the treeline, we'd entered another world. The stench of rotted fish that wafted up from the forest as we approached was nothing compared to the tendrils of decay that snaked around us, digging their way into my nose. I spluttered; my eyes stung. The fetid stench was stifling. How could I swing a sword in my defence if I couldn't hold myself long enough to walk straight for thirty paces? Around me, my chosen swords fell into a cacophony of plate that rattled louder as they tried not to break into their own coughing fits. I wiped a tear from my eye and continued through the thick, hot air, deeper into the pit of the oni.

As I reached Zaki, he bent down, putting his hands in something that brought back memories of the swamplands, and the goo-like wretches that lived within. I wouldn't be touching anything like that, but such were the ways of a tracker. He plucked, if that's what you could do with sludge, a piece of it and rubbed it between his index finger and thumb. Sniffing at it, like the Meater's dog should be doing. But where the shaman and his companion were was beyond me. It was the last of my worries right now.

"Fresh oni tracks." He said. "The Meater was right, it's alone."

"My boy," Cat Food said; I turned, and the freak had managed to creep up on me. "Disappointment isn't something I'm well-practised at."

"Is it close?" I asked.

* * *

"This underworld born smell should be a clue. The stench the oni carry is married to everything they pass, touch, or merely look upon. Urgh. My poor dog, there's a good, urgh. Daddy will give you a wash when we get home huh."

I turned away from the shaman; his words were more sickening than the stench around me.

"Master Shaman," Zaki interrupted. "I assure you I'd know if such were the case. The oni is not here. But certainly not far."

"YOU HEAR THAT?" I shouted to my men. "BLADES, EYES AND EARS SHARP."

"Then, we move on!" Zaki added.

With the clanking armour made when its wearer ran, broken bells hitting each other, a scout seemed to materialise from between two trees. If anything could be said about this place, it was that daylight shunned it. Catching his breath, the scout said, "My lords." He looked to me. "And Honourable Lady, we are not the only ones who travel beneath the Wuld, today. A small unit, maybe a score of men more than ours, is ahead."

"Within our lands!" I said. "The Oni Wuld is Dattori clanlands. How could—"

I stopped myself as the scout looked like he had more to say.

"The fieldclans. Their banners are fieldclan."

"Our damned taxes were raised for them. The first insult. Second, they tread into sacred clan forests."

"Masako, I think it is best we rendezvous with these...pests."

"And have the oni at our backs while we entreat with them, Hebi– Cat Food?"

"If not, we may feel their blades at our back."

"They wouldn't dare!" Zaki said. "Dattori is their liege lord. They fall under his purview, reside in his lands."

"Your honour might tie you to Dattori, but it seems our *friends'* honour was left outside of the Wuld."

"He's right, Zaki." I hated to agree with the Meater. "We must deal with the immediate threat before our quarry. We still have hours before the oni converge once more." I turned to the score of Wuld Guard behind me, each man standing as still as the dead despite the fatigue of a full suit, and swords, would be giving them. My pride and my honour, these men.

I pulled at my plate, and the cloth beneath it, trying to let the fingers of air work their way in, cooling this hell heat that gripped my skin. Sukami's flame burned around us. Stifling.

"Share the skins around." Zaki said as sweat dripped from his forehead. "We continue."

Just then, the Wuld bellowed. My jaw snapped shut so quickly I bit down on the edge of my tongue, tasting copper. Blood slicked into my mouth. As though thousands screamed at once, the cry of an oni ripped through my mind like hot nails. I clapped my hands to my ears in a vain attempt to shield my mind from the madness of the soulscream. Stealing a look sideways, I struggled to keep my feet beneath me as up nor down made no sense. My uniform, unwavering men gave in and clattered to the floor. My heart pounded, and I cried out, summoning the rest of my strength just to not fall. I will not be weak in front of them. I tasted the blood still as I straightened. My band broken. To my side, Zaki supported himself on one knee. The Meater nowhere to be seen.

As the cry stopped, I thought I heard his mutt in the distance but couldn't be sure. My ears rang like the morning bells.

I composed myself and turned to my men. A sad scene lay before me. Gritting my teeth and being nothing other than the strong commander they needed, I loped over to the front lines, who were trying to compose themselves amongst fallen bodies of comrades that would never get up. Blades that would were dulled forever. Zaki joined me as I knelt by the first victim. The oni soulscream; a noise that beckons you to the otherworld. It is why they are known as the keepers of hells' oblivion gates. The godless howl sends any who hear it, and don't have the will to resist, straight to Metsuku. It was by such a man that I knelt. Ujiyasu, he was called. I knew all in my company by name. Trained by their sides night and day only to lose some of them to this damned place. I gulped down hard and bit back against a wave of tears fighting to get out. I cut them back, rent them, sent them to their own hell; I couldn't lose it here. Five men I lost, and five men whose final rights were confined to this dank pit. Burned quickly is the last kindness I could do for them, to remove the dirtiness from their spirit and send it off to somewhere better than here.

The pyre was done, and the flames set quickly, efficiently. Wood in the thick heat of the Wuld only needed coaxing and it would burst into a flame that ate through flesh and bone.

Heads bowed, and knelt, just quickly, just out of respect.

Bodies of the earth released by the fires of gods.

The flames wash away your sins, wash away the pollution that clings to humanity.

May it deliver you unto the spirit world purified.

Ascend.

Again, I composed myself, stifled the trembling beat that ran through every inch of my body, that itched to draw my blade and drench the world in blood. I squeezed my hands into a tight fist, and then it washed away from me. I swung around, barking orders like it hasn't bothered me, "Up on your feet, you who survived the call of our hunted. You had the strength to face down the otherworld's call, not the weakness to go with it. If you don't think you can do it again, go, but lay down your sword here. That is the power of the godless we seek to face. The oni." I had to be steel always. "Well, anyone?" Silence, as I knew it would be. Unwavering were their expressions. Friends, companions, brothers and sisters perished beside them...and yet I cannot give them an inch. Cannot let them mourn, nor know that I mourn. It is the way of the warrior, to carry on bathed in the blood of your companions. For that is what the hunt, the battle, the war is. The godlord led us here. The fat wretches gave us no choice but to expend lives to line their own gold chests. To walk into hell with nothing but swords and armour.

Gold coins for cats. That is all this is.

I started to shake, to feel the fire more furiously, the fire that burned within. But I wouldn't let it take control. Now was the time for honour, for commitment, and for compliance. Master would see it my way one day, I'd make sure of it.

"Commander Dattori," Zaki brought me from my rumination. "We must hurry. That call, it must feel threatened. The other group...they have incited its wrath. We cannot let it fall into their hands."

A second bellow sunk my heart deep into the floor – just what mess have the fieldclans wrought on themselves, on us? "We have tarried too long. WE MAKE HASTE!" I shouted and broke into a run, ahead of my men, tears fled my face.

Damn this hunt to the gods. Damn this request. What kind of Meater worked with oni meat anyway? I asked myself, never wanting to meet the damned heathen, knowing I would. An ungodly freak. I'd rather go to the fiery pits bladeless than meet again.

Looking at the darksome trunks fly by as I ran, the darksome sludge that blotted my path, and the immense heat that threatened to suffocate us, I felt like I got my wish. I was in the hells alright, but at least I had my swords.

It was tough.

I waded through the fetid forest air; the smog of the underworld thick against my cheeks as I cut through it with the ferocity of a wolf fixated on a bloodied scent, tearing through the Wuld with my pack at my back. Zaki and his band were spectres beyond me as they moved unseen with a silence I couldn't. Only a faint movement at the corner of my trained eye told me they were there; facing the depths, looking into the dark void between the surrounding sentinels, I could see nothing, feel nothing as their very presence was stifled by some scout's trickery. Or maybe skill. Zaki was a fine man. In another life, my fine man. Gods, Master would've wanted it. But not me. A she-demon built for this way of life. Master knew not to chain my blade.

The forest bellowed again. My world shook. My body trembled. My spirit tried to break free, and I couldn't help but piss down my leg. The godsborne terrified the human part of my brain, the part that didn't yearn for this. Oh, I wasn't a woman afraid to feel her fears, but the whoresons that forced us into this job will pay one day. Somehow. If I'm to make it out of this place, I will make it true.

Zaki appeared, an apparition ahead of me. He guided his unit, with his signs, to a stop. He gestured to me, and I came into a crouch next to him as he wanted. Turning back, the unit did the same. I couldn't see that damned Meater anywhere. Vile thing didn't keep up. A pointless burden, then.

Something moved between the grey trunks far ahead. We signed, deciding what to do about it without uttering a word. Noise would cost us this close to them. Nor did I want to risk the tremble in my voice, it could be mistaken for nerves, making me look weak in front of these men. But it wouldn't be. I'm designed for this stuff. The heat of the wood clung tighter to me and mix in with my own swell of lava. Folding in on itself, swirling and fusing until it was a refined, heightened state, one that would fuel my sword, my anger rose.

Nothing, he mouthed. But I was sure it was something.

The forest was working its way in now. Anything home to the godsborne was somewhere humanity should steer clear of. You could taste it, smell it. Even feel it, here. Beyond the oni stench, and the heat, something different. It plucked at the hairs on the back of your neck and played with those butterflies in your stomach something awful as it throbbed through your body and out of the centre of your forehead. Over and over. Just like when Meaters performed their heathen arts, and when blood was drawn deep. The otherworldly sensation of sticking your hands and business where you shouldn't, where the gods could see them. It was all around us.

"No, Gods!" One of mine cried. "Make it stop!"

"Quiet!" Zaki winced as he grabbed his ears.

What...human. I knew it then. The screams raked through my mind, but my soul stayed in its place. "Human. It's tearing them apart." I went to move, but Zaki barred my way. No, his eyes said. We were here for a reason after all, and that didn't include saving the idiots that awoke the Wuld's wrath.

I winced at another scream. Much closer. It unsettled the leaves around me as a deathly chill whispered through them, cutting through the heat. I looked to Zaki who was draped in a shroud of concern; his lead scouts were still out there. I squeezed my eyes shut, feeling the despair of this godsforsaken mission pile up around me. When I opened them again, a bead of sweat dripped from Zaki's chin as he gulped, betraying my own feelings.

A slight rattle, like dropping nails onto tile, simmered behind me as even those trained by my own blade grew unsteady. Don't, I thought. It'll be the death of you. Don't let those ungodly screams in.

Silence.

I couldn't bear it as my own rasped breaths were all that filled my head.

"Gods, where are they?" Zaki asked, mirroring my own thought.

Again, something moved ahead, and I raised a hand, the hiss of katanas gliding up their sheaths at my back. Readying their teeth, my men were poised to attack.

The something stumbled forth. Unsteady like an undead, it broke the black veil between the nearest trees.

Zaki leapt forth and sprung through the forest paces ahead to catch it before it fell.

Not something. Someone.

He held his broken scout in his arms, but his face was concrete.

I signed for my men to follow and started toward Zaki. They knew the signs well and were at my back, but they spread this time, loosening the formation. No good to bunch up in a situation like this; our blades would only meet each other. As I made it to Zaki, I could barely hold my mornmeal. I was used to the fight, but not barbarianism like this. Only the gods know how that man left the spot he was injured on; from the left eye down to his waist, at a sharp angle, his body was missing. Cleaved, but not quite in two. One arm gone and his entrails spilled from his side.

One of Zaki's own shadows torn. Gone.

I heard his teeth grind against each other as he laid the man down, muttering his final rights. There was not time for a pyre now. He knelt, and that's when something was hurled through the forest, cracking against the trees ahead, a spray of something carried on and pitter-pattered against my plate like a light rain. But as I looked down and pressed my hand to my armour, something more sinister was revealed. Crimson and coppery.

Zaki moved as I blinked and knelt by whatever it was that had peeled from the tree and slumped to the floor. He looked back, Metsuku's ice shot down my spine. Pure terror as he held up a rounded insignia that could only belong to another of his own.

His scouts were shattered.

In that moment as he stared at me, it felt like seconds stretched into hours and days; I stared beyond, and above him as the blackness shimmered, taking form in an instant's instant. Monstrous club raised, mouth agape and shrieking with the chorus of countless tortured souls, an oni struck down on Zaki and his downed shadow with preternatural speed. Speed that defied its three-man-tall bulk. A fresh splash of blood hit me as the impact set me off balance. A breath caught in my throat, a scream stifled as I bit down hard on my lip, pulling myself from the spot. Gliding back, twirling my finger in the air scattering my men into their formation, I drew CrowKiller from her scabbard. She sung her metallic song. The hairs stood on my neck, pulled taut by the gods' own warning, I span arcing my blade upwards as the same oni charged from behind. How? Too late. It glanced off my blade, lifting me off my feet at the same time, I was hurled into a tree. The wind left me. My head pounded as I tried to rise, the bile burning the back of my throat.

I shook it off quickly and stood.

Clanging and hissing blades drew my attention. Screaming and shouting men.

The beast stood amongst them, my Wuld Guard, clawing and clubbing.

Two piss-yellow bent horns pierced through the greased hair on its head as it trailed down to its midriff; a hide rag spared its shame. It was unnaturally muscled, other than the potbelly that spoke of the easy pickings for such a beast in the Wuld. But its face told of something different, something shunned by all that's right in the world. Its eyes fish-like. Third eye closed, its top and bottom canines curled out from its lips and to the limits of its round face.

A demon in the flesh.

It picked a man up in its hand like he was nothing. Sentan, my friend, was torn as easy as reeds, in half. All those years spent with the blade were nothing in front of it. Twisted into pieces. The oni raised my guard's broken torso above its head, snickering as my men used the opportunity to regroup, to back away, to think in the moments before its next move. I couldn't blame them; I couldn't know it would be like this. The monster rang the torso out like a rag, its corpse-like skin splattered red.

The Dattori never had a relationship with our own godsborne like the other clans; there's no way to work with dread beasts, no benefit in the friendship of those who enjoy death – the heavens made them wrong.

My ears rang as the shouts dulled. My vision narrowed. Lips curling, I let the beast take over; nothing mattered now. I went to move, and something grabbed me from the side, shook me.

"Masako!" It cried. "Stay with me. Work with me, don't get any ideas. This is about us. We live as a group." Zaki. I blinked quickly to get rid of him, but it wasn't a vision. It was him. In one piece, blood splattered. Ninjato drawn in the hand that didn't have hold of my shoulder.

"Okay," I breathed deeply. Turning to the demon, it looked on at us, waiting for our move. I gave the signal for my men to engage. "Zaki, on me!"

I ran at it.

The oni scattered my men with a swing of its gargantuan club, and I ducked it, rolling and coming up within its guard, if you could call the oni's personal space such. My nostrils burned this close to the vile thing. I swung CrowKiller in my left and drew HighWolf in my right. And dashed between its legs, breaking out of it into a spin, taking a loose stance between, I moved to hamstring the wretch.

The blue oni jumped as my blades hissed against the nothingness it inhabited moments before. Darting forward, I closed the gap in an instant. Nothing escaped my blades. HighWolf skitters across shins, sparking, biting into the skin at the end of the slash. Gods, even with spell-forged. It turned and I brought CrowKiller up in time to redirect the club as it thumped down into the earth beside me, rattling me to the core, my teeth chattering as it did. To fight something so large and powerful scared me. My only advantage was in its own weight. I jumped backwards sheathing HighWolf and parrying its strike with a two-handed grip. Rattled again and sent off-balance, I dodged to the side.

Zaki danced in with his silent swords as it met me, cutting a chunk out of its leg, successful in hamstringing the whoreson where I was not; there were no finer smiths than his family, the Murakami, their spell-forgery was gods-sent, but it disappeared with them – the last two blades arrived with their last son.

He leapt back as it yowled and flung a balled fist at him. He was too fast for the oni and I closed in, I saw my men doing the same. The beast's footing unsure then, it flung its club and my heart fluttered as it hit a group of my Guards, armour clattering and bones crunching as the force of a speeding cart ended them.

I looked around for reassurance, but I didn't get it; a handful of my men still stood.

Diving in for a grab, as Zaki dogged it with small cuts in the openings he made, it screamed agony as the foolish beast put too much weight on the half-severed foot, snapping it clean off. It fell to its knees as I reached it and whistled. A signal of regrouping my men knew well.

On its knees, it was still a force only the gods should reckon with. It grabbed at Zaki, almost capturing him. I was there, slashing at its forearm. Slashing deep this time. It yowled again, but with none of the soul-splitting force I heard earlier. I almost felt sorry for it as Zaki ran up the arm of the slowed beast, blood trickled out of it from myriad cuts. That was its end.

The fieldsman and head-scout, master of the shadows, Zaki stood atop its slumped form, holding a ninjato above its head. I relaxed slightly, my part in this hunt played. He brought the blade down, it stopped. I cried out in horror. Enclosed around Zaki's arm was another giant fist. It stepped away, Zaki swung in its grip.

Red, deep red was its colour. Third eye opened and glowing, a red oni that dwarfed the first blue emerged from the pit of the forest, hidden behind a darkened cloak.

Shaking off the fear, I switched my guard into the dragon's tail, and it trailed behind me as I ran, not worrying about what my men were doing.

I jumped from the back of the oni that we felled and slashed wildly at the arm that held my dear friend prisoner. But it went dark, and I hit the ground with a thud, twisting and breaking as I was sent flying across the forest floor. I gripped around nothing as CrowKiller was lost in the mess I'd made for myself. Looking back, the red oni dropped his fist. Such power, to catch me unaware. Such evil. Foolish. We were all foolish. I staggered to my knees, and everything hurt.

My head thumped, but not with ache. I felt it cascading into my body, and out through my forehead.

That third eye, it called to the gods.

I staggered towards it as it gripped Zaki in both hands. Laughing, or at least that's what it felt like, it tossed him about. A ragdoll.

I staggered again and tripped, this time hitting my face as I fell. Something in the leaves underneath me cut my hand. I got up and found CrowKiller again. Hacked again, my blood splattering its blade. The oni wasn't even paying attention to me as it grew bored of the broken man, ripping into the rest of my guard. In my periphery, I noticed Zaki twitching, maybe he still lived. I roared with both of my blades in my hands and dived into my approximation of a run. Legs pumping, I'm sorry that I didn't rush in to help my men, that I used their last breaths as a distraction as I closed in once more. Just two paces and my blades would have had their fill. It swung a hand, and I dodged, lashing out with CrowKiller, slicing easily through armoured skin and bone, severing its free hand – dumbstruck at my own feat. I looked down at CrowKiller. Blood hissing and crackling against the blue of the oni's, consuming it. Madness. Accursed blood. A voice, something deep...within. But I buried it. At the time, I had no idea what awaited me.

I looked up in time to see its leg kick out and send me flying again. The wind smashed from my lungs. I hit a tree and didn't go far, and it turned to me.

Slowly, it walked forward.

A tune. I heard something.

What's left of my Blades picked themselves up. Fools. I hated them. I still do. Why couldn't they play dead? Why did they have to do that?

They cried out, and the creature turned from me. Weighing up whether the five of them were worth ignoring my broken body, or maybe listening to the tune, it tilted its head.

My men stopped dead. Two of them convulsed. The others looked on, wonder in their eyes at whether this was the machinations of the demon that stood in front of them. But it too was frozen. I wasn't so unaware, I knew it. As I tried to stop the tune from working its way into my mind, from taking hold of whatever it is looking for, I felt relief.

I remembered him. Cat Food.

The Meater's tune. Akin to whatever necromantic filth fuels the undead, it calls upon the meat you've eaten. Calling it back from the otherworld, allowing it a host.

A yap, then growl. And I prized my eyes open, beat away the tune's influence as it died out; for that reason, I don't eat meat. Against a Meater, it would be your death. But some warriors don't make that sacrifice.

Caught by the Don Yoku's lullaby, two of my men became twisted atrocities that resembled neither the eaten nor the eater.

I trembled as I pulled myself up onto my knees, and away from the tree I propped myself up against. At least the oni was distracted; staring, focused on something. The Meater.

Cat Food walked into the opening and stood amongst the gore. He looked beyond the oni, and to me and smiled a crooked smile. Patting down his robes, he walked towards the downed oni and drew a long, slender knife. He sized up the barely breathing beast and drew his knife-hand back.

The oni erupted, bounding towards Cat Food.

The result of the Meater's song shot out of the darkness behind its master. Rage and savagery incarnate. It intercepted the oni. Standing at half its height on all fours, but more monstrous than the dog it started as, Cat Food's pet snapped, bit and clawed at the oni as it attempted to grapple with the beast; neither dog nor lion, Cat Food's pet was a twisted, grotesque mixture of both. A shiba inu with powerful cat-like paws, fangs that twisted out of it mouth to match its prey's and a coat that shimmered with beads of ethereal water, splotched in orange spirals. It was a magnificent abomination. Its mane splattered with gore and flesh as it shredded the oni, the creature could only step backwards as it was mauled. Screaming, screeching it was pulled to the floor. And then, with a shake of its neck, and a crunch, the red oni was slain.

Everything went black. I relaxed into oblivion, then I pulled myself out again, blinking. Cat Food stood in front of me; he brought up a white cloth and wiped his long knife clean of blood.

A yap drew my attention. Dog-sized again, his mutt pawed at him, he put the knife away and rustled around his bag. He pulled out a chunk of something, and said, "Sit! Ah, there's a good boy. Here. Oh, you want some more? But you've just had something. There there." He turned his attention to my collapsed form, smiling, and said, "Job's done then."

I still hear Zaki's screams as Cat Food knit his bones back together, the chilling tune as he sang to him.

* * *

Now, as I'm dragged into the great hall Master used to preside over our family's affairs, I look up at the dais. Ignoring the savage leader who falsely occupies it, I gaze up at the giant skull that hangs above. Three eye sockets leer at me from the emerald-coloured skull. Teeth curl out from the jaw, smaller ones point every which way, reminding me of a rose vine; the horn, chopped from the skull, hangs in front of it, tip down. Master was beside himself over what we had to do. He said the gods would be allowed their retribution if it pleased them, as he sat under the swinging spike. I doubt the treacherous dog below it now would share the same sentiment.

The floors, now unpolished, are tracked with dirt and detritus. Some of the murals in the surrounding canvas walls remain, of great oceans, seas of trees, oni, gods and battles. Most of them are torn, kicked in, ripped from their runners. Candles weep around the room, their tears sprawling onto ripped up scrolls, and damaged trinkets. Our own bit of Sama's hoard is cracked, broken pieces of pottery that litter stands – nothing like that whore-lord's.

My house is in ruin.

Dragged at spear point, and forced to my knees, I now look up at the vile wretch that profited from all of this.

Chapter 13

"**G**irl." His voice is a rake against stones. "Why didn't you just fucking die like you were supposed to?"

Though my face is bloody, broken, I smile at him. A smile full of holes, no doubt. The guards gave me the once over in aid of their dead friends. "Imanta Nomin, your numbers dwindle every time we meet," I say. His eyes grow wider. With the scars that streak across his balding scalp and the great beard that makes up for that, I can barely tell whether I get a rise out of him.

I see he's no more elegant than the last time we met; Nomin wears the same tight hakama, the same tunic that the rest of the backwards tribe do. Rigid, he hasn't aged gracefully, as he stands from the dais and descends the steps with all the grace of a falling tree. The blade he wears at his side is familiar. I spit vile words as I notice it. Getting the upper hand in this was crucial but I've given it all away. The anger rises and I try to with it but am beat back to the floor; one of my captors presses my head against it with his foot, eliciting a scream. There's no fight left in me as I struggle to close my eyes, worried they'll pop out of their sockets under the pressure.

The pressure is lifted off and I writhe, trying to peel myself from the wood. Drool strings from floor to mouth.

The savage leader has unsheathed the blade, the steel glows brightly even within the dim orange light, green veins scatter across its surface. A spell-forged blade, no less. My – spell – forged – blade. CrowKiller. "Even now, you won't change. Even now that anger of yours will cost you...a finger or two," he snarls. The mutts around me jeer and whistle at the sentence.

Not one he will get to pass down.

"Empty...Threats." I maintain my smile. "A man like you doesn't have a big enough cock to follow through with it." My temper wouldn't be short among the fieldclans. Savagery is fed with it. And so, I rile him up, met with CrowKiller's cold steel to my neck. His eyes beg me for a reason to end it. "These halls, these walls are not your own. It was only a matter of time."

"Yer one to talk ownership again," says one guard. The rest of them snicker.

"He's right," Nomin adds. "What do you know about it? You never respected nothing of ours. Take, take, take, the Dattori way."

"Careful," I warn them, the word dripping with poison.

Nomin can't help but laugh in my face. He chucks my sword; it clatters across the room. Idiot. And he grabs my chin, forcefully pulling my eyes to his. Two guards entrap my arms. "So, you think you can come and reclaim this, eh? That this place is yours by right. But what claim does an orphan whore have over the estates of a dead man?" His grasp tightens. "We here, too, need a home."

"There's no home for poppy traders," I spit. "You're a blight on Basho. I'd do it again."

He strikes me, the room shifts and wobbles. He splits into two and then back again as I blink it away.

"Don't hurry it." The savage leader's hand flashes to his waist and he pulls a dagger from his belt. "You're gonna die anyway. I'd have offered you a place here. Impossible, though. A hawk sees everything that scuttles below it as prey. A feast. I can't have that here. The poppy is a lucrative trade, not done under the godlord's nose though. When you've but an unfarmable field to your name, what else can you do?"

"How dare you!" I bark, unable to control myself.

"She does bite, eh."

"Master paid for that! You'll pay for it. Growing the poppy on our lands."

"We came to Dattori with nowhere to go, and he ceded nothing. YOU laughed in our faces. Your own greed brought this on you. We had nowhere. We have nothing...Well, until now. This is ours. A place for us to be safe. Safe from tyrants like you!" With that, he swings back, then punches forward with the knife, straight for my face.

One of the guards flinches as if surprised by the brute action of his backward master, loosening his grip on my arm.

I don't dodge, there's no time for that. I meet his sharp punch with an open mouth, turning my head slightly as I chomp down on a mouthful of steel. It grinds, shrieks like a banshee across my teeth. Pulling my arm free, I grab his wrist with all the strength I can muster, elbow no longer creaking. It holds strong and I mutter thanks to Jinto. A trembling jaw and I can't quite lock my arm. Twice my weight, and naturally stronger. It's only a matter of time until the blade sinks into the back of my throat. The dagger slides, licks the inside of my cheek. A white-hot burst darts up the side of my face as it digs in.

His eyes are vicious, black, hateful.

I will die here.

Blood boils out from my cheek. And I hear it again, the madness that speaks, urges me on. I taste the copper, drink it, let it carry me away. There's no point in denying it. I speak to it, and it screams in anger. My anger. I stoke it, set it rolling down into the void, fuelling it with my own blood. Responding with a pulse, in that second, each muscle tightens, hardens, strengthens.

There's a drone, and I flick my focus back to Nomin. It's him, he screams, slowly. So very slowly. My fingers puncture his forearm, his blood drips. The dagger pulled from my mouth, I brace my legs underneath me and push, throwing him away from me as I stand. I can't hear anything but the heavy beat of the blood fever that grips me now, the echoing screams of the madness pumping through my veins.

I cross the room to CrowKiller, who lies waiting on the floor. The curve of the blade is a grin for her mother. For her return. I pick her up, and turn on the guard, they've pulled their long-handled weapons and make for me. But I'm too fast, I'm in amongst them before they register it, spinning on the ball on my foot. CrowKiller whistles through the air. I cut them all down in one stroke.

Then only Nomin is left. I stand before him as he clutches his arm, blood pooling around him, scurrying back on his arse. Desperate. Horror in his eyes.

"Curse you, demon! Fuc−"

I put the blade through his face. He doesn't stop it with his teeth, he just dies. I'm not a demon, those live in the mountains.

* * *

In the hours after I stormed the place single-handedly, took back my lord's estate and dethroned the savages that started the fires that led to his death, I shed more blood − their surrender wasn't an option. While I still had the 'Fever, I hunted them; the guard was an old skeleton that couldn't muster order even in the face of annihilation, so I cut them down. Even against four, a true warrior fights one by one. Their small numbers didn't matter now I have CrowKiller. Already I hear their women, and children whisper. I'm not only known as the Hawk. They call me the Butcher. But I don't care, the Lord Council will hear of it, will know what's coming.

I let those who aren't warriors stay. Or leave, there's no clear line where Dattori servants end and they start, and they're not a cause for concern. Only the sword-wielding were. I can't watch my back while the lords who didn't come to our aid, who turned a blind eye to the wrath we incurred, still live. My path still must cross theirs and my Way will be sharp, decisive. I'll act with blade in mind, not the scroll. The time ahead will not be one fought with policies in the small courts of the Samaki, nor will I seek retribution from the lawmakers, the Gods' senses, in Orika.

Not by me. I started this in a blaze of anger and will finish it the same way; the only way I know how to live.

I've sent for Kekkei, who will fight in the courts on my behalf. If there's one thing I've learnt about Thousand Hands, it is that there's much more to him than a simple mercenary; he's unmatched in charisma, a man people must follow. This is how Akate rose to prominence. Paid for war is not his only tool. When a time of secrecy and information was needed, he spun his webs in weeks. That much can be seen from the way he handled Tamikura.

I wait anxiously for his arrival, wondering whether he will come. He must. Although I don't trust the runner I sent, I'm certain that the horse he rides will find Jinto; its eyes are a cloudy bewitched green that the heathen boy must have something to do with. I don't fully trust the household staff that were left; all intact, but not my warriors, Yoji, Hatamo, Ganfi, Tane, my favourites, all of them dead. They followed me to my grave but did not rise again with me. If the Lord Council didn't burn their bodies, I'll find them, and I'll put them to rest as they deserve. I swear it.

The maids, kitchen staff, servants, nannies served the invaders without protest it would seem. And again, in this change of hands, they continue without protest, without a second thought. My household runs itself around me still, the servants drag the few bodies of the Imanta clan, preparing a pyre at my orders; they were my household's common folk first, but I can't help feeling uneasy at their lack of loyalty to anything other than order. What can I expect from low births, though? Honour is a word only those born in closer proximity to the gods speak.

My Master's study is the same as he left it, the scrolls and parchment untouched, tomes still shelved. Only the alcohol is gone, which alone speaks volumes about the late fieldclan. A shuffle, the door to the study is pulled open and I'm left slightly disturbed when Cat Food stands in front of me, alone. The Shaman always did unsettle me, even more so at his mastery of doors, while lacking the necessary equipment to open one.

"*You may come in,*" I snarl. "To what do I owe this early morning visit?" His smile is full of thanks. I saw to it that he was released, but his cell does not remain empty. The guards that captured me appeared to know their destination all too well. I'm to thank the woman who raised me for that, so Ozumi keeps it warm.

"Masako, Masako." My given name is liquid gold spilling out of his lips and I don't like it. "There's a subtlety to swordplay, a nuance in its teachings of patience and virtue, that you just don't have. Honoured, am I, that I know a purveyor of its...brutalities?" Cat Food comes closer, kneels in front of me, and fans himself with a stump, before stopping, his flinty eyes realising the folly in it. And going back to a grin. One of Master's dress robes thrown over him, green, finished with black floral designs; it reminds me of the estate. I love those robes, but I don't have the energy to reprimand him. I don't remember the last time I slept. "Had it not been so, I might have turned bad in there. My thanks, many thanks. My promise to the...late Lord Dattori stands, my oath to Don Yoku not-withstanding, I'm sworn to your household. Not...that I'm of much use now." He trails off, seemingly searching the room to focus on anything but me. The Shaman hides a deep sorrow behind that smile. For all Cat Food is, was, he's been loyal to a fault.

"Yoku Hebikawa, in a time when I can trust no one, you sacrificed all that is precious to you, in a bid to save *our* lord from the tyrant whose rule blackens the homeland. If you will, I would welcome you in charge of our estates. Your counsel, while I'm here. I've much to do before I can settle."

"Masako...Masako, please," he says. "Am I blushing? Look at what you've done, this is unlike you. You're usually so...abrasive." It irks me to hear it but it comes as no surprise. "There's no trust, though. No. How can you hear my counsel if you can't trust my words?"

"Those who were part of this household, even briefly, number you and I, now. If the right hand can't speak to the left, there's no hope for Basho. No hope for our clan."

"Oh, stop it." Hebikawa leans back, his eyes looking like two upturned smiles. "Accepted. Being a hand to you completes me. I miss those in my life."

"Under the dragons, please accept my sincere apologies." I bow low, rising again. His face is void of any tell, stunned. I surprise myself, however, with Cat Foods actions, there was some honour in our defeat. Our family were heard in its death throes. Most of my men died in the honour of battle, because of his lead. Even if the Lord Council wishes to pretend we never existed. It fills my heart with a warmth I'm not too familiar with.

"Well, er...I forget myself, Lady Dattori. I didn't come here just for this. Our messenger was too late. It appears. He should have left three days ago if he wanted to deliver our message. Come in, Little Brother."

I suck in a quick breath, leaning further over my desk. I fight to hide a grin, cut its heart out before it's born unto my face. I can't show him my elation. The wildboy, Jinto, steps over the threshold. Bunta and Oboro flank him. A misfit guard.

"Lady Dattori." Jinto pinches his lips together, bowing deeply and rising again chuckling. The guard do the same without the laughter. "Greed. Hawk, this is a change of scenery. Surrounded by all those scrolls, you'd look like a scholar if you weren't splattered with blood."

I touch my face, the grime, and crust of blood that isn't mine; I run my tongue along the newly jagged edge the dagger has wrought. Along the wound that it left. Pulsing heat, pushing needles into it as my tongue goes. I'm a mess, I know that. And I'm glad there's still someone who would tell me so, even while I'm seated here. "Boy Shaman, you're as delightful as a duel on uneven ground." I smirk. "The Wolf?"

"Yes. It was a concern when you didn't change your path. We didn't actually think you'd come here alone. Don Yoku." Cat Food flinches his eyes flicker and he thinks it goes unnoticed. "Brother!" Jinto catches the other Shaman's stray gaze. "That is why He didn't show me her demise; it aligns now. It all fits. He is here. His reach knows these lands." Cat Food doesn't reply immediately, he seems off guard, uncharacteristically so. Bunta and Oboro shift as if to address the rudeness, but they don't, for I've not spoken.

"Little Brother, you're mistaken. What can I do with these?"

"Don Yoku didn't take those. The pretenders did. Do not worry, yours is not lost."

There's a frustrated air that hangs over Master's quarters now, an air only Shamans of Greed and their repulsive, unanswered, unfinished words are familiar with. But now's not the time.

I stand, and say, "Enough of this. Bunta, send word to light the pyre. Oboro, Jinto, bring Kekkei. There's something we must do before this day breaks. Leave."

They obey without hesitation and again it's Hebikawa and I.

"Come."

"Wait...Masako."

I pause at the door, waiting for words that seem caught on the cat's tongue.

"Spit it out."

"Careful. Careful of the boy. Don't look like that, I don't intend to alarum you. There're layers to our...faith, that you cannot comprehend. That are not shared with the outside. Of those I've met, only those whose remaining time was counted in days ahead, whose bodies had withered in devotion of our God, were as close to Don Yoku as that boy is. I've seen even less whose Greed-sworn number more than one. None who did it without the Song. Even though it is my God, do not take my words lightly. Tread carefully, for I do not know what is planned. I hear a faint whisper in the wind where that boy hears a voice at his shoulder." With that, he jumps up, bows lightly, brushing himself down. And leaves.

I've known Shaman, they are numerous in Basho. That faith is overgrown in comparison to the rest. Even so, a nagging in my mind told me Jinto is different, told me that he is a kindred of mine. Neither of us belong. Not even to each other, so I mark Cat Food's words with importance, push it to the back of my mind. Albeit unknowns, they are not enemies. And I plan to strengthen that as I stride from the room, fastening CrowKiller to my waist. I note I must find HighWolf, then I can dispose of that wicked sidearm I left with my horse.

* * *

Warm, oppressive, the heat that billows from the pyre has an uncomfortable weight to it; spirits of the Imanta flee into the heavens, climbing higher with the smoke. But I feel their anguish, an unnatural fire is one that burns this hot. A bad omen when the dead hold this much heat within them. It tells of misfortune, flames that hot weaken bonds, the structure of things. But I don't care for it. They brought it upon themselves.

Jinto and his wolf pair dance, jump and scrap ahead of me, closer to the pyre than what is comfortable. Kekkei's retinue look onwards at him in disbelief. I see how the gods keep them wary of it.

At one side, Hebikawa, Mina, all I count trustworthy to witness this. To my other, Kekkei, Ropi. And Danzo, the last of Akate's captains who've returned from the wild, looking like a bent old staff. A gnarled thumb. While the unfamiliar faces in my estates number many more than those I know, I'm gladdened by the numbers. There's strength in those Thousand Hands has brought here.

The change in his heart, the fluidity of a man's decisions, I'll never understand. It leaves me confused, but with no choice. There's only one way to build my family, the way Master started it. Not with blood, but with oaths. I went to Kekkei with a fight in mind, and met only obedience, a willingness to swear to the Four; though, it is not so surprising. Leaving a *rōnin* for dead is one matter, turning down a Samaki lord is another.

I ascend to my proper seat as Thousand Hands finds his.

Across from the pyre, a shrine of the Gods of Creation sits. Carved out of one piece of stone, a rake and a katana cross over each other, a snake coils around them both, tying them together eternally; at the foot on the monument, there's a gutter cut into it, a reservoir of oil. I approach first, kneeling, and await Jinto.

He pulls himself away from his pack. With him, he brings a torch lit from the pyre which I dip into the oils, lighting a fire that curls around the bleak stone, completing representation of the Four. For this ceremony, Sukami's flames are borne out of the wrongs done to my family, destroyed so I can start anew. I stand and gesture for Kekkei to take my place, for all to witness what is done here as a new day forms once more. To stop this should they find reason to. But none do.

Few words are permitted once the flames are lit, so I speak the few I can, "Izenta, Meganako, Sukami, and Metsuku. First Four, watch now as our family is born again from these flames. Watch now as we grow under your names." I kneel next to Kekkei, bowing deeply. "Offer thy hand, one who seeks to become kindred." Kekkei does, as I draw the obsidian dagger from my belt. Ceremonial, it is carved with the words of my household. Wrought from the first oni felled by the Dattori. I've only seen Master do this once, and the butterflies swirl in my stomach as I worry over doing the gods a wrong. I take his hand, pushing the tip of the blade into the offered palm. He doesn't flinch, I note that. As the blood pools, I take deep breaths. Ignore the beat in my ears, the voice that speaks. Taking his wrist, we stand. I tip his palm to the flame, the blood crackles, hisses.

"It is done. Let this fire burn for four nights and as many days. Genaro Kekkei, Akate, serve my family as if it were your own. Die for it, as if it were your own. Honour it, as if it were your own." With that, it is done. I gaze at him for longer than I should, trying to find a tell in his eyes but they are stony, unmoving. The ease at which he agreed to serve under me, as a vassal to my inherited fiefdom, bothers me still. For now, the Dattori household rises again, stronger. But I will watch him with a hand to my hilt.

In death, all crimes are washed away.

The Lord Council must be careful in how it acts against Akate now that they share the clean slate of the Dattori.

My troubles have multiplied, I have a myriad of them to my name. The seas have calmed and it's the shark's fin that creates waves, not the salmons. If I am to continue on my path, I must spill blood into the waters, and watch them frenzy.

Now, whose blood will it be?

PART 2

"A savage, angry sword is the sea against the cliff face, battering the land it seeks to gain entry to, only to destroy its quarry slowly. Though, without violence, the sea will never touch the land. With violence, the sea will break the land."

Dattori Hojimoto

Chapter 14

The saddle wears thin. Myriads of sores line my thighs. My company wears thin, I've not travelled in such a healthy-sized retinue for as long as I could remember; Lord Dattori rarely made the trips with more than could be counted on one hand, the other hand should always be trained on your katana. Yet now I'm surrounded by Hands. More than I could count on two, but less than I could count on four. Eight horses to ride, two men to each, taking it in turns. One to lead, one to ride. Each saddle-packed. Some with rice, the others with weapons, trinkets, but no gold kobans; one thing that is gone for good is the wealth and prosperity of my clan, we don't have long enough left on this plane for that.

Kekkei, Oboro, Bunta and I ride front. I've none closer to me, these are the heart, the core of my household, bar the Shaman. What sick joke of the gods is this?

"Argh, Metsuku's testicles, 'urts," Bunta moans.

"Quiet."

"I've been in the saddle days, Oboro," Bunta snaps. "The gods dint curse me with a tiny set, like you. It rubs, aches. I need to get off—"

"QUIET!" Oboro's temper is quicker than mine, it doesn't suit his unremarkable visage. He looks more like a trader than of my household, but he's wearing our colours – deep greens edge his dusky robes, his daggers still a hidden danger – I'm not a strict lord.

"An' whys Jinto getting to stay again?"

"In all the hells." Kekkei spurs the horse level with Bunta's. "Stop! We've been through this. The Samaki lords are not known for their open minds.

The north is more open to the newer faiths."

"Right," I say. "My late master was the first of the Samaki in many things. Acceptance of the Greed-faithed one of them." His readiness to challenge, another. We fall back into a silent trot. Five days of slow, painful riding has brought us this far, if there's one thing that gives away that we've finally entered the lands of the Shuji-to, it's the many, many rice paddies. The immense farmlands, flat without even a finger of rock to break the monotonous display of wealth; it's not that the rest of Basho, for what I've seen, don't farm, it's that Shuji-to does it with meticulous efficiency. On a vast scale. To the dragons above, it would appear as an ant's nest, riddled with workers scuttling about. It speaks volumes of what type of man I should expect in their lord, Shuji Ayato. Kekkei insists this was not the right man to approach first. But, his family, his holdings, rival Dattori's peak, and now we don't hold a candle to them. It is power I seek, so I go straight for the lion's den.

That said, it was the only way to go. My clanlands are all but cut off from the rest of the Samaki. From our lands, the road to Shuji-to is the only clear path, the only path that doesn't cross the Sea of Jagged Sand; a vast expanse that rolls down from the foot of the Demon Mountain range, lying as far south as you can go in Basho. I'm not ready to let them know I live again. Not ready to call on old favours, to pay old debts.

A beggar would have more choices than one tied to a godsborne as I am.

The workers don't stop to watch us pass, that's not their job. Shuji-to discipline is a touch above all good measure, it seems.

We make our way to the main family's estate untroubled; their outer wall is the same chalky-white as ours, if not a bit yellowed by the dust fields that start where the farmland stops, surrounding the walls. The tiles on it too, are similar but it's mixed amongst the thatched roofs within. Neither striking nor particular easy on the eye, it displays their resourcefulness.

I dismount nearing the gate, as does Kekkei. He is the only one at my side as we approach. There's no sword upon which to rest my hand, and I'm all the more anxious for it, but I do not come as a warrior.

The two halves of the gates are drawn inwards slowly, the only thing in the Shuji-to lands that seems to groan with the effort its work takes. A small welcoming party awaits. I see five, no six, warriors dressed in full plain-undecorated silver plate; the Shuji's careful reluctance to move in the past has cost them the dignity of having histories to etch onto their armour. Even their masks are bare, simplistic. Each has the two swords permitted to our caste. An ungainly man steps out ahead of them, whiskers long like a cat's, a sandy robe far too big for him trails along the ground.

Kekkei speaks sideways to me, "We're expected?"

I stop. Wearing my own approximation of a smile, bowing half the way they'd expect of a warrior, and whisper to Kekkei, "Ayato is supposedly a smart man. I don't think workers is all we saw today among the common folk."

Whiskers stops at the threshold, returning the bow that the warriors do not, "Those colours. Ah, excuse me for my escort. The lord had not sent me expecting such an important guest, but the information comes from the mouths of the uninformed. If you would, follow me, *Lady* Dattori."

The six warriors split in half and turn to face each other as we follow the man through them and into the grounds.

* * *

"Dismissed, Naoyasu," says Lord Shuji. "Leave the tea, we can manage."

"At once, my lord."

Whiskers dropped all he was doing, the wind's haste on his heel. Still, he slid the doors with care. He made too little sound for a simple servant, the men that the lord keeps close; even those that head servants are well-met, functional choices.

Across from me, Shuji Ayato does not meet my stare. Instead, he looks around the room at the sakura painted sliding doors. An intense look as if he'd never seen such a thing before or was expecting someone to burst through. He's an old suit of armour. I'm aware of what that outwardly robust body was once capable of, but I wouldn't fight alongside him anymore. An elderly woman, with none of his violence in her eyes, kneels whispering in his ear. His face screwing, muttering. A younger man next to her, and one opposite him, there is but one space left around this table of abrupt meetings. It is all a bit too organised and leaves me wondering why or how the lord was expecting me. It would surely be addressed but on his own terms. Terms that sought to test my waning patience.

The two at my flank are stark opposites, as Thousand Hands is still as a rock, and Bunta shifts, groaning every second. I, too, feel the fires bubbling in my belly. But I remain passive, waiting. Between us, the green tea is poured, cooling. It waits for its lord's permission to be drank.

"A fine harvest this year, my lord," I say. The customary small talk, trading false compliments is lordly, it seems. "Golden fields, Sukami's blessing."

"Ah, I've been too relaxed with my farmers if it is indeed the divine lady's blessing." He lets out a long sigh. Looking away, he continues, "Nasty scars for a *young* lady. Black...My doctors could take a look? Though, they suit you, a warrior wears his thickest scars with pride."

I bite down my rebuke, back-handed old dog, "It would be too much trouble, my lord. I rather like them." The room falls back into silence.

The tired looking woman fiddles with her cup, seemingly agitated by the long pause. "Lady Dattori, while we await our final guest, please, drink."

The lord is the one who lifts his cup, drinks deeply and sets it down again, still without meeting my eyes.

I sip mine, and Kekkei says, "And who do we await? My lord sits ahead of me. My lady travelled long to discuss things solely of his own concern."

"Please, drink."

I bite my tongue, but it doesn't hold. A stifled moan leaves my mouth before it's interrupted by the soft whisper of the sliding door. I turn, expecting the servant but I double-take when I see a warrior. Two short blades hang from his waist, the pack on his back, and the greenish plate give the impression of a turtle. I'm offended by the lax way his hands rest on swords I'm not even permitted to wear in here, and by the fact all but his eyes are hidden by a wrap. Hair sprouts in a circle around his head. No, "*Kappa.*" I whisper. They take me for a fool? I speak up, "To what do we owe the pleasure, household Sikara?"

Now the lord looks at me, I feel it. "Pardon me, my lord," I quickly claw back control. "I speak out of turn." What game is he playing here? The Samaki are everything. The outer lands stand together. Yet, here, we wait for a member of the inner lords, the families who all but lap up the milk from the Lord Council's teat. If it were only proximity to the lawmakers in Orika that did it, I wouldn't be so bitter.

"What? Speak up, *Dattori*," Lord Shuji snaps. His face reddens. "How dare you let the chagrin spill into your face around my table. Have you been wronged? Do you have any sway over who I invite into this room?"

"No, my lord I−"

"This is a Samaki matter," Kekkei interjects. "My lady asked for audience with you, to which you accepted. From our reception, you had forewarning of our arrival. You dishonour my lady in making her wait for another household. Was my lady's time not as important as a simple guest?" Kekkei suddenly winces, grasping his head; my chest fills with panic, but he mutters his apologies, straightens and continues, "This is a meeting of Samaki diplomacy, as outlined by us. This...*warrior* is armed. Nor was he announced, so either this meeting has started under deceptive terms, or he is but a visitor who has no place around this table." Careful, Kekkei. Do not kill yourself in service of a good argument. Overwork, and the gods will notice. He washes away my annoyance. I take my cup in both hands, drinking tea to hide my pleasure.

Kekkei lets his words hang like thieves caught stealing rice from the lord. And Ayato stares back at him as if that were so.

It's the woman who breaks the silence, who clears her throat, before letting her lord verbalise the anger that boils within, "Genaro Kekkei, was it? You're a long, long way from Orika now. It is a wonder what circumstances led the *great* Akate leader here, as a spokesman and vassal of a house we thought dead. Pleasantly, we were surprised to learn it was not. And I'd also love to learn of that story in more detail. But you're right, we have Samaki matters to discuss." She pauses as if waiting for her lord to weigh in, but he doesn't. "As the lady of this house, you have our humblest apologies, we did not mean to deceive you. You see, our guest only made it known he wished to preside over this meeting a short while ago. And we are of no authority to disallow another household a voice at this table. Not one that shares so much in interest, or in common, with the other members present."

Lady Shuji. I had no idea Ayato coveted such sharp knives. A woman truly worthy of sitting in the high seat of the outlands.

The pause, this time, waited for us. But, as the turtle-man kneels with us, my breath catches. In front of the rest of the Lord Council, we're smaller than ever, weak. This other party means baring that to the rest of Basho. My jaw aches and I wince as I bite down a bit too hard on the teeth loosened by Nomin's blade, pain loud in my head. Kekkei shifts, but I silence any rebuttal with a nod. And it's worse still, in the corner of the room, a giant spectre appears, its muscularity, its stench, its screeches all try to form a picture in my mind, but I can't hold it. Neck and belly scars throb in remembrance of it; my breath quickens, but the rest of the meeting stare on. I blink hard, and it's gone, just a vision. One that reminds me of why I must speak now, of why I can't let the cats have my tongue on this one. "The lady is right, Sikara have a place in this discussion, where are my manners," I say, looking to the intruder, "if I may have your name?"

"Sikara Oji." His voice, oily, slicks through the mask. I know, or remember, little of their family structure to ascertain whether I've insulted an heir or a fifth son, but It won't matter when the north falls. "Then, my apologies, Sikara Oji," I say. Sick, tired to death of the formalities already. My sword speaks quicker, faster. "Please, my lord, all the players are present."

"Now," Lord Shuji says. "You have the attention of Shuji-to young... leader, my sons both blood and borrowed, my wife, my guest, we await with *bated* breath the reason you've graced our house with a summit, of sorts."

"Lord, we travel wi–"

"Dragons above," Lord Shuji interrupts. "I thought I posed the question to the Lady?" Not even looking at Kekkei, he insults my family. I'll show him this is not a trifle matter.

"Any member of my household present is fit to carry my words, my lord." Venom leaks into my words. "I have a proposal for you, join me. Join us."

With that, I've caught the attention of the room, each member snapped to attention. Amusement, and confusion, draw across their faces.

"In what?" The boy to the left of the Lord Shuji is a slab of a man, wrought from something different than the one across from him. And the lord between them now looks more offended than when we started. There's a quiet reprimand that I don't hear.

The lord brushes his floral, silk robe down and continues, "Join you?" He chuckles, it's theatrical, meant to offend. "And why would there be any need for the joining of our families?"

"War." My word falls flatly, not sparking the reaction I'd hoped. "The Lord Council is systematically ridding itself of those that it cannot quietly, effectively contain. The Samaki lordships. Murakami, Fenika, then Dattori. We're under threat of annihilation."

"Murakami? Pah," the lord replies. "Conspiracy, pure conspiracy. We know not of the Murakami's fate. However, you'd know all about Fenika, wouldn't you, Hawk? Word travels faster than horse, than the bird. That word tells of a family who played with a fire they couldn't contain."

"My lord, please," the smaller boy interjects before I say something I'd regret. "Hear her out."

"Quiet!"

"As a member of the Kasuki—"

Among other things, the Lord Shuji is well practised in the art of interruption as he says, "Around this table, you are Shuji. Vassal, or not, you'll be quiet." Ah, the Kasuki-to. A summit this is, indeed. Three Samaki representatives, and I have two-thirds of them. Careful now, Masako, hold the smile.

"Yes, my lord."

"I'll take my leave." Oji stands abruptly, taking me off guard. "The Sikara do not wish to know this. This would put the Sikara in a…problematic, position."

By the time the door closes again, the lord is the same colour as a tomato. Kekkei hasn't moved since the lord's insult and Bunta was never more than a number here. I'm alone, I've always been alone, but this is different. This is not my world, not the way I learnt to fight. It's as though the waters of the Kirisam surround me again. This time there's no branch to hold.

Lady Shuji's whispers are renewed, but she doesn't speak for her lord. There's no speaking for him in these matters. He's a skerry against the sea. A hard, old coot, if I'd ever met one. He begins again, "Did you look upon the many paddies of Shuji-to as you arrived, the farmlands? I suppose you can't miss them. Do you know the price of rice right now? Or how this season's crop has been plentiful even against my best advisor's estimate? Perhaps the silks we produce, the price of sugar or spices?"

"I'm not here to trade, my – lord."

"No, then. It is as I thought, the answer is no." The smile that upturns his frown is not shared with his eyes. "Then, why is it you are here? Why, when the Dattori farmlands are in disuse, the crop wasting, have you not come here under terms of trade? Or better yet, stayed to see to your land. I – CANNOT – fathom why you waste my time coveting WAR, of all things. You couldn't fund it; your land will rot before you can achieve it. Respect, learn respect." He stands. "Lady Dattori, you dishonour me with this tripe. What of your peers in Basho? You're a lord now. The head of your house. Act like it. Lord Dattori–"

"Do – not – dare insult me." I'm never good at stopping once I'm pushed. "Lord Dattori heard what was said, saw what went on when others didn't. Peers? What happened to you? The Samaki are peerless. We're the Old Steel of the Third, the lineage of Sama who brought the savages to heel. Our blood is forged in the shadow of the Demon Mountains, we don't look to the north. We never have. Do you forget that, *my lord?*"

"Stay," Lord Shuji sighs. "Let Shuji-to host you tonight. But be gone in the morning. Gone from our sight forever. The Dattori have done enough."

* * *

It will be fine, we expected this. This isn't a setback. The Samaki, of all Bashoan clans, are built upon ferocious pride. You wield the same as a bloody knife. We will show him, prove to him, we're a cause worth following. If not today, tomorrow. It

136

takes time, Masako, and we have that. Kekkei's words stir the anger in me as I swing at the training bamboo again, and again. It's soothing, but CrowKiller makes short work of it; it's not enough to bleed the fury out of me. I grit my teeth and step back from the mess I've made. But the Shuji-to are so brazen about their wealth, so I'll cut their straw men, their bamboo to bits. I run through my sword forms until I can't bear another, but it doesn't fill the void of the impact of steel on flesh. Though, I realise my body doesn't sing in pain, it adjusts to the sword, soaks in the training. Jinto's curse counteracts the mess my body is, still. I am fit to fight again, but only with the sword. These courtly matters, I can't take. Why does the merc always have to look upon things in such an irritating manner? Why does he remind me of *him*? This is not okay; it won't be alright. I came here to raise my brethren, my brothers, and sisters of the outer lands, against a common enemy and what? He might have just spat on me and saved me the effort. Pitiful, pitiful Thousand Hands, his tail was trapped between his legs before it started; where was all the charisma? Is he only of use when his Hands flock about him?

I scream and throw CrowKiller into the tatami mats around me. It slides through as if it were paper, stopping angrily halfway home. I go to the floor. Punching the ground for good measure, I collapse.

They're too similar, it drives me insane, makes this worse. Is this just the way the histories repeat themselves? Am I too bound by the gods' thread that I cannot escape this? *It will be fine; we can settle this without destruction.* Their words are almost a mirror. Zaki was wrong. Kekkei is wrong. Why must I go through this hurt again?

"E-excuse me." I jump so much that my ghost leaves my body, only to slam back into me again. "My Lady, the tables are set, my Lord Shuji has sent a summons, the entire family gathers. Attend to the main hall in one hour, a banquet in your honour awaits."

What honour? Shuji Ayato jests. "As the lord wishes." I get up, pulling my sword from the floor and sheathing it again. Before I leave, I turn and bow out of respect to the room that nurtures my trade.

Chapter 15

BEFORE MY FALL: ACT 3

There was something about that time of year that pacified my bloodlust. The spring shoots, the cherry blossom that drifted down from the high trees upon the hillocks surrounding my estate; a pink cloud seemingly fluttered down from the heavens, washing our home in a white-pink hue. If I'd have held onto that moment, really thought about what I was doing, maybe everything would have been different, but I'm never one to focus on the peace something brings, the calm in a moment. Because those moments make you weak. Calm is to my purpose as water is to fire.

My horse sighed underneath me, Lonestep wasn't enjoying the pink swarm above as I, no patience. I spurred him on, he was more than happy to carry me quickly through the black gates of Dattori Heiwa, my home. Everything that Master had built. All of it now standing on the edge of the knife the godlord had pointed towards it. I returned from Orika with all the haste of the great lightning bolts that struck the heavens, dancing with the dragons. But I hesitated. It was my mouth that had to deliver the words it'd wrought upon Master.

Where is Zaki? My first thought, I didn't want to be swept into the meeting that would surely come. As I unsaddled Lonestep, leaving him with the stable boy that might have been the same one who saw me off. I don't know, the common folk were unremarkable. To say the least. I have to give praise where it is due, they are more resilient than my caste. We burn brightly, at both ends, and fade in that same, tremendous flame. It is with regret that weak blood survives while the strong does not.

I turned, and an old, weathered stump of a man awaited me. Nothing got past High Captain Fenika. A name that would always ring screams, and horror, in my ears; strong men, deserters, and old warriors, such are the spoils of war. Lower household members, those not the immediate, direct family, can be spared in the terms of Basho warfare, if they submit to their opponents' rule. If they *agree* to serve, swear new oaths. Bound to someone else's honour like that, sworn off your own, I'd rather die. But Fenika Dabura was a smart, stubborn root. Intelligence is one of those things at odds with honour; it is intelligent to survive, but honourable to die. The Way of the Old Oak in his blood; *there will be a time for everything.* The Fenika words rung true with him. He chose the former, and our Lord was not an unkind man. Anyone welcomed into Master's caste was a free man. As long as they swore it under those Four of Creation.

If he bared any animosity toward me, he hid it beneath the black beard that poured, flowed from his face, a black river. Zaki and he were twin souls, plucked from the same fruit; born in plate to die in plate.

My travelling robes billowed behind me as I met him with speed and carried on past him as he hurried next to me.

"Lady Dattori." He said in his deep, cavernous manner. "Pleased, am I that you returned. Shocked, am I, too. The godlord is not a generous man." The pause in between his speech was long, contemplative. As if between every sentence, he relived the fall of his family, and what they did to incite such a wrath. The man surely was born out of favour with Metsuku. Or some other god I hadn't met at that time. "The charges?"

"Not now, Dabura. You'll know when Master does. Don't be fooled by my arrival, there's no relief to be had in it."

"Ah," he said, and fell back into contemplation.

In the courtyard, Dabura matched my stride, hurriedly filling me in on the elation some of the household expressed of my lone flight to the capital. The dissent the lord was met with over my return. Bile rose to the back of my throat, and I swilled it around in my mouth, spat it onto the floor as I looked up from my rumination. Dabura still droned on but my attention strayed from him with the ruinous congregation that blocked our path. Like grey clouds rolling in on a summer's day, Edan and his lackey Hima, flanked by the rest of their sort. Was it in the interest of those in a position of advice to shorten their lifespan? I still don't know, but my master's advisors were bugs that I'd not miss.

Without thought, my hand found a hilt. Only out of well-honed restraint did I not draw on them; no matter what danger lies ahead, I'd have rather seen to it as a butcher of men than get my hackles up over the words of those cuckolds. Only out of respect for my lord, did I drop my hand. "To what do I owe the pleasure?"

"Ah." Edan smirked. "Pleasant journey?"

"Out of the way." Dabura didn't ask. We might not have seen eye to eye on, well, most things, but the High Captain held these snakes in the same regard as I.

"Now, look here!"

"Hima." Edan turned to his lackey. "I don't need your intervention. Remember what I said." He looked me in the eye. "Short sentences, calm and patience. All a prerequisite to conversing with...warriors."

"Dabura, what did Lord Dattori said about snakes?" I said. "Ah. Unlike worms, snakes don't survive if you cut them in two." I went for my hilt again, and Hima flinched. The brute at my side blew out air in his approximation of a chuckle, and stood between the advisors and I.

"Move."

"Save us all some time, Masako. Allow us to report the charges to our tired lord and go crawl into a hole somewhere. You've done enough without having to deliver your version of events." He held out his hand and curled his fingers towards him twice in quick succession as if asking a child. "The scroll, please. I'm sure they issued one. That is all we need of you. If there is some pacification to be done in Basho, it does not involve the angry and unintelligent."

My face twitched. I closed my eyes, breathed deeply. And it went wrong.

My blade hissed as I tried to draw it from the scabbard. But, before it got halfway, the boulder of a man in front of me span on his heel, thrust his hand out, and blocked the draw. Whispering, "No," he forced the blade back home. "Masako, no," he repeated.

"What is this? What are you doing?"

"Edan, go," Dabura ordered, "otherwise you'll spend the night with me, in a cell."

"The scroll!"

"What is this?" Lord Dattori's voice was a quake that broke the dispute before it worsened. He charged over from the steps at the foot of the largest lotus. Even in old age he was a cat that hadn't forgot how to kill, he swept over to us with the fluidity of a killer; his beard was a wise man's length, his green robes decorated with the story of a man who conquered the 'Wuld.

"Talking, my lord." Edan and his group bowed together.

"Talking? I wasn't born in an age of peace; I know what a battlefield looks like. Scatter, all of you." The advisors dispersed, hurrying to wherever snakes hurry. I didn't meet my master's eyes as I started off. "Masako, not you."

I freeze. Around the strategy table, I could meet Master. But there, as a member of his family, a daughter of his household, I couldn't look him in the eye. Not with what I'd brought. I blinked hard; a tear tracked down my face, but I wiped it away. "Yes, my lord."

"What is this? Am I a demon down from the mountains now, a stranger in the road?"

"I don't know. What is it—"

"Away for weeks, it would seem, and I find you rutting in the yard rather than coming to see me? Masako." The slow, soft way in which he said my name hurt. "Daughter. Whatever it is, family is first. We are Dattori. If there is a way to sort this, I will seek it. We take the straight path. Whatever that is." He nodded, already knowing what that means. Already knowing what we were up against. Our family was in turmoil. The foundation had cracked, we were rife with the splinters of differing opinions. Factions were too plentiful for such the size of our household. Even advisors saved their true opinion for their peers. Not their charges.

There were those who wanted to feed the dogs, and those who wanted them dead.

There were also those who wanted to flee. Dogs don't bite demons, they whispered.

"Lord," I bowed deep. "Allow me some time alone before we meet, I would like to reflect on my journey."

He didn't reply at first, just looked on at me half bent over. "Of course."

As soon as I was out of Master's sight, I ran. Tucking myself around a corner, I propped myself against a wall and cried. There was a line. A point where I could see that the Lord Council would intervene, but I didn't stop. They would make an example out us. As they have before. The Samaki clans have a saying for it: *the hand that can't reach the bird will find a ladder. The ladder that isn't high enough to catch the bird incites the wrath of the spear. The spear that stretches out long to reach the bird will kill it.* I chuckled. It is blunt but that is our Way, blunt words and sharp swords.

I summoned the maids, before I went to our Tranquillity Pools. I'd not washed myself enough in the past weeks and wanted back some of the luxury that our house brings. While I could. They bathed me, poured the soothing waters, and washed away some of the ache. I went into our Rooms of Burning Scent. Sappy wood was thrown into the open fire, fanned so that the smoke filled the room. Trees entrap spirits, absorb them. Burning the wood again, bathing in the smoke, our bodies take it in. Revitalise ourselves on wood sprites and bark souls. Naked, my body drank in sweet, hot apple as I was slowly smoked in its scent. My mind clear. I didn't think, I just was.

I dressed myself. Paced around my quarters. Threw over my table and shrank into a corner. Zaki. Surely, you'd heard of my return now? I was off again, across the yard, through the storerooms, and out in the family rooms. Hatamo and Ganfi were there, they made their way over to me with the grace of mules. I shrugged them off, had no time for them. Their greetings were sincere, glad but I met them coldly. There was a time when the wine would've been on my breath. I reprimanded them, scolded them. They hadn't seen Zaki. And I made it their fault, which I now add to my regrets.

Their night off spoiled, they joined the east watch for the rest of the week.

Frantic, I wandered the halls but still nothing. So, I returned. Made my way to the Sanctuary of Strategy and confronted the despair that awaited me.

First to arrive, I found my place around the table; not set with tea, nor scrolls or maps, there was but one point to this assembly.

I stood, varying my bow for those that entered. The advisors, the ones who would feed the dogs; a small group of my Wuld Guard. I was there representing myself, if only I knew if they stood at my back. The High Captain arrived, then the one who hurt the most. Zaki, and two of his closest shadows, my friends, Yoji and Tane. None spared a look my way, nor recognised the respect I paid as they arrived. I tried to meet Zaki's eyes, but I couldn't. They were too far gone.

Whispers encircled the room, each with edges that cut me as I listened in. A consensus, of sorts, rode the hushed tones. There was but one way that we could avoid bloodshed. Me. If the Lord Council could have me, the sentence may be passed down lightly on the rest of our clan. I would do it, for Master. But that was not my own choice to make. Even so, my chest tightened as every side ran over their plans to bring Master to that conclusion on his own.

Acute, were my senses. Acute, was my suffering.

The door slid open a final time, the few Heavenists we kept entered, faces masked and carved in a sense to represent each old god; it was one of the traditions we share with Orika, one rule we followed. All charges are met by them, an eye for Izenta, an ear for Meganako, a nose for Sukami and a mouth for Metsuku, for the Lord of hells should speak of who goes there. The stone-grey of their robes bled a cold menace that I tried to hide myself from.

Lord Dattori entered behind them, wearing a silk blacker than Metsuku's last hell. As was the nature of the material, and of its lack of colour, it both shone as the candlelight washed over it yet sucked in the notice of every household member present. Unable to steer away from the Patriarch that built these walls from the dirt up. Whose blood was as much a part of these foundations as the wood, and the earth that supports it.

He knelt without haste, there were no servants to attend him, neither was he flanked by anyone. The rest of us lined the sides of the table, looking up to Dattori Hojimoto, who demonstrated that this was his decision to make on his own.

"Dattori Masako," he said. "First Commander and retainer of the household Dattori, you return from Orika with the charges set by the Gods' Senses, by the highest court in this land. Begin. Tell us the price of seizing our own land back from errant clans."

"Slaughter, my lord," Edan interrupted. "What she did was slaughter. Seizing implies there were hands alive to take it from."

"Swine!" A voice from the Wuld Guard. Gladdened, was I, by the bite in that word. I wasn't the only warrior there. Not the only one who practiced a strict code of honour. I was a fool to second guess them. A hollow death is nothing.

Shouts erupted from both sides.

"DAMN YOU ALL!" Master thumped his hands on the table, the ripples of anger felt even where I sat at the end. "Another word out of turn and I will personally cut the tongue that dares to. Masako."

My stomach bubbled and cramped. I suppressed the urge to let go of the fish it breaks down. My journey back from Orika was one of scraps, I've grown unfamiliar with richer, saltier food, that's all it was. Those men didn't worry me. Why would you fret over a room of men when you knew that not a single one of them could hold a sword to you?

My lip curled as I noticed Zaki's gaze. Hopeful, expectant. I guessed which way he wanted the charges to go, and what peace he hoped for. Well, true intent is difficult to hide in the glass of blue eyes, Zaki. I bit down before I spoke, hoping to trap the lava before it spilled from my mouth, directed at the man I tried to save from myself. Tried to give a chance at me, the only one I ever opened up to. But pride ran his heart, and he listened to that. If only he were simple, like the common folk, ruled by their cocks. It would have saved us all.

"Murder." I let the word hang, for an unjust, unsanctioned killing is the worst kind; the word was a bitter taste in my mouth. "They charge me with murder."

The room was a den of crows again. Squawking words: preposterous, truth, unjust, whore, demon, lawful. I was sick of it. Master slammed on the tables again, issued a threat again, asking me to continue.

"What cause do they have?" Tane said to cutting looks from those closest to him. An unexpected ally.

"That is not all, my lord," I said. "They wash us in the red brush of the fieldclans. For, the Lord Council uncovered the same truth as the Dattori inspectors. That the fieldclans learned of the way to synthesise Devil's Spittle from the black poppies; not only that, but they trade in it. The plague on Basho linked to the very fields their blood was spilled in."

"What, then, is it to us?" Zaki spoke, finally. "What charge of murder is to be had? No killing of criminals is unsanctioned, not in these lands."

Warmth, cold. Both, in flashes, washed over my body.

"Not true."

"High Master, what is it that you know that the scholarly do not?"

"Wipe that smirk off your face, Edan," Tane said. "Dabura is right, a large killing, a slaughter, even of criminals, must be ordered by Orika's lawmakers. It is unjust otherwise." His gaze brushed over me, and he mouthed an apology. Ally or not, the Dattori only took steps forward on truths.

"Murder is the least pertinent point." So many candles flicked around the edges of the room that they cast fiery shapes onto the canvas, giving the impression of an inferno, bodies danced within. Fled. Screamed, if I listened hard enough. I snapped back into focus, and began once more, "We seized fields tainted by illicit trade. Seized them with such an overwhelming force that it causes the Lord Council to consider an alternate story. One of disputes over land. Informed, by the Sisters of Aibo, supposedly, that we cut out the middleman. They see it that it was our fields, our poppy, our land from the start, so our crime." Only Master's face retained any warmth. The rest of the room was drained in a mute, bone white.

"Treason." The High Captain never said more words than were necessary, but the words he did say always struck true. The first to thread all of the strands into the black noose that hung around our necks.

"Stupid whore!" Edan spat. "You bring treason to this family?" He turned to Master. "Lord Dattori, there's but only one option. We'll execute her here. Rid ourselves of this charge. It is her's alone!"

"No."

"Lord, if I may, pay the taxes. Pay them the double they wish. Triple it," Zaki said. "We must do all we can to appease them. If then it is not enough, the crime must be paid with the criminal's blood." He looked down, not at me, but I knew of what he spoke.

"Out of the question," Lord Dattori answered. "The time for taxes is gone. Living in the shadow of the Lord Council has taught me but one lesson: fat cats never eat their fill. The Murakami," he looked to Zaki. "The Fenika." And to Dabura. "Each one of those should have been a lesson to the Samaki. The flame that started the fire. No, I will not sit by while we share their fate. The gold kobans will not pay the taxes that shackle us, it will buy the key that releases us from the Lord Council's rule. We will go to the remaining Samaki."

Agreement from the Wuld Guard, silence from the advisors, presence from the gods, but from Zaki, something more. "My lord, please. No, do what is right, lawful."

"The Murakam–"

"MY LORD!" The air was sucked out of the room as the silence gasped. Zaki didn't falter, adding insult to disobedience. "It was demons. Demon-men from the mountains, not the godlord that ruined my family. Our clan's stubbornness to leave the foot of those mountains destroyed them!"

"Stop, now."

"My lord, it is those same Demon- me...we butchered the oni at their request. To their order."

"Orders you brought us!"

"Orders that were meant to free us. Don't you understand, my lord. I put aside my desire for revenge, my hatred, so that we could pay our due. Live in peace and virtue under the Eyes of the Gods, and the law of the Lord Council. I gave that up. All of it, and now, you – insult – me by letting that go to waste?" His gaze lashed me like a whip. "For an errant child?"

"Listen to his words, Lord Dattori," Edan said. His tone was milky, fluid, planned. "We all sacrificed to get this far. We must do again."

For those few seconds, no one dare even breathe. I could hear the candle-flames sway, the chorus of heavy hearts that surrounded me.

"Out, Murakami Zaki."

Trembled, panicked words spewed all at once. "My lord. My...why. What are you doing here? M-my."

"OUT. This is a Dattori matter, off with you. OFF WITH YOU. OUT! OUT!" Master had never scared me like he did that night. Fury itself would have fled. Zaki blew out of the room a storm. As the door slid shut, the lord spoke the last, damning words. Death hung over the Room of Strategy, attached to the fingers of Metsuku himself. But the lord had something more to say, a wave for us to ride until the end. "The godlord has played his game for too long. I will not sit by while he tarnishes the name of the gods, spewing filth and lies in their name, courting foreign ideas. Foreign heretics. No, I will not have any member of my household pay his price. He will pay ours. DATTORI, what charges do the Samaki levy against criminals?"

"NONE−" We all said.

"−the sharpened blade wastes no time with words. Samaki have but one rule. Live in honour, righteously, or die. No time to waste seeking evidence, passing charges. Dishonour is death. The Lord Council wear dishonour as their robe. Well, we will tear it from them! Masako, what is it you wish to bring to the criminals?"

"War," I said, a wide grin spreading across my face. The advisors desperately searched the room for peace to cling to but found nothing but madness. I hadn't even noticed the Heavenists leave, the gods were no longer present. They turned away.

"WE MAKE WAR!" Master was madness. And I couldn't help thinking that I sowed it. The ravening smiles, the fish-like eyes. I knew something was off, but I couldn't see the puppeteer or his strings.

Chapter 16

Wearing an insult to Shuji code so openly is not something I can afford. Not when I still hope for much in the way of a relationship with the stone-faced lord; I'd leave that to the Sikara, and his foolish decision to walk around armed for war. Maybe only they had the foresight necessary for such blatant disrespect. I left CrowKiller alone in my room, HighWolf is still missing, and I dare not travel with the farmer's wakizashi, it still haunts what little sleep I manage. But I won't be caught unarmed again, so I insult them anyway. I walk into their Hall of Banquets with the point of Jinto's dagger digging into my ankle. I call it CutFree. For, without it, my estate would still be in chains. They won't know it's there unless I need it, no son of theirs will get that close.

I sit down across from the Sikara, with the slight, defiant boy from the summit at one side and a comely girl in richly embroidered silk at the other. The turtle man has traded insult for fine robes of a green probably only found in the swamp; but his face still masked, I wonder at its practicality at a banquet.

Kekkei and Bunta sit further down the table trading pleasantries with some of my caste. Wine has lowered their guard.

Lord Shuji heads the table in a kimono above his station, gold inlaid trees upon silver and blue, depicting his farmlands, perhaps. Wearing gold so openly could earn enemies quicker than even I do, only the ruling family are permitted gold. A rule as old as Basho. So what statement is Ayato wishing to make in front of so many outside eyes? The man is lit up in hypocrisy. But hypocrisy that oozes class and elegance.

Grander still is the Hall of Banquets itself; four long walls rise to meet a vaulted, wooden ceiling of such intricate design that I have never laid eyes on. In each beam, a story of our people is carved. The Purge of Demons, as they are chased from the waters of the Kirisam, up into the mountains; dragons descend from the Heavens, as man greets them for the first time; the storming of Fenika, I know, as the charge is headed by birds, but one beam is out of place. It is blank, an empty canvas left for the artist, perhaps. But what story does Shuji-to wish to tell on it, I wonder?

A dragon is carved into the wooden breaks between the sliding doors, spewing incense from their mouths. Jasmine, lavender, cypress. A sweet, resinous smell stays, overwhelming me as it lingers in my nose; the lord is a simpleton, a Barbarian of Scents, Master would be appalled at the clumsiness. Our family were deft hands in the Art of Scent that is so brazenly ignored here. The Shuji, too, display some of the bright oranges and yellow of our ancestor's hoard.

Again, I am distracted as servants pour in, laying plates of grilled fish, a sweet, white, and sticky rice spiced with something that seems so foreign to me I can't quite place it. The fish so fresh I wouldn't believe how it travelled so far inland and remained so; maybe the Sikara didn't come empty-handed, for their fish-craft is known in Basho. Miso soup, fresh vegetables, tofu, and boiled eel. Their kitchen combines both common and lordly food as if it is a small matter, as if both are inexpensive. The way this household flaunts its wealth numbs the flavours in my mouth into a bland mash, the only aroma in my nose is the copper of the blood that trickles from my thigh as CutFree rubs against with every uncomfortable shift.

The walls close in. I might as well sit here alone as I focus on nothing. My heart picks up speed and I wipe the sweat from my forehead. Pulling at my robes is not enough, I stand. Bowing, I excuse myself. Kekkei's eyes follow me along the table, I feel naked against the way he looks at me. He's not the only one who does. I slide open the door to the courtyard. It gets stuck in my haste, and a couple of servants come to assist me. Turning and walking down the steps, I leave them as they worry the panel free from its runner.

Out here, I can breathe, so I sit on the steps. I drink deeply in, the cold air is numbing, revitalising. It flushes my body. Never before have I been so overwhelmed, Lord Shuji is more cunning than I'd imagine. How could one fathom negotiation under those conditions? Kekkei's pacifying words mute. We have no choice but to return to Dattori Heiwa with empty hands. A lot of them.

This is not the place for me.

Someone clears their throat behind me, I didn't hear them coming over the raucous din the servants still make over the door. I have no shield here. Vulnerable.

I turn, but the Sikara is already taking his place beside me.

"My household's presence here is not malevolent," Oji says. "Those careful, gracious enough to befriend the kappa find help in irrigating farmlands. Fresh and plentiful fish." His eyes are an upturned smile. "Lord Shuji has many, many fields to irrigate, and the Sikara lack the former. A relationship born out of trade necessity, nurtured by choice."

Fine. What does he hope to prove, that's there no cause for alarum? As far as the northerners are concerned, I'm dead and buried. What does my opinion matter? I bite my lip, and say, "Do you have a point to this?"

Oji's eyes stay the same, and he says, "Mere courtesy. I know which lands I'm in. It was not my wish to be caught in these matters." He shakes his head, as one would after coming in from the rain. "I'm not here on family business."

"It doesn't matter to me whether you talk. It won't change anything."

"I don't look to change the way rivers flow."

I let a laugh escape my lips and he jerks away. What an awkward man, to sneak up on someone, to talk in riddles, but to be caught off guard by the reaction swine muck is usually met with. Odd, to say the least. Dangerous, I'm unsure.

Shifting again, a sigh of breath, his body seems to deflate as he relaxes into this. Oji lets out his approximation of a chuckle. "There was a reason I sought you out. Dattori was...is a Guardian Clan, like ours." I look to him, his eyes now flinty, cavernous. "Our kappa, they have changed. More violence. More kidnappings. They've a taste for human flesh, more so than ever.

Vigilance is key for us now. Your oni?"

The river's current does not yield its path. Secrecy is longevity. I chew on the words of the Sikara, but they don't go down well. I flex my foot, pleased by the sting of the dagger's tip. Two seconds, maybe three. I could gut him if it went awry. This is a man who lives in the Swamp Fort, not even the godlord is privy to its exact location. So too is the secret to traversing the godsborne infested waters kept. Outside of official Lord Council duty, their movements are unknown. Numbers unknown. By definition, the godlord would want them gone. Their lands lie north, in the shadow of the capital lands, a shoulder that can't be looked over. But there they remain untouched.

Yet, to the Dattori, a weakness is revealed. Does he realise what my knowing his dependence of Samaki trade gives me? Perhaps that is his point, perhaps he doesn't think the Dattori have long enough left in them for that to matter. But it is true our families are kindred in one thing: their homelands, too, lie on one of the Heaven Tears. That, they can't hide. Where the gods so lazily ascended again, godki leaks into the swamp, birthing droves of godsborne. So, I steady myself, aware of the shadows that unravel themselves to me. "They are not Dattori. We keep them in check, that is all. There's no kindred relationship there, I don't covet their good will. We are different in that, Sikara. Is that all? This conversation bothers me. I just." Something about him irks me, weighs on my good will. He wants to be friends but can't show me his face. I stand. Looking down at him, I say, "Apologies."

"Before you go." He does the same and towers over me like a beast. Maybe the rumours are right, the turtle demons do pick human mates. "We, the Sikara, weren't there when you died. Barbaric theatrics do not sit well in the Swamp."

"I know. It is why you still live."

Huffing out a laugh again, he continues, "The Sisters of Aibo had no hand in your downfall...foreign lies did. Your cause is just." He pauses. "For that, I won't speak of this, nor your...existence."

"W-what. How do you know this?"

Instead of answering, he ascends the steps, and I go to grab him, but he knocks away my advance. "Please, don't. I've said more than I set out to. One lesson, Masako, If I may. I learnt something from my years living alongside the kappa. Even when the water is clear, still and the bottom lies in plain sight, the kappa still lies in wait. For it is a master of the waters and wears its reflection like a cloak. I learnt not to trust the clarity in front of me. If it is ever too fortunate a picture, look beyond it. Maybe then, you will survive this change in waters."

He left me standing there. Confused, at his words. A smirk rips into my face. Then what do I trust, Sikara? If something appears in good faith, do I cry blasphemy in its face. What then are your words worth?

Shaking my head, I climb the steps. And sigh. Ahead of me, another patron of my time shifts and fidgets like a brigand with a conscience. "Kasuki, right?"

The smaller boy from the summit freezes, bows deep, and looks up, more startled than before, his face gleaming with the pale of the moonlight above. "Kasuki Tsujo, my honourable lady. Your quest is not ill-conceived. I believe in it, believe the words Lord Shuji did not. My father too would share my sentiments. I sent word ahead, please allow me to escort you to Kasuki-to."

* * *

Just two days' ride saw us in the care of the Kasuki. On the porch of their guest rooms, facing across a grey expanse, I shiver as cold wafts out from rain that pours so hard it hisses against the tile. The demon mountains are a menace visible despite the cloud in the distance. Rising like the thorny under-bite of a devil.

Another shiver, this time not from the cold. In the land that spreads before me, but not as far as the foot of those damned peaks, the razed estate of the Fenika lies in slumber. And to the east of that, the derelict, abandoned Murakami, who went before them.

I can't help but feel history is a short circle, that only repeats itself over and over; the last time I looked upon this land I rode under death's wing. The only thing then that troubled my heart was destruction. A family dared to pursue the demon's favour. Well, then, what else did that amount to other than treason, and what else is treason punished with other than death? To the Fenika, hauled up in their mountain-footed fort refusing summons to the Courts of Orika, readied their warriors. Mounted on horse with arrow, armed on foot with sword and spear. That is how they fell, trapped under their mounts. In the dirt among fallen spears, arrows, swords, they probably still mark their fallen, military graves. Honourable but wrong. The Murakami were closer to the mountain and disappeared, so why did Fenika make the same mistake? An audience with the demonic only incites the wrath of gods. And I've thought upon it much, that the precursor to their fall from grace was both times an invitation from the mountains, so it is said. And that it was those same mountains that I stood and faced in the Sea of Jagged Sand as my strange customer descended to meet his blasphemous oni meat prize. And it was in those following weeks that I was summoned to Orika.

A hand grabs my shoulder from behind, and I'd be dead if it meant me ill, for all I could do is gasp. Kekkei's familiar smile appears over my shoulder. Thankful am I to the gods that I am unarmed, other than the dagger; with anything in range to reach, I would have run him through.

Confidence did not carry him here after his treatment in the Shuji Room of Discussion. But he made up for it hundredfold upon our arrival, with the Kasuki already considering our terms. Kasuki Tsujo and his brother, and heir to the estate, Fingar, and their Matriarch Imari, welcomed our quest and the terms of our arrival with joyful consideration, buffeted by Thousand Hand's diplomatic tongue. We await their order, yet I would settle if it came sooner rather than later, we can't waste time on such a small household. I would like to greet Lord Kasuki, but I'm told the years don't treat him well.

"You'll catch your death out here," Kekkei says. "Looking at them won't do you any favours. The mountains are a wicked thing." He glances sideways at me, but soon the mountains pull him back. "Stories are a mercenary's mistress. It would be called blasphemy anywhere else, but around a campfire, on foreign land, it's a story."

"What story is it you want to tell, merc?" I snap. "I fear there's no point to this."

"Have you never wondered why the gods are gone, but the demons remain?"

"The latter is but conjecture based on the unknown. The men in those mountains are unknown, that breeds fear."

"Contrary to that, those on the Mongin islands shared another tale."

"Savages."

Letting my insults wash over him, he continues, "In the last days of Creation, when the Four were tired, overcome, and elated by all they'd done, they noticed the mountains that had not moved. The mountains that remained so, even after Izenta had carved the earth. Meganako, fearless and headstrong was picked to investigate. Upon reaching the highest peak, staring back at her kin, she smiled, gladdened she could see more from where she stood, and unafraid. There was nothing amiss. But then she turned, gazed upon the other side of the mountains, and stared into the abyss itself."

I shifted my weight onto my back foot and leant back in a mock yawn. One thing I never shared with my men was campfire tales, for they went on too long without a real lesson. "Are you done?"

"Do you not wonder what she saw in that abyss?

"*Enlighten me.*"

"The demons and their Bane Swords, who lopped off two of Meganako's arms, so that she was left with two, and so warriors carry the permitted two swords. Basho shares that belief. And they chased her down the mountains, to the other three gods, who scattered, panicked, they tore four holes and hastily left this plane." He raises his eyebrows, then bursts into laughter. "And that's why you're stuck with the onis."

"You were right."

"What?

"It is blasphemy. And I'd cut your tongue if you repeated it in front of anyone else. That talk is heretical, every Bashoan knows the story of the gods, and that isn't it."

Kekkei holds his hands up in front of himself in false surrender and backs away slightly. "Woah, it's the truth of the Mongins."

"And that is why Akate was ordered to subjugate the unlearned savages."

Sick of the rain, I go into our shared room. Kasuki-to isn't big enough to honour us with our own quarters, so there's a bedroll for Kekkei, Oboro, and I. Bunta shares the next room with the rest of the Hands allowed in these walls; the rest of our retinue camps next to the southern walls.

I sit and hold out my cup to Kekkei, who slides the door closed and brings over a kettle. Filled with room temperature sweet citron and ginger tea, it does nothing for the chill in me. He sits in front of me and pours his own, drinks, and grimaces. It is bizarre, the merc fusses over the temperature of tea more than I. Foreign excursions would have seen him a long time away from luxury. His behaviour is still off to me, and his ambition still wears a mask; a common man, who rose to mercenary leader, would not hold himself the way Kekkei does. I'd expect more of a base creature, nor would I have anointed them a vassal of mine. It's that something about him that seems to pull me in. A fool against my own heart, I took a vow to never trust but it stirs within me. Gods, how I miss Jinto. I'd welcome his childish distraction.

Kekkei looks at me, his eyes roughly cut gemstones, there's many facets that don't reflect the light in front of them. Many hidden. He clears his throat, relaxing into his sit, and says, "I only wished to distract you, my lady." He scratches the back of his head. "Never meant to offend. You looked troubled, and it would do you good to relax, we're in harmless hands here."

"Ah blasphemy, the fruit of relaxation," I say. "Do you deign to advise all your liege lords on how they should relax?"

His eyes go wide, searching every which way for something to break the chains of awkwardness, so I do it for him with the laugh that escapes my mouth.

"I think I preferred your company when we were merc and rōnin. As my vassal, you worry too much about your head."

Kekkei sighs. "I'd like to keep it until I'm done."

I haven't spoken to him about what that means, nor his turning his back on me. Or the revolution he sought to incite before I took him under Dattori name. There's a game I still see he's playing, and if I weren't playing a far more dangerous one, his head would not be so safe. *When you're surrounded by snakes*, Master said, *invite the one with venom you've tasted into your bed.* He had a penchant for advice surrounding serpents, the fool didn't see the ones he nurtured, though. "Done? What does that mean to you now?" The claws of fury. "You still play your game!"

"M-my lady." He throws his hands up. "When I agreed to join you, your cause became mine. They were one in the same from conception."

"Then, why do your eyes tell me something different?"

"My lady?"

"Stop with the honorifics, Thousand Hands." I never meant to lead us down this track, but I must know before I'm too deep to call for other aid. "Yours is upheaval and revolution. I would only see that my family flourishes again, far from the danger that culled it. It cannot be fought in the small courts, neither in front of the Senses, only the heads of those in power will suffice."

Expressionless, at first, he crumples his brow. Raises a finger at me and goes to speak but shakes his head like a fox climbing out from a catchless trip downriver. And says, "My Lady Masako, violence is a double-edged blade. I see that there are two ways about this. If you would allow it, there are other ways to satisfy your...our family honour, that does not end with risk of your dying."

The godsborne, my anger, does not allow it. If I thought I wouldn't die of my old wounds where I sit, I might tell him. If he wasn't so infuriating, I might even risk it, but I can't. "NO!"

"Hawk, plea–"

"HOW DARE YOU!" I'm a beast as I flee from the room. Seething, it wasn't Genaro Kekkei, my vassal and diplomat, that speaks to me here. It is Thousand Hands, the mercenary leader. Thousand Hands, who has his own plan for the rōnin, still.

I half break the sliding door on my way out as I tear out of the room. My breaths are animalistic, heavy. I stop dead. My storm almost collides with the quagmire of all things dull that is Oboro, who is standing with his back faced to our wall. A solitary guard of sorts "What are you doing?" I snap.

"Why are you armed?" I notice the short, curved blades at his waist, no longer hidden, I take full measure of them; the sheaths are of a slick black fur, the sea jewels in the hilt roll with waves if you let your eyes linger...I snatch away from them.

"My lady, I don't like this place."

"So?"

"I guard. They won't get the jump on us."

I shake my head and push past before my storm abates.

"My lady!"

"What?"

"Shall I escort you?"

Another base man unable to judge the situation. "No. Dismissed!" Back to the task at hand, I run again. By the time I slow down, an odd sense of guilt is a sludge that grows in my stomach. For he was only doing his duty, by our family. I make a note to remember why I started this journey, to what I owe my life. It's not my loyal vassals that scare me, it's the anger that does. Or lack of. It's losing its bite, I've begun to seek those around me, to note their presence with enjoyment. And their disapproval with pain; when it comes to the sword, it's straightforward. I cut. I win. When it comes to matters of discussion, of difference, I find agony in my articulation and find comfort in my flight, like some common coward.

I provoke the boil and bubble within my blood. Listen to its coarse words, its hunger. Adding wood to the fire, I try to stoke the flame. To remember the anger.

Chapter 17

These halls would tire the dead. Spider-ghouls tuck each leg into a shadow as I pass them, dust ghosts stir with each step, covering the spots where my footprints mark my passage, hoping to trap me in their wraith families. But foolish and simple are their routine, not able to distinguish the difference between a dust hovel and desert plain; in the mountains, and the Sea between them, I'm certain of their danger. Here they remind me that the Kasuki family is small and dying. Their servants not disciplined, nor numbering enough to scrub the dirt from their halls. To a Bashoan, a clean household is a clear mind, a mind able to see the enemies ahead, and count two steps in front of them. It becomes more apparent as the hours draw on that the Kasuki cannot be thinking straight.

There's a gnawing in the back of my mind. It leaves me wandering this labyrinthine estate. A murmur, something akin to a muffled conversation causes me concern, my hackles are up and my only claw is the knife still at my ankle. It's become my friend, my reliable surprise. I feel safe with it. My little wolf's fang.

I turn corner after corner. Every time, it strikes me that the household is empty. The hallways are lined with fading paintings, torn canvas and echoes of the past. A household, even a smaller one, should have twice again its number in servants and staff. Nannies, smithies, and visitors. The Dattori estate was alive while it lacked anyone who carried its name. The Kasuki's is a tragedy worse than ours, their family dies even while their patriarch draws breath. It's a wonder how a man of such sickness bore progeny; his sword, an easy one to lift, is wielded by its now matriarch, Imari. A woman in her prime, fit to lead, as I saw it.

There is wrong here.

These damned ghost-ridden corridors go on forever. I slow. Careful steps will keep me hidden from those who hope to use the din of the rain to hide their secret words, but not from my ears. As I draw closer, the murmur takes form, shapes into something more. There's pauses in it, as something quieter and much more familiar replies. But it's the unfamiliarity that has me. The second voice has a melodic rise to it and the blunt end of a hammer as it falls. My heart's slightly fastened beat ruins my chance of clarity at this distance, and my curiosity is that of a cat's, so I speed up. My warrior-trained footwork allowing me to glide over the wooden panel without noise.

The harder I listen, the more I don't understand. Lacking any authority, the tone of the first is a plead and a whimper in the face of the second's raw power. Up close, I hear bits, the weak Low Bashoan is easy to pick out. Natural. The second is not.

"F-fine, it will be so," the first says. "But, I-I don't under–"

The melodic reply faster, harsher.

"Understood. Y-yes. But father?"

And then the hammer drops, the striking tone is final.

"A-a...Yes. A-apologies."

Father? I thought his father bedridden. No, it can't be the Lord Kasuki. That language...no. I've been a dolt to eavesdrop, Master taught the swift, direct sword. Not the hidden blade. So, I rush around the corner. Stunned. I stumble back against something soft. I blink the daze away, let out the breath that got caught. What hit me didn't fare so well, it crumpled to the floor. He. He rubs his head, brushing his robes off. Kasuki Tsujo makes chaff look imposing.

"Sorry." Before he's fully recovered from our clash, he's on his knees in a bow so low it makes me feel uncomfortable. "My humble apologies, honourable lady."

"Up. Please, it doesn't matter." I pause as I remember the second voice, but there's no one else there. "What language was that?"

"My Lady?"

"Who were you talking to?"

He lets out a long sigh, smiles and says, "Father always did say I entertain idle thoughts too much. Speaking to myself is not a habit I quickly shed."

I treat him as if he's drawn a katana, my face blank, unreadable. As not to let the mistrust leak from my mask. Tsujo flinched as he said it, the uncertainty spread throughout his body. He struggles to find his feet. Shaken, still. "Do listen to your father's words, young master, you lead people to the wrong impression." Wherever the second has gone, I won't find them now. I'm not sure I can make the merc listen to speculation, but we're not the only visitors here. "Escort me back, will you? Your family estate is much...larger than I thought."

I see the relief wash over him. "At once. Of course! These halls are vaster than you know. The estate is not much smaller than that of the Shuji, you know." As we walk away from where he fell, his confidence returns in droves. "But it's all built on one big complex of interconnecting chambers. The Rabbit's Warren, I call it." I laugh with him, leaning into his guise. "We're always protected from the rains, like this. Never outside. Never have to."

"And that's why you've a revenant's complexion."

"Quite right, my Lady." Jokes are not his forte. "But the rains! Clouds roll from the mountains carrying devil's water and bad spirits! It's not worth venturing out. Never."

"I like the rain."

He tuts, and we both stop. Tsujo's face is riddled with apology, "Forgive me, my Lady. I make mistakes out of naivety. I've not your experience."

"Think nothing of it."

"I...be careful in the rains though, my Lady. You, of all, know the folly that playing with demons brings. Answering the demon's call was a poor charge by the godlord's account, we here in the Samaki do not believe that of you." His smile is weak, and resumes his escort, not knowing of his own folly. Not recognising his own slip up. Of all the charges, consorting with demons was not an official line of the Lord Council – even they only act on proof, though they tarred our family as heretics.

I've all the pieces but I don't quite see the picture. Yet.

* * *

Dancing without a blade is a futile, meaningless task. But Tsujo dropped me off at my quarters with news of entertainment at tonight's meal; he assured me that he was headed towards our quarters with such news when I found him. A dance, in their families' traditional upbeat fashion, would soothe our spirits of the evil rains that fall over us. The gods treasure music, which is always in their honour, and preside over dance. I know better than to insult the gods.

Thousand Hands sits in a corner of the room poring over a blade I haven't seen before. Wrapped in cloth, I'd thought it a Bashoan weapon, but he tells me it's plundered from one of Akate's island campaigns. Why the Lord Council sort to restrain and quiet every piece of rock that floats off the Endless Shores is beyond me. A petty task set by cruel men who are aroused by subjugation. Nevertheless, the sword is strange. The blade is as thick as three Bashoan swords, the steel has seen less folds and both sides cut, but not with the grace and finality of a weapon worthy of a name. The edges would slash and crush, not the clean severance I'm used to; neither was the craftsman concerned with beauty, it is blade grey throughout, only the grip is different, the hide of an animal. A filthy way to hold a weapon.

I leave him to his peace, keep the strange voice to myself. My trust falters over the merc, the gods' displeasure will be felt if I can't find trust in my vassal, for it was their name he was sworn under.

Oboro is still the diligent guard.

The others now join him as I commandeer their room. I prepare myself for the eve-meal by reluctantly shedding my warrior robing and fitting into the skin of a lady; with me, I brought the pink silk of a kimono master had made for me. Its spring blossom embroidery, and tailored fit bother me, every breath I take it constricts, tightening its grasp as it gropes my breasts. I hate it, but I must don this mask.

Bunta stumbles through the door to our quarters, and sits with all the grace of ice rain, crashing against the earth. A bitter, alchemical smell whirls around him like flies to a corpse. "To what do I owe the pleasure, Bunta?"

He looks up at me, blinking long and slow. The realisation of what he almost barged in on draws across his face as he takes note of me. His lips tremble, and he breaks into a mash of words. "M...mi. Hawk, I'm. I–"

"Drunk. You forget yourself."

His eyes widen with haste. A smile tugs at my mouth and he belches a laugh. "Milady, mi. I apologise."

"Please, Bunta," I say. "You're the only one who forgets your manners and doesn't mean harm by it. Continue."

Belching, he really starts to test my patience. The world I grew up in is vastly different, I consider, but the world we started in was somewhat the same. I too, am not of noble birth, but that is what it meant to be Dattori. We stand out because we're the mountain rose; a snowy white beauty, flecked with the blood of lost hikers, thorns for each one covers the roots and stem.

"Milady Masako, I...er. Thanks."

"I don't recall being owed any gratitude."

"For givin' me a place in your family." He pauses. Stifling another belch, he starts again, "I'm no noble. Master Genaro only noticed me for my routes." A smirk blossoms on his rotund face, whiskers bristling. "None carted rice so far. B-but...that's nothin' to be milady's kin."

"There's not that much to it. Your thanks are misplaced. Master Dattori was of low birth, not even born into a trading family. A pauper. But he rose from it, blossomed. Became a Lord of the Samaki." Eyes glassy, confused. "There are no set rules, no traditions but the ones you make, here. In the outer lands all you have is your honour and what you prove yourself to be with it. It's why we're feared, shunned. Nepotism fuels inner Basho, your blood dictates your worth, no matter your strength. Those in the north, born from family name and writs fear the south carved in stone and forged in steel."

I've got him, his hands tremble. He clasps them together to stop it but I don't think he fully understands what I mean. That, or he's filthier drunk than I surmised.

"You're carved of rock, Bunta." I rise, letting the silk fall around me as it were water. "Never be sorry that it isn't a name that holds you up. You're Dattori because it was earned."

Bunta bows with his head touching the mat, muttering something. I'm certain he's not steel. However, he's worth our name. Worth feeling of use. That is what Master gave to me and I'll never forgive them for taking it away. What I build here fills the void. What I cultivate here is anger. Anger in their oppression. Anger in their mistreatment. Anger in their destruction. Now the Kasuki are my kindling; in the coming days I know they'll join my cause, I feel it. With that, I will fan the flames across the outer lands, and unite them in a pyre that'll burn the body of the Lord Council.

* * *

I'd never considered such a disorderly sound could be made with stringed instruments, fatter and louder than the shamisen. But as the three musicians play at differing speeds, there's a medley that incites the surrounding madness. A flowing stream, birdsong punctuated by the notes that splash around the throng of dancers, who themselves are stranger; the scions of the Kasuki intertwined with newborn Dattori.

Caught in a storm that sees me in front of my patron, and matriarch of the Kasuki, Lady Imari. I exchange pleasantries with the woman deciding the fate of our alliance, she takes my hand and wishes me well. The deep-rooted wrinkles the powder can't mask, the deep grey rings around eyes that don't befriend her false smile, unsettle me. She must have been a beauty. Her hair is a tight nest of blue gemstones shaped as tears, or drops of rain, I don't know which. The glum family could take either as their crest. Imari's kimono is a fine silk, a near copy of my own. At her side, Kasuki Moka remains lifeless. The gods' great mirror would reflect nothing in her image, the girl is mute, or invalid. The younger children share more with Tsujo in the way of confidence, the little twins too young, though, to grace this dance. Still, the room is filled with cousins and retainers that have some touch of normality in them.

The Kasuki know this type of affair in their blood. In finery passed down, and robes that look like they're crafted from spring flowers, they move with elegant steps, the sword is in their makeup. My name is muddied next to theirs in bland grey and blacks, stained in plum wine and whatever else they pilfered from the Kasuki stores. The family has been too good to us. Though, guilt has me in its grips, for I don't trust them. A farce is all I see in front of me.

The blunt-ended singsong is what I hear over the music.

Out of the throng, I stand, eyes darting about the room. Bunta and Kekkei forget themselves. In the midst of the jostle, they cannot be missed. Arms flailing, wine spilling, theirs is a high-kneed stomp to the beat. The mercenary's trot, I would say. They lock arms, circling each other, then swapping each other for one of the Kasuki ladies who marvel at the brutes. Again, and again. To the rear of the room, near the exit. Oboro and his appointed are sentinels. He gets a chuckle out of me for his persistence, if there was ever a man that knew duty, it is he.

The spiced tofu soup, vegetable mash and unpolished rice sits heavily in my stomach. I'm too well fed – there was much in there that a warrior doesn't need – the sweets were a step too far and I consider retiring. I don't get far with that thought. A large man splits through the crowd and flies towards me, an arrow loosed from a bow. Kasuki Fingar, in every way, is Tsujo's elder. The Heir to the Kasuki line is of a swordsman build, lithe yet largely muscular, his gait is that of a water wheel. Wearing the sky blue and white lined robes of his family, he presents himself to me. I let out a shallow sigh. My smile masks my disapproval, I'd hoped to remain unbothered throughout, but ours is a meeting of powers that I've yet to conquer.

Fingar bows slightly, as he looks up there's a flash of something in his eyes that I can't place, the whole picture still writhes out of focus. "Dattori Masako." He holds out his hand. "A dance, if I may?"

I allow him that, and he pulls me in close. He smells of a sharp, heavy spice and sweat. My feet quickly match his beat. The battle is won if the enemy falls into step with you, so I lead him as we circle each other, eyes locked. "My lady is more beautiful up close."

"Unnecessary flattery. My late lord father always assured me a long life of serving the blade. He said the hawkish and uncomely are fortunate in creating their own path."

Fingar forces an inhuman laugh through his teeth. "The Lord Dattori was a harsh man. Perhaps a touch too protective of his adoptive daughter."

The latter elements of the sentence strike me as rude, not something common in the knowledge of the Samaki. But I smile anyway. "A realist. And I was thankful to him for it."

"It pains me so that our families won't be joined in more than cause, I would have liked a bride that knows our ways here at the foot of the mountains."

"I am lord. Not a daughter anymore." His laugh is a cackle laden with discomfort. I push on, "How is Lord Kasuki fairing?"

"Not well. The gods are cruel, bless them."

"Gods? Does age not come for us all?"

"My lord put his soul into building our family, exerted too much effort. The gods know, the sleeper's illness won't let go. He hasn't risen in weeks, opening his eyes once a moon." Focusing too much on the triviality of this conversation, another pair hit us. Tsujo expresses his apologies, as does his lady cousin, and he adds, "Brother, you're filling the honourable lord's head with conjecture. Our lord father tires of such close family." He smirks. "The gods' illness attacks nightmares, bad memories, things of ill-omen, of which father has none to worry about." Tsujo's insistence on his father's condition leaves the hairs standing on my neck. The boy is nothing short of strange. He offers me a dance away from the bore of his elder, to which he's chided. The Kasuki younger dishonours himself, I'm embarrassed for him as his cousin drags him off.

"Apologies, honourable lady."

There's a silence that draws on too long, the music pushed to the back of my mind. To his credit, he doesn't miss a step as the music changes, pulling me back into his lead as I almost stumble with the abrupt change. It's as though he knew it was coming. It bothers me. The revelry around us quickly finds its feet again and he says, "Stay longer. Our families have much to smooth out." I'm drawn away from his distracting intent as Oboro sifts through the dancing and whispers something that stops Kekkei dead on his feet. A few words exchanged and they make quick for the exit. Bunta close behind. They don't come for me, leaving to me as what might outwardly appear as the coming together of houses, but I don't like this. The lord heir still whispers to me, but I block it out.

"Excuse me, Lord Fingar." I stop and pull away, but he grips my waist. "Excuse – me, my lord. You run the risk of offence if you hold me so." I go to pull away again, but he grabs tighter. Now I know what I saw in his eyes, it clicks into place. They're fishlike, void of any tells. The eyes of a corpse. Yet I don't have time to understand why he is so. I push him back in anger and his steely grip falters. I rush towards the exit, and he screams, "WAIT!" The music has stopped without my realisation and the notes of his voice are clear. Lord Fingar's voice stays with me as I rush from the Hall of Dances, overlaid with a melody not belonging to the Bashoan lordling.

A shout ending like a strike against an anvil.

My heart thrums in its place as I close the door behind me. I decide in this moment that my vassal must know, he and his Hands might be able to finish the puzzle.

I don't turn too many corners before I find the hushed meeting I'm looking for. Oboro gestures to one of his guard. Kekkei fidgets impatiently while the man speaks. As I approach, I hear part of it.

"No, sir, not a thing."

"How? This is what you're there for."

"Sir, I know, but there was nothing. Not a whisper."

"Impossible."

Kekkei rubs his forehead, squeezing his eyes shut. I recognise the way he holds himself, a man at war with the anger he wants to inflict on the messenger. They notice me finally and straighten up.

I hold my palm out. "Save the courtesies. There is a problem?"

"No, ladysh–"

"Not you!" Oboro snaps and sends the guard away with orders to double the watch. "Master Genaro, shall I?" He nods, smouldering where he stands.

"Our camp. It has been beset upon."

My eyes widen before I can stop them, I say, "But. By what?"

"It is not known. We were on the way. Lady, if you please."

I'm already past him, not needing to hear what he has to say. The place of the crime holds the answers. My men shadow closely behind, only Oboro keeping up with me as I thunder from the Kasuki-to's gates and into the camp. Two score of our good men have been braving the elements here. I follow the fresh tang of blood as I navigate the tents. In the midst of the others, centrefold to the camp, the tent looks none different from the rest. I taste the rancid last breaths of a struggle. The tiny specks of copper spread about the place. Yet, there's no sign anyone left, and as I enter, there's no sign of a struggle.

The bedrolls are neatly made, if not a little too perfect.

"Gone." Kekkei's voice is short, sharp behind me. "Deserters."

"No." If only Jinto was here, there'd be more credibility to what I say next. As I cannot share my cursed blood with Kekkei but must convince him of the signs that point at me from beyond the grave. Though, I don't have the chance to.

Oboro kneels down, wipes his fingers on the waxy tent floor, and says, "Blood. They died here."

"No, who would do it in front of the Kasuki Fort? They'd have to." Kekkei stops. As I meet his eyes he knows where this is going. "They couldn't. To what gain? We were invited as a family of high standing in the south."

"They've not the choice. Foreigners have invaded." Oboro jerks his head around. "Let us return to our quarters, I'll explain on the way."

"It is not safe," Oboro says.

"It is safest where my sword is!" I snap." I'll not spend another second here without it."

* * *

"You've kept something from me?!" Kekkei's words are so savage spittle flies as he speaks.

"We need the Kasuki. Until I was certain, it was my business alone."

"Too late. My men are gone, dead."

"Our men. I am your lord!" – he mutters something about them being Akate men first, and a watery, sinking feeling bubbles in my stomach – "Kekkei!"

"Wait." Oboro still crouched, absorbing what was said in silence, broke our argument. "Monkitan."

Kekkei's face washes white, and I blink in disbelief. How could I have missed it, after all that has been wrought by their hands? The final piece I was missing, the name of the strange language that bothered me. Monkitan. The High Tongue of Taos. The language of the Soshists. The vile mages of the bordering nation that can't keep its paws out of Basho affairs. The same mages that brought down my household. "There's a Soshist here, Kekkei." I can't hide the tremble in my voice.

"Gods," Oboro says. Leaving the room at once, I hear him in the next room yapping commands to Bunta and the others.

"If the dragons watch us," I say." I pray it is a single one. Two is the death of our cause." I try to sort through the panic, but my mind is ablaze with the flashes and screams that still haunt me.

Po, is it you? Gods know I'll have your head.

"But they don't!" Kekkei barks. "This is folly. We must leave at once!"

There's a crash out in the hall that startles me. I already struggle to focus over the blood pumping in my ears.

A murmur. The distant noise of a crowd. Closer still. A roar tapers out into a gargle, a shadow nears the canvas wall between ours and the next room before it hits. The impact sends splinters flying. A body bursts through it, toppling backwards. Bunta tries to rise, but a wicked creature is upon him. Its knife flickering in and out of his chest, he gurgles a scream, but it is overwhelmed by the blood that escapes his mouth. Where I'd expect anger, there's only despair, my stomach is a watery mess. The strength to move seeps into the earth in the face of what stares back; why eludes me. Even my blood's call is distant, muffled, subdued by an invisible hand.

The creature is not that at all as it looks up. Eyes bewitched with the same fish-like glare as Fingar. A purplish tinge to them; the only bit of it that is Tsujo is the fleshy mask of his that it wears. There's only madness that inhabits the body now. A familiar madness. The picture is clear.

"Taosii puppetmen!" I shout. "Kasuki-to has fallen!"

CrowKiller is in my hand before I know what I'm doing. I hear a shout that isn't mine, its fury resonating in the marrow of my bones.

Kekkei, double-edged sword whirling, hits Tsujo as a storm unchecked. He is a force of nature as the lordling is cut down. Limbs flying. Not even the beast the boy had become can stand up to the raw power of the mercenary.

Then, the canvas splits in a myriad of places, the whole wall falling as creatures bewitched with the same lavender insanity arrive. Kasuki cousins, common folk. There's a jolt of pain through my chest as our missing clanmen litter their numbers. A horde. They converge on Kekkei. But are kept back with hacks and punches, his sloppy swordsmanship brutally effective. Unmovable, rooted for a moment, he's an oak against harsh winds. Blood splattered, he slashes up and across his body in a wide arc, giving himself breathing space; a sharp thrust glances off his shoulder, he winces as he's on his back foot, stumbling.

I dart between him and the attack that would have stamped out his light, severing the arm of one of the cousins, still dressed for the dance. I grab Thousand Hands and tug him towards the door before the wave of bodies crashes down on us. Shaking off the daze, he passes me first, checking the hallway, but not before another mass of bodies takes him from the side.

In front and behind. I'm cornered. My own madness still an echo, desperate to help. It begs I let it loose. If it were an option, I'd decline. I need a clear mind. My true enemy is near. This same scene would have enveloped Dattori before its end, but that was a drop in the vast sea of troubles that came for us. For the Kasuki already dead, who hosted this heresy in its walls, I will set you free. Another great family lost.

A sharp whiff of something reigns in my focus. The burnt peppery smell of Soshist sorcery is there, thick in these walls that ooze its miasma. The same sorcery that blinded me from itself until now.

They come for me. Mad men and women, a sharp jostle of mindless stabs.

The minutiae of the sword lost to inhuman savagery. I dodge one, parry another, running my slash up the length of the blade and taking the hand. A club hits me. And I'm sent careening. Getting my feet under me, I narrowly divert a thrust as it rakes the side of my neck. Blood springs from it. But I pay it no more attention as I drive forward. My breaths are heavy. I swing round, slashing with all I can muster. But the puppets still don't falter, I need the one who pulls their strings. Like the undead, they don't take check of their injuries, pushing on with exposed bone, and severed stumps. I change my tactics and run along their numbers as the invalid puppets squirm on the floor, a pause in the torrent as gods-damned sorcery knits them back together.

I cut an X into the wall ahead, jumping, arms crossed in front of me as I erupt through wood and paper out into the hall with ragged breaths. To the left, devastation, the murmur of madness regrouping. To my right, Kekkei is pinned against a wall, teeth snapping. The hilt in one hand and the end of his blade gripped in the other, barring the hordelings' way. Blood drips from the desperate clasp. I've a moment to worry over the cut I make. I take all three heads at the neck, and Thousand Hands slumps against the wall, breaths rasping.

"W-we. We…"

"You're okay?" I ask, he nods in the face of trying to talk. I glance over him. A slick red seeps from within his robes, his shoulder stoops and he's covered in new bites. Something he is used to, so I don't worry for him; the merc is made of more than the wounds that cover his body. The ravening murmur floods back into the hall behind us. "The lord and lady have been spared of this! Come." I take off, placing trust in the man at my back.

Between our quarters, and the main family's, there's nothing to suggest a small Soshist led army of our undead patrons lurks within its grounds; the candles still flicker, painted walls of bamboo, storm clouds and rains still intact, vases and trinkets sit in place. Kekkei keeps up, but I see his strength is flagging, the blood runs in too many places at once. I still hear the chatter of madness behind me as we come to the grand doors of the Family Rooms, but they stay back. I try to shake the bad feeling, but I can't help but feel as though we've been herded here.

The lavender haze coalesces in the room ahead. A pulse between my temples and the pepper of the sorcery is so strong it numbs my airways. I can't feel my breaths anymore. If I think about it any longer, I'll second guess myself, let the shadows of the past carry me from this place. For Master. For all those that died, I'll put it right. Even with one of those wretches that move the ki of the gods as if it were their own limbs in my path. Against my true nature, I still cannot summon the anger that usually drives me, only a hollow despair. There's more in this miasma – a damp cloth thrown over my flame.

I check over my shoulder for Thousand Hands. With his nod, we enter. Trepidation on my heels.

Chapter 18

An oily serpent coiled around its naginata, the Taosii sorcerer waits with a grin that touches the edges of her face.

I recognise the bitch. Po's nameless lackey. I want to cut that grin from her face.

She unwraps herself from her weapon, slinks from a grand, raised night platform, upon which an occupied bedroll lies. Lord Kasaki didn't stir as we entered, nor with the evil at his foot. There is wrong here.

I snatch my gaze from it and look over the Soshist with disgust; her bald head gleams as the candlelight licks over it. Her face so childish it's the antithesis of what she's done here, the strangeness she wears; the Soshist is so tattooed the untouched skin that zigzags between the runes and sigils gives the impression of tawny-gilted, obsidian scales. An animal hide strap only just covers breasts; a skirt of feathers sweeps from her midriff onto the panelled floor. She giggles. The sorcerous air pulses with it. My sense of dread thickens. Around her, my thoughts worsen, I'm in the clutch of her ungodly machinations. She must die. But I hold fast. Looking sideways for Kekkei, he grips the double-edge's hilt in both hands, his body trembles in tune with his ragged breaths.

"Dattori whore!" The Soshist's Low Bashoan lacks the lyrical rise to it but has all of the hammer. "Ruin. That's what you are, dog. I play here. This is mine. My break, you oni-minders didn't go down without a fight." She twirls the weapon above her head, amusing herself as if we aren't a threat worth her full attention.

The words cut deep, release me from the daze, and I step forward, bringing

CrowKiller into a high guard. The rich clove oil wafts from the hilt; I take care of her, and she takes care of me. I'm angry beyond all good measure, but it's bottled.

"Why're you here you foul bitch?"

"She never left, Kekkei," I say to him, not taking my eyes off her. "She sowed a similar kind of madness the night Master was captured. She's stayed here." To her, I say, "If I had the time, I'd make you tell me what business you have with Basho, but you won't live that long. As a Lord of the Samaki, I charge you with no crime. I note your slaughter and murder of the most insidious kind." I change my guard, in an instant, it's a steel dragon's tail arcing out from my waist, knees bent slightly. "Death. Death awaits you." I explode towards her, expecting the long reach of her naginata. And she falls into my step.

The Soshist strikes out at me, viper fast – had Jinto not reworked my muscles, I'd be dead as her blade skins the hairs on my head, death close – but I duck. Using my momentum, I pull my blade from the tail, it's a crescent moon as it parries the gargantuan weapon upwards. Thrown wide open, the Soshist doesn't see Kekkei, his eyes show his intent. His strike true.

The purple miasma pulses again. A hiss from above, the spear strikes out at Kekkei's slash of its own accord, it is now a viper in the flesh. Fang and metal clash and clatter. The merc cries out as it strikes his arm. He moves backwards, slicing in the room he's made but it's not enough. Metal on metal clang as it becomes a spear again, before he can sever the snake's head.

I move into the opening, but as her eyes wash over me, my kimono tightens, constricting at my waist and throat. I drop, gasping, but don't let go of my katana. As her glare detaches from me, I can breathe again. She dances backwards, flipping like the lithe performers of Chisai. She lands at the foot of Lord Kasuki's bed and shrieks at us.

My guard is heavy, my breaths are laboured. Each step feels as though it'll be my last. One of the heathens who ensured our family's demise is before me, my blood's screams still muffled. It's never been as quiet as it is now. If I wanted to set it loose, I couldn't.

I catch Kekkei's eye with a nod and hope he knows what I mean.

"Uh-uh. No." She smirks. "Not again, you don't get another go. No, no. COME!" Her command resonates through the room. The murmur is close again, I feel the mad crowd as it closes in. From the shadows of the room, two figures peel themselves free.

"La. La-ady. Lady Hawk," Fingar says as he emerges. Next to him, Moka drags an odachi much too large for her. The Soshist watches with glee as they split off, one for each of us. Fingar stares me down. "What's w-wrong? Don't like young lords?" He says as he rips his robe open. My chest tightens. Where his heart should be there's a hollow. "It's why I couldn't give it to you, my lady." His grin is inhuman, crazed. "Mistress Ti took it." With that, he rushes me. Knocking my sword aside with the savage strength of the undead, I kick out and it barely registers, sending me stumbling backwards onto the floor. As I land, a fleshy cacophony of chatters starts behind me. I turn, and the horde looks back.

Kekkei roars as his slash cuts the girls in two, his mercenary stamina prevailing.

When I think it's truly over, there's a glint beyond Soshist Ti, who presides over the battle with glee, spear-arm twirling the weapon above her. She doesn't notice the hells approach. A rat is deadly in a corner, and the wasp you don't see stings the worst. Oboro is a death sentence as he springs from the darkness. At the last minute, something gives Ti the nod, and she moves her head out of his sword's arc, but it takes the spear-twirling arm at the elbow. The sword licks through skin and bone indiscriminately. Her shriek is deafening, the pulse dies, and the horde drops around me.

A man of duty, indeed.

I'm up on my feet. The spear is a snake again, coiling around her stump, arresting the crimson fountain. As I start towards her, an undead hand trips me. I look up and Oboro cannot finish the job before Lord Kasuki grapples his legs. Emerging from the bedrolls, his body decayed. A corpse left to rot. In that opening, the Soshist disappears into a side door, clutching her severed arm. I slam into the ground.

The first thing I notice, searing heat in my veins. I bite the insides of my cheek and slam my fist down. My knuckles split, but I've a hold of myself. With the miasma gone, it's difficult to hear anything else other than the hunger that curses me. It's a shout, a begging scream that I let it out. My head throbs. I try to look up but Fingar's fitting corpse blocks my view. My hand wrestles for a hold on him, pulling myself onto my knees, then up. A low fever burns without my invocation, and I spend a second wondering how long I can keep this monster bound, or whether I have control over it now.

Kekkei is knelt, hunched over his blade. Oboro has gone, I can only hope he doesn't mean to finish the sorceress by himself, a tiger with one paw is a deadlier beast. Scared, hurt, furious. I need answers, although I would settle with one less of those wretched Taosii in the world; Ti, I have her name now. She didn't take centre stage, the only reason I didn't see this happening sooner. Nevertheless, she was there the night they took Master and I in. She is privy to secrets we need. I take pause. Should I stop here? Should I regroup? With both arms, she shattered our ambassadorial party. Bringing the other Samaki lords to heel is but a ridiculous fallacy if I let her go. I search the floor, find CrowKiller, and sheath her.

I'll not give up.

My orders for Kekkei are simple, gather all we have left, bring evidence. We regroup at Shuji-to, I'm not done with them. I'll drag the Lord Ayato out by his whiskers if I must. He must see this. But I'm not finished with the Soshist.

I prick my finger on an errant blade. Teasing a drop, I lick it, drink the offering. And I let the 'fever take hold. It's only light, the ache in my muscles distant, senses sharper. Step quicker still as I sprint through the passage Oboro, and Ti before him, took flight from.

After a handful of steps, it's just dirt and darkness. I run as best I can in a crouch, if not for my curse it'd be a lightless void. Until, up ahead, the darkness thins. Dirt and dust whip up from a light breeze ahead and I splutter. My legs yield. I go to one knee, wincing as a sharp rock slices across it. I force myself up and push on, the fever not strong enough, it is all I could do to continue. My body screams. And I scream back.

Moonlight is a white blanket over the farmlands that slumber while their lord family's rotted corpses finally go to rest. In the distance ahead, a lone horse gallops away at the edge of what I can see. I muster all that I can, taking long strides towards my quarry, in a vain attempt to catch her. But I fall. I can't. And when I want to give up, the thunder of hooves is closer. I look up confused, hoping I fell close to her by some miracle of the gods. It isn't.

Oboro reins his own horse, and a second, in as he stops by me. His mare whinnies, the second is unsettled. It thumps the earth and pulls hard enough to almost unseat my gaunt saviour. "Come, Hawk!" He wrestles the steed under control, passing me the reins. "Her lead isn't strong; the winds don't lend themselves to it. Come!"

We're a medley of hooves and heartbeats that rage into the night.

Chapter 19

The fleeing horse rider, only a blot on the horizon-line when we started, is now a thumb-sized scourge in the distance. She's reduced her lavender plume of godki into a weak shawl that cradles her.

I waste precious energy on a smirk I can't suppress.

We ride into the rising sun – an open wound pouring molten amber into the failing night. Each laboured step into the day sends a painful jolt between my eyes, the throb in my head returns hundredfold. Limbs heavy, unwieldy, I can only balance in the saddle. The horse beneath me is dying. Her flanks heave and she stumbles, righting herself before she falls and traps us both in death. I gulp, my tongue is swollen. Teeth too big for my mouth, the last of the wine gone.

If I ever question why Kekkei keeps the gaunt ghoul, Oboro, at his side again, may the godkin undo his work and strike me down. The man has a tenacity not even I possess, we put his horse down after the first half day, and I've nothing to get the taste of her out of my mouth. Beside me, he presses on, horseless, even after the second half of the day. A man that can face down a horde of undead with his own shadow plot, only to sneak up on their beast-mother and maim it, is either mad or cut out of the same stone as the gods themselves. Stone and steel. I talk of praise and he only of duty. And yet, he surprised me still when he pulled a wineskin from his robes. Now empty, without it, we would have perished alongside his mare.

Every step forward is an accomplishment. We close the gap, only perhaps because one of the gods favour us today. Because I'm greedy and need this more than she does.

Woodland and rusty plains have passed us, we now enter a land rich in shrubbery, the morning skies are brighter still. Edging closer to Shuji lands, we skirt along fields of barley, cutting through wheat tall enough to brush the withers of my steed.

This is folly. It must be, there's no sanctuary for the Taosii mongrel here. She rides into the clutches of someone more terrible than me. I only wish to kill her; Lord Shuji would surely want more. Bamboo shoots and fingernails. Much would be learnt. But maybe her arrogance leads her astray. "A fool's path," I say.

"Yokusei borders," Oboro mutters. "Closer."

He confirms what I know. The Soshist puts her faith in my failing horse; if she can outrun us for another half day, doubtless she would get away. The Shuji farmlands sweep for days east and west, but are spread thin in the middle, the Yokusei reaches out on the Pig's Rump, a set of hills contested by both families, but owned by the Ghost-bedders. Salvation presents itself, and so she grasps it with both hands, stringing her last breaths out. Stretching herself across her own pyre. Had she turned it would be the end of us. It still could be, but a reliance on the gods breeds arrogance. And arrogance masks anxiety. Which comes to the fore when you've nothing to feed the mask; deities are hungry beings, they drink deep, leaving nothing to spare for when you need them the most. Which is where I'm stronger. If not, I'd lose myself to the cruel curse that lurks within, a bloodline of secrets.

When the sun tightens into a pale-yellow orb, veiled by the low-hanging cloud, she makes her move. I've just missed a crucial moment surrounded by these damned wheat stalks. The haze of godki seemingly evaporated from around her. My stomach flips, and the beetles scurry across my body, I'm unnerved. After a few more yards, I spur the horse, Oboro croaks something. And the horse bucks. A wink of purple catches my eye. An ear of wheat wearing a tinge of godki I'm too late to react to, the spikes swell. Each are a footlong before they explode. I throw myself from the saddle. Lances of pain sear across my arm. The horse next to me spasms, toppling toward me as I roll before I'm crushed. My steed is pin cushioned in wheat spikes. Flesh is torn in streaks from its belly up, blood pools into the pink rivets. I tip my head to the noble beast, thankful to Metsuku that the death was clean; part of the ear found the horses eye, brain is spread around its exit.

A dry sob comes from my throat. No. I can't let this be the end. Wheat rustles behind me as Oboro catches up. I don't wait for him; I don't know when to give in. A red stickiness leaks down my arm. My body is numb but to let it go would be dishonouring Master. I part the stalks and force myself on with a limp.

Minutes stretch as long as a day, and I count two score of them before I hear something. A moan, tapering off into a shriek. A long moan. Hurried breaths and a hiss. There's a shout of three hurried Monkitan words, laced with fear. Those three words cost more life than they are worth. Three quick strikes beat against flesh. I go faster, this is not to be missed. There's an opening, the wheat thins and that's where she lays. Trapped under her horse, Ti is still. She still grips the viper-turned-naginata in her only hand; clutched hard around the creature crushing the life out of it while its fangs still cling to her neck. Her eyes are glassy with the fish qualities she left her puppets with, a cape of crimson at her back as it spills from Oboro's wound. All her secrets die with her. I let out a scream that's sorry I didn't do this to her.

Wait a little while longer, Master.

Oboro crashes into the opening on hands and knees and freezes. A chirrup of laughter escapes his lips, and he collapses.

I draw CrowKiller, she's heavy. If Kekkei cannot find enough evidence to sway the skerry-faced lord, I'll present Shuji-to with a face of the likes it can't explain. A couple of meaty slashes spray blood into the crop. This defiled area will have to be burnt; the gods only know what plagues hide themselves in the Soshist red.

Approaching footsteps, they don't try to hide themselves as they wade through the fields. Not that they could. Farmworkers aren't especially known for their grace, we're deep enough in Shuji territory to have raised an alarum.

The crop parts once more and dirtied, harrowed faces look upon the scene. One of the workers' faces rinses of all colours and he drops to the floor. The other cannot still their trembling, a dark patch spreads down their leg. Cowards. And animals. Though, the scene about me looks like an offering to the demons. I'm grinning madly. "Well," I say, "take me to Lord Shuji." I cut the hide wrap from the Taosii and fasten it around her head. "He would like to see this." I hold it up. My prize.

* * *

The Room of Earthly Bodies in Shuji-to is small, unused. Scrolls hang around the room with symbols of the gods, wards of lake chrysanthemum and cherry blossom are wrapped in twine, hanging from the ceiling. Walls of a clean, ivory colour are deftly painted with pictures of souls, and their gathering at the mountains before Metsuku's hells open; his servants circle above them. The embodiment of death. It is unlike the room my family kept, for we had no wards or paintings of the gods. It was crisp, clean, functional. We fear no gods in such a place. To look into the body is the great gift only curious humans are bestowed, for the gods only dabble in souls. I'd never taken Ayato to be a fearful man. He who fears what cannot be changed is a man uncomfortable in the ways of fate. Dangerous.

Ti's head has been tarred and spiked, for it'll decorate Lord Shuji's gates for as long as the birds stay away. That needed no investigation. But here, in front of me, lays a corpse among the many Kekkei brought with him. Unlike the others, the heart hasn't been removed, but the body is still decayed by the weeks it spent in the earthly air awaiting the pyre. Decay, an insult only heinous criminals deserve. Tsujo was none such a person. Yet, having been butchered by Kekkei's hands only days before, even I can see he was dead long before. I, whose days spent in the study of medicine can be counted by one finger.

The Art of the Body is not an entirely futile undertaking for a warrior; to take apart an adversary in the least steps, knowing where life will flood fastest from is key. The Five Points of Heaven. Which is where the Earthly

Doctor, a village elder from a neighbouring hamlet, starts. He takes out a small surgical knife and plunges it deep in the Stomach Point. I want to look away, but I force myself to watch. There's something off-putting about the delicacy of surgery that I can't stand. It's a trifle too personal. My lip twitches and I notice the same discomfort in the faces of Kekkei and Lady Shuji.

The lord is still.

But, as the doctor unsheathes the knife, there's an eruption of moss green and yellow biles that challenge the composure of the room. Faces twist in disgust. I do nothing to hide my own as the doctor hacks and coughs into a cloth. Fighting for control of himself, the doctor says, "Months, my lord." He retches, trying again. "How long did he serve you?"

Shuji Ayato nods to the lady, who answers, "The spring delivered him. His father took a turn, he sought a stronger, more experienced teacher. And our lord is that."

The doctor stares at the offensive liquid bubbling from the corpse, and then back at the lord, the words visibly turning behind his eyes. "Then, he never served you in life. Terrible, terrible." The doctor is muttering to himself. "Gods' great mercy this is heretical. My lord, what is this? What does this mean?"

"Out."

"But, my lord, what practices are these? Should I fear for my life? Surely the demons have descended the mountains?"

"Your life is safe, your family too, so long as you speak nothing of this."

"M-my honourable lord–"

"We're done. Out now, don't test my patience."

The doctor packs his things, rolling his equipment in cloth, and hurries from the door.

Lord Shuji hasn't taken his eyes from the corpse. I worry this is not enough, that he will find fault in the evidence before him. Then the change in him is lightning, he barks commands to his servant, who appears quickly at the door, "Pay the good doctor handsomely."

"Yes, my lord."

"And bring his eldest to Shuji-to, I would see that the man keeps his word, the child will benefit from it."

The servant repeats his hesitant words and scurries out.

A tad too cautious. Does he not look to the future? The doctor will not work for him again. Not in good faith. A short-sighted decision, one that rubs me wrong, no matter how trivial it is. Tells me more than I need to know. Shuji Ayato is a man I'd rather have no dealings with. If common law permitted it, I'd slay him, take his lands and his men. But I won't get that lucky, he conducts himself in the view of the gods. He is not as giving as the fieldclans were.

"Come," he turns and catches my eye. There's something fierce, burning about the way he stares through me. "Lady Masa–"

"Please," I growl, interrupting him. "Was it not you who suggested it? Address me as your peer, not as what you see beneath these robes."

He smiles, for the first time. "Ah. Yes, Lord Dattori. This room is no place for discussion. And we have a lot to discuss." He turns and barks once more, another servant at the door. "Prepare the Room of Musings." The servant responds with the same courtesies as the last and disappears.

The day draws long ahead of me. I yawn.

Out in the courtyard, the sky is bruised with clouds, and the Shuji household moves with heavenly precision. Not missing a beat, even with the foreign head hanging from the gates. Members of the household are like bees as they hurry around with purpose. I miss this life in my own estate and spare a moment's prayer. Whichever god is listening, I hope it has not been razed by the two Shaman who watch over it.

Kekkei falls into step beside me and says, "Lady Masako, we've found her."

"Lady Kasuki lives?"

There's a telling pause, and he says, "Well, she lives...yes."

"Kekkei."

"Ravening, mad. All that can be expected from a woman who lived with the corpses of her household."

"I find discomfort in it. I ask myself why the Taosii spared one. However, the machinations of a monster will always be found to be bizarre. A human mind isn't so capable as the answer cannot be found in logic." And my words worry me still, as I have my own idea of why the lady was left to suffer. There's no innocence in those who survive a massacre. I will broach it with her myself. "Where was she found?"

"Heading north. Mumbling of mountains. Devils-tongue, we call it. Plain mad."

Then, maybe I'm wrong. "She is here?"

"Yes, confined within our camp. Will you see her, my lord?"

And the mercenary slips into place. "Not now. The *honourable* Shuji Ayato wouldn't have the patience for it. Nor would he welcome the ki-touched to his doorstep. Soshists make nasty work of their victims, they can't be trusted."

* * *

This time, Shuji-to honours me with the respect deserved of a Lord of the Samaki; the meeting chamber is decked in finery. Red camellia and daffodils are arranged in bunches around the centre table. A mongoose wrestles with a snake, both run through with a blade, backed onto a syrup-yellow on wall hangings around the room. The Bashoan symbol for struggle beneath them finishes the Shuji family crest. Ours is the hanging oni head, on viridian. Our symbol, bond, for Master saw worth in nothing above the relationships we build, that tie us as family. Now, the struggle is mine, as I try to fill his shadow. I strive for this moment, for this steppingstone into the world that'll break the Lord Council for me. I see the godlord's head upon a spike. Either side adorned in the lords who watched my family fall. And yet, the piles are vast, higher than I can climb. Here I am, at the bottom still. And I tug at my dress robes for air as my breaths comes in short, quick.

Lord Shuji sits across from me, his lady at his side. My retainer, advisor, mercenary, and friend at mine. Friend, the word weighs heavy, I don't think I mean it. I wear the mask well.

My opponent lifts his cup and drinks first, and I do the same, sipping the tea personally poured by Ayato.

They say in Basho that in the midst of war, on the battlefield amongst foes, even then there's time for tea properly poured. Ill becomes those who forgo proper etiquette in favour of a hasty victory.

As I sip again, the green tea is bland, bitter as it goes down. I take check and regain control of myself, hoping our hosts don't hear the slight grind of my teeth. Even now, I'm at odds with this, Master. There's a pride that wells in me, but it's easily melted by the flames. There's no time for this. It doesn't matter how hard I try; I'd scream in the face of those who take note of such irritating traditions. A hasty victory is what I need, death is what my blood desires. I ache for it. Feel the excitement of the battles to come in my loins but I hold tight to the mask.

"So, I am to believe that the Lord Council is engaged in foreign affairs." The lord's tone is pensive, tired. Without my provocation, the evidence would still nurture extreme measures. "I've had little dealings with the Taosii; they claim to believe in the same gods but cannot agree to even the same names to worship, or the number of hells." He travels down a stream I did not expect. These lords love the sound of their own thoughts. Room of Musings, indeed. "I have little patience for those who seek to undermine what is already written in the Heavens. We know our gods and what they brought us, but still, they broach the matter. Do you know, Masako, that I hosted one such storyteller here? In the advent of our looser borders, when the Crossings were first sanctioned, he came. He shared a likeness with the head you bring me, a likeness of his people."

"My lord," the lady says, "they seek your approval, not this tale. Let us move over this."

"No. It is important they understand."

"Not in this way!" Her tone is clipped, she lowers it to a hushed whisper, but she cannot hide it from my ears. "Ayato! You wish to tell them of the unsanctioned murder of a foreign ambassador?"

It's testing now, to keep my face stone, disguising my elation. But I do, the lord continues without heed to the warning, "He told me I sit beneath the cradle of the demons. He told me these lands were cursed, ungodly. He spat on them. After I invited him in and played host to him still, he deigned to *adjust* the stories of our gods. Chased by demon swords? Pah, heinous lies." He stops, pretends to spit, working the disgust on his face. "I boiled his hands. I cut his tongue, and I spread his liferopes across the *cursed* soil."

"Just, Lord Shuji," I say. "Blasphemy is intolerable."

A small grin curls at the edge of his mouth. "So, you see, there are no negotiations to be had. I merely invite you here as a courtesy. That heretic's head serves as reason enough. The Taosii scourge must be kept from our borders. For the Lord Council who covet their words, accept their *stories*, there can only be one punishment. An act against Basho is treason, and here, as a representative of my beloved gods, I pin that sentence on Orika itself. They will learn to fear the Samaki before I'm done."

I'm he says. Treason? How very northern of him. A petty man. Pettiness that eclipses even my own. Men of his kind make for terrible allies; when honour runs so close to the surface, even a tiny prick against it causes unimaginable damage. I know, at least, the full measure of the man whose alliance I seek. Although I'm not so foolish to know I could bend him to my will. And I know, as I look sidelong at Kekkei, that the glint in his eye is of victory. But my stomach churns with it. I cannot see that it is a victory shared. It's the same look he gave me at Kasuki-to. Those are the eyes of the mercenary, not the loyal vassal.

"Let us seal it in blood," I say. "Is it not our way?"

"Blood." The lord's grin thickens. "Why not join our families, pay the price in matrimonial blood? After the Lord Council crumbles, united, our families' rule would be unparalleled. The true might of the Samaki. I have many sons, Masako."

Rule? He has designs for the highest seat.

Kekkei's smile is wry. The merc sees me, flattening out his expression. "Consider it, my lady," he says. "A family as powerful in influence as Dattori and Shuji combined could win the Lord Council without destruction. The foreign poison would be dredged from the wound, Basho healed without adding to the damage."

"Genaro Kekkei. Hmm, I wronged you. Lord Dattori, you court intelligence

185

in your family."

"Lord Shuji, you are too kind." Kekkei continues to talk out of turn. "I merely share the same wish as all of those present, it is why I switched to my lady's side. All resources intact." His sentence sharpens at the end. "I assure you, heresy is first and foremost among myriad other heinous crimes the Lord Council partake in. I'm sure, Lord Shuji, you're aware of my past. Before I was cast out of the northern feast, I ate plentiful in its dealings, drank deep in its knowledge. This, I'm sure, my Lady Masako would be willing to share in with Shuji-to, given its cooperation."

"Yes." My words are coarse. "Thank you, Advisor Genaro."

They share a slight nod. Lord Shuji's salt-dotted whiskers bristle, crow feet deepening with cunning he can't hide. Claws grip my chest. I will not be some Shuji whore; my rule would be proxy to his. I will not live in his shadow. Still, I tread carefully. Kekkei has started his game, he thinks me too naive to see it. "With every respect, honourable Ayato, it is not the Dattori way. My late lord father never took a wife, nor did he sow his seed; Dattori are chosen, not born, or bred. I cannot see that my family traditions are dishonoured."

The lord doesn't blink, his stare cutting. But the stone breaks, and he chuckles. "Can you forgive an old man for trying?" He sighs. "There's naught for an ambitious boy southeast of the Kirisam."

I mirror his amusement. "Agreed. However, on one other point my dear Genaro has me wrong." *And so do you.* "I have no love for rule." I let the words hang, straighten in my kneel. If there's a slight change in their temperament, it's unnoticeable. Their breaths, however, give them away; the rasp stopped briefly. "Was that the intention of the Lord Council when they beset upon Samaki families? Did they offer new rule? Did they extend the hand of the Lord Council? No. They had no designs of bringing the outer lanes to heel under tighter law. They bled us dry, until we turned to the mountains, then brought the sword to our necks. Annihilation, death, destruction. Call it whatever you want, but that was always their point." Dramatics add fire to my words, so I pause. "That is my point."

"The Samaki deserve reward. A long campaign will strip us, wear us down, so it is foolish not to plunder what we can from the northern cravens."

"Lord Shuji, you will have your reward. You will never again feel the hand of death reach from Orika. Land, aplenty, will be left in wake of what we do. But we must not allow a broken, corrupted way of governance to continue. We must start anew."

Kekkei shifts, I think he's going to speak. Instead, he claps. Laughing, he gets up and bows to us both. "All-honoured lords, today we truly make history." His eyes betray a different message. The lord shares in his cheer, and in something else also. In a look that screams danger in the recesses of my mind. A look shared between men that they think goes unnoticed because they don't see the monster in the room. They look past me because I wear the skin of a woman, a woman who they perhaps don't think deserves what she has brought.

What she lays on the table.

I look across to the lady who has all but shrunk into herself. Wilted, the flower loses its beauty. If watered, it'll reveal itself once more, but only for those who care for it. Nothing is hidden from the one you lay with, not even a lord. Ayato's bedmate will make a fine friend. I will pull his secrets from her petals.

Getting up, I savour this moment. Like the last drop of plum wine in a skin, days deep into a ride, the rich, aromatic taste redoubled as it leeches in the past alcohols the hide has kept. The rest of the Samaki will follow where the Shuji tred. If they can let go of the past.

The difference between Lord Shuji and my late father is that the latter acted out of honour, balancing the powers of the outer lands against the growing laws and taxes aimed at them. Master was concerned in longevity, order, and peace. The Lord here is only concerned with power, not the balance. True it is that he has never wronged the Samaki, never played party to its bloodshed, like the Dattori. My namesake battle, where I became the Hawk, hangs over me. Shuji-to's blessing stole the poison from the bite of those snakes who would circle around my weakened clan. For now, it is a victory. My victory.

"We are not done! Wait."

The lord's growled command rips through my reflection. A stone splitting

187

the surface of a calm lake. So, I sit.

"Tell me," he orders. "What possessed your lord to pay for your own crimes?"

Fury. I bite down so hard my teeth shift about in the gaps. I swallow, my face goes numb as I try to contain myself. While he couldn't turn my cause away with the evidence mounted against the north, he vies to provoke me. To give him reason to sever my part in this game, letting him reap every reward he imagines. He has the impetus to move the other southern families who're stiff from subservient inaction.

I own it, though. This is yours, Master. I won't lose myself to this fool.

"My lord," I say. "He didn't go of his own accord, they sent the Wolves for us, dragged us to Orika. I'm sure you've heard of the Hawk who clawed herself out of their den?"

Again, his amusement fades. It is like the tide. "Hmm, I heard something of it. Rumours, inflated stories, we are too close to Chisai here. Yet, nothing of your...*escape.*"

"The Kirisam never tires, my lord. Past Orika it flows, not stopping, even for the mountains. One just must trust its flow. I threw myself into its waters so that I could live to bring this news to your household. So that I may take vengeance on the Lord Council."

"Truth. It is always harder believed than rumour."

"Oh, but truth it is, *my lord.*"

Chapter 20

BEFORE MY FALL: ACT 4

They came for us. I couldn't stop it, didn't want to. I thought I could ride it, harness it, but it burnt me up.

I searched for Zaki in the hours following his dismissal. Looking in his quarters, everything was untouched, his bed still rolled and tucked away. A lake chrysanthemum drooped on his desk, the petals slowly dripping from its head, the soft watery aroma dissipated. I sighed. It was never good to watch decay happen in the room you slept. A promise of sleepless nights and a clouded mind awaited those who did. As my eyes glanced over the room, one thing startled me; his twin blades were gone. A warrior left only with their blades for battle or for travel. Panic fell on me like a shroud, clutched at my shoulders and chest. I searched, then, for his robes. Gone. And as I faced the entranceway, tucked into one of the wooden beams, a piece of parchment fluttered in the draught. Cool air snaked through it; a chill raked down my spine. On the note, a single High Bashoan symbol etched atop the Murakami's owl. Not theirs of PATIENCE, replacing it was CONSEQUENCE.

The wind caught my step as I barrelled into the stables, the stableman looked up just in time to see the anger boil towards him. Grabbing him by the collar I pushed him into the wall. "You let him go?!"

"Milady, I-I...It's above me to."

I dropped the boy, who slumped to the floor in a shriek. Lonestep whinnied as I passed her stall, bothered briefly by my presence before worrying her straw bedding once more. All horses accounted for, except for the middle stall. The one that I saved for last, hoping it wouldn't be so. My eyes fell on the empty stable; a void where my anxieties laid, punctuated with a sharp loneliness. He was gone.

Consequence. I mulled the symbol around, swilled it but I didn't quite get the taste. Was that the consequence, Zaki? That you went and stole everything I truly loved in the world with you, because you couldn't stand up to the godlord? Or because you daren't. Well, you will never know that I drew the courage to take on this land from you. My twin sword. There's something blunt about his leaving that never sharpened again. Zaki wouldn't return, I felt that.

My lips curled, my face scrunched, and I stifled a scream. What came out was a growl. I turned on the stableman who let it happen. An elk caught in the field tiger's gaze. I must have looked the picture of one.

I pounced.

He shielded his face, I hammered down his frail guard with a couple of wild punches, he was not built to take it. My next punches beat him to the ground, and I couldn't contain myself until my knuckles were raw, and his face pulped.

I heard only my breaths. I felt a hunger, but then I couldn't place it.

Innocent blood pooled around me, overwhelmed my senses. I staggered backwards, slipping in it and stumbled to the ground. Only then, was I undone. High Captain Dabura, Tane and Hoji. My confidant. My friends. Grave were their faces, each set of eyes wooden.

Dabura said something I couldn't hear against the beating in my ears, Tane winced as he knelt by the stableman, searching for a pulse but finding nothing but hopelessness. He shook his head when the High Captain said something more and turned back to me with what I could only describe as hatred written across his face.

In the eyes of my men I was hope, I was fierce loyalty, and change, but now just a murderer. That's what Tane said, I read it on his lips. Never would I tell a soul of this part of my story, common folk don't die like we do. Aren't made of what we are, so the killing will never be just.

I wonder if it was in that moment my cursed blood truly awoke.

Tane and Hoji heard their orders. They marched me straight to the cavernous jails at the foot of the cold rock standing at the back of our estate. Our enemies had been imprisoned here, thieves, traffickers, we'd held the lieutenants of the fieldclans to draw out their families. Common folk, those of low birth, those dank, depressed cells were designed to hold their like. I'd roused a mighty ache in my hands in the hours that I was held, trying to force the hinges of the solid wood door. It would not yield to my punches, unlike the fool that had me sent here.

Darkness here was absolute. The sliver cut into the wood face, so that my captors might look in, was framed in an orange hue that dare not imprison itself with me. Knuckles throbbing, the pitch-black seemed to pulse with it. Blood boiled as it fizzled out of my wounds, hardening in the air. I heard it clear for the first time there, whispering.

Master had spoken of it before. Once. That my birth would have been bloody. If ever I was wounded, maids and doctors of the household flocked instantly. Not a drop was left. Master scolded me for paying too much attention to a droplet of my own blood, pricked on the tip of my blade; I was not to lick it like the other children, who wore their scrapes as a badge of honour. No, my blood was that of outcasts. Sired at the foot of the mountains, bathed in the demon's bile that spilled like streams from their peaks, I had tainted blood. Poisonous, deadly to even my own consumption. It was the only time he beat me. The only time he checked my behaviour. Taught by the best, I learnt to fear the spilling of my own blood. To our people who found honour in death on the battlefield – I was an anomaly. A wretched being. Those were the only times he would talk of my coming to the Dattori, I could not broach the topic of why I was so – not twice.

I wondered whether the dragons above had seen it. Did they watch as Master pried me from my birth family?

The taint lived on when it should have disappeared. For that, the gods would punish my lord. Their designs were cruel, slow, over those past months I could almost watch it coming, but ever is the Hawk blind to those above it; it sees prey below, field mice, things that scurry beneath it, never imagining something could strike from above. Swift, sharp but arrogant.

My mind was not built to be confined. So, within the throbbing darkness, I laughed the night away.

By the morning, I could hear murmurs, voices coming for me. I waited that entire day for them. Working my fingers through the slit, I tried to force the wood, but it was beyond my strength.

When I awoke, someone had slid a stodgy bowl of porridge and a gourd of water from the moat into my cell.

I screamed blasphemies through the tiny slit that entire night, for someone waited out there. Someone beneath me, under my own command. They dared defy my order.

Master did not come. For two days, no one paid me the respect I'd earnt. How would they face the Lord Council without my lead? And for what? I'd slay that stableman a thousand times for what he wrought.

I laid against the chill of the unyielding stone, listening to the silence within the earth. The calm that spread beneath me was a friend. It alerted me to something amiss. I blocked out the whispers of my blood, the coarse gurgling, as best as I could and pressed my ear against the stone until it hurt. There, amongst the beat of my own madness, a tremor. A tiny patter. In all my years, there had been no earth-tremors in the south, the land held still by the surrounding mountains. The demons that inhabit them did not incite disaster on their doorstep, so they thrust their machinations further afield. It was different. Sure, consistent. No, it couldn't be. Not enough time had passed, had it? The days in the Caverns of Penance were impossible to discern.

"Guardsman!" I croaked. "Get me out of here at once!"

I listened in case I missed the reply, but there wasn't one.

"GUARDSMAN. MANY APPROACH ON HORSEBACK!"

My throat raked hoarse with unanswered shouts.

The whoreson only replied when it was too late. A longer rumble, a low *whoomp*. A night frog's slow ribbit, but magnified, muffled. The earth shook with it.

"M-masako?"

"Gitaki, you wretched swine!" As I thought, guarded by a sword I'd trained. My whole body tightened, muscles cramping as I contained myself – it was no fault of his that I was there. "Let me out!"

"The honourable High Captain's orders."

"Fuck his orders! Does the earth usually belch so? If it is nothing, boy, bring me back for all I care, but release me at once! That's a direct order. Did I not place that sword at your side and not before teaching you to wield it?"

A jingling. Then a grunt and as metal clanged against the floor. Again, a rattling. The earth shuddered. With a clunk, Gitaki swung open the door and I bolted out. Legs shaky beneath me, I stumbled before falling. A direr situation there had not been. I was weak, much too so for what awaited me.

"L-lady...orders. I just wanted to follow–" I waved him quiet, it did not matter. He was true to his post. A good man. Plate hissed and clattered. I turned, and the warrior. No, the boy, that stood behind me could barely keep himself still. We'd not discovered what lay outside and already he was overcome with Metsuku's fear. A cruel god indeed. He was far too young for the fate that awaited him.

"Your katana." I held my hand out.

"I c-can't."

Even weakened, he wasn't a warrior capable of following my steps, so I drew his sword from its scabbard and turned. My robes were cumbersome, not light like their warrior counterpart. I needed to get to my quarters.

In full plate, Gitaki took lead, wielding his side-arm as we emerged into what I could only describe as one of the hells summoned to our forsaken realm. The night sky was lit up with flickering reds and oranges. Smoke billowed from a fire that consumed maybe the entire eastern wing of the estate, where my quarters had been. Smouldering ash and debris punctuated the grey cloud, glowing in place of the stars. Destruction rained down on me. Grabbing a handful of my robes, I hacked into them, unable to breathe properly. I held it there as I followed Gitaki into suffocating mist.

Shouts were continuous, as was the din of steel on steel. A battle took place. The ground shook once more.

Through the cloud ahead of us, three figures emerged.

Gitaki froze, as did I. It was never good to use the element of surprise if you didn't have the measure of what you were up against.

Three warriors clanged towards us. Their masked helms snarled like wolves. Their silver helms decorated with battle etchings, guilted in a shiny obsidian finish; the Okami's Wolfpads had come. At the time I couldn't understand how. My sentences were read, the Lord Council should have awaited our arrival. And yet, they sent a death squad to our doors.

"Go!"

Gitaki reacted clumsily to my order. He was not quick enough to close the gap or take note of his impaired reach. He swung and missed as one Wolfpad closed in. I was a step too far. My warrior parried a riposte but was too inexperienced to see the feint. One move behind the blade that cleaved through the side of Gitaki's face, I parried the blow that took his life too late and botched the killing blow. He screamed, but not for long as I slashed backwards and made space for the oncoming charge, ending his suffering. As his body dropped, I positioned myself so it fell between the Wolfpad's cut and I. There would be a time to reflect on this later, a time to put his body to rest as he deserved. I swore to him I would, and lied. There was no coming back from the death that came for me. Not in that life.

As one Wolfpad tripped over the body, his hands occupied, there was a meaty slap as he fell face first within the confines of his helm.

The other two were separated in their charge as one dodged the bodies between us. I rushed the gap. Jumped into his guard. With my sword in both hands, hilt tucked to my side, blade pointed outwards, I was ready for the closed quarters. He wasn't, tried to slash downward, but had no room as his wrists thumped my shoulder. I thrust outward, my blade skittered across plate before it found a gap and punched into his side.

Crying out, he fell as I unsheathed my sword from him and spun on the other Wolfpad, again hitting plate. My slash diverted groundward with an elbow and returned with his own, cutting into the top of my arm. I grunted but that's all the notice I showed the shoulder immediately screaming in daggers of pain. We traded a few strikes. Not one of us getting the upper hand. On the last parry, he hadn't realised I'd led him back around to Gitaki's body and fell backwards. I finished him on the floor. There is elegance in a fair fight. There is only survival in an effective one. A successful warrior keeps one eye on the opponent and the other on their surroundings. A clever warrior uses those to their advantage. Defeat is defeat. Victory carries the only honour to be earned.

I took a breather, checking my shoulder. Blood pulsed out of it; a flesh wound that wouldn't slow me.

The ground still *whoomped*, there was more than steel and cries in the ashy fog. It glowed to a beat, crimson, amber, a giant heart. It wasn't indiscriminately flooding the grounds, the shroud was something the Dattori were caught in, no other. The Wolfpads seemed to navigate it with ease. Which was apparent when I followed the closest shouts and found a small unit of my Wuld Guard. Those who faced the oni were a splintered mess. Michita and Yoji headed the group, the distress loosened on their faces as they saw me. Eyes glassy, bewildered. On our own grounds, we should have fared better than that. Ganfi had Hatamo under his arm, blood leaked from his mouth. He was dead but wasn't ready to admit it.

"Tane's gone." Yoji delivered the news fast, blunt. Rolled over it. I had a brief second to consider that Tane died looking upon me as a murderer and moved on as he continued, "Routed. We can't get a foothold in this. They're everywhere."

"She ain't commander."

"Quiet, you fuck!" He said to Michita. She scowled back. "We're dying here. *You're* gonna lead us?"

"What of the fire. What started it?"

"No idea, my lady." He stopped to listen. I heard it too. "Fuck. I can't see two foot in front of me but those swineshits are on us already?"

"Two-forks!" I shout.

They split off into pairs, swinging room between them. In the hope of using the smog as a veil, I dip into it and follow the sound of plate in a wide arc, before diving back in again. My men engaged, three pairs holding off double their numbers. There's no other set of warriors in Basho worthy of being outnumbered by the Lord Council's elite than my Guardians of the Wuld. No matter whether you're against two or three, or five, there's as many single battles within that. Not a battle of three on one. Three battles of one. Men and women that I trained were the only ones there who knew that. That is our Way of the Sword.

Two pairs needed no help, the enemies fell into their step without realising it and were slowly overwhelmed save the already injured pair. Ganfi took a slash to the arm that protected Hatamo, but that was only before I swooped from the smog, the wings of death beat above, claiming two more wolves.

Still, the hawk didn't look above. At the apex of its own hunt, it dared not think of another.

On our way to the epicentre of the battle, bodies were charred, strewn about. Smoking parts of my comrades lay indistinguishable from the burning debris of our house. Our home. Before we made our way to the pit of hell, Hatamo yielded to his wound, and I made another false promise.

I would bury them all one day. After everything is done, I would see that they rest properly.

As we rounded the corner, a gnawing in the back of my mind made me stop, I said, "Go on, I'll follow you soon. Find the High Captain!" And I left, slinking between two buildings and out into the yard before Zaki's quarters. The doors were open. My heart thumped. I would not let them be raided by the scum, lest I took something of his with me. Save it from the fires that would consume me.

At the threshold I sickened, my stomach turned into a putrid swamp.

"Z-Zaki."

He stopped dead in his frantic packing and spun with fear painted across his face. Eyes flicked to his twin swords that lay atop his pack. My breath caught as I saw it. In part because of the betrayal of searching for his weapons before he looked upon me, the scene begged me ask a question I feared the answer to. "Why're you unarmed? Our household breaks around us, and you're concerned about belongings, Zaki? I've only these robes and a borrowed sword. Gods, it would seem my fucking quarters drift back down to the earth as ash."

"Masako. Masako, come with me. It'll end quicker if you do."

"Run? We can't! Lord Dattori is still in there!"

His eyes grew sad. I only heard what I wanted to hear, ignoring what lay before me.

"No, come to Orika."

"WE CAN'T GO THERE!" I ground my teeth, started again. "Zaki...please, I'll be executed. We need you! We're losing out there."

"Go to Orika and pay for your crimes." His calm words were betrayed by the tremble that coated them. He looked to his swords again.

"Drop this! We don't have time to finish that quarrel. We must go to Master!" A third look to his weapons cut me. An insult that pushed the missing piece into place.

"I brought them here. You cannot bring Basho down with your nonsense. Look at what your anger has wrought!" My blade firm in my grip, I still don't really think he expected it. "You are poi—" *I brought them here.* Four words numbed me. Erased that piece of my life completely. Two quick strides, I cut across myself in a sure arc. At the last second, he realised what was happening and tried to dive for his swords, but my blade took him through the side of his mouth, raking across teeth, through cheek and the back of his head.

I don't know why he felt so strongly as to bring the Lord Council down upon me, I didn't want to hear from his traitor mouth. It's something I'll hear from the godlord himself before I gut him; perhaps the Mountains weren't happy that one Murakami escaped their wickedness. It was their evil that brought this, but his own inferiority that called them.

A clap interrupted me before I could pull the blade free from Zaki's head, my body numbed still but not by my own emotion. At someone else's command, I turned. A hooded, feminine figure, flanked by a purple haze I only now know, stood next to the slender, smiling child-faced man who clapped. His body was draped in a patchwork cloak of different hides, myriad animals stitched into one; bald, save for a braided ponytail that sprouted from the top of his head, running down to his waist, eyes like upturned katanas. He was already enjoying this, Soshist Po. The artificer of our family's plight.

Their look was not of Basho, and although I'd never laid eyes on them before, I'd knew enough to recognise the Taosii. The scourge that the Lord Council bargained with.

I tried again to move but could not. A wash of fear ran over me, like a bucket of freezing water poured above my head. The purple glint, the fires, the smog. I spoke of what they were but only a hoarse croak left my mouth. Again, "So...So-Soshists."

"Smart," is all the man said before he left. I was dragged behind. A doll without control.

I swallowed a lump of dread, Master knelt in the ruins of our east wall. At the same time, it dawned on me that the debris surrounding me once belonged to my own quarters; sadness draped over my shoulders as I'd not be able to leave with my precious CrowKiller, nor would I break free with HighWolf. No fires would undo the magic that binds them, but they were too lost to help me.

Next to Master, I'd thought him a pillar of flame, a smoke-spectre, but only because his plate made him look so. Armour forged by the same means as my blades shimmered with the fires around him. The white and silver so perfect it was a mirror, the edges of each plate finished with a gold only the godlord was allowed to bestow. Green veins swirled on its surface, acid-etched with family histories. Kitsutana Kita, All-honoured Captain of the Okami Guard and personal guard of the godlord himself. A man recognisable in Basho from his swords: law dictated two blades, but this man had eight. The only warrior permitted to break that law. Two blades at each side, he wore four on his back, a true demon.

The Fox, but he didn't have nine tails, yet.

He stood in an opening seemingly surrounded by walls of flame. Wolfpad reserves scattered around him in two groups that made a score.

A roar sounded in the night. From the far edge of the hellish arena, two units of Dattori guardsmen appeared, quickly met by the Fox's men. A final battle took place. The despicable Taosii choose to stop our approach in favour of watching the battle unfold, whispering and chuckling to themselves.

The High Captain, Fenika Dabura broke off from the battle, tearing a Wolfpad in two with his great halberd, a polearm with a giant curved blade on the end that only the treelike man could wield the way he did.

"Couldn't you stop him?" Soshist Po said in a clipped Low Bashoan.

The female, Ti, answered in the same language, "Yes. This is amusing, though."

When they could speak their own tongue, they chose mine as an insult.

I will still have the last laugh.

Struggling with all my might against my bonds, I could only watch as Dabura charged the Fox like a spear thrown by Meganako herself. He hit the armoured in a torrent of thrusts. How one man could be as immovable as an old oak, but as quick as a serpent that slithered between its branches, only the Mistress knows.

The Fox wielded two swords with ease, parrying everything Dabura threw at him, even while the tree-of-a-man held a distance only his polearm could assault from.

Disbelief. I blinked and I still didn't understand it. The Fox didn't only use two blades, as much as I could follow, he'd used five of them so far. Sheathing and drawing seamlessly. Each blade a different length fulfilling a different purpose. Until Dabura left an opening. It was swallowed whole. A minute gap as he tired faster due to the sheer size of his weapon.

Kita was not a muscly man; I could see that even behind the armour. His body was not one that strived for perfection, for absolute efficiency in its makeup. A man of my height, Dabura towered over him. I saw something else that chilled me to the marrow; he was sharp. That is all there was to it. A born blade. Simply, he moved as water, fluid with no gaps, responding to everything in front of him, a flame. Unavoidable, the wind. Immovable, the earth.

Within that moment the halberd dropped, quicker than I could follow, he sheathed two blades and drew one. Threading it into that minute opening, he felled the Dattori's Unyielding Tree.

Soshist Po clapped again. A slaughter continued around us.

And Master and I were dragged before the godlord.

* * *

To his credit, Lord Shuji listened to the tale without interjection.

His neck red, blotchy, cup trembling in his grip; during my recount, the rat servant delivered a fresh tea. A bitter bite with a floral note to it, lavender, perhaps. It did nothing to ease my tale, it could only be delivered in anger, could only evoke anger. The plants relaxing properties wasted in this room. The lord didn't say anything immediately, his lady advisor hurriedly whispered pacifying words in his ears, that I could gather. Not that it worked.

With a yell, the lord smashes the cup against the table. As he let go of the porcelain pieces, blood drips from his hand, which he brought up to his face as if scrutinizing each droplet. He squeezes, wringing his hand out like a cloth as the drips turn into a stream.

"Lady Dattori," he says. "Here!"

The smell of his blood is a tendril that sweeps across the room, it is the only thing I now smell. The only thing relevant to me. I get up and follow the lingering scent back to its master. Lady Shuji pulls a small knife from her robes. Jewelled, old, ceremonial. I politely decline, picking a jagged piece of porcelain from the mess.

I cut my own palm with a rough slash and await the blood to pool. When it's sufficient, I take his bloodied hand, we recite the words of the Samaki, for there is nothing else that would tie our households as one: *bond, struggle, endurance, cultivate, patience, unity,* and *restraint.* These symbols remind us of why we live in the outer lands, why we do not have the luxuries of the north, and what we share with each other; Master said the Samaki take a symbol so that they only strive for one thing in their life. So that the focus, daily, returns to maintaining that. Whatever it is, it grounds us.

We bow to one another, no other words worthy of our agreement.

I want to feel the same pride that Kekkei wears so brazenly on his face as he joins us. I want to feel the same anger that the lord cannot shake myself free of his form. Instead, my hand throbs against his, the blood seemingly alive between our vice-gripped agreement. A song, a bloody chorus pulses through my veins. An urge, a throb between my eyes. A compulsion. And then back again, through my veins, into our grip and out into his veins. Anger untapped, he finally has me where he wants me. *There's never been a Godlord of the Samaki, has there? He asks himself, suppressing a grin. Mayhap this is my time, I'll let the girl fail first. She could surprise me.*

And I'm sucked back out again, my thoughts are my own once more. In the seconds before we part hands, something changes forever. I'm reminded of the farmer, and his readiness to save me from the claws of the Okami. Now he who saved me is embedded in torment in his own blade, his screams still haunt my sleep. I feel something of a similar connection to the lord who plots behind a warm smile. It doesn't scare me this time, no. Somehow, at his end, I know he will play a crucial part in my campaign. Not the part he is willing to play, though.

Chapter 21

The same evening that our families are bonded, we say goodbye to the souls of the fallen.

Many Shuji servants were enlisted in bringing firewood and kindling, the lord spared no expense in erecting a pyre the likes of which I'd never seen.

Servants bring round fruity wine, bitter sakes, something else stronger, abominable in taste, in glasses that shine like jewels against the moonlight. Distasteful. To flaunt such wealth in the face of the gods is a dishonest, impure way of sending their honourable spirits off. Honourable, for they died in service of our lands. Dishonourable were the festivities around me. The Shuji cry blasphemy, tremble in rage, anger, and bloodlust at the mention of foreign interference in the physical plane. Then turn a blind eye to the lavish, uncouth behaviour that would act as an insult to our Four of Creation, and as a beacon to new, hungry gods who covet the sins of the mortals, hunger for converts and careless practitioners.

As I survey the crowd, watching the finishing touches to the pyre, I'm certain that Don Yoku sits somewhere above. I cannot be sure. A thick, dark cloud rolls in, shrouding the stars; some of the spirits will tire before they reach the heavens tonight. It's a deep, unmoving night.

The pyre is lit, I'm flanked by my newly appointed High Captain, Oboro. There was need for that Dattori seat to be filled, no quicker has a warrior gained my trust than this man. He sips from the same wineskin that gave us nourishment enough to see the Taosii die like a dog. He calls it SavedHide and finds amusement in his own way with words; I realise it's the first time

I've seen him smile. Offering the 'skin up as the fire blazes high into the skies.

I, too, offer my glass. As his lord, I do not owe Bunta more than that. His death solidifies him as a member of my household. Not as a vassal, he died Dattori, and there he will always belong. There's a chill in the air tonight. Despite the pyre, I shiver. A good day for a send-off indeed. Perhaps it's not the night that touches me so. I look across the congregation of Shuji and Dattori and spy two men in the throes of massaging each other's ego. They take it in turns to laugh at every bit of dribble they must speak. Kekkei pats Lord Shuji on the shoulder, sharing a nod. That Ayato does not put my First Advisor in his place tells me all I need to know. For a low born to touch a lord as if they were birth friends, no matter how high he climbs, speaks of snakes and shadows. So they think, but I've heard your thoughts, Ayato. You fool. Ropi and some other unfamiliar faces mingle near them, the Shuji slab-for-a-boy gestures towards the blaze, their faces painted in awe as he churns out perhaps a tale of the gods that captivates them all apart from the arrow-loving whore, who chucks back the alcohol like it's her last day on this plane. Pulling her from my estate leaves fills me with dread, not because I cannot stand the woman, I'm at peace with that. There is now no one to watch the Shamans – the entire courtyard will be defiled in meat and rituals by the time I return. I sigh.

Oboro notices and shoves SavedHide in my face. I don't hesitate to drink deep, to deny her that privilege would wrong it. A bad omen. And so, a new Dattori tradition is born. I wonder whether I'll be feeling in good fortune when I break my fast with a sore head.

* * *

I thought the summer done but Sukami's orb blazes overhead. Overzealous in its second wind, I fear it means a quick falling, the cold is fast approaching. I pull down the opening of my tent, fastening it shut. I'm not ready for today. The seasons strip away my options; it means we neither have the luxury of time on our side, neither the funds for our household to run itself; Kekkei assures me that Bunta's trade routes are so bountiful I wonder whether they are lined with gold themselves. The fieldclan had their own illicit wealth that they do not need in death, but that won't last us long.

I sent instruction to Cat Food with a runner to gather our common folk, to rouse the small villages dotted about Dattori land, and those further afield who fall into our authority. The paddies need dredging, re-setting, if I'm to trust Lord Shuji – our fields too need cultivation – but even with that truth there is no time for a crop. We can do our best to prepare the fields for when winter's spiteful grip gives the lands back, but it will do nothing for us now. Our host lord opens his coffers for *allies.* However, the interest owed will be no different to those of foe. My great family needs to blossom once more, and it cannot do that from under a cloud of debt.

Before I mull over it anymore, my head flips, stomach cramps. Waves lash against the inside of my skull and I pull the bucket closer once more and vomit into it. Oboro is a swine.

I dress myself in a light silk robe. Grey, embroidered in silver with the oni head of our house, over and over again, dizzying. The seamstress is masterful in her work. I still don't forgive the woman for her loose legs. Neither will her hands work thread in those caverns. Perhaps I should have written some reprieve for the woman in my last message, maybe I'll do it in my next. Fastening my katana to my waist, I try the scorching day once more. My eyes are too big for my head as I squint, they swell, soaking in the brightness. *Throb, throb.* The familiar, but painful, beat is twin to the alcohol's ravages. Our Earthly Doctors knew little of it. So, I came to my own hypothesis. Sensitivity. Heightened sensitivity to Sukami's light means my sight doesn't fail even when her moon reigns supreme, and that is overwhelmed on days like these.

Ropi greets me as I exit my tent, I try to hide my scowl. Though, I was never masterful at it. Around me, I stand at the centre of a sea of tents, greys and whites. Shuji-to stands as a thatched mountain in the distance, our campsite sprawling at its foot. As soon as the eye is turned, Kekkei's Hands number a small army. Resourceful doesn't cut it.

"What is it?"

"Master Genaro sent me as escort."

Her smile bothered me, already too close, and even more than the bundle she hides. "That?"

"Master Jinto sent it." She pulls it from behind her back, and my stomach does another nasty flip. I brace for another spew, but it settles. I know it. Sword-shaped and small. A sidearm. I hear it, and snatch it from her, immediately feeling its revulsion. "Master Jinto said he could not sleep with it. The demons would not settle either, not with something like that so close." She chuckles. "Sorry. I did think twice about repeating it word for word, and I regret it. Silly words. Don't leave again without it, a warrior is allowed two swords for a reason."

"I know well our Ways. Thank you. Dismissed."

"But the escort."

"I can traverse my own camp without a bodyguard."

She disappears between the white sentinels, and I'm free to breathe again. You don't have to tell her twice, her only redeeming feature.

I stagger, propping myself up against a tent pole and am sick once more. This will be a testing day. Not least because I carry this burden with me now. Unwrapping the sidearm, I wear it for the first time. My whole body feels out of kilter with it, but it is something I must bear. For the sake of the little man who showed me a path other than impatience and anger. Kekkei tries in the same vein of thought, but he does so behind closed doors, in the veil of shadows and hushed tones. Trust is not something that occurs to the man. I will not stop at negotiation; I won't give the Lord Council an ear when they only brought me the sword, but that doesn't mean there will be only bodies in my wake. I seek change. The godsborne has bound me to it.

That creature's words weigh me down, it must be shared before it consumes me. I scour my memory for a warning and cannot find one. Head-splitting, anger rises unchecked. Must this path be mine alone or can I share your words with my kindred?

I claw the bandage from my wounded hand, pull open the porcelain wound, the blood comes quick. In a moment of madness, I kneel, slamming my palm to the ground. *COME. COME AGAIN. HEAR ME.*

Thump.

My heart skips a beat.

Thump.

There's nothing but the annoyed nagging of my palm as grit and dirt works its way into the wound.

Ropi is back with a couple of Hands in tow. Smiling, her grins stretches too far across her face for them to have only just arrived. Mad, that's what the whispers in the camp will say. "Master insists I bring you."

The plain robed men either side of her are both adorned in grey with a short sword tucked into their red sash...Kekkei is so brazen now he marks his Hands as his own? Glancing skyward, I sigh, shoulders slumping. Why is it that I feel like a *rōnin* once more? Godsborne, I'm not done with you. Ignore my call now. You'll rue it later.

If I could cut through Ropi with a look, I would've now. "As your lord, I outrank your m*aster.* Did I not tell you I can manage alone?"

"Master Genaro joined the Dattori as a vassal. A vassal lord, perhaps. Akate did not disband. A vassal's people are their own. We swore allegiance, not obedience. Call Oboro what you want, he's still Master's man."

Demons take you, I want to say, but I will take it up with the dog's owner. "Onward, then."

We thunder through the camp, each step ricocheting from the earth up through my head like a spike; the camp stretched further now it seemed, engulfing the field the Shuji leant us, overwhelming my eye. Was not a single one of these tents loyal to me, then? I suppress the thought. Content was I in the dream that my family could be remade overnight. Bunta suppressed Kekkei's ambition, having a Right Hand that strove to be more a part of our lord family clouded my vision – now that the bitch takes his place, Thousand Hands, leader of the Akate, lives again. His guise as advisor shrivels away under the beat of this gods-awful sun.

I fear I am a mere platform for Akate to stand on level grounds with the Samaki lords.

To the back of the camp, one tent is our destination. The unknowing eye would perceive it as no different to those around it. We made it so. Screams carry in the wind, as it whips around the edge of our site, there's a hope that they'll be carried off for only the mountains to hear. I'd kept myself away from what we do inside as I do not wish to dirty myself with the dishonour – there is an *art* to making criminals talk, not one that befits a warrior.

Two red sashed Akate guard the entrance. Their spears bar the way, not the most inconspicuous tent, but our hosts allow us some discrepancy, only our people patrol.

Spears part, one guard cracks open the tent, my nose turns at a waft of air that smells like vomit mixed into a cattle trough. A metallic tang lingers beyond it. Both my head and stomach swell and I pull up my robes as I hack into them. Luckily my stomach has nothing left to purge.

Ropi and her crew don't follow me in.

Propped up in a kneel, back tied to the centre-post, Lady Kasuki rasps shallow breaths; surviving mother of Tsujo, great matriarch of the rundown family and *sole* survivor of the *Kasuki-to Incident* as the whispers of the camp refer to it. With Chisai nearby, I'm sure the rest of Basho will know it soon. I fear they will. None will know of this woman though; she would have died with the rest of their family. That's the way it should have happened, no one who survives a massacre is innocent. I know this myself, for I survived in the wake of Master's murder – the Lord Council would have me believe I brought it upon him. So, I look upon this woman with something akin to pity but nothing that'll let her leave this place.

She's only recognisable by the fact I know her. Her once silvery black locks cling to her head, hardened with sweat and dirt. Dried blood cracks all over her face as she notices me and looks up with a weak smile. Her robes are a rotten stench.

"Murderer!" She croaks. "The murderer arrives!"

A shift towards the back of the tent breaks my stare. I hadn't noticed Kekkei's presence until he peeled himself from the shadows. He wipes his hand on a stained cloth consciously, as if he cannot rid himself of what he has done. His hands are clean, from what I can tell, but his eyes are deep, hollow.

"It was right that you see her, my lord." Kekkei's voice is flat. "She speaks more to your arrival than she lets loose over a nail."

I don't press him on the matter, gladdened that her hands are tied behind her back. My involvement here is that of ignorance, a lord knows the weight their orders carry but sits above watching them realised in these situations. "Leave us. Rest."

"I'll stay. The right questions need to be asked, we can't waste–"

"Does no one in this damned camp recognise what I am? Leave! Stand guard if you must. But do it outside. This will play out better if it is one matriarch to the other. Look at her, she holds her tongue at the sight of you all."

Dipping his head slightly, he leaves.

"Murderer!"

"It was only you that brought down your family. Trust me, you're amongst friends in that respect." The words bring an ill-fitting smile to my face. As if one in such a dire situation is concerned with trust. "Why did you invite the Taosii to do that to your family?"

"Murderer!" She rasps once more.

"The only honour left for your family can be regained in your truth. Do not dishonour their deaths by withholding this."

"Pah." She leans back, wincing. "I care not for their honour. My Lord Kasuki was of a weak strain. Sickly, even my eldest had trouble with his sword forms. Mistress Ti saved them! They didn't even know they'd died... just wanted to serve!"

"Listen to yourself, woman! That was your family."

"Family? I was dragged from my village and sold to that sick wretch. My children, yes. I loved my children. Mistress Ti gave them to me forever. Freed them of their father's strain. Tsujo was with me until the end...you did that to him!"

My nails curl into the palm of my hands, tightening until my wound weeps blood again – I imagine her neck as it snaps in my grip. I let the feeling slip away with the pain. "That Taosii murdered your family." Flames, it boils over. "YOU DINED AMONGST THEIR CORPSES." I spray spittle at her in my growl.

"Murderer!"

"Pray tell me why you care that we carved up the living dead of your family when you invited them in?" Useless. I'm arguing with madness. Calm.

"NOT THEM!" She breaks into a fit of coughs and it's as though she's stabbed with each one. "Mistress Ti was doing the gods' work and you murdered her! Only death awaits you. Mountain fuckers – all of you. Demon breed, we're too close to the filth here."

I decide to push my finger into the wound. "I didn't kill your *mistress*, she did that herself. Gods' work? She's a dolt who rode her horse until it collapsed on her. A *whore* who fell on her own weapon."

"Bitch! Demon cunny! How da – ack – dare you. Pay. You'll pay you will. You'll pay." She's broken, the words repeat over and over until I backhand her. Writhing, a sound of choking, her wheezes are the rattle of death. They quickly peter out into a hoarse laugh. A cackle. Evil. "You know him...though, the King of Furs."

"What madness woman? I know no king."

"I tried, oh tried to run to the mountains. I wanted it, master." She looks through me now, the mumblings of a mad woman. "I wanted demon blood for you I did." Now to me, her eyes are wild, familiar. I stagger away from it instinctively going for my sword. I stop before I draw. And she speaks once more, "That mark. You live at his mercy? You know the King of Furs, so why do you get in his way? For him, the mountains will fall. He will knowhewillknowhewillknow." She bursts into tears, and I'm done with this madness.

Outside the tent I tell Ropi to do whatever she must with her, trying to shake off Kekkei's questions as he struggles to keep up with me. I can't take this brightness. "I. Need. To. Retire for today. What is it?!"

"You spoke at length; we could hear it. Tell me, did you discover anything?"

"Madness drives her. It still does. She has love for our foreign invaders. That is all."

"Masako!"

Not yet. I'm not ready to tell him, but I yield and give him all he desires.

"The King of Furs."

It's the first time I've seen Thousand Hands so confused.

"Perhaps the ravings of a madwoman. That *king* put them to the task. Do you believe there are peoples in the mountains, Kekkei?"

"I–I don't know. Tamikura's meat goes somewhere...I believe what is in front of me. I have yet to have had one present themselves to me."

"This King of Furs, he has a quarrel with them. His quarrel is killing our peoples, it would seem." I pause. "You have the means, see if you can verify this. Use the Sisters of Aibo if all else fails."

"You insult me. We do not need to pay such a high price for a name spoke in madness, my – lady. I'll get my people on it." He pauses, something washes over him, and he's distant. I ask him again and he flicks back, snapping out of the gaze, bringing his fingers to his chin.

"Do what is needed. Save your ego." He walks away engulfed in the cloud that seems to have fogged over his mind. "Wait! Kekkei, you realise what you were sworn into when you shed blood for the Dattori, don't you?"

"Yes."

"Blood is blood to the Dattori. If your servant dare challenge that again, she will pay her own. Make sure you all understand your oaths."

Swift he is in his wordless flight.

I'm neither sure whether my act solidifies my grip of things or crumbles it. Neither do I care. *The King of Furs.* The godsborne that I owe my life to fancies himself a ruler...by that ruler's hands our people die. By that ruler's hands we move on the Lord Council.

The wheel turns and I can no longer stop it. As long as the godlord's head rolls with it, my family finds peace.

Chapter 22

I n the days after my meeting with the madwoman, the camp around
Shuji-to grows, but not with my people.

Mako and Daichi – the final two pieces to the Samaki puzzle – make
camp around us. The word that Lord Shuji sent held nothing back, the picture
around me is sure of that. Our scouts tell us of two-score or more tents in
each new camp; they don't come as ambassadors towing a small retinue,
they come readied for war.

Nearest to ours, a picture that speaks and symbolises unity, the four
crossing hands of Daichi-to flaps in the wild winds that blow down from the
mountains. A bruised, thick-with-cloud, sky lessens the things that bother
me in this world by one. I don't see the cat's claws, but I know it is amongst
the frantic banners.

"A gathering the likes of which I've never seen."

I didn't notice his approach, but Oboro's silk tones don't surprise me, they
are a pleasant greeting; the only one there is to be had surrounded by snakes,
dogs, and vultures.

"Where you're from they don't bow," Ropi says, "backwards breed.
Wouldn't have left that island if not for us."

"In the shadow of the Demon Mountains, it is easy enough to pretend
there's nothing worth leaving for. The mountains are generous." The mouse
grimaces. Oboro continues as a smile snakes across his face. "Bowing, Ropi,
demands there be a superior present. My peoples saw no such being among
your landing party."

A cackle I can't control ripples from my mouth. Oh, Oboro, I couldn't have put the fool in her place better myself – I share his wry smile.

Ropi's fingers drum against the hilt of the daggers at her side, one longer than the other as if she wears a miniature set of my own sword and its sidearm; both Oboro and her dress as warriors today, trousers over their underrobes – Oboro wears a jacket akin to mine, reflecting his station, my oni crest on either side of his chest. The summit that calls requires our show of force. We cannot be a house divided by factions, today we are Dattori, four-score strong.

"You've a few hours, gather your thoughts, go swing your weapons at a strawman, or a real one if you must." I eye Ropi. "Do something to clear your mind. For you'll represent our great household amongst others who would rather it we stayed buried – these men believe they gained release from the Lord Council's grip when we stopped stoking the fire, today I will show them that the flames continued to ravage their lands."

"Yes, my lady." Ropi has grown ever obedient. Kekkei listened well, but the fast change of it sends a shiver down my spine.

"I wish I could see their confusion," Oboro says. "They cannot see Kasuki banners and I'm sure it lends itself to much speculation."

Patting his shoulder, he is immovable, I say, "You're a man of my own blood."

One eyebrow raises, as seemingly he struggles for an answer. He bows his head and replies, "My lady does herself dishonour, I am island folk, as the rat tells it. My blood runs too close to the waters that run off the mountains. I thank the Lady for her kindness, though." With that, he disappears.

My High Captain shares something of the same with my old; the image of the tree felled is forever etched into my soul – find peace, Masako, if for only today. You veer closer to the true enemy. Do not waste it in pettiness. Lord Shuji will ensure there is plenty to go around.

There's a knot in my chest that won't go. A voice in my head that will not quiet. An itch in my hand as it brushes over CrowKiller's hilt – stifled by the cold ice of the farmer's sword. Had I my way, I would have crept into Orika a shadow, severed the godlord's head while he slept and delivered myself to Metsuku already. I'm at war. And I'm the only participant. Every word I utter in act of politics, in the act of unity against the northern aggressors infuriates me; one thing can be said about lordly men, and it is that they waste countless hours around small tables with stiff cocks over the next lord's posturing. Patience is one of the virtues I do not possess, but this cannot be solved in blood. Not yet. I must again play Lord of the Hard Cods and convince these men to follow me. I cling to the nuance of the words the King of Furs spoke when he pushed my arseropes back into my body.

"You will not leave these lands without a leader, do not presume to think that you can do this is selfish haste, mortal. You will shatter the lands and rebuild them in my stead."

Patience, then, it will be. Now, I must turn my head to the summit, clear my thoughts, pray to the gods that I'm not found out. I'll be damned swinemuck if it's discovered Dattori are a patchwork of mercenaries, and whatever refuse Chisai couldn't hold.

* * *

Sweat. A musty aroma clings like mould to the soft, sweet caress of the incense in my nostrils; a lot of these men seem to have dusted off their fine dress robes for this very occasion, there's more than a handful of motheaten family crests dotted about the Shuji's Hall of Meetings. Back to the room that first entertained our family, a long, rectangular room that looks more like a jostling barn full of livestock now than it does the summit that will decide the fate of the Samaki lands.

Kekkei, Oboro and Ropi are pressed uncomfortably close to me, allowing for the Daichi to my left, the Mako to my right, headed by the Lord Shuji, flanked by three sons that look like they were cut from the same stone, each differing only by the years that weather them; I'm introduced to them one by one, it seems their father still has a mind to join our families in the way he flaunts his brood. The eldest, Ken Ichi, I know. Sada, the middle son, arrived with the Daichi; his long face is a picture of honour and discipline. His chest expands wider with every breath like a ground bird in courting a mate. Yoshi next, the youngest, brightest of the three. Against two rock-faced hillocks, he is the jade stone buried amongst them. Hidden in stone, its real beauty unearthed when the rock splits. I'm afraid for the youngest that the stone that surrounds him will never yield.

"It is pleasing that father's tutorage on the sword may finally yield results," he says with a wry grin. You may be too hasty to die, my young friend. The battle-readiness must have skipped a generation, for the Battle of Fenika was void of Shuji interference – father expected resistance, or a hand. Not abstention. Shuji-to only awakened for personal gain, he'd said. I fear this stares me in the face now, but I can do nothing about it. I'm at the mercy of those who eat the lion's scraps.

Incensed sticks line the middle of the table. A cold tea is served, mint and nettle, good for the soul. Mint sweeps through the mind as a gust of fresh air, served at all meetings of importance, before the posturing and politicking begins. The sting of the nettle there to sharpen. I only feel the cloud over me still, there is much too much to flush out. Out of courtesy, I've turned into a slave to the gods-damned stuff. Fried milk sweets are a step too far, watching most of these lords scoff their fill is dessert enough. I don't know what they symbolise, or if the host lord felt peckish.

I chew a hole in my cheek waiting for Lord Mako to finish his speech about this year's crop, the struggle he must sell his rice for a high price when he has to send it through Shuji land to do so. A proud idiot, both Mako Otsutan and his first son present are far too slight, however there's something in the way they move that screams pack horses, cultivate is an apt choice for their family.

"Please, honourable lord, these are words for your own advisors," Daichi Maki says, "it is on their heads that your negotiations with Shuji-to bear no fruit. But not here please, are you not intrigued by the head that met us above the gates?" The Lord of Daichi-to is the antithesis to everything Mako, stocky, his visage is strength. The lines on his face tell me that smile rarely fades. His younger to his right looks ready to draw the short blade concealed in his jacket; I want to test it.

I feel Kekkei nudge me, shaking off the fog.

All eyes glare back at me. I remember Jinto's wolves.

"Well?" Lord Daichi says. "The head. Surely, you've brought us here for its story? Lord Shuji's summons called for war. I rode here half-expecting to see this place razed, but I find an encampment of the recently unearthed Dattori clan, so I've learnt. It appears the Kasuki are too sickly, now, to respond."

"Father!"

"Oh Tetsuya, quiet. They know I jest. You know that, my lady. Don't you?"

"Quite. The honourable lord's humour is lost on me though, I fear mine was left in the grave."

Lord Daichi freezes. He convulses, erupting into bellowed laughter. "No, my lady. I think it is still there."

"Let us move on." Lord Shuji's voice splits through Daichi joy.

"I don't know, father," Yoshi says. "I rather like this...joviality. What, it's quite amusing that we gather here while the north cannibalises itself."

Ayato turns on his son, who feigns shock as he slips his hand over his mouth with a wink. The lord is a cunning old fox, he keeps his cards tucked away, intelligence perhaps the young lordling wasn't meant to share. I go to verbalise my annoyance, but the young Mako beats me to it, "Strife in the south? You mean to hide things from us?"

Lord Shuji sighs, rolling his head around his shoulders before sharing his scout's spoils. "The godlord has fallen ill to madness. I'd say too much of the poppy, but madmen do not steep themselves in such...dishonour. He hunted his own son."

"His heir?"

"No, Baraki."

"Baraki is Okami," Kekkei says. "My lord, excuse me for saying it, but I think your scout must have tasted the poppy themselves. His own guard?"

"It is true."

"Thank you, Lord Daichi." Ayato ignores Kekkei. "There was a clash between the Okami at Taras Crossing. Several sources confirm this: there's infighting among the godlord's closest. His son met the Tanuki and the Fox in battle.

"Gods be damned."

"We need to speak with him!" The words escape me in excitement before I know what I'm saying. If there's a hole in my enemy, I need to exploit it. But control yourself, Masako. These men know not why we're here yet.

"He's with Metsuku." Lord Mako says. "One Wolf against two? The outcome was written before it started."

"Not a swordsman like that, no." The younger Daichi speaks as though he's met the man, of which I doubt. Intriguing, what an intriguing boy. His tone so sure. "If the godlord produced one good thing, it is Baraki."

"I'll send men." Kekkei's words are attacked with daggers, a long stare from Lord Shuji – they must be itching to know of this brash stranger who sits beside me. "If there is any indication of changing tides in Basho, this is it. We need to monopolise on it." He turns to me. "My lord, please, tell these men why they were summoned."

I smirk. Not only because Ayato looks on in disdain at having been removed from the seat of control in this summit, but also knowing none of these men will be smiling when I'm done. "The head–" There's a different angle I can take than this. "Despite the pleas of my late lord father, you refused to listen. He was captured and killed. Murdered. As a result. Now, my lords, do you know how the Lord Council brought down our household?"

"Do. Not. Insult us, Masako," Lord Mako spits. "Provocation leads to a certain response; your lord father knew well who he refused to pay taxes to. Hmm, you sit here a girl trying to lecture us on...what? Well deserved–"

"Let me stop you there. Lord Mako." Lord Shuji's tone is clipped. "Are you not a lord of these outer lands?"

He displays some intellect, there was only a fool's answer to that question. So, I continue, "I'll answer for you. Taos. Our *government* sent foreign sorcerers to my estate, left it in partial ruins, slaughtered our family, captured Master and I. I dragged myself from Orika to avenge him, and what do I find here?" I gesture to the unfortunate servant at the back, she scuttles towards her lord, trips, righting herself in time. Praise to Lord Shuji for allowing me the dramatics of this as the servant opens her robes and rolls the tarred head of Ti across the table. Daichi Tetsuya stops the head before it rolls into the incense meant to cover its stench. Only he smirks, and all but the Shuji flap about in disgust. "This is Ti. Was, excuse me."

"Remove it." Lord Shuji has had enough. The same servant retches as she collects the head and quickly removes herself from the room. Brave. However, the obedience of a dog can sometimes be mistaken so.

"Lord Dattori."

"That woman was one of the Taosii sorcerers. Our government sent foreign curs to do their work."

"Why do you have the head?" Lord Daichi snaps. "Enough of the dramatics."

"She never left the south. Lord Mako." He jumps as I say his name, I doubt it surprise, the old ghost flinches because a woman addresses him at a table of equals, I'm sure. "You presume that the Dattori brought this on ourselves, so then tell me why the Kasuki were massacred by a Soshist? Did they, perhaps, provoke their own slaughter?"

"Impossible!" Lord Daichi's attention darts to the Shuji patriarch. His nod all but confirms the horror written across the room.

I recount my capture, the liberation of my estates. And spare none of the sickening detail as I retell the Kasuki's plight, the undead horde they became at the hands of the wicked Soshist; there are no questions during it, the room is ghost quiet only my own erratic heartbeat interrupts my tale. After I finish, the room still does not stir, household Mako flits between the hanging jaw of shock and the plain ignorance of disbelief. Daichi simmers, the laughter lines now taut in rumination.

"A-and, how is it you expect me to believe this?"

"Why would she lie?" Shuji Yoshi, the youngest, brightest son says.

"Lord, Yoshi," Shuji Sada the middle son corrects him. "You forget your manners." My mind is slowly defeated with the many imprints of our host lord dotted around the room, an amorous man indeed. I pray they're as good in battle as they are at sowing their seed.

"Lord Mako, on my blood, I was there, too!" Kekkei lurches forward, trembling fist pressed to the table. "By my honour, I vouch for Lord Dattori."

"Familial honour is shared, a Dattori cannot vouch for Dattori."

Kekkei tips his head in thought. Pausing for a second, he stands, pulling

217

open his robes. "The red of this sash is the blood that runs through our people. An unbroken circle of purity, I will not allow it to be traded or tainted, murdered or sold!"

My throat tightens, chest constricting. This is not it. Kekkei, you've sold us out. Before I move to stop this, there's a tight grip on the inside of my arm. I glance backwards and meet Oboro's eyes. Calming, reassuring, let it happen, they promise it will be okay.

Both Mako men scoff. Daichi still taking measure of what is going on.

"Mercenaries?" Lord Mako looks me dead in the eyes. "This is how low the Dattori stoop? Kekkei...Kekkei. The Yokusei had such a prisoner. Thousand Hands. Hmm, no. Legendary, were your island campaigns. I'm sure you know a thing or two about what makes that bastard government tick. Your coffers were lined with their gold. Fine. Fine." He mumbles to himself; I'm stunned but I don't mind it. His younger cuts in and he waves his hand at him. "My son here is rather fond of the Yokusei." That he mentions them first, he is a cunning man, two steps ahead already. "Not everyone in these wretched lands hates the North. Dattori Masako, you still wear the name of the Samaki. I know who must fall first, but I pray we can find a way to... soften that fall. For the Yokusei's part in this, I will seek...change. However, I cannot condone a war only of destruction."

"You're wrong, father!"

The lord turned on his son rage incarnate, his eyes a beast's. Hisao catches his father's swinging backhand before he connects, I cannot see what they share in that hushed moment before they turn back to the table. A house divided. Every young warrior has much to prove, especially a Samaki lordling. But he was a babe during much of the strife, and this time of upheaval is not one that will be fought on the bonds of trade.

"I only ask that you consider another way," Mako Hisao blurts out. A boy eager to move in on his father's seat. "Allow the northern lords to this table. The Yokusei could let us through, they are as honourable as any other family in Basho."

"We'll send them your head, first, then." The Daichi younger takes his turn now, wicked smirk flicked up to one corner of his mouth. His left hand worries the hidden blade still. "And save them the effort of coming all the way here to get it. The Yokusei bar the first path to the Lord Council. We will cut it away!"

"Tetsuya!"

Dipping his head, he whispers, *father.*

"The Daichi join in unity with your cause," Lord Daichi says. "We're being hunted, one by one. They'll destroy us down to the last if we let it. And I'd rather it be them than me."

"If there is another way, I will find it. But for now, the Mako, too."

"Well then–"

Lord Shuji is interrupted by a commotion out in the halls. *Make way, servant.* A familiar raucous tone but I can't quite place it until the door is almost thrown from its runners. The incense gives up. Blood and sweat notes are doubled with the two fully armoured warriors stood in the doorway, even with their swords sheathed. One straightens to his full, proud height, while the other skulks in the first's shadow. Fidgety, armed men and anxiety make for a bad mix. New blemishes mark their armour; they've not come alone nor has their entrance been peaceful. The haunting etching on their yellow-tinted plate and the ghostly screams of their masks mark them as warriors imprinted into my memory – the ghost guardians, the Yokusei. Caretakers of the vast lands that largely border Samaki territory.

The eldest Shuji tries to stand, but his father grabs him, taking his place. Even against armoured foe, Lord Shuji's presence matches their own. "Yokusei, how dare you tread my halls outfitted for battle! An insult that will be rectified at once."

The forward warrior unclips the mask, it falls away revealing the face which the masks seem modelled after, the Yokusei share a lot with their godsborne. Neither will I forget the face of the one who unlawfully captured me. He catches my glare, screws his face and says, "Prisoner."

"Look. At. Me. NOT HER! This is my household, my estates, my land. What business do you have here uninvited? Your *lord* has taken leave of his senses allowing this behaviour from one of his sired!"

The ssht of steel whispering out of the second Yokusei's scabbard cuts

219

silence into the room.

"Goro! No."

"They insult our lord father, Satoshi."

The heir to the Yokusen throne. Yokusei Satoshi. Never has a second son been in line for such a seat, this fool looks to waste that here. I itch for my sword, my fingers run over my unarmed side. "Is this what you've brought? A drawn blade in a meeting is an act of war I pray you've the confidence to backup," I say.

"This is a meeting of Bashoan lords, is it not?" No one answers the ghost. "I see no representation of the north. I come here for that purpose. With only Samaki lords here, this is tantamount to conspiracy. What other reason do the forgotten lords of the south meet in secret for, other than to conspire? I'm thankful to the gods *one* of you has sense to include us." His nod to the younger Mako disconcerts me. Followed by Lord Mako's fist as he turns on his own son – the rest of the room carries on as if it were nothing, imprinting it into memory for another time.

"Fine. What is it you bring to the table?"

"A warning. I see your encampment. Disband this...game at once. Come near the Yokusei borders with more than a handful of men and my lord will bring down his full might upon you."

"Do not dare threaten us!" Lord Daichi's words are met with steel.

As the masked Yokusei levels his blade at the thickset lord, he's made his last, and maybe first, mistake as a warrior. The younger Daichi's twitchy sword-hand needs no further encouragement, the concealed blade is lightning as it tears through clouds of incense and then flesh and bone. Goro's mask muffles his scream as his sword and hand fall to the floor.

The scene of violence unfolds before I blink again; Satoshi wheels on the young Daichi, his sword only half drawn as the Shuji brothers stop it in its flight, restraining the Yokusei heir. His fury is contained but it does not abate. An entrapped tiger does not relinquish its claws, does not forget the prey. When it is released, they remain sharp, nose trained on the prey that thought it escaped – I fear Tetsuya has incited a wrath that will not die, for it is the wrath of those who guard ghosts. At the same time, it brings me joy. The Yokusei heir has single-handedly destroyed any notion of the negotiation. And the Daichi heir has set it in stone, forged it in steel.

I grit my teeth as I look upon the invaders again. The struggle continues, a mess of bodies as each son tries his best to shield their lord. Each willing to die, but not considering such a fate awaits them from the conceited rag-tag assailants. Their arrogance pumps my heart a bit faster, my muscles clench tighter. Without invitation, the Yokusei are a picture of what is wrong with the Lord Council: serve and obey or die. Suppression. It is all the northern vassal lords know. Above even their own command sits the godlord, and the whip that they so fear; it is only us Samaki who can lead the change, only our outer lands that fall out of the reach of its lash. We will never surrender, it's not in our blood, it's why they hunt us. It is why we're here, why we must begin the hunt – I've had enough of what takes place before me. Shedding the weight of all I hold, relinquishing any care for what the others think, I stand. The dagger, CutFree, hidden at my waist, drawn in a blur. I slam it point down into the table, screaming for some semblance of order. Only Goro still squeals, he's allowed that. He'll never be a swordsman again.

"Yokusei, you play into the godlord's hands. It is not with care for your own family that you freely spill blood in Shuji-to, it cannot be," I say in a growl. "Had you any care for your family, or the traditions upheld in Basho, you'd have sent runners. There's a proper way to do this. Instead, you provoke war."

Satoshi tries to speak but can't wrestle his mouth free of Sada's chokehold. With a nod, he drops it. The room tenses as the Shuji back away, but the assailant sheaths his katana, and says, "War? This summit is of that design. Do not quickly forget the Lord Council's might."

"Boy." I pause, shaking off the shout that wells in my throat. "The outer lands have slept so long that the north is the only one who forgets – see the gathered might that'll surround your flight from this meeting, carry word back to Orika, for all I care. Be glad, too, that you're allowed to leave here unscathed, Satoshi."

"Lord Dattori."

"No, Lord Shuji, if you will allow the insult, I will not."

Satoshi's eyes narrow, shock and confusion turning into realisation. "You actually mean to, don't you? All of you have a touch of the madness." He searches the room, eyes falling over the Mako. "Lord Mako, long have our families traded. Much longer than this...cretin washed up in the Dattori's lap."

The lord ignores his plea, the weight of the meeting he interrupted washes over him in a pale, bloodless picture. More and more he resembles the ghost.

"Murakami. Fenika."

"BY YOUR OWN HAND." Satoshi screams as I mention their name. Ken Ichi needs no other excuse to turn on him with a ferocious backhand that ignores his armoured mask, sending him reeling.

"Murakami. Fenika. Kasuki. The Samaki know their losses and won't stand for it any longer. Satoshi, how long is it before the Taosii foreigners convince the godlord that Yokusei is no longer useful? No longer obedient enough?" I smirk. "How will the godlord take the news that it was your household that started this war?"

Clutching his cheek, he spews abuse, "Madness. This is all madness. Taos has no reign over Basho."

"Oh, but it does. I fear you will learn your lesson too late. Go, take your worthless brother with you. Carry word of war to your lord father. The old stone of Sama comes!"

Pointing sharply at me, an arrow nocked for flight, he says, "Demon! Do you think we do not know what you did at Orika? Do you think these men ignore rumour? We will come for you, demon spawn!" He draws his sword, dancing away from the Shuji, and shocks me for the first time – his sword is a viper as it lashes out, slashing his own blood across the throat. Goro doesn't have enough hands to stifle the flow and gurgles in horror. He writhes as the blood seeps from him, but his brother pays him no care. "Useless! You pay the price here, brother!" He turns on me for the last time. "I do not believe for a second that my brother's life will pay for the insult, Lord Shuji, nor that his insult provoked anything here. Know this, the Yokusei will meet you in the field. We will meet you with overwhelming force. Might? I see nothing but dead men here. Dead men fall under our jurisdiction to quash.

We needn't worry Orika. You will come to know us. You will come to regret turning a blind eye to *that* which courts you in the guise of a woman. Ghost, spirit, or demon, they toil in the senses. Never trust what is given freely!"

With that, he flees the scene of his brother's murder. Better that than a life struggling to relearn the sword in his offhand. I do not pay him any more mind.

"Pah." Lord Daichi breaks the silence. "Desperate idiot."

"Mhm."

"CLEAN THIS MESS!" Servants come running in at Ayato's order – the only evidence of their being here is the rage Satoshi leaves with. I hear him all the way to the gates. Each stomp marries with the pump of the blood in my ears. He goes unaccosted.

Lord Shuji is the embodiment of a storm out in the endless seas, its fury plain to the eye, but it is contained, distant. "They wrought this," he mumbles to himself, and then louder, "to have lost time and surprise in one meeting, the gods' want this rushed. So it will be. What side they favour remains unclear." Shuji Ayato picks up his cup, swilling the cooling tea around. A bit spills. He seems to regard it with disdain, sips, sighs. "My lords, make use of my estate tonight. Luxuries, I have unchecked. Wines, oils, baths, books. Drink in whatever you desire. In the morning, we prepare for war the histories haven't seen since the First Reckoning of the Mountains. No. We set out to make our own place in history." He raises the cup, spilling more. The others join him in toast.

I pluck out the knife from the table and raise it instead, stealing the host lord's thunder for the last time, I say, "Let the Wolves know we come. We hunt!"

The room is a cacophony of cheers save two.

Ayato's gaze has fixed on me, the Yokusei's words settle over him. Kekkei can't hide his silence.

PART 3

"Greed."
Yoku Jinto

Chapter 23

THIRTY YEARS AGO

"Loosen your body. Don't watch his blade, you'll see it slice through your gut before it's any good to you. Too soon. Masako, watch. Wait. The crow...your feet." The old bat lets out a sigh, what does *Master* think I can do with all his gibbering? "Bah, child. Patience, you'll make a useless swordswoman without."

The sword this. The sword that; I didn't ask him to pull me from my village, what would I care if I died there? I didn't even know mother, nor do I remember a father beyond this pain that is inflicted upon me every day.

Zaki smirks in front of me. I hate the boy, he's better at the sword, wants to be the lord's pet.

We start again at his order. I step in first, I've always been faster, and his guard is loose, not like mine. Why doesn't Master scold him? He shows himself up, we're not little children anymore, so why does he act like it? Dodging to the left, I swing my blade out, blocking his lazy overhead swing. He lets his arm swing with it. Not even going to try and close the opening? That brat. I'll teach him.

"Masako!" Master's shouts are followed by a drone that I block out. My heart thumps hard, my lips curl into the shouted growl I let out as I bring my blade back across his body. I want to hurt him. Drawn blood would wipe the smile. I hate it.

Zaki catches the swing in his off-hand, and my eyes widen with the realisation of being caught in the same trap – both his arms are blade-strong. The Mistress blesses him young. He pulls on the sword, and I can't stop myself now, the momentum already carrying me towards his knee which lashes out. It hits like a thunderclap forcing the air from me in a scream I can't hide. I drop to my knees, hiccupping as air won't come, my lungs burn, throb as it feels they'll never fill again. My face warms. I want to disappear. Then the air is back, it floods in and I'm renewed.

Master wags his fingers in the Brat's face a few steps away, but the pat on his back tells me that he's prouder of him than he's worried for me. *A warrior uses every opportunity, there's nothing below a victory, terrain, sun, hands, feet. All of it, as long as you live.* Cowards, then. Warriors are cowards? I want to look at a man as he feels my blade, not watch him trip on it. Blood, Zaki's blood. They laugh now. Spare nothing for the loser, damn him. I pick up my sword again, they don't see me. I grin. Is this what you meant? The battle is never over, aye, Master. Before they notice, I leap, swinging with both hands, I smash Zaki around the side of the head with the flat of the blade and watch him crumple in slow motion, blood flying. Little droplets arcing in the air, fleeing each way. I feel my heat beat in each of the little beads that fly. I'm whole.

I win.

Not that I'm greeted as such, I took the opportunity, like I'm taught. My enemy's back turned, but I'm met with eyebrows pushed together in pure rage. Master is shouting but I only hear a *thump, thump* still. A whine, my ears ring. Master's open-palmed strike sends me to the floor.

"Call the doctor!" Master shrieks at one of the servants who stand ready. The only audience who knows my prowess. "To the Healing Rooms with him now. No, don't attend her. I'll deal with it."

I shrug the servant off. My cheek throbs. Master is tomato red and stews in it as he waits for them both to carry Zaki, blood drips from his head as he goes, and I can only smirk as there won't be a grin painted across his face now. Teaches him.

"You!"

"He turned his back on the enemy."

"It was over, Masako. What is wrong with you?"

"*A warrior uses every opportunity.*"

He leans in and grabs me by the scruff of my robes, his breath stale and hot in my face. "Don't you dare. I know what you're taught. This isn't it! It was won." He lets go of me and paces; he's thinking, wondering what lesson there's to be taught here, what words of wisdom might steer me from this – there's always words to learn from. Always lessons. "I don't know what to do with you. Your...anger. I don't think it's patience. Gods, I don't. With a careful sword, and well-timed strikes, we'll make a fine warrior out of you. Yes, that's not the problem. It's anger, Masako."

"He grinned at me! He enjoyed it!"

"So, you try and kill a member of my household?" That look worries me. "Anger. Look at you, wild-eyed, it seethes in waves from you still. Try me, will you?"

I bite my tongue hard, screw my face with the effort. "NO!"

"Young, a babe when I found you. I hadn't thought the *water* would have taken hold, but I'm not so sure now."

I ask and ask and now he throws this at me here? I fight against my first urge; I would not get the jump on Master. Instead of going for my sword, I dig my fingernails into my leg. "T-tell me!" It comes out as a croak. "What am I? Why...why d-does it grip me so?"

"A day's ride into the Lower Fangs, there was a small hamlet."

"I know where I come from! Even if you've never said it, the servants kids do! *Demon Girl,* that's what they call me in Teachings. The mountain was my home, but what am I? Why did my village burn?"

"The water that runs from the mountains is as impure as the demons they house. It is the blood of the demons themselves. Drinking from it is enough to inherit their fury. Their rage against the gods who kept them there." He sucks in a breath, then continues. "Your people, they grew up drinking those waters. They razed villages far into Basho, so far it became a problem. I know little more than the insanity that met our force."

"Insanity?"

"The demon's own brood." He pulls up his sleeve, bringing his arm towards me. A scar, not blade born. Four deep rivets of gouged skin as if it had been raked. Not raked. "Bitten."

"I was most fortunate." His eyes glass over, he sees only memories now. "As we entered, there was no chance of negotiation. We were met by anger, violence only the gods could explain."

"Why wait until now?" I feel *it* rising in me and can't stop it. "I ask and ask, and you never say a word! You keep it from me! Why tell me now?"

He's in my face. "Because I never wanted you to be that!" He throws his arms around me and I let go, tears run down my face as I sob into his shoulder. "I wanted you to be you, Masako! Not the anger that cursed your village. I feared if you knew what you came from, you'd grow into it. There was hope that you were too young to be afflicted. I don't kill babies. You weren't the only one. But you were the lucky one! The Fenika brought another under their wing, the lord murdered it for a tantrum...said the anger had taken to it. I'll never forgive him." As he pulls away from me, his hands are heavy on my shoulders. I try not to meet his eyes, but they have a way at pulling me in. "I tell you now because I see it blooming in you, see the anger taking hold. You have this chance as the only surviving member of your clan to prove them wrong. Prove the Lord Council wrong, damn the Fenika. As soon as it speaks, you listen. I tell you now because I ask you to step away from it. Do not listen, you are more than it. Much more. A fine swordswoman, Zaki has none of your skill, only the strength of a man. You can overcome him. You will overcome anything. Trust me. But do not let your blood overwhelm everything you'd become."

"When I lean into it, I know. There's power in it, I feel strength. Master, strength beyond men."

"The blood in your veins, it is a curse. A weapon not to be used. I witnessed it, evil. The gods will deny it. I deny it. Do – not – use – it. We are Samaki. There will be no threat to follow, you know that. Only action." His eyes are watery, sad. "It will never come to that, will it? You are a good girl, Masako."

* * *

The soft way he said my name, eyes that bore into my soul, reach me even through the passage of memory and time; the incense I brought of Master's curls around the tent in oppressive wafts of sweet grasses, it presses over my shoulder as if he leaned in, stealing a gaze at what I pored over. It aches, hurts, the scent of it without him is empty – perhaps I'll set a fire with them all, burn away all that reminds me of him. What good are they to me now? Why is it only now that I realise, I was loved? I threw it all away for what... My chest tightens, cramps as if the feeling itself has claws. I felt love, it is why I wanted war – there's nothing you wouldn't do for those who love you so. I just wanted to make it right for my lord.

There are tears in my eyes as I turn the page; regret is a hand that strangles my sobs. Why is it only surrounded by enemies, false allies, and liars that find time to pore over my late lord's life, trapped between these pages in his own words? Master, you never were strong enough to follow up on that threat, not even when it cost you everything.

I'm sorry. But without this weapon, your honour will never be restored.

My breaths catch as I hesitate to turn the last page. What I see in front of me when I finally pluck up the courage hollows out my being. Chewing on my lip, my heart is crumpled as every *liar* I shouted at Master comes back to me. Bitter. He never lied, what is written here and what he told me match, word for word. He knew no more. And so, neither do I, save for one final note that catches my eye. *Bloodworkers*, he called them. Us. But finally, because he always had to play with the information in front of him, never settled for the given truth, he writes *Children of the Bane?* It is incomplete but my mind wanders to the story Kekkei told me of the gods that were chased by the demons and the *Bane* swords they carried. These stories of other *truths* converge on my path, and I don't know what to make of it.

Nonsense. It must be.

Why are men so bent on positing their own truths? There's no need to look between what is written, in the blank space there is only emptiness...the lord at Chisai suggested such foolish ventures, didn't she? All are afflicted. It is perhaps because they wish to scrub out the last author's name and etch their own into history.

I only wish to erase mine, and the rest of them with it.

Chapter 24

We ride along the outskirts of the great spirit forest, not daring to enter. Not my unit, anyway. The plan has gone awry. The young, reckless, with a lot to prove can be blamed. Gods-damned Daichi Tetsuya, he's thrust us into the grips of hell.

The clash that's started among the ghostly rise my unit skirts is carried in the winds; there's the clang only swords hoping for death make as they're repelled once more, looking for a way into the enemies' flesh.

A few days, a week, I don't know it all melds into one – as we Samaki lords brought our camp to the Shuji-Yokusei border, our night fell to the Ghosts. Spectres appeared amongst the tents. Horror written on their masks, the Yokusei hit hard and fast. Guerilla tactics, not meant for honourable battles. Grotesque, not the way to wage war, but meeting us in the open field is too far above them. Thugs and brigands murder people while they sleep. I had the measure of Satoshi in our first meeting, there was no problem showing his face when there were bars between us. Using your enemy's weakness is another thing entirely. Vassal lords are truly dogs, eager to please their master with no fear of how stooping into such filth looks to the rest of *honourable* Basho.

Not today, we were ready for their night brigade. Hushed, enveloped by the curtain of night, we waited far east of our camp, a score of us on horseback split into two units along the banks of the Winding Rush, the river takes a harsh turn north from the edge of Shuji lands, splitting the hills of the forest in two along a diagonal ridge into its heart. Mako information – their scouts are unrivalled, even amongst unfamiliar surroundings. For a breath, I feared

231

their relationship with the Yokusei ran deeper, their scouts got us around our enemy with too much ease. But Lord Mako is a sly, skilled tactician. The whole trap his idea, assuring me one must know the way to slide a blade into their *friends'* heart better than they know their enemies. For it is friends who wield the most damaging words. We were upon them as they slunk out, a mist from the trees, Tetsuya's group was to follow the 'Rush in a flanking manoeuvre along the sheer path cut into the northern brae; orders of chase, not engage. Flush the rats.

So as my unit races along the treeline, wind on our backs, the ghosts are spooked. I spot ten, maybe closer to a score of men makes for the treeline they emerged from. Spurring my horse on, not caring now for the thunderous cacophony our hooves make on the approach, we slice like a scythe across the edge of the wheat, missing the men by seconds. I signal behind, and we turn the horses, bringing them to heel. My gelding rears, thrashes in the excitement as I fight with the reins. The night is alive amongst the trees.

"We go in!"

"No, my lady!" Oboro shouts over the din. "The boy's unit is lost."

I snarl at the night, the eight with us are worth more than those idiots, but I balk at the idea of fleeing, Tetsuya is worth more than them all. Intriguing, born for the sword. Fearless. I see myself in him, so I give the order. And we're a sweeping wind past the treeline and into the treachery of the incline, spread out, careful, but swift. Roots and branches have a terrible hatred of horses, more lose their lives to those than battle. I follow the harsh cry of steel. The lantern at my back leads the way, for I don't rely on the struggling dawn light to see. A spectre unfolds from the shadows, aiming to unseat me with his spear but I see him. Drawing my blade, I hack his weapons shaft, splitting it in twain. There's a gurgled cry behind me as one of my men rides up on my flank. A shrieked whinny and I pull my reins up across my body, turning sharply. Another Yokusei pulls his blade from my man's leg, pinned to his horses' side with it. The horse is done. My chest tightens. I ride back, trampling the opportunist. And snaking back towards the clash, I cannot spare a thought for the soldier, his life is in the gods' hands.

I'm alone, my heart thumps with the hooves, cresting the hill it flattens out. Greens and yellow flash by as the first light breaks ahead – I close in on the rattle of plate, the shrieks and cries of lives gone. Until, I emerge along the river; my horse only just making the turn before we'd have plunged into the waters below. Other men emerge ahead somehow. We follow it deeper. Signs of the battle appear, Yokusei bodies line the bank, two, three, five. One of our horses is wheezing, slowly succumbing to the polearms that protrude from it. Blood leaks in pools from the wounds but I still race by. The rider is hacked to bits a ways on. A quick prayer is all I can offer. Turning away from the river as it rises up to meet the pass – snaking around a jut of rock that separates it from the opening we arrive at, the trees have died back to reveal a bloodbath awaits.

Tetsuya, three of his riders in tow, hits a handful of Yokusei; they're scattered in pockets amongst their own dead. My heart skips a beat. He's knocked from the saddle, I charge then. I pull up the reins and launch myself from the horse with its momentum, a hawk swooping it on its prey. I'm amongst them. The first falls to a thrust that takes him through the neck, others wheeling on me as he goes down. I parry once, step aside. Another man attacks wildly; it catches my arm, but I ignore it and push a third. He's torn at which of us to target so I slash across his throat, kicking his wrist to deny his final strike. My foot planted, I spin adding momentum to a two-handed strike that ignores another's unsure attack, costing him an arm.

More enemies fall, and I'm face to face with Tetsuya. His breaths are ragged, he wears blood but a lot of it isn't his own. He has a smirk for me, and raises his katana high, "The day is won!" he cries, despite turning on two more enemies as they approach in a sloppy formation that he quickly picks apart; separating the two, driving one back, he steps into a feint, allowing the poor idiot no room for his real strike. The Yokusei goes down run through. My heart lurches, I bolt towards him moments to late. The second assailant finds the opening too enticing. The young Daichi still worries his blade free from the abdomen it's stuck in, he doesn't have time to turn. Not enough time. A reaping strike from the enemy aims to take Tetsuya at the throat, who I swear glances sideways, smirk still painted on his face. He is a blur as he drops his katana and swings out his sidearm in an impossible backwards rising arc that punches through the man's throat. Blood sprays.

"Fuckin' close," Tetsuya says.

The boy's a demon of dexterity.

I grab the back of his head, pulling him in close. Forehead to forehead I scream, "Idiot! Don't engage...do not engage. Orders."

"Look," he gestures as he pulls away. The Yokusei are a scattered force around us. Before we can move to them, a couple more ghost warriors emerge into the opening; distress on their mask-less faces, Oboro and the remains of my unit emerge behind them, riding them down.

"Swordsmen of your own ilk are rare, young Daichi." I struggle not to smile. "The deaths of these men are not worth that. Your lord father would have me hanged."

"Ma'am." His bow saves me from the childish laugh; it's hard not to grow fond of a boy that continuously fights against the stream. Only a warrior of my own heart would so ruthlessly punish Goro the way he did at the summit. A rare breed. To nurture, to keep for my own. There's promise for the Daichi, beyond the plans that Shuji-to has for them.

Our horsemen make quick, bloody work of the remnants.

The Yokusei take their first loss.

* * *

"They're a vast family. Killing a few rats doesn't destroy the nest. This is no victory, if anything it is a waste. Four horses, half as many men. We have to be smart about this – we're of finite numbers in comparison to the north."

"–but of thicker blood."

"Hmm, quite, Lord Daichi," Mako Otsutan says, "and what do you suggest, mercenary?" They have Captains, but the Samaki lords trust only their own decisions over this table – each eager to make a name for themselves – the Shuji might have something to etch before night falls on this...skirmish.

"Strike the heart. Engage them with numbers they cannot deny, numbers they have to respond to. Give them the hells as they muster a response; their casualties will be many before they can. There, we will drive home the knife."

Lord Mako pauses, you can almost see the possibilities flickering in his eyes. "Yes, yes. But the terrain is a problem. Only my scouts know it well, and the hills are not something taught. Learned." He stops again. "There is surely a forward base, it is just not found. Yet. The forest moves, is alive with something. I fear they bring their numbers close, but the tracks...there isn't any."

"Godsborne," I say.

"Nonsense." Ayato is quick to interject when I speak. "They do not move at the whims of mortal men."

"*If* it is so," Kekkei starts, touching his fingers to his chin, "we grab what we can from under them first...the river at our backs would be advantageous. The river at theirs not so. Base or not, if they have one, it isn't this side of the river − they couldn't risk trapping themselves between our forces and the 'Rush. So, we make a grab for the land and then strike onwards all the same. We move our forces up before they've had a chance to gather themselves and finish them."

"Yes, yes. Excellent." Otsutan rubs his hands together. "It...could very well work."

Lord Shuji watches on, for once, a slight nod as Kekkei speaks. No one has more experience in warfare on unfamiliar ground than my advisor, but still, this seems wasteful. He smooths out the plans over the next hour. Mako mapmakers are diligent. It is a contradiction to his cause, not an oversight. He doesn't make those. Akate are the only mercenary group in Basho's history that remain, our country's foreign incursions are few and far between, only rising out of necessity to quieten small neighbouring islands − to bring seas around us to heel. Now the savages are taught, ruled, and subjugated, there is little need for them; yet, where the other groups died, Akate consumed, survived. Until he gave into the cat's curiosity. Burning his nose, he'd made himself a necessary resource for the Lord Council, even in peaceful times. I do stop and wonder whether this upheaval was a way of fanning the fire before it went out. A cause for the causeless. We, in equal measures, created this. Kekkei is calculating, he doesn't make oversights. Playing my desire for an end to this, he proposes annihilation. The Yokusei become one of his island quarries, and I am pacified, happy.

But no. I see through it. I see the twinkle of deceit in Lord Shuji's eyes, his silence is only bought by obedience; Kekkei is surely the voice of a plan devised by him and the lord, they only show the fin, we don't see the body of the shark.

I hold my tongue, agree. This is what I want. I will ride with their plan for I will get what I want out of it, but there is little the hawk won't see from the skies as long as it knows where to look.

We convene and I exit the Command Tent, a monster erected in the middle of our camp. I know exactly where I'm going as my feet carry me past a lot of the same. Lines and lines of tents resemble a field of upturned tulips, their white mud-spoiled. Entering a tent, I'm met with warmth. Expectation. "A pleasant evening, Lady Shuji."

"Goya, please. I've told you! I've never liked formalities, not especially from people of your...station, *my lord.*" She smirks, her eyes shift about the tent, she doesn't trust the secrecy of our meetings, nor do I. This is necessary for me to keep my head about me. I can't ask those in my inner circle to do this, so I pick the petals closest to the thorns, for they are most perfect. The Lady Shuji herself is a rare flower, her lips are poised, full with secrets. Her hair rolls over her like silk, black waves seemingly a part of the obsidian gown that is thrown over her. At the lord's side, she is the obedient Head Advisor that cowers from every harsh word of dismissal. Lord Shuji's advisors may only stroke his ego, only his voice wields merit. She plays it well. The lord may never note her worth – a spell-forged blade housed in a ceremonial sheath. "Do you know why the Outer Lords never marry within their own class, instead looking to hamlet and village elder's daughters?" She licks her lips as she finishes.

"Is this pertinent?"

Raising an eyebrow, she pouts at me, breaking into a smirk, "*Masako,*" she pauses. I've not recommended she address me as such, even after a handful of meetings. I let it slide. "Come, sit." She gestures to a silk cushion next to hers. A small, ornately carved table separates us; so, too, do our upbringings. "Better. Oh...so, we're to be grateful to them."

"What?" Ah, my mind is a fog within her presence, orange, and lavender scents swirl about the tent. "Yes. Grateful?"

"Why the *great* Samaki marry low. Come on, Masako, dear."

"Grateful for what, precisely?"

"Everything. While the northern lords marry for gain, the southern ensure their bloodline runs pure – they don't get caught with a cousin's cousin or even an aunt, like the north. Instead, marrying below their station keeps their brood clean, strong. And their blood pure, in most parts." I hear Kasuki in that sigh. "But that really isn't the most important reason."

"Lords do as they please. They always have, the south just has more honour about it."

"Not quite. I was a village elder's daughter, akin to common folk, to you. Still, a cut above them, worth marrying – perhaps. Thrust into a lordship, wealth beyond any measure of my birth, gems, riches. Enough warriors around me to call an army, and enough ladies for a harem – and that just in my personal retinue. I'm to be grateful for it all, and in that gratefulness comes untold obedience. No, the Samaki wives don't plot and play like the northern heiresses. *We are grateful.*"

She stops for a second, but there's more to this. Sipping on a fine glass of wine, plum, from its scent. Her eyes are bright, full of fire. I don't grow sick of her company; though, the games she plays better my cause, in the shadow of her lord. "And so, here is the grateful lady, courting another lord's company over her own."

"Now, now. The Dattori always were different." In the way we are selected, maybe that's what she means. Her eyes still, and she looks down, beyond this meeting here, into another time. "My birth village was razed by the Yokusei. My lord did nothing. *Gratefulness, I was gladdened that my lord saved me from such a fate.* Such obedience means that the lord is not challenged, the Shuji rule as the Shuji always have, the Daichi, the Mako and so on. They don't share their decisions and interests with another family."

"So, what does the Lord Shuji mean to do... he has other plans in mind, doesn't he?"

Goya claps, frantically, chucks back the rest of her wine, wiping her mouth. As she pours, she offers me a glass, but I decline, like every other night. "Quick, sharp. You pluck the information from me – I do not deliver my lord's business to anyone." She winks. "We share a goal, in some ways. The Yokusei must fall for a foothold against the Lord Council. I gather that much from my lord's snoring."

"Yokusei territory is a barrier to the rest of Basho. I say burn it, but even Samaki uphold the laws of the Guardian Forests. They must not be harmed."

Even Goya winces at that. "Correct, correct. Ayato proposes that you follow up a crushing defeat with an open table. He will allow Yokusei a seat amongst us, if they swear fealty to our cause."

I flush warm, hot, cold, at the news. Even if I suspected it, the truth is a dagger in the back. "Gods damn him." I'm wild with anger. My façade breaks. "Why tell me? A plot?"

She stands with me, gripping my chin. I mistake something else in her eyes for longing, she bites her lip, and my body settles on a flush of warmth. Beautiful, ripened with age. Her skin flawless. Resisting the urge to kiss her, before she speaks again, "Don't – move. Sit." I take two calm breaths, centring myself before I pull away and take my place again. Though I know she wants it, I'm no lord to take a mistress. Not a Samaki's lady. She sighs. "I remind you, the Yokusei razed my village. Killed my father. I will not allow my lord to negotiate with this scum. And, if he won't listen, you will. We can't let them ruin this, Masako. You ignited a fire in my lord like I never could, the *coward*." Her words are slurred now, alcohol is in control, the demon's tongue forces her words. "I will not let him waste it."

As I make for the entrance, she asks tomorrow? Can she see me again? It is only a maybe, now, to her disappointment. I run the risk of spoiling what she has given.

Chapter 25

Despite my night watch, hours after dark in the saddle; hours in meetings of strategy, rumour, *bonding*; swing upon swing of my katana, I sleep fitfully if at all. Days pass while we prepare, we are not so eager as to rush this now. The cry of the morn jay is not a welcome delight, I want to strangle each and every chirruping swine, but my muscles sigh at the thought. A body that whispers in creaks and nags in pain is one that wears the years of experience like an old, battered helm – it has survived many a fight, many a life, but worries whether its metal will fold, give in at the next battle.

Jinto's magic mended and soothed, but it could do nothing against age's ravaging. My blood pumps fierce, angrily. My mind will not rest. But it is with great difficulty that I brush off the morning sleep.

Hazy, I walk out into a morning much the same, a mist rolls off the hills, the breeze has a bite to it now. The Fall is here. Trees arcing high in the distance, the fields we stand on, both have lost the green vibrance. It is quiet, almost, the singsong of swordforms fills me with energy to go on – my stomach rumbles but it is never fed before my sword. I follow the whisper of youth to a clearing amongst the tents, our Training Grounds. Battles of war are not the place to train, that is where you show the enemy what you've mastered or die. Between those you survive, we make the mistakes so we might avoid them in the next battle.

Daichi Tetsuya huffs, pants, and dances around an immobile, straw enemy. There are lines of them. Yet, only he is here. It's why I nurture him, why he could not be lost, only those up with the dawn birds will make excellent warriors. We have many great warriors in our forces, but none that cut the air so fine and quick it sings sharp, melodic like his forms do – given my years, his is a blade that would reach the Okami – they're perfect.

Above us the heavens are glum and grey, but I'm met with a wry grin that brightens that; Jinto would like him, but Kekkei fears the wrath of the Shuji for the wildboy represents the very heretics that move them. It would be remiss of Ayato to distinguish one magic from the other. One devil from its mate. Shaking my head, I rub my eyes. I hack and spit on the floor – ridding my mind's mouth of this useless longing – why should I care whether Jinto and Tetsuya would get along, let alone what the Greed Shamans are doing past protecting my estate from likely besiegement. If they send messages, Thousand Hands doesn't tell me. My runners report to him first because that is their duty, but it irks me some. So does the young Daichi's unmoving smile. That fucking smile. I want to wipe it from his face just once, teach the boy some humility.

"Let's go." Tetsuya speaks first, with none of the formality. Indeed, this will be a good lesson.

"I'm sure you have siblings, boy, spar with someone you can handle."

"Steel then." He nods at CrowKiller, not knowing that's the only way we Dattori would train. "We're both wearin' ours."

"Drawing the blood of a commander-and-heir to an ally family will do nothing for morale, I assure you."

"Don't bleed then."

"Brat. To first blood." Because it's your last on the field. "If we're going to do it this way, we'll drill forms. You've got defence first." It's the only way I can guarantee I won't lean into the fight, get carried away. At least it gives him a heads up.

At the same time, I dash a couple of steps to meet him and draw in an upward arc from the sheath – there's a speed only the first drawn slash is capable of. Some warriors swear by the Way of the Draw, but it's a trifle too risky sheathing mid-battle. Ibano the Draw fell with its usefulness in the last age. I doubt Tetsuya would have fought it before.

He half draws his katana across his body, jumping backwards at the same time, he uses the momentum of my strike to throw himself. Smart. A switched grip is unconventional – but I do so, and bring my blade at the top of its swing down. The back of the blade is a scythe that'll reap its reward. With an overextended arm, he has no strength to muster a block – first blood is mine so soon. Tetsuya steals that from me. Instead of blocking, he brings the hilt of the blade towards my face. A bludgeon, forcing me to retreat.

I chuckle. A prodigy, perhaps. Only one at peace with their sword is capable of overruling the body's automatic need to defend.

"Switch," I say, and it's his time to come for me.

He twirls his sword in one hand, rolling his shoulders – cockiness oozes from him. His grey robes darkened in patches; the bottom frayed, worn in already by the effort he's exuded. I wonder if he even slept.

We go through two more turns, trading flurries of slashes. It's a long time since I've had a chance to go through all of my forms, some of them wake groggily from a long rest within my body. There's a few my family hold close. A few only those in death remember.

One final time, when the boy thinks he has the measure of me, I show him the distance that lies between us. A reminder that he's not to fall too deep into his own arrogance until he stands atop a pile of the numberless corpses of the Lord Council's warriors with me.

"Go."

Again, I move quickly, trying to enter his guard. He is good at back-pedalling and steers me away. Before leaning into his steps, I break out and spin against his lead and explode from it in a two-handed slash. He's caught against the momentum of the battle, but drops slightly, bouncing in an angle upwards. Elbow catching the bottom-side of my blade, he sends it skyward. I'm open. He extends from the elbow, in the hope to slash across me. *Drills*, I said. Drills! He's too eager for the win, I see too much of what I am in him. For his lack in patience, I show him why the Dattori warriors were a feared breed, the katana is only an instrument – at the top of my swing I let go of CrowKiller, she somersaults above me.

I drop, like a stone, my unexpected palm diverts his slash towards my face but I'm too quick, already out of the way. Driving forward with my shoulder,

I send him off-balance. A punch to his face sets me spinning the right way. Honed are his skills as it doesn't connect the way I want it to. His feet shuffle, his steps are flawless. Daichi breeding is strong, Daichi training is better. I let my body swing round; my sword-arm lashes out to CrowKiller. Pure spell-forged blade doesn't cut the wind. It is the wind. Everything is so slow now. There's something about being this close to the blade that brings out a peace within me. This is but a dance, one where I lead the steps. My final slash is not meant to kill, just teach. CrowKiller licks out, tasting the skin of his cheek, but is stopped dead. Buffeted by his off-hand arm, his blade seems to have materialised into a cross-block.

I only meant to leave him with a scar, but I've barely pricked him. A small bead of blood wells on his cheek and there are all but heavy, carefully measured breaths between us; we sound like a couple of work mules before we burst into laughter.

"Woah." He pants, bowing deep. "I'm done, *my lord*. That would've been permanent, you know!" He wipes his hand across his cheek, smudging the blood on his face. He looks at his bloodied fingers once, the smile falters, but remains strong when he meets my eyes. I have failed. "Gods." Bowing again, he says, "Thank you, I needed that." And turns and walks off into the camp.

Thank – you. I lift my hand up to my face, it trembles. I breathe a couple deeper breaths, purging myself of the smell of his blood. Anymore and it might have been dangerous. What is wrong with me? This blood fuelled anger rises too quickly now.

I look back to the empty space Tetsuya left as he walked away; he is a true marvel. A prodigy, indeed. To walk away having blocked me at my best, even if it was not a killer's blow. I let it creep in, hope. There's that foolish thought this won't have to end in my death...that the bonds I forge here are a steel that will hold until the end – could possibly hold my cause down until Master's honour is restored. I...want to live in that world.

"My lady." I cringe. A messenger awaits. "If you will, come with me. The other lords say you are to lead the morn raid?"

"Ah. Yes." I'll be the spearhead the Yokusei feel in their side. We make a push, today the ghost-fuckers lose part of their precious forest. A campaign can go long on rations, soldiers can hunt far and wide – pillage if necessary – but can go days, if that, without water. Unsanitary conditions have been the cutthroat of many a campaign. Not ours.

Kekkei dazzles the other lords with notions of a sweeping, absolute victory. A simple capture, and one violent push. He knows differently though, we plan this attack together, both knowing this is better fought in pieces; a swift push tramples those opportunities. We plan to collect those pieces, building foundations that'll last the length of our campaign. Only Lord Daichi pays close attention to our plans – with his backing we undermine the rest. Though, I'm sure Kekkei doesn't keep this from Ayato's ears, but it is at his wife's behest that I do this. I must be careful to make permanent changes.

* * *

"We need their river! We need the fresh waters of the 'Rush! We will take them!" I face the six-and-thirty mounted beyond me; Daichi, Mako, Shuji, this is a mixed bunch, experienced bunch – we need those amongst the trees, they're unforgiving – the lives we lost before owe mostly to terrain, know-how within it. Three units to liberate the Ghost's Arrowhead, as we've named the piece of land we want to possess. It makes it all the more prize-worthy.

In the distance on my left, Kekkei will strike past the river. Oboro, Ropi, and a unit named the Hands of Akate at his side. I allow him that. To the other, Shuji Ken Ichi takes his debut command, a flanking manoeuvre in mind.

"The Arrow-Head will be ours! With it, we will drive into the heart of the Yokusci! DO NOT GIVE THEM AN INCH. WE ARE THE STEEL AND STONE OF THE SAMAKI!" A roar ripples through my men; I wheel around, my plate chattering – etched in our family black in green, I wear it not with pride over the clan who fell at my blade, but as testament to why I still fight. The pike unfamiliar, heavy in my hand, but I raise it high; my bannermen gives the signal; I know both sides have finished a similar speech as the rallying cries erupt around me, and charge across the field. Steel and stone roaring on my heel. The sun rises behind us. The dragons above move it to our favour. I'm certain the gods watch, for it is their land that is about to change.

Our forces split and stream along the treeline, only my unit mounts the rise. My heart thuds at a thousand beats per second – our night scouts said the trees are abuzz with movement, spectres in droves hide amongst them. I say a silent prayer to Meganako and the Mistress.

The trees flash by. Ghost-light sparks up ahead, their aquamarine flicker is scattered amongst the forest in uncountable numbers, each a deathless gaze already upon us.

"GODSBORNE!" I – was – right. Fools!

A cry erupts somewhere beside me, and I remember the undead who tried to defile me at the start of this journey, a cold shiver runs down my spine. But I burn it away, stir up the fire within, spur on my horse as it hits a pocket of them, my pike left skewering three into the earth. Though, they writhe on. I draw CrowKiller and pull on the reins, my horse is built for war. He whirls on them stamping as I slash. We split along a ridge. There's screams of the living and moans of the godsborne around me. Again, I dig my heels in and break through, charging to the aid of my men. Two are surrounded but I punch a hole in the undead but, unlike the Kasuki, there's no stopping these. Bit by bit, they reform – Kekkei and Ken Ichi need to hurry, the godsborne will surely retreat with their Guardians. There's a sorcerous tang in the air that says magic orders them. Though, I don't know of it – I draw my blade across my palm, lathering her in my blood. *Heavens, gods, forgive me. The spirits broken here will be replenished, repaid in tenfold by the time I finish.*

I shout orders and break away with the two soldiers at my back, the path I carve through this time stays dead. My blood knows only destruction.

Despite the odds, we lose few, and regroup on the crest.

Push after push, we're met with a resistance we cannot overcome. With each ragged breath, we survive, we are a slow spear that pushes its way into the body, searching for the heart – every half a dozen yards are won by the slow, powerful tread of our horses and the sweat of my men. Our flank is clear, the godsborne mean to stop our advance, though the rotted teeth and brittle fingers are more a tiresome annoyance than a danger; but there's method to it. If only the oni could be bound in such a way. The Yokusei will go to the hells for this. There's a break in the herd which two of my rider's mistake for a chance, they ride into the trap; a whistle splits through the groan, an arrow takes one in the throat and another in the side. They're unseated – the horses spook, one of them charges my way. A clatter, I'm thrown to the floor.

My warhorse joins their flight.

Yokusei riders burst through the brush, tearing into the ranks of the godsborne. A deathly horn sounds, like nails on tile. The godsborne break, corpses dropping as the spirits flee. The ghost-light disappearing from each as they fall; their retreat is called.

More enemy riders hit our own. Swords clang against plate around me. I dash to a tree. A rider thunders by. Diving sideways, I miss being crushed by inches. A Yokusei falls from his horse as it hits the earth, where seconds ago, I stood. I run him through. A whistle pricks my ears and I go to my knees. An arrow rips the air above me. Two more – a shrieked whinny and the thud of the tip biting into bark. Legs pumping, the arrow's path leads me back to the archers, not ready as I emerge from the brush. I'm a child at war, so a chop across the first's bow for effect, rendering it useless, wheeling on the second; he brings up his bow and looses an arrow at point blank range, but I'm already moving, already chopping the projectile as it leaves the hemp string. The loosened half of the arrow spins violently, skittering off my plate. I catch his hidden thrust at the bottom of my blade. The guard holding it steady. A sweeping slash takes him at the throat and the first, who scrambles in a panic for anything to end me with, across the face.

I clamber over the bodies, hooves beat around me, men wail, and horses cry in a way they shouldn't. Chest tightening as another rider whips up dust and mud in its wake. Another barely missing me as they chase past. I don't even recognise friend or foe now, it's a blur. Further on there's death. Both sides are strewn in blood and guts; wrapped around trees and trampled into the earth. A struggle, one warrior straddles another while she tries to force her blade home, into the other's face. Dashing to her, I recognise that *unity* marks her Daichi plate, and sever the resisting Yokusei's hand leaving her free to do what she must.

Picking her up, we limp in a direction, I follow the sound of the river. She's pale. Her weight doubles, I want to ask her about herself, but an arrow takes her through the chest; I dive behind a tree but another finds the flesh of my shoulder – my grip loosens on my blade. *Curse the gods.* I rip the arrow out and lick the head, an explosion ricochets throughout my body. Pain numbs. Grip tightens. Muscles harden. Senses acute. Every breath, every groan, slash, and movement threaten to overwhelm my exhausted soul. I'm wrong to do this here, the coppery smell of blood is heavy in the air, droplets everywhere like a bloody rain. Trembling. A whisper, a promise of more. Power pulses through every muscle fibre; it's a well tapped, unchecked. A waterspout, a shake in the earth, a seaborne wind, the thunder. I turn, a beast in full plate. The oni snarls still on my kabuto helm. Hooves rage around me, bursting into view – a stampede that materialises like the spirits – riders' ghost-helmed. I've no time to dodge, so I brace. Power.

I am power.

They offer me death. Ride me down like a dog? No. I offer something different. The horse is upon me. Slowed, its eyes wild, muscles rippling, I meet its pure, animal strength with hatred, frenzy, anger enough to turn its charge away. Its knees buckle against my terrible swipe – the paw of a lion. The other rider passes me. I don't see what is written on the man's face as he's thrown from the saddle, but I imagine horror as CrowKiller punches through plate. Before the other rider can turn, I throw my blade, send it spinning. It cleaves death along the horse's back and tears through the rider before lodging in the plate. Control. CONTROL IT! Get a hold of yourself, Masako. *Never lean into the anger, please, steer away.* Master's voice is the only bit of sanity I hang onto as I retrieve my beloved katana.

We're broken, my forces again in disarray, the Yokusei formidable in these trees. Against the 'Rush, I wonder whether they've mustered the same strength against our other two units, was it foolish of me to leave such a task to an untested warrior and a merc? Men have too much to prove, it always leads to avoidable death.

* * *

My losses are grave, at least ten dead, and as many uncounted for – my blood fever simmers, abates as the seconds draw on. Tiredness, so deep and heavy it's like the veil of death, leaks into my muscles. I struggle to stay on the saddle, thank the gods my horse didn't go far, that he is unscathed; the creature is a being cut from my own cloth as it nips and shrieks at my surrounding soldiers. A dozen of us cross the river at a shallow point, the horse managing to wade through. We rest, soldiers splash, drinking in the crystalline prize for their efforts. I welcome the revelry. Morale is high. I pop the top off my water gourd and drink deep in celebration, stashing it back in my robes when I'm done. We cross the river without resistance, only Yokusei bodies litter the banks. Kekkei's led a massacre, but I don't see him. We follow the marks of their crossing, the distant din is unsettling, they've no reason to overextend themselves. Men and pride. Have Ken Ichi and Akate pushed too far?

Mako scouts lead us on, following hoof marks in the hundreds, there's no doubting they pushed on – why, Kekkei? Is this just Shuji ambition?

The undergrowth thickens, but we still have their trail. A damp clings tightly to me, a sweat ever closer. The forest is lush here, not knowing the seasons change. I stop to consider my next action, the mesh of trees now stifling as we go on only seeing signs of our allies. My plate is heavy, so I unbuckle my cuirass, saddle it with my helm. I knead my shoulder with my hand, pain scatters away from each press like hot needles. A flesh wound, the muscle is punctured but it'll heal fine. My grip is weakened, though, I won't be able to fight. Poison tipped. My blood will burn it up before long. Retreat to our encampment, my mind screams sensibilities but I also know that if the other two units are lost, so is our campaign. So, I ready myself for the idiotic order.

"WE PUSH ON! COMMANDER GENARO'S UNIT HAS PAVED THE PATH TO VICTORY – LET THE SURROUNDING BODIES OF OUR ENEMY KNOW

THEY'VE TASTED DEFEAT!"

We plunge into unknown territory. I'm uneasy. The forest watches us.

My soldiers, too, have cast away their plate. We're in no fit state to fight, but ours might be the push that tips whatever lurks ahead; the air is smoky, ashy tasting – I'm surprised the Mako notice it before me. A worrisome fatigue that has me. We push until that damned, elusive forward base comes into view.

Kekkei's unit have broken the enemy; a Yokusei forward base smokes, burns as flames creep up the wooden curtain wall. Still horsed, the Akate scream like the hells, encircling the wooden fort. A handful of my missing unit ride with them. Tiles hiss, break. The flower wilts, as the centre building catches. The air cools around me, suddenly crisp like the winter's breath as the flames flicker, and dulls, turning raging tongues into embers. The Chill of the Ghosts. It doesn't matter though; we're not even needed as Akate guts the base.

Kekkei pulls his horse up beside me, and says, "They're done, Masako. We've forced their hand; a single family cannot muster many more men than have been lost today. We win! Our first victory!" His smile stuns me, such nonchalance against a crime aimed at my command. The mercenary's initiative is the same as the fool's, but I hide it. "So it seems," I say. Something nags at me, something wrong.

"Why'd you not bring the Shuji boy and his unit? They tire of all that galloping they did?"

"What?!"

"Lighten up, I jest. It's lucky there wasn't a larger force, his tardiness would have–"

"Not that, you fool!" My heart races. "They're not with you!"

"I don't."

"Kekkei, this is folly. The Shuji boy – that noise – they've pushed on too far. He's missed the river."

To his credit, Thousand Hands is instantaneous in his orders. Not a minute is spared before we're hammering, again, through the undergrowth, spurring horse and soldier beyond exhaustion. An hour feels like an eternity as we veer northwest, hoping to pick up trail of the Shuji-led group. The scouts finally catch it. Metsuku has a hand here, the group of young lordlings were to be out of harm's reach, lying in wait for the enemy as we broke them. The immovable stones of the Shuji, Ken Ichi, Sada, and young Yoshi – Tetsuya, my heart weeps, the Mako boy. Curse them. Youth is foolhardy.

The forward group, led by Ropi rides back into view with something horrible written on their faces. They lead us to a filth that disgusts me, a reckoning awaits the men that did this.

"Butchered. All of them."

"Look!" Kekkei grabs me, shakes me violently. "It's only horses, they still may live." Even to me, who has led such massacres, the way they're lined up. Throats hacked indiscriminately, left to bleed out – it is cold, ruthless. Not even I can discern the coppery, sweet smell of blood from the suffering that happened here. There's evil deeply embedded into men who do this to steeds, to animals who wish no death on anyone.

We press on. Spirits low.

Ropi says they've been herded. Double their numbers lead them on horseback. Fresh, this was done not an hour before. I hear nothing else; my senses are numbed to uselessness. I cannot carry the weight my curse has piled on me.

Oboro offers me a drink. SavedHide is little comfort now.

* * *

"BACK! STAY BACK!" Satoshi bellows, his ghost mask flapping from his helm. He cannot hide his insipid grin, pale skin brightens. Glee has him. Beyond their line, I see the Shuji boys, blackened with bruises. The Yokusei waste no time.

I don't see Tetsuya. Each thump of my heart is slow, felt – eyes darting around – where is that idiot? My injury pulses, arm numbing still. I cannot repay Lady Shuji with the heads of her boys.

"What is this?"

"This is your reckoning. This is your might undone, whore."

"Release them. Your numbers are not enough to survive this." They're no more than two score strong against our forces with ten on them. "Let. Them. Go!"

"*Masako!*" Kekkei's whisper has a sharp edge. "What are your terms? Lay them out, Yokusei."

He cackles. The men around him add echoes to the snicker. "Terms? I told you what'd happen if you stepped foot on our land – now you push, you grab, you take. So, too, will I take." Throwing a hand into the air, he cries, "BRING THEM FORWARD!"

On the edge of what I can see, a shadow slinks between the trees, horse-shaped; Tetsuya and horse are a wild dog that stalks its prey. They are one. A perfect blend of surprise.

Kekkei shifts, I turn to see his eyes widen but the Yokusei are too bent on their performance to notice. The fox that slips the chicken pen will be back again. I try to signal to him but I can't risk anything that would give his position, nor does he take notice. Those around me see him now, shifting, uneasy. The call for charge trembles on my lips. It's the only way I would save him from the mess that is about to unfold at his hands. But I can't, for there are many lives that hang in this balance.

All at once, this standoff erodes into chaos; Tetsuya rushes in to claim the arm of the first soldier he meets, his horse is a bludgeon that breaks their formation, scattering them as they lose seconds in the surprise.

"NOW!" Kekkei's scream is behind me as I've not waited for it. Oboro at my side, we crash into their ranks. A wave of muscle and steel. Deep in a jostle of bodies, I slash, doing what I can with my loose grip. Head-butting riders as they get close. My eyes searching for a way through.

Ken Ichi momentarily visible as he pulls a rider from their horse by their pike. Our ranks encircle theirs. This is not a battle they'll win.

My arm drops, and Oboro and Ropi are between me before I pay for it, cutting their way through.

Sword and sword rip into men and women as this gathering cannibalises itself. Men fall in droves. My horse buckles finally and we're forced into a skirmish. Those Yokusei caught in the initial charge, as we did, fight us tooth and nail. Ropi's hands are a blur as she looses arrow after arrow, wielding it deftly at any range, crushing their numbers. Oboro whirls his jewelled blades next to me. Not one of the Yokusei who've stepped up can match him. I'm surrounded in a protective throng as we push through.

I glance back, Kekkei has split the remainders of our mounted forces, meeting theirs who do the same. Somehow, gods, I don't know how but I'm thankful; the Shuji are back-to-back, along with Mako Hisao in a formation of pikes that keeps several horsemen occupied. More fall. Dozens still hack and slash at each other.

Tetsuya is a fool.

I rush forward and batter into a man, taking him to the floor. My knife is out and in his eye. Oboro pulls me up. Ropi is with us.

We're not going to reach them.

Satoshi is on his feet. Sword spinning, as he cries, shouting at his men to stay back. He will take Tetsuya alone – "COWARD COME!"

"SAMAKI!" Tetsuya chants. He's the surging wind, undeniable, he works his way into gaps other warriors wouldn't see. He's the fire, eating away at Satoshi. My mind eases, the Yokusei end here.

I'm reminded then, of the brutality of the north. Of the men who covet gold over honour, of the men that dragged my master from his home, spilling his blood into unfamiliar soil.

Tetsuya parries, sees the feint, and shuts Satoshi down. His response bites deep into the Yokusei's side.

The cry of the Ghost Leader is not that of anguish. It's one of action.

I force all my weight into a jab that brings me again to the floor, covered in another's blood. I scramble but can't get to my knees in time.

There was never enough time. The gods steal it from the Daichi heir; Tetsuya has a second to pull out of his slash before he sees the rider. A second for it to register that the Yokusei has defiled the sanctity of the duel he called.

The rider's kabuto is horned like a demon. The mask is passive, unchanging as he rides up on a warrior with so much promise, so much skill, one day he would pull these lands down with me. His white gelding doesn't register the death it sows. It rides on, as it's bid.

In that second, Tetsuya whirls on the rider in violence, hacking through his leg, and into the horse's flank as his own head flies with the Blades of Metsuku. Tetsuya's body drops with my heart, which dives into a pit.

Ropi's arrow takes the rider through the mask's eye in an impossible shot. Impossibly late...

...The Yokusei break and flee.

When they're gone, I go to him. His blood seeps into this strange, unfamiliar land and I weep – the others give me space, they know what I invested in him. Blood. There's something I can do with blood, something... I don't know. Can I help? In my foolishness, I pop open my empty gourd, filling it with his blood. It is wrong. The gods will have me for it, but Tetsuya must live on. Like the farmer, there has to be more.

Chapter 26

My warriors are sick – the waters we won spread plague. These northern families are a vicious, rabid dog – just when you don't think they can do you any more damage, it takes you by the throat. Put it down, I say. Put the fucking thing down.

And so I will.

In their deviousness, the Yokusei filled the 'Rush with the corrupted bodies their godsborne spirits dumped. While we harried their main force, another of theirs slipped by sowing a slow death. It was hours before we fished the rotting bodies out, days before I dare drink of their waters. Too late for those who drank first, fought hour by hour, pushing with everything their life was worth, fighting honourably with everything they had alongside their comrades. Only to be overcome by the most cowardly of methods. Our doctors can't touch it. The insipid bile that seeps from their every orifice is noxious, a hint of the ghost-light flickers in their vacant gazes; the ramifications of this leave a pit where my heart is. Can the gods really be so cruel?

Its spread can be contained, though, I can't risk the nurses, servants, and doctors. They are the spokes to my wheel. There's nothing else for it, there's no doubt I owe them more than this, but I have no other option.

I give the order to purge the plague. The servants bring porridge to my temporary quarters. I haven't left them for the last day – the other lords continue their plot without me. I don't have the stomach for it, greater commanders have lost more and continued. The one who came first, Sama of the Everlasting Dirge conquered Old Nodo, where the Bashoan capital lay before the Warrior Age; taken from the Savage Kindred with less than a third of his force. It is that third we're all forged from, we don't know how to bend, to flee to the islands as did the savages. We live in victory or break and die. I don't have the luxury Sama did, they say Izenta themself raked plain-land into field, sowed seed, brought about the Heaven's Harvest that allowed them to besiege Old Nodo for a year. I have weeks, maybe months, before the Lord Council recognises our threat, mustering a force that would dwarf ours. I need the godlord's head on a pike that marks my grave by then.

We Samaki are the closest to Sama's Third, Old Nodo was seated in the south. Our blood runs close enough to it that we haven't been watered down by pomp and entitlement. Samaki have the tenacity, the rage, and the skill that would usurp Orika, but we don't have the numbers.

A plague? I will bring them a curse. The ghost-fucks will know me.

Satoshi and his retinue escaped our hands, the riders too fatigued to give chase. We don't know the Forest of Souls as they do – not even with Mako assistance. It would've been folly.

I'm inconsolable, heavy with sadness, the black dog of despair has me in its maw. Leaving my tent means facing a dawn that doesn't ring with the young Daichi's blade. Kekkei says I knew him for a moment, that my sorrow is unfounded, but I dare anyone to know the Way of the Sword as I do and not anguish over the potential the world has lost in Tetsuya.

They come, Oboro and Ropi, for it is time. I don't know how many hours have passed since my last thought, but I gather them now. Donning my finery, a silk kimono, still I wear my swords. The maid worries over my face, plasters me in powder and ink dress paint, but I'm no Painted whore. I lash out. Harder than I wanted. She clatters over my bed roll. I apologise. I'm not in my right mind, hanging by a thread. She tells me it's her fault. Of course it is, you were born to take fault for my caste.

Outside, the dragons hide themselves, they wrap the skies in plumes of cloud that is melancholic as it engulfs them like a new bruise. The camp is a buzz, it doesn't stop for one, it moves as runners, nurses, and servants wind like snakes through the sea of tents ahead. The land dips before me so I see it all – take stock of what I've wrought. The forest sits hunched beyond.

Charred, rancid notes hang in the air, an unwanted reminder of the weight my last orders carry.

We arrive. Everyone is here. Faces I don't recognise but I know by reputation all the same; Lord Daichi is the deepest lake. A void black depth unreachable now. His next steps hidden by grief. I will go to him soon. At his side, the triplets: three women of differing beauty, that they shared the same womb is only noticeable by the steeled way they hold themselves. Two model themselves in the quaint, quiet yet comely way of the northern ladies; their silks are bright, sophisticated – a continuous waterfall rippling over them as they sway. Haru and Aimi. The third, Hira, has her hair cropped in a warrior fashion, knotted at the top. She too is beautiful, but it's hidden behind the stoic, hardness only a true Samaki woman holds. Tetsuya's katana trembles in her grip. I'll be sure to test the worthiness of her to that blade, less I take it for myself. Lord Shuji, Sada, and Yoshi are present, the latter two are still painted in the injuries the petty Yokusei saw more important to inflict than fleeing. For that, I thank them. Ken Ichi cannot be found. Akiko, their daughter, takes his place. Her eyes are sharp like her mother's. Camp rumour has it that Ken Ichi has taken a vow of silence until his next command, he punishes himself from the tragedy of his first.

This campaign is mine; I sit at the helm through good grace, deep pockets, and shared cause. There's a way to put this right. Two ways, I mull it over. How long is it until the lords, Ayato namely, decide that I'm not worthy to carry their sword? How long until they discover I'm not up to it?

Lord Mako and Hisao amble in late, with a look of disdain on their faces. The surrounding families return that with a look of distrust, eyes shift over them. No one wants to ask it but everyone is thinking the younger feeds the Yokusei runners that skirt around our camps nightly. Looking for holes where they will find none. Unfortunately for the old Mako crone, his heir is his only child – he carries the look of a weak swimmer. Instead of beautiful daughters, the three Mako Captains flank him in a full red suit of plate. Tatahi, Mizen and Ishiga. Each wear the three-bladed cat's claws at their waist, the armour purposely etched with slashes and claw marks. Ornaments. They've yet to join the battles, so it is despicable that they show their faces here – although hidden behind a growling tiger's jaw. The Mako tread the line of treachery by lending only small numbers of foot soldiers to our cause. Regardless of the intelligence they've lent us, while Dattori and Shuji numbers dwindle, grow tired, theirs are fresh, unaffected; restricting numbers in smaller battles, where you foresee a larger one on the horizon is smart, but I start to question their methods. Perhaps they seek to win profit from this campaign with the assurance of never having their names written in the histories if it goes awry. Whatever it is, if they do plot, I'll save them from themselves, cut off the source.

At the back of the congregation, stooped in the shadows cast by the flames, Kekkei whispers to a hooded woman; my cursed eyes cannot hold onto the image of her face. It twists and contorts with the rising smoke. It is unremarkable, a face for the shadows like Oboro, but different still – my hands curl into fists, trembling. Even now he plots in the shadows.

I do not pursue it, relinquishing my anger as the pyre is lit. Lord Shuji bears that weight. For he is the benefactor of this war. It is he who will earn a sobriquet remembered in the annals of history. I just wield the blade.

I watch on. Already, since I pulled myself from the Kirisam, I've born witness to too many pyres of my own kindred. Was it a plan to drench Basho in Samaki blood? If so, I've succeeded on every front. Again, the flames engulf one of my own, eat away at hopes, dreams, hours of training. A lifetime of missed achievement. It is a deeper despair, more personal pain to watch a lone warrior burn. There's something special in the pyre, my people believe. To be Bashoan, witnessing the relinquishing fire, is to be complete. Calm. Pure. My people believe it is only those flames that truly connects us to the gods, only at this moment do they receive our prayers, hear our pain and pleas, know our worship. It is why we solidify relationships, make promises, accept new members into our families in front of the pyre. Only when we lose our love ones can we forge new, lasting relationships; but this time I only make a promise. *Blood.* I will honour Lady Shuji and the wretched King of Furs, too.

I want to pray for Tetsuya, tell him he's earnt his place alongside Meganako, and the Mistress, whichever he prefers. I never did ask him.

Instead, my stomach cramps, rolls with the cloud. My head is heavy, pins prick my temples. I cannot lie to the boy, sick with anger, wild with rage. I cannot pretend that the loss of such a warrior is fine because he died for the sword. When Warrior Godlord Terinda died, did Basho sing praises for a warrior lost? No. It brought on the Distress. A year of mourning, an age of decline as his uncle, the Fifth Godlord, still ruins this land. The poison that claimed his nephew still said to age in Orika's stores. Basho knows it so but does not contest the rule; of the many large and small northern lords, only those who uphold the lies and deceit, oversee the land, have the title of *Great Vassal* Lord to Akuto Takahashi. The only ones who truly profit in this era of peace. Until they notice the war I bring them.

If Terinda's greatest achievement was unification, purification, his uncle's is the antithesis.

It takes the death of a great man to level me, to remind me that it is not my own personal stakes that I carry on my shoulders. With my victory, I'll end an age of tyranny. My cause is far-reaching. And I thank the young Daichi for making me see this.

The Yokusei will be made an example.

A feast for the souls lost will be held tonight, but I shrug it off. There's nothing to celebrate. Nor is it a good cause to consume two days' worth of rice and the only fish we have – we're still too close to Shuji-to for Ayato to understand his wastefulness.

In the coming days, we pack up camp, move along the river, push the advantage we earned, and onto the eastern edge of the Forest of Souls. The Yata Fields will be our base.

Moving from the comfort of the Outer lands and into the toes of the Lord Council, it'll be an unsettling move for the lords, but one that will necessarily force their mindset into that of war. With Chisai at our backs, we may still not feel the true discomfort of war. In a few weeks, as we move onto the Kirisam, Tetsuya's death will feel worthless. For the small river won by it will be useless, and the Yokusei will no longer exist.

"Masako."

I roll my eyes and turn; Lord Shuji approaches. His eyes are quiet, a tide ebbs within. The campaign is treating him well, his beard plaited, he almost looks learned. His robes are plain, grey, animal, a wolf pelt draped over his shoulders – metaphorical, Ayato. "My lord, do you not have festivities to see to?"

He walks by me. We walk a ways out of kilter until I fall into step with him, and he says, "Do you only know provocation?"

"It was a mere question, my lord. Do not mistake the shadows for a hidden blade. It tires the soul."

He finds it funny. "The Taosii head rots, although the crows leave little really. Bits they cannot worry from the skull. Each passing day I watch it, it resembles our enemy less and less. Just a skull. I fear my patience, my need for this slipping away with it."

I wheel on him, my hand reaching for his robes, but I snap it back. "You lose faith in the face of victory? We're mere weeks into this. By Sama's Third, our losses only suffered in the naivety of command, the foolishness of youth!" I stop to catch my breath; he's stoked wildness I can barely contain. "The river – is – ours. The Yokusei have little to muster against us."

"So you tell me. A greater victory was promised. Is Kekkei not the famed Thousand Hands, or do I mistake him for a better man? I trusted his words."

"A victory made in haste is an estate built on sands."

"This is my coin, my reputation, my family that feeds this. Reports tell me you spent the battle drenched in blood, drugged like some sort of beast. Your focus was on butchery, I'm told – it's not faith in the campaign that wanes." His stare starts my heart racing. "Am I to believe these...heretical rumours coming out of Orika? Lord Dattori was foolish enough to let you have your way, I will not be."

"*I am Lord Dattori.*"

Ayato lets the silence answer for him.

"Dattori Masako, I relieve you of your command."

"NO. You cannot!"

"Do not deign to tell me what I can and cannot do. In our first battle, you not only embarrass yourself, but you ensure the Daichi clan will die with

Maki, less the lord plant a male seed." Ayato almost talks with himself. "Perhaps the north will yield a suitable woman – there's some merit in the Daichi continuing." He folds his arms, ensuring he catches my gaze. "If he stays. Through your failures, the Daichi threaten to pull away from our campaign. Do not mistake my words, I mean to see this through to the end." You won't, I hear on the end of that.

"My failure? You remove my command because your heir took it upon himself to make his own strategy – the Shuji maids filled their heads with too many stories of heroics. The boy needs grounding. Do not forget I did nothing that wasn't sanctioned."

"He did as promised! It is you and that despicable mercenary that failed. You were to capture the river, only. Not forge ahead, killing more Yokusei. You let the momentum of small victory carry you. Bloodthirsty bitch." The laugh that curls out of his mouth is forced, theatrical. He's a swine. "GO ON. Stop caressing that sword. Cut me down! Coward. Go on...that's how you solve things isn't it, Hawk?"

I go to stomp away, done with this arrogant imbecile, but the camp folds in on me. I'm surrounded by guards that wear the plain plate of the Shuji. Fully armed, they level their spears at me. "Do not be foolish, Ayato!" I growl. "Do – not – make this mistake. I'm a far more tenacious enemy than the north."

"Take her," he says, "I don't need you in the way when the Yokusei bring their terms of surrender."

Surrender?

His command void of any emotion, I'm being disposed of as he would of trash. Not expecting me to flee, they wait for me to give into his taunts. They wait for the tiger to swipe, but instead the hawk flies. There's an opening. They're still too weary of me. I dash between the lord and the closest guard. Between two tents, I flee. Light-footed, my legs pumping as hard as I can, avoiding tent pegs and strings. The alley too thin, pikes too long, battle regalia too heavy to follow me.

In the heart of the camp, I jump over fires, spits with dripping rabbits. The main carriageway is empty. Lord Shuji made his bid to silence me while the other families remain occupied by the feast – if I bring this to them, there's a chance I can remain. A chance the other lords are not in this. Ayato is rash in anger. If he loses the Daichi, loses momentum, his riches would have lessened for nothing, Shuji-to would be marked by the Lord Council. I get it, but I won't take it. For my people, it could be overlooked, but I'm not that level-headed. Instead, too prideful. I don't head to the feast, avoid the gatherings, making for my own quarters instead.

Inside I gather bottles of oil, the incense master loved. Lavender and orange, cedar, something that smells like fresh grasses somehow. All of it. The tinder box too. Wrapping it up, I sling it over my shoulder after changing into dark robes, and a cloak to shrink into the shadows.

My horse brays softly as I approach – the beast's tended to only by my trusted a short way from our quarters. I take his face in my hands and stroke him gently, sorry for asking more of him again so soon. Wounds, gouges, and scratches, ooze from his left flank. One particularly nasty slash was close to spilling his guts. Twine, spare arrow strings, hold it together, healed by Earthly Medicines.

No pressure is needed in my heels, he pulls away like the wind with a gentle nudge.

The Forest of Souls is among four great expanses of wood that hold a sacred place in the hearts of all Bashoan. Oni Wuld, The Deep Pond, and the Expanse of Tails name the other three. The forests stand for the Four themselves. Long have our traditions abated, relaxed; two ages before now, only the godsborne inhabited them. Men, instead, skirted them, treated them with absolute care – gifts and carvings to the gods were etched into the outer treeline. Wood chimes that worked the air spirits and offerings to the Four were laid on the outer limits. Only a few caretaker families, those who the Guardian households of today model themselves on, were permitted entry. Times have moved on, even the special measures for the godsborne wane, the respect dwindles as do the walls that keep Basho isolated from the rest of the Endless Lands.

One thing still holds true – the destruction of the forests is a grave sin. A crime worse than treason, for you would act against the very gods themselves.

At the edge of the forest, I set down my pack. They won't deny me now. The Lord Council knows nothing other than complete annihilation. If you will not heel, roll over to their taxes, their demands, you will perish.

And what do we Samaki offer? We hear their terms.

I spit at the thought.

No, their surrender won't survive the night.

I am the flame, the perfect fire. The all-consuming. I open the tinder box, pricking my thumb with Jinto's knife that I pull from its place at my ankle, and sheathing it again. A wolf howls in the distance. I snicker – this is all too poetic. Don Yoku, eat up. My blood drips onto the tinder, it hungrily soaks up every drop.

Fire, by its nature, is destructive. Emotionless destruction. That is not enough to burn down a place of the gods, which is why I add emotion to the flame, my own blood is a rotten pit of wrath. Striking the flint, a flame shoots into the air. I drop the box, diving backwards, away from the monstrosity I've unleashed; the flames rise, orange, red and black – the tongues lick into the night with an oil-ended gloom. An impenetrable blanket of horror. My horse whinnies, shrieks, thrashing against his reins.

The fire lashes out in every direction, searching for something to nourish its anger.

I grab my pack, heavy with oils, and smash them onto the nearest tree. Spilling a thick line of it back to the flame, it grabs holds, and explodes towards the forest, engulfing the first tree and the next, and another in the blink of an eye.

See this, Ayato, I've saved your marriage. Your wife's family avenged.

Sukami's vehemence rips through the forest.

Without any encouragement, my horse carries me like a divine wind up a rise, from where I can watch my scheme unfold. Simple madness, really. Awfully effective. Everything that is Yokusei will burn in the hells before the night is old.

I can't help but bellow a laugh, but it too is lost, consumed by the roar of the black flames.

A curse? No, no. I've had it all wrong, this is a gift. I rifle through my pack and pull out a final item – my gourd where Tetsuya's blood sleeps. Watch this, boy, they will pay for what they took from you.

Us.

Chapter 27

The fire doesn't roar, no. It's the cry of a peacock, thousandfold, and the birds' have cried themselves hoarse. Screech overlaying screech. My blood is a gate. It's not fire I've inflicted upon the horizon, it's the very hells themselves. So bottomless are its flickering tongues, a black frigid, so cold it sucks everything in, a fire that would burn worlds – loosed by my own bent anger.

It grates on my ears. Grates on my being, I go cold, the warmth leaking from every orifice. My teeth chatter. I tremble now as the entire frontline of trees is alight. The entire Samaki border burns. From end-to-end, all I see is fire. The glow is radiant death. Quickly it moves, eating further into the forest, it crawls so far into the distance it reaches up to burn the heavens. My heart erratic, it's a spasm more than a beat.

The picture before me is the very realisation of what I brought on my household, my family.

You will overcome anything. Trust me. But do not let your blood overwhelm everything you'd become.

"What use are your words now, Master?" I ask the night. "Why do you plague me so? I did this for us!" A pit where my stomach should be, watery, it squirms. I convulse and vomit down the side of my horse. I breathe in deeply, only to hack and cough. Thick ashy plumes burn my airways.

My horse bucks beneath me as embers flutter down. I've decided this horse will be Lonestep, too. For he alone carries my burden; much is the requirement of my steed. Hold on a little longer. I must see this out. If this is the end, I will watch it turn to nothing. The world is afire, out of my control.

"WHAT WILL YOU DO NOW, GODS?" I cry, "IT IS BY YOUR HAND I AM CURSED! BY YOUR HAND I SUFFER!"

Almost in answer, the skies summon their own hell. Lonestep bucks, whinnies as the winds pick up. It circles above. I struggle to right myself in the saddle and keep hold of the reins as my steed fights against the rough whisper of the winds, the growl of something above.

The blaze is harried by the invisible foe, but they only fan the fire, feed it, irritate it; the tongues lick out across the fields. The winds batter it, some streaking as far as my campsite, lighting it up; it forks like horizontal lighting above.

A deep howling, the skies are an old wolf. They crack open, a white glow pulses; the clouds seem to coalesce around a single point above the fires that reach up like a serpent towards it. And then it's dashed to the earth, split, the flame's curiosity cost power, its force abating somehow.

My throat tightens so much I rasp. No... how can it be?

In the midst of the vortex, the gods are known. A godly finger pierces the clouds, each scale illuminated against the surrounding glow, glistening jade water. Two whisker-like tendrils protrude from its face, riding the airstreams, manipulating the winds – it uncoils, not from the cloud, it is the cloud. Wreathed in lightning, onyx claws matching the flame, its eyes stream sky dust, the glow emanates from them. Its fangs molten starlight. Filling the skies not a hundred metres from the top of the blaze, It's a giant. A thousand onis wouldn't wield the monster's presence.

I'm numb. Insignificant. Weak. This being is the gods on earth.

Tendrils still working the winds, they converge in front of it, the smoke and ash giving form to its otherwise invisible nature.

I've made history, but what have I wrought? A disaster worthy of the Eyes of the Gods.

A great sora dragon answers.

It lets out a bellow that silences my world. A ringing is all I hear, my horse is frantic, horrified as it throws me from the saddle. Vivid lilac spots my vision, writhing against nothingness.

Trying to find my feet, a great pressure hits me, forces the air out of my body – my lungs useless as I'm pressed into the earth.

* * *

Nudged, I wake but my vision is blocked, clouded. I inhale, taking in a lungful of something bitter, soft, and sandy. I sit up sharply, whatever I've breathed in falls from my robes, an avalanche of a grey substance with the qualities of snow. The taste is that of unmistakable ash – charred flora and fauna form a sludge in my mouth, spitting doesn't help.

Nudged again. I turn to reprimand whatever it is. My sooty hand fumbling my hilt as I meet two bulbous black eyes – they say a horse lacks real emotion, that it is driven by whatever fuels its rider, but I notice a glint of relief. Hear a low bray, a sigh. There's no bond stronger than that with the animal who's carried you into battle, taken slashes meant to cut you down, carried you past exhaustion so that you may fight on.

Taking his face, I caress his mane, press my head to his.

I get up, survey the borderlands around me, look at what's left in the wake of divine intervention. Like the lands when the Cold comes, the fields are blanketed in a sheet of grey, ash still falling around me. Closer, the earth rolls left and right, unharmed, untouched by my flames. But, where the Ghost's Arrowhead was once a lush, green, vibrant part of the forest, it is now grey ruin; what's left of the trees poke through the blanket sporadically. Charred pins. The Winding Rush now visible, saved from the hellfire. I...still. I have no words for what happened. Is my journey watched so closely? When I next act will the gods smite me down? My head is a torrent of questions, my chest fluttering, my body a trembling mess. Will the histories ever know it was I who summoned the wrath of the dragons? I who the gods could no longer ignore?

Yes, they will. It will be I who writes them.

It is not a bad omen, no, it is a second chance. A chance, again, to change these lands, rather than burn them down. Foolish. They do not silence the anger but instead change the weapon, reset the pieces. Maybe, no. A cold bead of ignorance shoots down my spine. Yes. Maybe the dragons acted on their own, maybe it couldn't bear to see its charge burn. What, then, would be their use? Blasphemous thoughts but the dragons might be protecting their own worth.

Whatever it is, the skies are clear in every direction. The dragon is nowhere to be seen.

Eyes widening as I take measure of my camp, the divine wind, the great pressure that destroyed the hells' flames did not lay a finger on it. How can such a titan be so careful? I feel amongst my robes, even Tetsuya's gourd remains intact.

Gods, then. It's decided. Only they could be so discriminate in their magics.

A glint catches my eye on the horizon, and as I squint, I notice the distraught masks of the ghost; the Yokusei many-faced ghost flaps above a retinue that surrounds the proud white horse, the high-horned helm of their leader. His bronze plate catches the sun's glare like the facets of a cheap jewel. A warning signal to death, your quarry approaches. The Four want this done the right way, so I will oblige.

Checking again, at this distance, the flashing light hides their numbers; ten-maybe-fifteen or twenty. A score would be most right. His warrior-escort is the colour of the setting sun, a vibrant orange dress plate – they come displaying their wealth but wearing the colours of the Saman Period to a meeting with the Samaki would be an insult. A start on a bad foot. I'm sure Lord Shuji would forgive it; he has proven his family blood thin.

Gods-blessed, the Yokusei probably figure themselves.

The dragon has paved the way for their demise, not for their terms.

Lonestep's sure hoofbeat is the quake of the earth. The Yokusei's arrogant canter leads them slowly into my charge. I intercept the unlucky fucks halfway to the Samaki camp – the ashfall is enough to obscure a normal set of eyes, our scouts might hear it, but they won't see it.

This won't take long.

"Tsk, out of my way!" The front riders part at Satoshi's command. "You! So, Lord Shuji failed?" He snickers. "I'd first though Ayato had taken leave of his senses. But, no, he's a sensible lord. Look at you, wild, rabid. You've spent the night in the ash, haven't you?"

I say nothing. Feel nothing. Straightening myself, I don't let my mind carry me in any which way; it flows, as the river does, where it is natural.

Satoshi is a brat brought up to worship his own voice. "Brigands, common criminals, cannot resist watching their crime, can they?"

There's a mumbling of agreement.

"This fire was yours. I won't hold the other lords responsible, that you meet us here is proof enough. Aren't the skies beautiful? You failed. The dragons above saw to it, then delivered you into our hands. You poor cunt."

I take the gourd from my robes, popping the cork. Not sure of what another's blood will do, but Tetsuya deserves to see it. I sip it. Twice. The Yokusei are laughing, chattering, as two dismount. I won't go back in their shackles, but they bring them forward anyway. "I promised I'd repay you for that filthy cart," I say, but Satoshi is ignorant, lit-up with glee, the fuckwit is probably hard over this. It takes hold. Washes over me. Where my own blood is a ravenous hatred, Tetsuya's blood is satiating. A blanket of confidence. A smile tugs at my mouth, I can't resist grinning. My muscles strain, still, stretched beyond any normal measure as my body falls into the blood fever. It is still, like never before, a pond that knows its strength; my muscles stretch further, one body struggles to contain two, the young Daichi's being forces its way in. Memories now, in floods, my head throbs – fit to explode. *I'm in front of the clan High Chair, my father smiles knowingly, I am a warrior but an heir first – the weight of it all heavy. I smile anyway, my sword is trained. I will not fail father. The girl from the hamlets is most beautiful. Father presides over it all, the Daichi rule. You can have her. This is yours to take. But I don't want it that way, father. I want to win the girl with the man I'll become. She really is beautiful; does she notice me? Of course, she must. Titika is a goddess, her hips wide, built to carry the weight of Samaki lordlings. Shoulders broad to push into the fight, a body built for the sword. Her breath catches as I run my hand across her breasts, pulling her into mine.* More. A storm of hopes, desire. A life unfulfilled. *The Hawk of Fenika, ugly. A warrior with no equal, not that I've known. Nearly cost me this perfect face, what would Titika think? She'd love it anyway...Will father approve, though? I hope a boy, she says a girl, but I don't care either way. I only care for my lord's approval.* Tetsuya doesn't deserve this. Am I no more than a cruel leech? An eater of dreams. His last moments real again. *I step to him, he's nothing. Not worthy of the sword he holds – hooves – too late. He's coming with me.* Gone. It settles, our flows meet – two rivers converge.

"Monster!" Satoshi shrieks. "They're true! Kill it KILL HER."

I don't ask what he means, I don't care. My body is one, from my shoulders, straight down my spine, to the power that wells in my legs. I concentrate it there. His men are squawking, flapping like birds as some break from his command. I tighten the wedge, abdomen taut, unbending braced by my scabbarded sidearm.

The ropes are dropped, the two approaching guard go to draw their swords. Satoshi moves to wheel his horse around. The coward will flee while his men die, but I won't have it said that I cut down a fleeing man. I push off and I'm water, fluid as I pass his men before they draw on me. I'm the wind as CrowKiller is drawn, whispering her deathly whisper. I stand before him; his men scatter around me. Satoshi digs his heels in, but I slap the horses' charge aside.

It's dazed, frightened. He falls from the saddle, somehow righting himself. Rodents know how to fall – but the cat does it better and I'm the tiger as I pre-empt him. Stepping forward with a mighty thunderclap, I slash; it takes his drawing arm off horribly just below the elbow. I almost step through him as momentum carries me forward, my attack rending him in two. Blood showers down around me. His men are in disarray – the fleeing not far. The wind in my stride. I hunt them all. Not a single one survives Tetsuya's Reckoning. For him, I carve them all up. After I'm done, I don't miss a breath, I'm not tired. The act washes from me. It is a drop in an ocean.

Ripping their banner from its pole, I hack off Satoshi's head – it is the way of wartime, the way my caste proves a killing. It isn't butchery, that's already done – and thread the banner through his mouth in a loop that meets in a knot around the back of his head.

Lonestep waits; he grazes nearby, indifferent. His kin scattered to the wind, other than Satoshi's, who foams from the mouth. There's a pang of guilt in my chest that the beast had to pay for his cowardice. But you will be remembered.

I tie his head to the saddle and start for the camp with ash still falling around me.

Chapter 28

I don't make it back to the camp before something is terribly wrong. The light burns my eyes, I'm blinded. Tetsuya's strength leaves me. I'm a barren waste. I tremble, not able to hold the reins, I freeze. Hot and cold. Fury and calm. The ground meets me with a dizzying thud as I fall from Lonestep. Nudging won't work this time, horse. I'm numb – so hungry. A many clawed beast raps at my ribs from within, pains lance in every direction. Each breath laboured. Muscles throb, deep aches over rivers of fire that navigate every fibre of my being.

The price. Something whispers with Tetsuya's voice.

I curl up where I fall and let the hours pass – gods, I hope the horse doesn't arrive without me. The credit for it should be mine only.

The sun reaches its apex before scouts find me. Unity. They're Daichi men. Kind enough to peel me from the ground. One takes Lonestep's reins, he's close-by, they suggest I ride with one of them, but I say no. Tell them to help me onto my horse. So they do.

"Is that?!"

"Yes," I croak, "take me to your lord."

"At once!" There's a giddiness to his tone.

We enter the camp, soldiers, servants, camp followers, they all gather as we wade through the tents. Some notice the Yokusei head, their whispers travel beside me. The crows of rumour circle above. Yips, raucous cheers. I'm greeted a hero. The dragon was herald to it, this great victory, they shout. Good fortune to the Samaki.

I feel like I've caught been caught on the wrong side of a stampede of oni.

Lord Daichi's quarters lay not far into the camp. His men help me from the horse, help me untie the head, lend me a shoulder and part the tent flap. He and his daughters sit around a small table, they take their mornmeal, small bowls of rice. The sly devil still has fish to grill? They look up as I take a step forward. Legs buckle and all I can do is fall to my knees, the head hitting the floor with a bloodied squelch. I bow low first, waiting for longer than I should as I summon the strength to pull myself up again.

"What is this? Explain yourself at once. Lord Dattori, you dishonour my family by fleeing the celebrations, and now you present yourself here, a mess." He blows out a long breath. "Gods above, the dragon...did. Never mind. What is wrong with you, *girl*? Need I-"

"Father, the head!"

"Yes. Aimi. I. Notice. Who is...the Yokusei boy?" Beneath the stern mask, a light flickering. Disbelief parts way for recognition. His lip trembles, eyes watery. He gets up, turning to pace the room beyond him, hiding his tears. The triplets don't hide theirs.

I bow again, and as I come up, I force words into my mouth, "My...Lord. Maki." Formalities aside. We're brethren in blood. I hold the head above mine. "Here I bring you the head of Yokusei Satoshi, heir of the Yokusei and the Forest of Souls, leader of the treachery that saw your heir, Daichi Tetsuya, fall in battle. The responsibility was on my shoulders." I look up, catching him in the eye. "I'm a warrior first, Maki. A lord by circumstance. As a warrior, only blood pays. Please accept my apologies – I will strive to bring this war to the end promised. The Yokusei are conquered."

He goes to speak, but stops as he first tends to his daughters as they sob. A man worthy of his title – he brings all three in close before he addresses me again, not as a lord, as a father. "*Thank you.* From the bottom of my heart, thank you. Ayat– when it was decided we'd hear the *scum's* terms of surrender, I knew then my family would never know peace. Lord Dattori, you restore our honour." Maki's eyes sharpen, narrowing. Closing briefly, before the lord takes over. "But you *murder* under the oncoming white flag of peace. Guards!" It wasn't white. It was yellow – crimson, now. "I hope you understand this is not what I want, only what must be done. This act threatens our credibility. The Samaki are savage, they will say. This will only fuel their desire to eradicate us. It may even turn the entirety of their numbers on us before we can get ahead. You bring ruin."

"No one survived."

"What?"

"I killed them all, his entire retinue. Word will not reach their lord. Not yet. If we bring it to them with the rest of our force. This was always the way, *Lord Daichi*."

"We?" He gestures and his guards grab me before I react, I'm too weak to fight.

Dragged through the camp at its displeasure. *Boos* and *hisses*. A hand grabs one of the guards, Mako soldiers try to splash through the Daichi numbers, crying of a misdeed. Their lord wouldn't have heard yet. Wouldn't have issued the same damning orders.

They bring me to my own quarters; our camp isn't fit for prisoners. Tying me to the centre pole, a thick trunk that supports the rest of my tent, I'm reminded of the late Lady Kasuki, smiling as I may share her fate yet. The guards search me, leaving me with the gourd. "OFF!" I growl as they try to take my swords. "I promise I'll kill you." They break my gaze, unnerved. They check my restraints again before they leave, placing my swords away from me.

The hollow feeling in my stomach groans.

It is hours before I'm fed like a babe, the guard spooning rice into my mouth. I slurp on a rich, salty soup, bite into the bread. Biting into the hand that feeds me crosses my mind but what use would that be?

Shuji Sada delivers the news – I'm to be executed.

It is off that Thousand Hands does not come to reprimand me, to scold me for ruining the empire he plans to build of traders, thugs and brigands. Fit to rule the new world he plans to negotiate. Neither do Oboro or Ropi. I grow paranoid, troubled that they'd all desert my death.

I won't give up – I bring my ankle up towards my face, thanking the gods that I'm still as dextrous as my younger years. My robes slide down my leg, revealing Jinto's knife. Working my neck against the ropes, I loosen it slightly, my skin tingles, and burns. The rope tears into it. With the knife in my mouth, I sigh, letting it drop to the floor. What the fuck did I think I'd do with it?

I fight against my restraints until the skin on my wrists and neck is red raw. And somehow fall into a sleep.

There's something or someone in the tent with me, I'm sure – but I don't see them. I woke up with a start, the gentle patter of feet. A shuffling that I can't place. Breaths. Steady, composed.

"Lady Dattori?" A whisper snakes around the room. I cannot see her, but it's definitely a woman.

"Where are you?" I ask. "More importantly, why're you here?"

"Answer. Are you Lady Dattori?" Her voice is sweet like honey. Seductive – a whore's voice. "I'll leave."

"*Lord* Dattori, yes. I am her. Where are you?"

My heart clenches as the picture in front of me is all wrong, it unfolds itself like a cloak, revealing a hooded woman – familiar. Yes. The hooded woman that was with Kekkei. Up close, I can behold her, she's comely, but in a plain way. A face that suggests it could be any woman. Magic. I smell it on her, splitting through the ash, a bitter sulphur that sours in my nose, finished with a hint of roses.

"Don Aibo is pleased to meet you. Aibo, the goddess prefers."

Damn it all, tripe-talkers again. "You're a Sister?"

"Yes."

"Get me out of here!"

"Wait. The goddess is owed – we come to you in search of your charge, F– Genaro Kekkei."

"Whatever you want of him is my business. Get me out of here and I'll pay you whatever you want."

"Our goddess doesn't work in that way. It wouldn't please her like this. From Genaro Kekkei's mouth we hear a request for information. My goddess covets information – feeds from it. We do not work without price. Kekkei flees the price? Where is he?"

"He's here. You slink around draped in magic and you can't fin–"

"Not. No, he's not, that is a lie. That isn't truthful."

He's gone...this isn't right. Kekkei wouldn't. "That is as much of the truth as I know...I wasn't here."

"Yes. You beckoned that...thing to this place. The goddess doesn't like the dragons – you brought discomfort." She craned her head up, tilting it to the side. Raising one eyebrow, she says, "Fine. We need you, then." She seems to listen again. "Ah yes, Kekkei is captured."

"Captured? BY WHO?"

"They came during the storm – the last night was tumultuous. Fate lines collided. Oh, that is not free. What do you pay the goddess for that?"

"Damn you woman! who?"

"The Soshist Po."

I scream in her face. That whoreson still! The one who took me from my home now breaks my family renewed. "Free me and you can have gold, whatever you wish. Weapons? Horses?"

"No. The goddess does not like those. Ah...help?"

"With what?"

"Leave, tonight, help us find Genaro Kekkei."

The Sisters of Aibo. Those whores and prostitutes that collect the secrets of this land – a sect of spies built from the very women who lords, elders, noblemen share their beds with. There's not a secret you can't extract from the bedside. I'd thought it only that until she moved reality in front of my eyes, you can't hide from my eyes.

Don Aibo, sister to Greed, and just as potent it seems.

She picks up my knife and clumsily slashes the ropes, biting into neck and wrists as she does, only just. I think the bitch does it on purpose, but I say nothing. "Wait."

"Yes?"

It bugs me again. "Your secrets brought down my family."

"No."

"The fieldclans. The poppy!" I snap, tired of all the lies. "You helped Takahashi pin it on us!"

"Clan Sikara told you, that was not us. Our goddess cannot see who did. It reeks of furs."

Furs. "The King of Furs...Kekkei paid you for that at my request. Tell me!"

"No. We cannot tell of the King of Furs. We are paid. Paid. Genaro Kekkei wanted more. We told him we cannot...only that it is the one who rules the Taosii. There're clouds, many clouds in the way – strands we cannot see. It confuses Aibo, she is angry for the first time. Will you help Aibo? She grows agitated at this. We need to move. The Taosii, they collected Genaro Kekkei with a mutt."

My mind blanks, the world folds in on itself. And then starts up again, I cannot grasp why this is happening. Why history repeats itself. We go after the spectre of Master and I – what can I do now where I've only failed before?

I pack what I can, rolling my swords in cloth and wrapping my face. The Sister insists we leave before we are seen. It is ridiculous to me, I say, because she can fold the shadows in on herself – but it is not her, she answers. It is Aibo's cloak, it only works when the Goddess can't find her debtor. Aibo is not the generous god that Greed is. I cannot stand her, my skin itches around these... disciples of half-sentences and foggy words. This woman speaks less sense than Jinto yet brings the message of a *deity* who prides herself on knowledge. My patience wastes away. My family is split, in ruins. My advisor is dragged along the same path to destruction as I was. I have no one again. The tent spins, the canvas walls loom inwards, breathe shallow. I can't do this again, I rasp. Fall to my knees. I can't. The Sister pulls me up, the flowery scent of her really fills my head. She tells me that the mousy one and the Islander await, and I steady myself. Calm, by its own small measure, trickles into my being once more. I check my robes for the gourd – I will need it.

Our horses are saddled with cured meats, cheeses, and rice. Wineskins, too. The Sister has been thorough, almost as if she knew I'd lend my hand to her cause, whatever it is. My head is more of a mess now than when I consumed every living memory of Tetsuya's. The Lord Council have finally come for Kekkei. Is this why they didn't respond to our war? Are the secrets Thousand Hands carries with him more important to smother than the Samaki armies that lay waste to a Guardian family? I don't get it – I cannot make sense of this.

Only Kekkei can.

We gallop through the camp, past the guards that have no chance to stop us and into the night.

Ropi and Oboro wait on the road between our camp and my slaughter, my stomach cramps. They'll just have to see it. I cannot hide what I've done. Both look relieved to greet me, their faces stricken with worry.

"What of the Hands?" I ask, "how can we leave them to the lords?"

"We won't" Ropi says.

"–They scatter to the wind," Oboro adds, "slowly, they steal away. The lords are too wrapped up in their own affairs and bloated egos to notice our numbers dwindle."

"Where will they go?"

"Back to your estates," the Sister says. "The fast ones go to collect our cousins. The Shaman of Greed will be of much help in this."

"Akate will fortify Dattori Heiwa," Oboro says. "We need Jinto...but they do not respond. The Hands will see to it." His cheer spoils if that's possible to notice in him. "The Fox and his Wolfpads came. Only the Taosii entered the camp, not as secretive as he thought. I could but watch." He tips his head. "I'm ashamed, my lady."

"Fool! You'd have died. We'll get Thousand Hands back. Come."

PART 4

"On the road to the Fangs, demons present themselves. Do not accept what they offer, for they operate only in pain and never-endings. A demon may offer you immortality, but only amongst the flames."

Ibi Sama, A Treatise on the Demon Mountains, FT1045

Chapter 29

The road to hell is long, arduous, and full of saddle-sores. I clench the reins tighter, my hands throb from it. There's a hole in my lip, I can't stop chewing.

Lonestep whinnies dismay as we're buffeted by the winds – the heavens weep for Kekkei, worried we will never see him again – and sodden hooves of rain beat against my back. I'm soaked to the bone. The Sister that trots beside me is little comfort, no longer can I hear her over the din, nor are her words worth the time. Aibo, it seems, does nothing without payment. I fear I'd rack up several lifetimes worth of debt just conversing with the goddess' bitch. It's what's wrong with a cult comprised of women of the bed and night – they'll do anything to get paid and nothing without it.

Ropi veers westward, following the Kirisam and the large trading road that snakes alongside it to Orika; the Sister does not think the Fox acts on order of the Lord Council, here. Godlord Takahashi acts out of his own interest – so they would not take the direct road. I wonder how much I owe for that. Oboro rides ahead, he's faster, more experienced in the saddle. We need to know what awaits us without spending everything we own; the campaign has all but drained my empty coffers, Ayato cut me out before I could reap the rewards of destroying the Yokusei. Cunning, I wonder if this was his plan. He will let Lord Daichi go, and that'll give Mako and Shuji the lion's share – with my help, he has settled years of border disputes with the ghosts in one fell swoop. To go further, he now owns the trading agreements they have with the Mako. Ayato is a dog, he'll have his day. Is he so wicked enough that he played a part in Kekkei's capture? The riches that would be in his grasps...I turn my thoughts back to the road ahead. We await Oboro's return. Though, we are sure of the news he will bring – it is likely the Fox travels this dishonest path.

The road we follow weaves up through the villages, along the Fisher's Basin to Dabi, a village that sits before Oshima, the town of the Painted Ladies, Aibo's home. The town is a little sister of Orika. One who will do anything to please. If the big sister has something to hide, the younger obliges. A smuggler's haven. The main road is proud of its proper business, traders, honest men and women. Ours is not so; it stinks of lost children, the poppy, and the wronged.

The rain abates, and the Sister chirps again. A morning bird that longed so for the dawn. Nothing gets by Aibo, who picks the lucky women and children the smugglers won't miss. She is both the Goddess of Knowledge and the Saint of Forgotten Things. The Sister is proud of her mistress, to break up the journey, I ask of her.

"What interest does Aibo have in the affairs of lords, the upheaval?"

"We don't. We have interest in the truth."

"Why withhold it then?!"

"We don't. But men will pay. Bad men more. Aibo doesn't like bad men."

"Her knowledge only adds to their power."

"–Takes from their wealth." Blasted woman has an answer for everything. It is as plain as that? I'm talking to a trader, but they trade in broken families and back-alley murder. I try to impress on her the importance of their information, the importance of the change I seek, but she only replies with the cost of change. The price, again, for what they possess. I press the King of Furs, but someone with deep pockets holds their tongue. It irks me. My fingers caress the hilt of my blade. I cannot reply in force, nor can I win their allegiance with good cause. I don't have enough money. A stabbing pain in my chest, I realise I miss Thousand Hands. He would have the words, would know what it took to convince the goddess.

We ride for another half a day before we stop. Neither of my captains return, nor has the weather got any better. It is that time of year in Basho where Sukami's glare still doesn't want to give in but hasn't the strength to carry itself to its full height. The air carries a frigidness, making me shiver as it works its way under my cloak, still thick and damp with the rains. The Forest of Souls is so vast and great that only after three days we ride past its boundaries, up a steep incline that juts out of the heartland. Rice paddies are set like steps into the side of the hills, a mist clings to them.

The canter goes against the hurried beat of my heart, the pace of action too slow for what troubles me. "This isn't right. We move too slow while my family is in peril; you know of what haunts my past. Of course you do. Is that not cause for haste?"

The Sister is expressionless, there's no weight to the way she sits, fumbling the reins but never holding too tight. "We have arrived."

I look around but don't see anything. Rock rises out of the land ahead of us, a miniature version of the Demon's Fangs. Though, there's nothing else. It doesn't surprise me when she leads us around the stone, down something akin to a sheep path and there's a quaint little hamlet carved into the hillside – a large, tiled shack sits most prominent. A sign reads *The Monkey's Falling.* "You're thirsty?" I look sideways, not hiding my disdain.

"A place to sleep, where rumours are free. Patrons of Aibo."

"A whorehouse?"

This is the first time she's displayed any sign of emotion; her lip slightly curls. I can't help but smirk.

"Do not think your work above ours, Hawk," she snaps, "every soul plays their part in the games of fate, only those pig-headed enough to think they're above everyone else do not notice. *Of all flowers, the cherry blossoms.* Don't let your pride get in the way, warrior. There's help in many places, do not be so arrogant as to only look at those you see from the horse." Her cheeks are rosy, brow furrowed; I take check of her now, it seems you need only anger a Sister for them to drop the convoluted godspeak. Still, there's a bite to her words that sets me aback. I'm to be put in my place by common folk? My lip curls and I fight back a rebuke that would have me lose my company, and she speaks again, "A wolf licks his wounds. This is a meeting of fate lines, of shared interest. With this, my first debt paid to Genaro – he said you'd wanted this meeting." She wears a mask of neutrality once more. I don't push for I doubt I'd get an answer, but her words resonate with something I'd misplaced. Intriguing.

* * *

We mount the threshold, the Sister drops away, backs into my shadow. Fidgeting.

I turn back, and say, "Lead the way."

"No. Wolves are violent – Aibo."

"–Doesn't like violence? I thought these patrons of yours? But fine."

I throw the door open, drawing CrowKiller at the same time. There's a glint as steel catches the light from beyond me. My only warning. Blade half-drawn, I pull my sword-arm shoulder back, giving me the room to draw upward, across myself. The hilt guard brushes my nose; another's blade caught just below it. The hairs on my face are less. Blood trickles down my lip where I've only just braced the blow. CrowKiller is a sharp bitch. I thank the silly little woman behind me for the warning, had it not been so I would have lost my head, and knee the assailant, who dodges backward. Falling into my step, my legs moving in complimentary steps. I'm two beats ahead, as many slashes batter his guard, before he stumbles. And my decisive slice strikes down but is met with a bright hiss, another blocks my assailant's death. The momentum carries me, these brigands won't have known a blade of my ilk – thieves perhaps, either way, they will learn to choose their marks better – I run my blade up the length of the blocking weapon, green sparks flying as two twin metals meet – *spell-forge*. These are no brigands.

This one diverts my upwards arcing slash, creating an opening. The warrior's a blur as he uses it. I'm overextended but I bring CrowKiller down with all my strength forcing the opponent to block – I boot their blade away with the ball of my foot, but they're quick to counter, driving me back. I fall into a two-beat counter, then three, he drives me further. This is a warrior beyond me as I can't quite turn a fourth, blood runs down my cheek, his blade nicks my side. I've no room, backed against the wall. Ducking, I drive hard into his abdomen, coming down on top of him. I've lost my blade now.

Though, it doesn't stop me raining down punches. They buck me off – like water, I cannot hold, neither perceive the next move.

An explosion of noise ricochets around the room. I'm dazed, ears ringing.

"STOOOP!" The voice is a drone. Low Bashoan like I've never heard it before – the word is uncomfortable, too deliberate.

Blades, from every angle create a steel jaw around my neck; I'm surrounded by yellow-eyed snarls. Wolves. Craning my head sideways, there's a new hole in the wall behind me, smoking, crackling. Sulphurous. Magic!

"Who are you?" One of them yips.

"Rōnin."

A smack, my head jerks back. "Urgh." I spit blood and thank the fool for opening an exit if I need it. The blood pools in my mouth, but I let it dribble out for now. "Just stopping by."

"She's with me." The Sister waits until now to speak up? Her voice carries all the authority of a chick that cheeps in front of its mother's caw. "This is Aibo's business, mutts. I'd appreciate it if you didn't wreck the place, our goddess hides you out of her own good graces."

"Fuck you, Fini. You deal with this. Your fuckin' fault we're cooped up here, Baraki. I've got better whores back in Orika." One blade pulls away, the rest of them following. Dragons above, beetles skitter across my skin. *Baraki.* So, the men that back away are the Wolfpads of the Red Dog of the Okami – Akuto Baraki, third son of the Fifth Godlord. Intriguing, I grit my teeth and suppose that I'd have got this far without almost losing my head if I'd anything to pay the goddess. Kekkei...you thought this far ahead but didn't cover the service?

Aibo slowly works her way onto the list of things to kill.

The rest of them skulk away, leaving one man. He offers me a hand, and I take it. His grip is incredible, he'd crush my hand if I let him; standing a head above me, he wears a frown like his life depends on it. Young, his long goatee is some kind of attempt to hide it – but being void of wrinkles works against him. A fresh, pink scar cuts sideways through the bridge of his nose, arcing up over one of his murderous eyes, biting deep into his brow, ending before his scalp. His brown gaze flecked with fire. A true warrior's knot in his hair, sides cropped, razored. A wolfskin falls over the shoulders of his white-muddied robe, two priceless blades at his belt; Baraki is born and bred for them. He is still like a lake, the control showing his pedigree – the third son of a godlord still has a duty to lead, a duty to uphold common law. So then, why is he here? The rumours are true? But, how can they be if he stands before me alive...and with men left in his guard after clashing with the Fox and the Tanuki – to drive two Okami off is madness? Impossible. "How are you here?"

"I ask the same, Hawk," his eyes widen, tilting his head back. Smiling. "I watched the Fox carve you up. Demon."

Searching for CrowKiller, I have to cut him down. Have to leave, he knows. He saw.

"Don't worry. She's safe." That strange, ill-fitting usage of my language rings out again.

"Come, sit. I do not care at what I saw." He turns, leading the way to the table. I search the room but don't see the Sister anymore, the Wolfpads kneel around tables, some with women under their arms, cards, gambling and drinking as if they didn't almost gut me minutes ago. All in the same dress as the Red Dog – the alcohol den, whorehouse, looks like it doesn't know the end of the Terin Period came, ornamental plate suits, weapons and spears line the walls – silk hangings depict the ocean, a woman of beauty.

A stranger fellow sits awkwardly at the low table. Foreign. But not Taosii. His eyes are big, round like a fish – but what's most terrifying is the icy cold complexion of his skin, apart from red blotches where it peels. Cloth clings to his body, a strange tunic of hide is cut off at the shoulders, sinewy arms sprout from it; Soshist-like tattoos sprawl as vines down one arm.

I kneel and so does Baraki, the other man sits like a thug, knees up, arm draped over it holding an object with a curved knife's handle inlaid with something that has a theurgical reek; out of the handle sprouts a hollow steel spout – like steel bamboo. He catches me eyeing it and says *Gunna*. That...thing is a weapon worthy of a name?

"The rest of Basho are happy believing what I did was rumour – even your peers. Does it not scare you, Okami? Why let me live?" These two ooze danger, a fight I could not win, but I need to know why he hides so close to home. Keep your enemies close.

"The Soshists bend elements, the Shamans of Greed mutate into beasts, the Sisters of Aibo know my thoughts before I speak them, and my Okami armour shakes off battle scars like they never happened, infuses wind into my muscles. What does one more freak matter to me?" His tone is mocking, one only the young and confident can muster.

"And you?" I look to the round-eyed man. "Where do you come into this?"

"Freak."

"A *Whitan*. From across the endless seas, their...shipus lie out in Orika's bay."

"*Ships*." He corrects.

"The black sea dragons?" I stand. "You bring other gods with you, heathen!"

He laughs, swiping his hand in a dismissive way. My blood boils at the disrespect. "Boats, no dragons. Believe something else. Everyone own story, eh?"

Heretic! "Baraki!" I spit. "Whatever it is you're doing, what in the hells are you using this man for?" The iceman raises an eyebrow, I speak fast purposely – so he doesn't keep up. Though, when I stop, his laugh is a rusted knife.

"Captain Dickson," he says, nodding his head. "Sell and trade guns. My god kind, magics." He waves his strange object in the air.

I look to Baraki, his frown an upturned smile, as he says, "So, the Samaki march on the Forest of Souls. That your doing?"

"The ghosts are dead," I say, "their line cut."

"Hmm, not quite. Yokusei Kabutomaru, the Tanuki, still lives. Just." He pauses. "Don't be shocked, I'm the best. Now, when the Sister told me she'd found someone who shared my cause, one lord and her mercenary, I thought you'd come with the Samaki in tow – tsk, what am I going to do with just you?"

"What...what are you trying to do? If you knew I was coming."

"We need test."

I grow to dislike the *Capitane*. "I've got nothing else to give you. My resolve and two of my trusted."

They both look around the room, down to my blades. "Not them, I've forward scouts. The Fox has my mercenary, my First Advisor. I plan to take it from him. But why should you need me? If you know I rallied those fuckwit lords, you know what I plan to do – you're the Lord Council's do... wolf. Quite frankly, letting me leave here signs your father's death warrant." I bring my hands together, cracking my knuckles. "Still, your blood or mine, I guess."

"Kill him. Matter's not to me." My breath catches, and I know he hears. "Your little speech all but reassures me. I share your cause. The Lord Council, as it is, must die." *Only half right.* "The lack of the other Samaki is fine. Lord Shuji is an arrogant swine. He already sought my aid; did he tell you? Oh. Guess not. Well, then we share more in common than you'd imagine. We're not lords, you and I, no matter whether you're Lord Dattori or not. Warriors have a code of honour, we have duty, but what of those men above us? They set their own rules, treachery in the name of good. Just so they can have another's land. My father was a conniving cunt even before the Taosii came. Then he changed, until recently, walked around like a puppet at the sides of Po and Ti."

"He's to blame. He let them in!"

"Did he?" I have no answer for him, so he lets it hang. "They turned up as ambassadors and within a week move into father's private estate; he walks around with a stick up his ass, and a purple glint in his eye. Yes, I know."

"Imbeciles! You had the means to stop this, the Taosii could not deny the Okami."

"Fuckwits? That's the word you used. The others will not question an order from the godlord's mouth, no matter whether it's manipulated or not." The Capitane chucks back whatever is in his mug and bangs on the table. The skittish waitress fills his mug and disappears again. "I'm amused, in some ways. Father spent his years finding ways to counter foreign magics and he falls straight away. Should have had an Okami suit for himself."

"Why act now, then? You've let it go for years. My family *suffered* at his... their schemes."

"I dishonour Basho. Dishonoured all those I took a vow to protect, I know. Our formidable country falls apart, our common folk are pacified by the poppy – dependent on it. The north is in ruins, it has Taos all over it. I cannot watch it anymore...more importantly, father broke the spell. A couple months ago he raged, tried to send the Soshist away then, but I could do little before he was wrestled under control again. It steeled what I thought I knew. Tsk, I was banished when Po wrestled back control."

Well...my, it seems the Kasuki were not so damned useless after all. The gods have mischievous ways of doing things, the ramifications of one's actions are so far-reaching – the entire ocean feels the ripple as a fish breaks water. Bunta, the echo of your death brings tell of good fortune. "It wasn't broken. I killed Ti, *the puppetmaster.*" A lie of sorts, but he takes it, his eyebrows raise, and he seems to relax for the first time. "We can do this. I have Akate, you your 'Pads. And...he?" I eye the tattooed brute.

"His people number two hundred, but their ships lay behind a sea stockade. Taosii barges came upriver, and out into the sea mouth, blocking our bay. How this one snuck by is a mystery of their one god. Why or how he came to me another." He smirks. "Then, we have a small army, and I was right in trusting the little Sister. Akate, can you gather them?"

I shift, uncomfortable. Is this not what I wanted? There is some poetry in using the Takahashi's son to usurp him, to end an era of heathens and degenerates; Zaki was the same kind of puppet, and although I despise the man now, would it not make him rest easier knowing the same treachery undid it all? "Okay. It can be done, but not without Kekkei. I promised them that."

Baraki pulls his katana, sheathe-and-all, from his belt. Brings it in front of his face, slowly drawing it, the singsong whisper only spell-forge makes, he stares at the blade, muttering to Meganako. "The Fox and the Tanuki, *my brethren*, let's send them to the heavens."

There's a special place in the hells reserved for the Fox, but I let it slide. The foreigner erupts into a wheezed laugh, drumming the table.

Savage.

Chapter 30

The air is frigid, the chill is a knife that cuts between my robes as I exit the 'Monkey; to my right, a path sinks into the hillside and snakes off out of view to the way we arrived on. In front of me, the ground drops into an abyss; I walk to the edge and see what looks like clustered glow flies getting smaller further into the depths but is really houses belonging to the common folk of Hugi – the village hidden in these unnamed hills.

My breath is white as I exhale, and I'm left wondering where my youth has gone. To be so afflicted by the change in seasons is to be an old crone waiting for death – and with the realisation that the Cold is already here, I know I've warred past the Festival of Liberation. The day before the cold signifies Basho's relief from the Savage Kin; important most of all to the Samaki who remember our old ways, who are all too fixated on personal gain to notice the movement of our plane. Master loved it. Pyres galore littered Dattori Heiwa, common folk gathered to the estate, lanterns shaped in the fashion of the masks of the *Gods Senses* littered the skies, fried foods – the day of indulgence, all of it missed, spent in hatred. Sighing, perhaps I am just an old crone. Time to die, but not before I dance one last deadly dance.

We've only been here half a day and I already tire of this; the Okami and his men are too laid back, their arrogance rots their skills. A man on the run from the enemies he's made should not relax easily, there's something to be said about a sharp knife left in the warm waters of calm for too long. It blunts.

As I breathe in deeply, my right lung aches. The Cold is the Saint of Old

Wounds – she never lets you forget them. For the entire season, old breaks throb, scars tighten, all remembered. It is a time to slow down and relax, to be grateful for life, sitting by the hearth with your soul still tied to the body despite the ruinous things the warrior ways do to it. Under the sheet of snow, Izenta renews the fields for the new season, decides the yield of crop for the year to come. Riches depend on the luck he brings; so, I kneel, saying a quiet prayer to the gods and their cold. Not wishing for luck but begging. Once more, I am a beggar for forgiveness as I shed blood and wage war in a time of peace. To bring my estranged vassal back to me, to save Kekkei, Ropi, and Oboro from harm. To ensure Jinto and Cat Food remain safe, and prosperity to our estate in their care.

A wolf howls in answer, and I look over my shoulder to the compound that lurks in the shadow of the rising hill behind it. A yip and a growl. Are there more than one? Communicating...this is bad. With a spin, I draw my blade, a couple of hesitant steps lead me closer to the low grumble – has the change of seasons already pushed them to lurking around in human settlements? There it stands, to the left of the two-story inn, a shadowy wolf. It's hunched on one side. One of its front legs is malformed. Mutated. That boy! I dash after it and it rounds the corner. The wretched thing has disappeared into smoke and air as the only thing I find is the glare of the moon. Fat and icy.

The grounds of the 'Monkey go further than I'd explored. With a waist high, tiled wall surrounding it, it sits separate from the village; to this side, there's little adjoining buildings dotted about. They're unimaginative boxes with a slanted roof and not enough tiles left to keep out the cold. With the complexity of the inn, I wonder if a minor lord fell into trouble, had to sell off his land back to the common folk – they're more hardwearing than my caste for sure. *Back to the wolf, Masako.* If it catches a servant, there would be the hells to pay. Another yip draws my attention to a larger building; the roof is finished, the many sides of it curl out, flicking like the petals of a lily. A newer, Orikan design – striking, but I shake it off and search for the mutt. Above the lit-up canvas, atop the hill that hugs this settlement, the silhouette of a wolf stares back at me. Its eyes glow green in the dark.

"Jinto...Do you not trust me to look after myself, wildboy?" I whisper, and the wolf leaps out of sight.

I take a step forward and my foot crunches on something; I pick up all the pieces – it's one of Master's jewelled necklaces, a blue gemstone inset into four eyes. *To ward off evil and demons, all four of the gods' eyes must see it.* Then...why? Jinto, what do you mean? We send our forces back, send a plea for aid and you send me an old charm. How are we supposed to move against Orika if this is all we get? Weeks without notice and you still play riddles. Fuck Don Yoku. Will you watch us burn, Kekkei and I?

I tie the string around it and shove the necklace into my robes. I'm too far into this to turn back, with or without the Shamans' help.

My katana has but to reach one last neck.

The King of Furs can take my soul after for all I care. I have no wish to see beyond bringing Kekkei back. I can't place it, but now that he is gone, there's a hole left. What feeling is missing I do not know, the merc was never much of a friend. A companion, maybe.

Groans in the wind – moans, lots of them carry themselves away from the Orikan building still lit with candles where the others sleep around it. It stands a stranger in the night; there's a flash of memory. The undead horde roll out from the broken canvas, encircling me. I brace myself – *you're a fool.* I edge closer to the building, grip straining on my sword. Not again, surely no. Closer. The sulphurous smell of magic entwined in honeysuckle. A permeating and heavy aroma draws me closer. Pulls me, its tendrils beckon me in.

Stopping to take measure of it, the small hut doesn't just seem aglow with candles, it pulses a rose miasma.

I'm at the door not knowing the steps I took here. The corridor splits off both ways, a heavy blanket of sweat pushes against me. I should've known. Sheathing my sword, I stride down the corridor, somehow knowing which way to go and open the door; my robes aren't thick enough to fight back the ghastly smell, but I bring them over my nose anyway. I should have turned back; curiosity leads the cat astray. Not moans of the undead, the opposite. The heathens don't turn to my attention, they carry on.

The floor writhes, a human-skin carpet alive with frenzy. Fine silks and cushions envelope the room. Candles burn on tiered hangings that swing above my head. Bodies slither over each other, beneath the silks and on top for the eye to see. Men, but more women. The centrepiece is a woman whose face shifts with each partner she comes into contact with as she buries her head between one's legs and comes up looking like another. Shrill ecstasy. Men and women entwined in a knot; I've stumbled upon a rabbit's den. Fuckery of all sorts.

I don't know why I'm here. They'd be hung for debauchery in all parts of Basho; the Sister that brought me steals my gaze, plucks herself away from her lover – her breasts are small, perfect. Nipples pink, she has bite marks all over them. Ravening freaks.

She's supple, a tigress sizing up her mate. Her face changes as it catches the light. A diamond revealing a different face as it moves against the rays – she's upon me. Grabbing my chin, my lip. She unties my robes, warmth floods to my face – between my legs and I can't – she parts my robes. My breaths are heavy in my ears, the room absorbs me. Pulls me in. Her searching fingers slide across my naval, down into my small cloth. No. Stepping away, I plant a slap on her face, breaking the wicked spell. The Sister recoils, only slightly. Holding her cheek, she smiles. The crazed seductress says, "Why resist us, Masako?" She looks to my chest. I grab hold of my loose robes and pull them back around me, the bitch. "Your body desires but your mind is a barrier. Why has it been so long...does the death of your last still weigh heavy?"

"Careful, witch!"

"There's one you miss. The islander, what about him?"

My eyes go wide, there's something about this place that erodes the control I have over my own body, a tinge of the Soshist's lavender mist, perhaps magic in the same vein. "What lord doesn't worry over their closest?"

"Not a lordly feeling, Aibo knows." She reaches out her hand again, I grab it. "Ow. So rough. He's fine, though – he will come back." She pauses. "Relief, yes. Maybe needed in more ways than one. Would be much easier for us if you'd taken him before." With a wink she pulls me around, my grip still on her arm, and we leave the amalgamation of bodies. They don't stop for us.

In one of the adjoining rooms, she pulls night robes around her, beckoning me to a small table; the room is bare, only the materials of its making, a bedroll, and her pack. We sit in silence while she fastens the front of her robes, pulls her hair back, pinning it. The Sister pours wine, offers me some, and I indulge her. A bitter aftertaste but a heavy bite of something sweet. I drain the entire cup – I need it after this filth. The gods punish me tonight, turn their eyes away from me; and as they do, the others descend. While our Four of Creation are distant, the other gods, the new, very human, very close sneak in. Like carrion birds, they peck at what was left, the dregs of our kind who need something more...immediate to worship.

Aibo and Don Yoku scare me, for how close they circle.

"What was that? You bring me here so you..." Something about her smile makes me stop. Turns my words into a clenched fist. To punch that smug look from her face would be more of a relief than anything they could offer me in that room.

"Meat...and blood," she starts, "when the god is coated in death, you don't flinch." The light through the door catches her face again. Her eyes seem to swirl, seeing elsewhere. Soaking in knowledge. "But when it is offerings to my goddess, offerings of love. And unity. You turn up your nose." She leans in close. "Hawk, does death get you off more than life?" A wretched look crawls across her face. I snatch out, pawing to no avail as she dodges. "Aibo needs only love. Our power is strong in these places. Do you not wonder whether the woman turns to sex before or after Aibo?"

"If I'd have known how much of a whore your goddess is..." I catch her frown and change tact, this goddess is already less helpful than the one of Greed, and twice as vindictive at a guess. You don't hear much about the Sisters of Aibo. Which means they have a means of keeping their secrets...one I wouldn't like to test. "There's more at stake than these base conversations you new godlings are fixated on. What is it you bring to Kekkei? What information does he require and how do I pay you to leave me with it?"

"*Whore.* Only those who fear intimacy would call her that; there's nothing to learn from us with such a narrow view of things, Hawk."

"*Masako*...or better yet, Lord Dattori."

"The price is paid – it is not clan business; Genaro Kekkei must know first." *I cannot stand this any further.* Biting my lip won't work. That bubbling. "Uh-uh. Push your sword back home. Do not draw on Aibo. Tonight, here, we are strong."

Sheathing CrowKiller, I listen. For I don't want the retribution of such an...unfussed goddess to return for me. Though I could cut her before she blinked next, I worry how many throats I'd have to slash as her face morphs once more. Or did it...I don't know. This woman.

"Quiet. But your mind rages. Share with us." She hands me another cup of wine, but I bat it out of her hands. A purple splash across her bedroll. The Sister tuts. "We knew you wouldn't. I saw you." Her grin is wide again. "We felt you...so we owe. A little. The Samaki continue their campaign in your stead; the dragon's appearance filled a lot of pompous heads with divine purpose. Including Lord Shuji. The Yokusei have folded, Ayato retains what was theirs. He is a bastard, yes. Striking deals with the Yokusei, summoning the Sikara, calling for Orika. You've stirred an awful beast – given it confidence.

"That whoreson. I..."

"The Yokusei will not give up – death surrounds him. The Tanuki may still yet be their heir."

Damned fucking gods. "You mean to say if Baraki slays the Tanuki, we're playing into Shuji-to's wretched hands?"

"We do not know. Aibo loves truth...not speculation. Should it not be joyous your campaign struggles forward?"

I let go of a long breath. She fetches the cup and I take the wine this time, emptying it in one gulp. "Shuji wants me dead. I have a beast on both sides of me." And they aren't the real issue.

"There's still another on your mind," she says, stealing her way into places she doesn't belong. "The King of Furs. One owns that knowledge, we have said." Her eyes narrow, her visage finally fixes upon a face I don't quite grasp, don't remember. But the more I look at it the more I remember the one I saw with Kekkei. Perhaps her true face. "Another thing...our goddess is not scared of much; but if she looks at him, he stares back. His beady, yellow animal eyes – there's a hunger. A hunger!" she trembles. "We cannot see again; he's one of us."

What does that mean?" I lurch over the table, both hands gripping the front of her robes. The mumbling, nonsense infuriates me. "What should I do with that?"

The Sister's eyes fall from mine to my neck. "Too late...this is all too late." I go to leave but she stops me and says, "We want the same thing!" But I pull away and leave towards the main building.

We, she says. But I don't know if she still means us, or her and the whore goddess.

* * *

The courtyard is still blanketed in the white haze of the moon. There's a pregnant silence in the air. The night is not done with me yet. I check my robes are fastened and take a few deep breaths before I stride over to a figure who thinks it sits in the shadows. The Red Dog, Baraki, stands glaring at me as I make my way over. Raising an eyebrow, he says, "I didn't think you'd be into that sort of thing." A grin rips across his face. "But you are a lord... so." He bows a mocking bow. My cheeks warm, chest tightens like a lady caught with a lover. I jab back, "And you don't take part? I didn't take you for a cuckold."

Baraki laughs, patting me on the back. "Walk with me."

"I don't know, my lord." I jest. "This is an awfully peculiar time for us to meet."

"Tsk, not at all...damned wolf woke me. I thought I'd get to try my blade on a real one. I then thought better of joining that midnight gathering. Now I'm a sorry soul for not." I ignore that. We walk down the ridge afront the 'Monkey, down past the glow flies, even too dark for my eyes, but his voice doesn't hide the curved edges of his mouth.

We end up in a lit clearing, what's left of bamboo training men are placed sporadically. "On the run," I say, "yet you still spare time to train. A warrior worthy of his armour, I propose."

"The Mistress is a wily old goddess. I wouldn't upset her. Praise be."

He draws his sword, taking steps back from me; I don't follow how many. A sinking hole opens in my chest. I shiver slightly, as the cold suddenly redoubles.

"Tsk, you don't trust me? I want to see it. Whether that devilish anger can reach the Fox this time. It...there was as much surprise on your face when you used it as there was probably on mine. Tell me you know it now?"

"Not here. Against the Fox, I will wield it...it is not Taosii elementheurgy to be shared in awe. It's dangerous." Without noticing it, I caress the black scar at my throat and hear a huff. I don't look at him in this moment. I dare not see the eyes of someone who openly knows my...*bloodworking*, for I'm ashamed; I give it the name Master knew.

The young Okami clears his throat, and says, "It's a good thing the gods made me to thrive from disparate odds...we may die, but I don't see anything else for it."

"Why?" I can't help wanting to hear it again; he defies his very birthright when it is easier to roll onto his back. I cannot have him drive a knife into mine. "You have a clear path back to your own...why waste your life?"

"Because family is as important to me as it is you, did you not already get that? Basho has forgotten its values and I will teach it again or burn. Fine, we work with what we can."

A deal with the demon, but it must be made, so I say, "Train me. Show me the ways of the Okami. I will reach his blade."

The moon revealed a glint that suggested he didn't think it was possible. But I've found a companion who wants to reach into the hells...together. Will we be a divine wind that sweeps all the way to Orika's walls, or will we fall in sight of it? We start right away, and I fall to the back of his blade before I can trace the movement. The accursed bubbling starts in my blood; I don't know why I struggle against it, why I remember the old teachings of Master instead of coveting his final words.

That night there was not a trustworthy word spoken for the godlord's words were not his own, the cackles of the lords belied wild intent, the entire congregation was swept into the mad designs of just two vile Taosii.

Before I leave, under the song of dawn birds, Baraki reaffirms the battle we face. We're doomed to go alone.

The Whitan fled, *Capitane* Dickson got lost in Low Bashoan the first time. Baraki says, "We clashed in misunderstanding. Down alleys of nonsense, he led me. He was hurried, frantic. Said his *one god* called, his ships needed him. Wrong, wrong, wrong. All I could get out of him. I couldn't convince him otherwise." He wanted assurance of a trade deal, but that is only possible after the heads of the Okami roll, not something he was up to, he says.

"If we do succeed in bringing down this corruption, think twice that I'll watch you hand a slice of what we establish to that...heathen."

Baraki remains silent. Pensive.

A trader's courage only stretches as far as their coin purse, and I didn't see one on him. These Whitans have no interest in formality or honour, it seems. I cannot court something so barbaric; their god would threaten our own. From the wild story he told, they rather fancy themselves as men of action, but is quick to create a false impetus for his flight. If he's made it as far as Oshima now, I'd be surprised; if he makes it further, there's no doubt he'll be accosted – not much moves through the capital without inspection. Though, he's a coward with sea legs on him. I laugh at the thought of him swimming all the way upriver to the Sea Mouth. Cowards never tire.

"He will be missed." Baraki breaks his silence. "That strange *Gunna* moves faster than me...I do not see it. In my armour, I could not catch the projectile. Trust me, we needed him. If the wrong he spoke of is true, it could only mean something amiss in Orika. His force is on our gods-damned shores."

Worrying, indeed. A shame, perhaps, but I'd rather not pit my family's redemption against cowardice. Would he not turn such a weapon upon us if he mistook a jibe for a threat? There's too much to be said about the barrier an unlearned language presents.

"And where did he pluck the message from?" I ask. "Do not worry on it Baraki, thieves, brigands, and liars will craft stories to save themselves."

He nods.

Chapter 31

No matter what I try, I cannot follow his fourth beat – will never reach the fifth.

* * *

While the Red Dog's words were sharp, decisive, our actions cannot be. With every minute that passes by here on the nameless rise, on the edge of Sikara land, my anger wilts into frustration. Not for eagerness, no. My body trembles at the mountain I'm to overcome, as it crashes against one made of the same ilk here. I'm not yet ready to face the might of the Okami. Baraki teaches me so with every swing of his blade. There are some monsters you just can't overcome. It's a tightened chest, a light-head that grips me; I cannot escape the feeling that we will be too late, that poor Thousand Hands will die a dog's death. A great man, cut off from unlimited resource; a body without hands to grab hold of the situation and bring a blade down on his captor's neck.

Oboro arrived the day after I, the Sister led him back. I hadn't even noted her disappearance. Time seems to move slowly here, the hamlet is small, sleepy and hides in the mist from attention. Enough pass it by without notice – but the right traders stop, and there's a gods-be-damned amount of rice in these hills; the proprietor of the 'Monkey is a whoreson with a monopoly on a small fortune out here. Though, I expect that's no insult.

Every passer-by, trader, common folk; amongst the Wolfpads, even Baraki, the sora dragons overwhelm any conversation, the lands have become obsessed with it; my teeth strain against my clenched jaw every time I hear it, *retribution for the Samaki, a bad omen for the South, the gods recognise the North, the Four's blessing on a rich crop next season.* Every gods-damned person attributes it to their own pitiful existence. I bite my tongue but want to scream it was me. I am the one they recognised! I am the madness they couldn't turn a blind eye to! But no, it was a Guardian forest that burnt. The stray wolves would feast on me where I stand – the common folk would hang me, damn me to this plane. So, I let it go, turned my mind to Oboro, who sat worrying his cup, who knew but didn't judge. Who came back from within the jaws of death, but first sat with his *lady* on trivial matters.

It was with grave concern that he turned to me with what he found, the dolt is as mad as the demons, he's walked the Fox's camp, and came back with a punctured shoulder to pay for it. Seen off with an arrow, I count him lucky he got back at all; it heals well *thanks be to Aibo.* Kekkei is safe, for now. Oboro sighted him, not tied, but guarded, confined to the tent they allow him. Allowed movement around the camp which leaves a sinking, bottomless feeling in my gut that I can't get rid of – it shouts, screams wrongness in my face. There's something off and I can't place it.

Oboro pleads for me to regroup with Akate first, to go back to my clanlands. He doesn't trust Baraki, but this is a chance I cannot give up, though. He thinks it's all a show, to bring us into a false sense of courage. But, if I know Kekkei, his mouth, his loose-lipped charisma has won him more freedom than a prisoner ever has under a Wolf's watch. The godlord is more arrogant...No. The Taosii are snakes. The Soshist Po thinks too much of himself. It is their arrogance, their need to bring him before a proper death, paying a proper price in ceremony to their gods that buys us time. I cut my enemies down as soon as I can. Damn tradition, that only breeds failure, encourages a chance for them to stab you in the back.

They're a day's ride ahead of us, encamped in Oshima's rolling grasslands, a prize ready for picking – I hear Oboro again, *a trap. Forgive me, but it's foolish to take an opportunity so ripe and well presented. The fruit is poisoned. Why do they spend days in reach of Orika when they could ride on?* He had a point. Something is amiss, but Baraki's words settled me. The capital is full of spies, a place where Kekkei's scattered Hands could gather, where Aibo and Don Yoku flock in numbers.

I have a reason to rejoice, the godlord is not well. Officially, he is sick with the sleeper's bind. *If you're overworked, the gods lend their favourable hand to you*; his sudden relief from the magic, the wild anger. An attempt to close the borders again, all buried under lies. It seems the blow we struck with Ti's death has been lasting, thus far. The godlord hadn't shifted easily back into the puppet he once was, Baraki supposed. In the last weeks, as we clashed with the Yokusei, the sickness claimed the Fifth Godlord, Taos saw fit to remove him from his seat entirely for now and that is no easy task; parties, gatherings and public appearances were all part of his weekly schedule – never had there been a more egotistical, vain *warrior* leader. *The God's Senses* issued the ruse at the Taos order, and Orika holds its breath for the godlord's return. The common folk ignorant and gullible as ever. No one with the sickness will awake before the new moon. A foolish person spurns the favour of the gods, an unlucky person awakes early, tainted by the bind forevermore.

With the banishment of the Okami from the capital, they must wait a week until the new moon rises, there the godlord will awake, granting their entrance. There is our chance.

We have five days to prepare. Five to rescue Kekkei from Metsuku's grip. No charge other than treason awaits Thousand Hands, no penalty other than death. Baraki doesn't know what secrets he holds, only that the Lord Council need his end like the sun needs to rise.

* * *

I drop low and put all my weight into a forward step under Baraki's crescent slashing blade. He's overextended, too much confidence into that attack. Too large an opening as my upwards piercing thrust seeks his neck, but again, like every other time, he pulls out of the swing. Impossibly, in an attack he is fully committed to, he pivots on the tips of his toes, sweeping the blade in an arc towards himself, crossing his body. Deflecting my attack.

I let the momentum carry me and sweep around with a foot, he brings his knee to block. In the frustration, I let go of CrowKiller, and wince as pain lances through my knuckles against spell-forged steel. I batter him with a flurry until I'm bloody in my own red. I'm pushed back still. Manage to grab my blade from the ground somehow, one, two, three – I can't go for my sidearm, won't – the fourth I can't keep up with, it's not normal. And I'm in the dirt, ears ringing as he's spared me with the back of his blade.

"Whoreson!"

"My mother was the best in our family." Baraki laughs. "A rose too close to the thorns." He pulls me up, his frown is taut seriousness across his face. "You can't do this. Excuse me, *Lord Dattori,* but an old dog cannot possibly learn new tricks. If you can't reach me, you cannot reach the Fox. We cannot kill two fully-armed Okami with the men we have."

I hate it. I hate his words...the truth is a heartless bitch – I couldn't keep in step with them when they took my master, when they thought they'd ended me. And I can't now. Their footwork is a mastery only the gods could give. The crow step taught by the warrior cast pales in comparison. "Show me again! I can do it!"

"The *Falling Step* is the first words I learnt, the first steps I took. You cannot now teach your body to lust after falling, when you've spent your life fearing it. A long life." He smirks, never have I been so insulted. By a man ten and twenty years my younger, I'm made a fool. "To commit to every move, every slash, every beat as if it were your last, like your life depends on it. To put every ounce of strength into it, then pull out. Back away, and do it again, and again – every time you swing the blade. That is what it is to be an Okami. They tell us these were Ibi Sama's words when he passed it down."

"Nonsense!" Here, at the end of my world, I find Sama's step – before I die, I must see it, must have it. It is my birthright...this should never have been kept from the Samaki. But Baraki is a son of a whore. He won't listen to *entitlement.* No matter the history, he says, I must take it from him. Brushing off my robes, wiping the blood from my face, I lick it from my fingers. This madness takes hold. I must use this. I'm wild. "AGAIN!"

An eyebrow raises with the corner of his mouth. "Okay, demon."

CrowKiller scatters across the ground, Baraki pants as he finishes his disarming sweep with a hit to my ribs, the back of my knees – I'm down – resting it across my neck. "Demon. I was right. Like that you are a beast. Wolves are cunning, clever. A beast will always lose. We're done here."

"Trust me! The plan goes ahead!"

"I'll get what I want, but I cannot guarantee your life. If you fall, I don't come back for you."

Through my laboured breath, as the raging, unsatiated madness thrashes within. I still cannot believe it, would not, if I were not in the receiving end of this...insanity. In front of my rage magic, that has felled countless men, he is some god of storms, controlling, harnessing the winds no matter how they fight. How destructive they become. Though, there's a calm that drips into me, cause for a smile as he turns and walks away. For the first time, I beheld it, his step. I watched it in my wicked eyes, saw the fifth strike. The farmer's way? Impossible...could this be the same? The way Tetsuya fought matches the Wolves I was certain he could meet. Boy, your memory is all-honourable, the gods were lucky the day you joined them. Sama's blood is strong in you...and will be in me. I'm sure Meganako has found her muse. Your blood will live on.

* * *

While the preparations took place around us, we trained still. Not that I could reach Baraki. His blade eclipses mine in every way and that is that. But I grow used to dying to the wolf every day, know how it feels for them to cut me down. Each time, my death is harder earnt. In my muscles, in my mind, a knowingness.

* * *

I place the final candle, arranged in four points around my blades. CrowKiller, and the farmer's sacrifice. I wash my hands, pulling my robes off next as the Mistress needs to see the warrior as they are. I kneel in from of them, bowing my head low, reciting our warrior words:

Great Mistress,
Your blood in the earth is our steel.
Your steel folded is our weapon
Your weapon in our hands is our offering
I take up your sword so that I may die by another one day
On my honour, I will spill cleanly the blood of my enemies.

For each line, I offer clove oil onto my blade, so Meganako's blessings seep into the steel. That my blade remains as strong as it was first forged. So that my grip is tight, my attacks light. To ensure she sees what I'm about to do, pays attention to my fight. And if she deigns it, may she bless the duel in my favour.

For that is the message we sent.

Our numbers are not even half the combined strength of the Fox and the Tanuki's forces. We couldn't beat them in an open field, nor could we guarantee we would push as far as their leaders. The head I want to cut stands upon shoulders I just cannot mount. Anger redoubles through me a new flame. I swill its madness and spit it onto my blade for good luck as I finish buffing it with a cloth. Like a cornered mutt, I'm forced to yap and bite at the whoresons that took my family, begging they do me the honour of the *Mistress' Mercy*, a duel of ultimate consequence. Live and walk away with honoured restored no matter what or die with the gods in witness. A warrior's death. Not a warrior's burial, though. I slam my hands into the small table, throwing wax everywhere as the candles roll, catching an errant drop of oil, bursting into flames. I grab my bedroll and suffocate the flame, coughing and spluttering as the small, private room fills with a pleasant char. Idiot.

After everything I've built was scattered with the dragon's divine winds, this is all I can do. We cannot muster the force, the Capitanc has gone – the icemen already prove themselves unreliable. His men are out of the question. There're no gods I can turn to, the Endless Seas are godless. What's more, the Fox's camp does not reply. They send no runners with an answer. We will march on them anyway. Baraki's arrogance cannot be quelled, with half a unit of Wolfpads and his armour, he's an undeniable force, if only to himself.

He has a bone to pick, scraps still left out in the sun, with Kabutomaru. Oboro fears I've been swept into his bravado, into the lunacy of monsters. But it is done. The duel requested. Meganako beseeched. I go to duel, or I go to die. It cannot be changed.

I will do it. If I cannot silence the mouth that ordered my family's destruction, I will cut the blade that carried it out.

It is not a matter of failure. It is a matter of what I must do. My duty. Dattori honour. Even so, I tremble, slept fitfully; I'm resolved to die, and yet, I want to live to see my master's enemies at my feet and his honour restored. The ache in my heart tells me I can do it, but the acute pulse in my shoulder, the creek in my knees, the cramp in my stomach, tells me I can't.

As the sun comes up, it splits through the shutters, daggers of light scatter around me, casting away the shadows of doubt in my mind, unveiling the upturned ritual. This morning the gods receive my wish. Today is the day I should be concerned with my friend...My ally's life, but I am a fanatic of the stage his capture has set.

There's a rap at my door. With the soft chirrup of the dawn birds a signal is carried – we leave now, while the day is young, before the gods are fat with prayers. "Come in."

The man that appears is haggard, he has not slept or the rings around his eyes lie. His silver flecked hair is pulled back tight, black robes and the twin short swords inset with island gems – the only difference about him is the warmth that his appearance brings. If I were not a lord, if I was not rage incarnate, Oboro is a man I'd take to my bed. But that is a weakness I cannot afford. I watch the light fall over his blunt, focused eyes, caressing his lips and I want. For the first time since Zaki, I need.

"My Lady, we're ready." He bows, his tone and formality casting my feelings aside. The man is all the efficiency of a knife to the heart – final and trusty. But you wouldn't straddle it. So, I brush off the thought, misplaced lust. What I desire is the Fox's head.

"As am I." He raises an eyebrow, tugs at his robes. Awkward. Maybe he felt it? Never mind. "Lead the way. Oboro...Thank you."

"My lady?"

"For all that you've done in service of an old bitch that doesn't deserve it."

He opens his mouth but says nothing and leads the way to our horses, he never wanted this. Of course, he still thinks it a trap. I offered him a horse, food and a start towards Dattori Heiwa. He won't go. Something about his own duty. Fool.

Around our small table next to the kitchen, the smell of cooking drapes us in a homely warmth – the tofu soup is bland, watery despite the lingering salt notes. One thing they have right here is the pickles. I finish off a second portion of the rice, and some of the fried burdock root; it's a veritable feast, all that this establishment is capable of. Baraki, Oboro and Wanrin, the Red Dog's Wolfpad Captain, join me in a pervasive silence that reaches the rest of the Wolfpads in the 'Monkey. It feels like a final meal. I've dragged myself from the hells before – let the gods notice me again.

Baraki, in full gold-trimmed-white Okami plate, leaks a sulphurous, bitter tang. It looks etched by the gods, a different scene on each piece. Suppression, destruction, victory. All that he is, fronted on the chest by a wolf with all fangs bared, each a blade; the way Meganako is sometimes depicted. But it is woven in a magic that turns my nose, making the formidable warrior a demi-god of power. Under his stoic demeanour, beyond the frown, there's a confidence that pulses in his eyes. He is disaster coated in armour. Oboro opposite is a concealed blade. There's none of the brute, undeniable strength, but it'll kill the same.

The willingness of youth to die in bloody battle suddenly seems alien. Flicking my gaze between them, I allow the doubt to spread; I'm old, hate has sapped my strength. I remind myself that it is for my master and my honour that I still breathe. My warrior-caste don't believe in failure, not occurring to them even against impossible odds. It was in that mindset that I died to the Fox. We're taught never to fear another, death is a welcome part of the order of things. But what if you've died to those same blades before, is it not natural to fear them? Gods, is it okay? I've come this far needing this opportunity, needing to sow death to these men, but now I am reminded of that sharp, unforgiving steel.

I let out a long sigh, my own plate rattles. Borrowed, it is Wolfpad armour that matches Wanrin's unit, without the magic of Baraki's. My family set is with the Samaki.

Swines.

The river does not fight its current, for it is the very flow of the water; the ferocity that drives follows one path. Do not fight the current, Masako, become it.

There was always a fucking convoluted way of saying something, wasn't there Master? I've lost sight of what is right, you hear. I am driven by the one thing you pleaded me to ignore. Will you truly rest in honourable sleep if I do this? If I kill this man? All that's left is to find out.

Baraki rises with a burp, pig, "We leave!"

A resounding drum on the tables, a cacophonous snarl of readiness.

In one motion, we're outside. A wave that's started rolling. Lonestep grunts, nips at the Wolfpad gelding next to us. A grin tugs at the corner of my mouth, I'm in capable hooves.

"Ready, Hawk of Fenika?" Baraki shouts down the line, wheeling his horse around. "The arrogant mutts have never tasted defeat; they are fat with pride, too sure of their own blade! Well, what do we tell them?" Another growl ripples through the men around me. "We bring them death! Death to those who defy heavens, death to those who corrupt our way of life!" He finishes by kicking his heels in, his horse flying off down the goat path, and we follow – he would surely fit in with our southern ways.

Chapter 32

BEFORE MY FALL: ACT 5

"My gracious lords," I say with difficulty, fighting to keep the poison from leaking into my words; I bite it back at having to beg in front of these whoresons. "Under the dragons, this is folly. There's but one clan in disgrace; the fieldclan's deceit knows no bounds. It was on our land they wrought the wickedness of the poppy, so it was on our land they paid. Just, my lords. It was a killing with the gods in agreement–"

"Mhm, we've heard enough of your backward justifications!" The godlord interrupts, his neck bulges over his plated cuirass; etched in family history, gilded in the gold allowed of his rank. The only time his armour has seen a battle is when the smith scratched one into its surface – that topknot is an insult to my caste. How do the gods allow such a cretin to pass judgement on me? "The scroll! This bitch is irritating me. On with this!" There's a raucous clatter of ceremonial plate as the presiding lords trip over each other to deliver the message. Lords Dorakon, Yokusei, Kitsutana sit with him on the platform, judging me as only the gods should. I'll await each one in the next life, they won't get away with this.

Their platform rises out of the courtyard, giant golden waves frozen before they crashed back down to the earth. The cowardly lords line the higher most tier. Torches flicker, fight with the night's bitter wind, its fingers snaking under my robes; the Kirisam roars beyond me – if I can drag Master

307

to its waters, we will live. I cast my eyes in despair around the yard, not looking at him. I can't bear his eyes. The godlord's bodyguard, the Wolfpads, encircle the edges. An insurmountable barrier of steel and thousands of hours training, topped off by the monsters standing at the foot of the wave; a sulphurous draught emanates from their armour as it crackles, spits into the night – spell-forge steel. Warriors afforded its like are cut from the cloth of the gods. The four captains of the Wolfpad army, the Okami guard. Only their beast-masked helms snarl back at me. The hopelessness leaks in as I notice his gaze; High Captain Kita, the Fox. Eight blades in all hang from the prized mutt.

Pockets of noblemen, minor lords and their servants stand as witnesses to this barbaric misuse of common law.

Lord Jizu steps out from the shadow of the wave, he has all the presence of a robed rat, whiskers and that overbite adding to the effect. The snowy old whoreson should not survive me. Fighting against restraining hands as he scuttles over, I'm bludgeoned to the earth by the guard that hold me still.

"Masako!" Master's taught rasp scolds me.

Taking my eyes from the dogs in front of me, I'm in anguish at having to see him this way; two guards hold him to the earth as they do to me, an incomparable man made to kneel in front of lessers. His eyes are tired, the fires simmering in the low light of the moon; sick of everything...sick of me. He won't leave this place. There's a watery swamp in the pit of my stomach. A man of honour, Master wouldn't waver for anything, much less the gold these despicable lords covet; from the ashes of a pauper family, he rose to the seat of lord in the outer lands, without so much as a silver coin from anyone else – and now my anger takes it away from him, my inability to steel myself. I'm not worthy enough to be a warrior of the Samaki. Sama's Third would fall from the heavens if they witnessed how their blood thins. There's no hope here. I only pray I hold my anger in check as it rises to meet Jizu. Master always said it would ruin me if I let it.

Honour and emotion are at odds with each other, one must die while the other lives.

"Now then!" Lord Jizu cries. "Swift and absolute is the order of our

Heavenly Godlord. With it, the judgement of the gods will be done. Let them be known." As he throws one arm up in a flamboyant arc, four masked figures mount one of the platform's lower tiers – the Gods' Senses. An eye, an ear, a mouth and a nose, a sense for each god drawn onto the masks of the plain robed law-presiders. It's why I've been undone; they've tarred us with the Lord Council's law – those that mean we must go to these cuckolds and beg before we're allowed to act. No. That isn't the way of the outer clans. But here I am, in a plot that runs deep into the heart of Basho. "May they look down on you with mercy–"

"On – with – it, Jizu!" the godlord says, "read them out!"

"Ah, er...yes, my heavenly lord. At once." Jizu unravels the scroll, hands trembling – the man knows the falseness of this, but his eyes betray a rotten core. What would those who can't wield a sword know of the importance of cutting truth? "The charges imposed on Lord Hojimoto Dattori and his commander, *the Hawk*, Lady Masako Dattori, are most heinous. They are those that act against the Lord Council, our very way of life. Those that anger the gods themselves and threaten this Time of Peace: the illegal seizure of land from the Imanta, and the slaughter of those who lawfully protected their rights within; the manufacture and distribution of Devil's Spittle, this plague that ravages our great country. Treason." He pauses, I only hear a buzzing in my ears. Numb. I daren't look at Master now. "Treason, of all crimes, carries the penalty of death. May you never enter the heavens." I surge to my feet, screaming, before the Wolfpad guards drag me back down. Again, bludgeoning me until I quit. "The charges go on, but our all-honourable godlord deigns them too damaging for our good peoples' ears." There's a gasp that ripples through the audience. *Demons?* I hear it question. Zaki, your traitor mouth went too far. Was it not you who brought their attention?

I cannot let them do this to us, the dishonour, "LIES"

"Masako!" Master says, lowers his voice to a whisper. "*I said quiet. We've no chance at honour for our family if you carry on! We must go into death with it intact! It is done...done!*" There was always a lesson to be learnt, wasn't there, Master? But who are they to decide where we fall? Blood bubbles, beckons, speaks to me as it always has – if they would just draw it, give me the chance. "NO. You will not silence me...you send foreign sorcerers to do your bidding? The Soshists you invite into our nation soil it!"

The cawing of crows erupts around me – there's a chatter that the Wolfpads try to silence – "Listen to the rumours," I say, "I implore you look into this...government." A flash streaks across my eyes as I'm hit again, pressed against the cold, wet earth. Master's grunts are heavy next to me. The fury of my bloodline still costs him.

"SILENCE," the Fox shouts as he closes the distance between us in a matter of seconds, the magical tang bitter in my nostrils now – his sword arced up over his head in the Guard of Heaven. I didn't even see him draw. "Speak out of turn once more and I swear you'll not leave this plane with honour. You'll die a dog's death!"

"Kita, stop!" The godlord waves his hand from the high tier. "This has gone on long enough – the knives, bring them."

Master cannot offer me reassurance; his wheezing hollows my chest. I struggle, straining against my captors. Desperate. The man I revere is a bundle of blue and blackened robes – blood runs from his mouth, it beckons. A sob rises in my throat, but I swallow it, breaths coming quicker, faster. Out of control. I can't do this. The silence strips me of my nerves. I look up and see them approaching, the godlord's grin stretches from ear to ear – the Fox as escort, and the knife-keeper flanks them both – this is it. Out of my control. A lifetime of blade swings boiled to one single cut. I need to survive this; Master, I need to. You can't ask me to go in honour, there's none of it left in this life – we need it regained. We need justice, "You sacrifice a great clan for a lesser's crimes. This is not the gods' will, you hear? Jizu... you know this. They will not rest while the culprit goes unpunished." I look to the godlord now. "The laws dictate it! It was our land...let Master go, I slaughtered them alon–" His chuckle stops my plea dead, there's a giddiness in his eyes that won't let this go. Deeper, something else, a ghost-light in them; someone else pulls the strings.

"Did you not plot against me, girl? Treason...that was the charge was it not?" He raises an eyebrow, making a show of looking to his peers, the audience. I have nothing to say to him. "Treason. Yes, I will make a concession...of course, I am a benevolent leader." The godlord leans in close – the guards' grip strangles my arms; they numb. He whispers, "*My brother was offered this same chance, don't let history repeat itself over and over.*" I'm hauled up when he steps away. The godlord turns, saying something to the 'keeper but I no longer hear anything – just the throb in my ears – the 'keeper steps forward, two ceremonial knives on the pillow. He bows, holding it outstretched. The godlord brandishes one with a murderous smirk. I'm a wild beast as I struggle but it's to no avail. The knife is presented to Master, who goes to take it, but hesitates first and says, "Please rethink this, Takahashi. It is your laws my retainer sought to uphold, she saw a wrong and righted it. Those fields are Dattori land...we Samaki protect what is ours, but make no mistake, it was not done as insult to you, my lord. Allow her into your charge, if it must be. She is a great warrior. One of pure code and honour."

The godlord grimaces, slowly nodding his head. "You play on my good nature?"

Master's eyes go wide. "No, my lord." He bows, taking the knife. "Not at all...it was mere suggesti–"

"–Silence, beggar! You've said enough. Fine, I grant you one thing. With that knife, you may take her life – I will not carry out the judgement myself. That's what Samaki honour is worth here. Do it yourself. Is that not what you...people pride yourself on? End her!"

A cheer erupts around the room, goading Master on. He's right, there's no honour here, no hope to be had.

Thump, thump.

Master steps towards me with the knife – "A clean stab, through the heart," the Fox says, "I'll take her head, you've not to worry about that, wretch."

"No...NO. Master! You can't. Don't let them." Time slows, each moment draws out into a lifetime, the sadness written in his eyes will follow me to the grave – my lungs petrify in my chest. Master moves in quickly, placing one hand around my back as he pulls me into a sharp embrace; the knife

311

goes deep, nicks my lung – white agony. He misses my heart, and whispers, "*I'm a fool to want this now, but it can't end, Masako. Bring it back, bring honour to my family once more.*" Light, dizzy, my head seems to double in weight as they pull Master away, I drop to my knees.

Laughing, or something I can't make it out. I bring my hands up to my face, they're covered in red – blood – hunger...just take it. Mumbling, shouting. There's the singing rasp of a blade being drawn, and I catch what's going on in time to see the Fox's reaping slash, taking my master's head. Blood erupts from his body. I leap for it, taking Master in my arms, the boisterous pain in my chest ebbing against the cold that fills me. Cradling him in my arms as they try to pull me away, I push my head into his chest, nuzzle it like I did when I was a girl – there's a scream – I'm screaming; there's no stopping it, I must do it. MUST GIVE IN TO IT. So, I lick it, his blood. Taste the honour lost. A lifetime in ruins.

It must be paid.

Only blood will pay.

Mine or Master's, I don't really know whose blood incites it – but it rips through my mind, an explosion of heightened senses, crisp, sharp. I taste and smell the copper I'm drenched in – that pulses through my veins. Muscles, pumped, tightening. Steeling. And I see the ceremonial knife. Taking it, I turn, parrying the Fox's blade that comes for me impossibly. It sends his attack away, the knife shatters in my hand. I take the jagged stump and look for the godlord but he's unreachable, beyond the Fox. The courtyard stands frozen – not enough time has passed for their minds to make sense of it.

I don't waste a second as ferocity wells in my body, forcing it into my legs. Master has to be avenged. I have to survive this. The distance to the Wolfpad wall vanishes in a moment. Crossing it as if I were wearing the Okami spell-forge, weaving the winds on my heels, I hit their ranks like a force of nature if I ever was one. They're not expecting it. To be fair to them, only seconds unfolded since my master's head fell, and they're faced with a demon. They hesitate, and that's a moment too long for a swordswoman like me. A quick jab to the face of the first one I meet, a red flower blooms slowly from it. To me anyway. Reaching down for his katana, I draw it and leap into the thick of them, as the lines converge. I cut two down before they've half-drawn their sword. Another two just manage to get theirs free before I lash out, one parries me, so I catch the other on the backswing, taking him at the wrist. Kicking out, the next one falls, and I stab down as I trample over him – heading for the rush. The gods favoured me tonight when the godlord set this stage so close to the Kirisam. Behind me, there's a madness of screams unfolding – a roar of something else. Clashing steel carries in the wind. But I put it behind me, legs pumping for my escape.

The Kirisam is fierce with the gods' fury, winds whip across the darkness from it – pure primal force, a fool would swim in it, a madwoman has other designs. Injustice has been done in your names, tonight. *Please*, I beg. *Take me from here!*

A few steps more, the Wolfpads haven't followed over the curtain wall, they couldn't hope to chase, and I'm undone. Something glints in the moon. I turn, throwing it away from me with the borrowed blade, down across me in an arc as a second appears. A third and I'm on my backfoot, wheeling away. Laboured, impossible breaths. Parry and parry, not being able to return a strike. Not even my curse, let loose, is enough for him. I break away, the Fox's mask snarls at me; the white plate rippling as are the foaming waters beyond me. A katana in both hands, he's the only man I've ever met to wield two the way he does – the ruin of my family met by one man. I can barely hold myself up, bracing one hand on a knee as the power seeps from me. A ruined husk. He watches, waiting. There's no need for him to rush. Driving at him with desperation mustered force, I'll take him with me. The Fox feints low, moving into the viper guard and striking heavy. I turn it with a two-handed grip away, spinning, evading the flurry he launches at me. Anger fuelling anger. I become a living torrent of rage and break out of it, catching his stab, biting down with all the strength I can – one of his legendary blades gives way. It snaps against my force. I am everything.

I – am – undeniable.

But a third blade has appeared where the second just was. Hot, wet agony. I cry out, staggering backwards. I'm run through. Unbearable. I vomit.

Razors shoot through my body.

The rush is but a step behind me, so I leap back with all my might, his blade follows me still, won't let me go. It slashes my throat, and I fall into the waters, letting them take me.

Gods, please...let me live. Let me rid these lands of these heathens, the Fox, the Soshists, all of them must pay.

Chapter 33

I watch Oboro ride all the way back, he makes no effort to hide his scowl, or the fact he's just rode around the enemy camp in daylight. Blasé doesn't suit him, it's anxiety that has him retie his sash. He straightens the folds in his robe again, and once more for good measure after he dismounts his bark brown and white steed; geldings are more reliable creatures, but he says there's a bit of wildness in mares that suits longer rides. "I warned of treachery!" Oboro's words are coarse. "It is all wrong!"

"Are they armed for warfare or not?" I don't care what else there is. We need to ride in with a chance to settle it cleanly, not a barrage of arrows.

His eyes narrow, thinking better of whatever rebuke he intended. "Ropi. She's there now. Among the camp, following Kekkei around."

"Tsk, do they look war-ready or not, man?" Baraki's patience is tested, his captain seems here to rein him in, else he would've ridden into the heart of the camp upon arrival.

From where we stand, on a rise east of their camp, they surely see us. We do not hide. Instead, our men fan out amongst the tall grasses, making us seem more numbered, more formidable than we are. There's just over a score of tents, double the horses. The camp is awake, men scuttle about. Nearing the back, something forms. We thought it a muster for battle – but they encircle a patch of the grassland, working. Soldiers pass something between them. I cannot quite see it.

"An arena, my lady. They carry away the grasses." Oboro notices my glare.

Baraki barks a laugh and says, "Fools. Their pride has dishonoured them. Their deaths written." The more time I spend with him the more I'm sure it is not the Taosii that turned Takahashi tyrant, they only nurtured the seed the family already bears.

Checking my blades again, CrowKiller, and the farmer's sidearm. Even now, if I focus on the small sword that braces my abdomen, a faint scream works its way up my side into the recesses of my mind. The blade has sat firmly in the sheath since Chisai. The hells. They ebb and recede back and forth inside the blade. Only their torment would rend the farmer's spirit so – but I keep it by my side, maybe to remind me of the failure at Okami hands before, again and again. I will not make the same mistake. The chance the farmer gave me may be immortalised in the steel he lost.

The gourd hangs next to them. The lives that have got me this far converge on one point.

I look up as the Sister of Aibo wades through those clustered around us; I hadn't seen her on the ride up here, but that doesn't mean she wasn't present. I'm uncertain as to whether this is the same woman. Though, the unfamiliar air to her, the white-painted face, has Aibo's marks. "You can do this?" she says, finally standing at my side. "We need you to do this. Aibo doesn't like wolves. Their magic, she can't speak next to it."

"Yes, I can."

"You don't believe it, but we do. The fates, they squirm in the skies above, crying Hawk!" she looks at me, eyes searching. Smile wide, wild. "Kekkei is owed. Aibo is owed. Take us to him. Win him back from the shadows." There's a glint of something as the light catches it in her hands, she plays with a glass bottle. When she sees I notice it, she snatches it back beneath her robes.

A pressure on my back, I turn as Baraki pulls his hand away. "No more time. We go."

I don't feel ready, our force counts a third of theirs, win or lose, we've not the presence to guarantee our safety. I can't ignore the fact that Ropi is there. That Kekkei swans around the camp with his First Hand. The hairs on the back of my neck stand, a prickle of energy runs to my tailbone; I think it only cowardice that steers me away but it's something else.

"After you, Wolf," I answer Baraki. He studies me looking for something to infer from the way I spoke, but it wasn't a jibe – I've grown fond of him. It would be a shame if he cut my throat.

He throws his hand up, fingers flicking forward, and we start to move. Oboro next to me, the Sister pulls away, it's not her fight. I won't see her again unless Aibo is satisfied we can deliver what is owed; what exactly is that Kekkei? The secret is a claw clamped around my heart, I follow blindly into the abyss and don't fully know what I search for.

Thousand Hands, where did you come from? I've been so caught up in my own anguish that not once did I ask anything of the mercenary. Now it is all wrong. I search my memory still and nothing points in the right direction, the picture askew; our flight through the woods from the Yokusei prison wagon, the signs already there, he knew where he was going; the missing family crests on the robes; the lords wrapped around his fingers – a *mercenary*. What secrets would Aibo have of his that were worth besieging the wolf's den? I'm missing the point of it all, but it ties something towards the man I offer myself to *rescue*.

I give my life now, Meganako, not only to honour the old Dattori, but to find the new. Yes, it is all wrong. Though, I turn a blind eye once more because the mercenary, the wildboy and their men are all I have. Mine was never a family of blood. When ancient family lines run dry, heirs murdered, killed, lost, those housed in Dattori Heiwa will remain mighty; bonds found and earned, not born, will withstand the years where blood will run dry.

Family is everything, found or not. Kekkei is family.

I will take everything, this time, from those who seek to destroy it.

Like the cook's pot, readying the rice batch for the day, my blood heats; it starts to simmer, the change rolls over me. Doubt boils away. Anger is stoked.

We roll down the hill in a gentle canter like ants spilling from their nest. Though, there's not many of us to make that comparison. Less...now. The men that surround our descent are not enough. I pull the reins, my horse sidled up to Baraki's and my High Captain follows. "What is this? You plan to fight your way out with a hand's worth of men? This isn't the plan," I spit.

"When the wolves circle, it's too late to check our fangs."

"Plainly, boy."

He flicks his head back, looking down his nose at me as we edge closer to the Fox's camp. With a chuckle, he says, "Relax." There's a pregnant pause. "The wind tells tales. Rustling, chattering plate. Listen." He's mad. There's nothing but the raucous welcome ahead of us as enemy Wolfpads line up. "Don't think because you've offered the *Mistress's Mercy* Kita will take it. Honour sits differently when you've only ever won – the Fox slew his first as a boy, and none of them came back from the grave."

"So?"

"Tsk, you're a done deal. He's killed you once. There's no honour in it twice."

I shift, uneasy, my tone a whisper now as we come into arrow range, "Why're we here then?" My chest thumps.

"Don't," he growls, "his pride will get in the way. It's a heavier burden than dishonour, but not every warrior covets death, Hawk. We need assurance. Ours moves to their flank, Aibo leads the way."

Dismounting, the wall of wolves part to allow us entry into the camp. We puncture the camp-line like a needle that lets out the stale sweat, camp refuse stench that swirls around me; oil, a low *thud, thud*. An excited pulse beats around me, pulling me closer. *Thud, thud.* It's as though I'm carried on the wave of it. A wiry figure saunters over to us, decked in wolf plate, scars crisscross his face. Someone grabs my arm, Oboro. He nods. We're met by the Scar.

"Giju, where is he?" The name belongs to the Fox's Captain, who takes no notice of Baraki, his gaze fixed on me. A low snicker as he nods. Baraki goes for the hilt of his blade. But I grab his arm, wincing back as his plate sizzles under my grip. "Mutt," I say to the Captain. "Ignoring a superior is met with a swift knife to the throat in my lands."

"I don't see none here. Superiors." His voice is the drawing of a rusted blade. "Nothing to it." He looks me up and down. "I just wanted to see you for myself, demon. Before Lord Kita dices you up." With the same cockiness, he starts back the way he came.

On the outskirts of the arena, tall grasses sway in a light breeze; I shiver as the frosty fingers cool my plate. Oboro, Baraki and his Wolfpads flank me. I think back to the arena at Chisai, the odds mounted against me, hatred my guide. Common folk stacked at the edges, jostling for a better view, vendors selling fried foods, shouts. It all washes away into the scene before me – the only similarity is the enemy, and now my anger as my lip curls. The simmer turns to a boil. There's no audience but the soldiers. This is no spectacle; this is a matter of finality. An end.

Honour commands it.

A monster in gold-edged armour stand before me. The man who killed Fenika Dabura, last of the Fenika line. The man who killed Dattori Hojimoto, my everything.

The man who headed the ruin brought to my household. He is a pawn, yes, but one whose death will sate my thirst.

I run my hands across the taut black scar on my neck, parting my robes in display of my other. "You thought this enough? Fool. I come for your head. On my honour, I offer you a duel in sight of Meganako and the Mistress." Unsheathing CrowKiller, I continue, "Draw your katana, highest Captain of the Okami, Lord Heir of Kitsutana, I offer you a warrior's death. Scum." I bring the hilt of my sword to my face, point tipped towards him in an ox-guard. "What say you, do you protect your honour?

Kita goes to his helm, chucks it to the side. His wrinkled eyes search me, one is glassy, white from a wound that cuts across his forehead, and crosses it. He's much the same as the Okami to my left, but experience ages his skin, stubble prickles as he frowns; a katana, and wakizashi, to one side, as common law dictates. Three more swords at his back, and a short sword high on both of his sides – any other warrior would look at fool, but it only proves the Fox's skill. A kitsune matures with the addition of more tales. Though, his ascension was foiled, for I cut his *unbreakable* eighth blade.

Baraki says, "You kept my gift, eh." He interrupts my offer – spoiling the ceremony of duel is bad luck. Immaturity and pomp anger the gods. Fool. "Well, are you a coward? What say you?"

"LOOSE!" the Fox barks in answer.

The word is foreign to my ears, I can't make sense of it, not in this circumstance. Honour. Honour is this duel. Honour demands it.

There's one breath before I realise what he's said, but I'm not running a fever. My hand reaches CrowKiller's hilt as a great wave of arrows rises to its peak behind the coward Okami. I cry out something blasphemous. I have time for nothing else as I wait to be buried underneath a myriad of thorns. I try to pull my sword anyway. Not even half drawn as they fall – the gods have never acted quicker. My heart is a slow *whump*. The arrows slow in their descent. Time crawls to a halt in my final breath. Even so, in my periphery where Baraki stood, there's a blur. Surging muscle and plate barrels in front of me, a strike of lightning wreathed in storm wind – a god of them all. I see what he does, but it's so fast my brain doesn't have time to perceive it, to turn it into anything useful.

There's a cacophonous roar as I'm brought back into the flow of things, my katana is half-drawn in a feeble attempt to block the inevitable; around me, enemy Wolfpads fall on my position, I pray to the gods the small unit we've brought is behind me.

Baraki holds his sword arm out, extended at the end of the arc that split the sharp rain in twix. Fletchings and arrowheads litter the grass. Oboro flies to meet two oncoming 'Pads.

"Now, demon!" I'm torn back to Baraki as he's bashed towards me – forced to backpedal. He sends me flying, my katana spinning from my grip. I twist, landing like a cat ready to pounce. CrowKiller is gone. I don't see her; mind racing, my heart is a bludgeon in my chest. Baraki has raised a high guard but struggles against the Fox's driving sword. There's a blur of exchanges. "What're you fuckin' waitin' for!" Baraki spits. "I'll kill the cur if you don't move!" The Fox leads, feinting in a sweeping arc, "Pah," he says, and parries Baraki's sword with one of the daggers sheathed at his side and pushes on, catching the young wolf on his back foot, crying, "years too early, brat! Stand down!"

I grab the gourd from my robes. I wanted to try this on my own, but I'll see to it that Tetsuya eclipses the potential he was meant to become. Popping the top, I drink deep. Consuming all that's left of his blood.

Baraki's guard is broken as he slips to one knee. His opponent throws a wild, nonchalant piercing thrust. Baraki brings his blade up in time to deflect the strike, the Fox erupts into the opening, pouring towards me. A tsunami of power. Before my vision is blocked by it, I see the wolves descend upon the Red Dog.

Idiots.

My thoughts echo, the blood takes hold – the next beat is a pulsing flame of power blooming from my centre until it engulfs me. Muscles throb, steel, grow; the burning quells, everything sharpens; the metallic scent, the song of steel, the grunts of struggle; the next breath fills me with power that shifts through my body, into my legs.

And he hits.

Crashing around me in a savage delicacy of stabs and slashes. All committed, killing blows. But I become Tetsuya's light-foot, an incorporeal wind that flows around every one of the Fox's murderous moves; he cannot hold me to his strike. I don't make effort to move away from him. I'm pushed to avoid them, scattered like the air if you try to grip it, squash it.

Only, slowly, his fire consumes it, wears me down. I've no sword to parry but the wakizashi strung tightly at my side. The Fox switches tact, sheathing a wakizashi, drawing a katana from his back and in the same fluid movement his off-hand buffets the downward lash of his blade, added brute force making the swing not entirely avoidable. I lunge forward with my lead foot, stepping around with my back. I miss the angle, not getting low enough in time. The sword bites into my shoulder, the wicked fang sending lances of pain throughout my body. They're dulled, distant – and feeding from that, I react. Instantly striking the blade skyward with the palm of my other hand. Instead of cleaving deep into my arm, it cuts a shallow gouge. Hot warmth spreading from the wound is the bubbling, swelling power within my blood. I cannot be turned. The Fox's blade skyward, even the god-like wind imbued in his armour will take two breaths to recover – so I take my chance in one. For a warrior like me, born for the sword, raised under its swing, the steel is but an extension of the real weapon. Thousands of hours packed into sinewy death. *Father, would you be proud of this?* For a moment,

I'm not sure whether my thoughts are my own or the wrongfully pilfered memories of the boy warrior who never got the chance to live. Still, it only adds to the ferocity, the blaze stirs. I pull back my arm, ignoring the throb of my shoulder. Tightening my pull, squeezing every ounce of blood-given power, Tetsuya's presence inside me is a raging wind. A puppeteer that moves my body in ways I could not alone. It reacts to what I can't see by myself. I offer my palm outwards. Striking the Okami in the ribs with the clean wildness of a tiger's paw. Still, Kita pivots, turning away from most of the force. I carry on, letting the momentum take me and dive out of the way as he brings his sword down again into the earth.

I get up with a start, putting distance between us, searching for CrowKiller but not finding her. Around me carnage unfolds; a full-scale battle has sprung to life. Turning to the Fox, it's as though our duel is a skerry amid the crashing sea waves, the rest of the fight flows around us. In my periphery there's a sudden flash, fire whips along the grasses – a group of riders flow from within the inferno. The men Baraki left out of the fight charging in to turn the tide.

"Here, beast!" the Fox growls. "Your fight is with me. Don't you dare steal your eyes away from it. You'll die here. I'll have your gods-damned head to make sure this time." *Beast.* No, that's all wrong! He took my family from me. I'm not the monster – but my body swells still, muscles stretching with every heartbeat; I scream at him not recognising the hoarse shriek. Tetsuya cries within but I hold him close, need him still. It's not long now, boy, just a little further.

The Fox moves to me but stumbles on his second step, going down to his knee, wincing. He hacks up blood; the scent of lost pride lingers around the thick metal of my victory.

I pick a katana from a dead Wolfpad I didn't notice fall near me, the fight has since moved on and I don't stop in my stride until I meet my opponent as he rises into an upward-arcing slice. I move out of the way and attack him with my own. His hands are a blur again as he sheaths his katana at the top of his swing and pulls two short swords from his sides before I can finish him. Grunting, roaring through the pain, he launches into a burst of movements I only just avoid. A nick in my cheek. Two slashes to my arms. The last rakes across my ribs as I jump back. All drawing blood. All making my curse seem like a child's tantrum.

I stumble, catching myself as he brings a massive double over-head swing down on me, stopping his twin fangs on the edge of my borrowed blade. My off-hand props up my guard as my gods-forsaken curse struggles against one man.

My chipped and battered sword snaps.

Both pieces fold inwards. I try to dodge but not fast enough for the magical plate he wears. One of the short swords pierces the same injured shoulder. My arm goes limp. His other slices through the opposing side of my neck, both swords positioned to cleave my head; I feel the movement that ripples through his body, to the ends of his blades before he does it and I tear myself out of the bite as the jaws snap together in front of me.

The Fox drops both blades instantly, drawing the katana that sits in the rightful place on his left hip. Ornate, the hilt shines with the grimace of a wolf. He draws the fine grey and red spell-forge, putting all he can into one final swing.

I don't think; my hand goes to the hilt at my side and draws it to meet his. His steel meeting something changed. As my side-arm arm shrieks something ungodly, stabs through the wind like a dying bird, it cleaves his spell-forge in two. I press on, curving my blade amid thrust.

Masterfully, Kita pulls out of his fully committed strike, his wolf-step avoiding certain death. Peerless. There is no other human warrior like him. The wretched cunt.

I am no human warrior.

I am hatred.

I am anger.

I AM BLOOD.

So, I step to him, with my howling blade. Everything around me greyed as if something has sucked the colour out of my surroundings. The world is bleak, desolate. The blade in my hand feeding off life, giving power. To his credit, he doesn't flinch at the broken katana. No matter the implications of breaking spell-forge in such a way; drawing his final two swords, he braces them against my oncoming attack

My wrong-blade cuts through his cross-guard like it isn't there. There's a little more resistance as the magic in his armour crackles against the tip of my sword, but that breaks too. Slicing across his stomach, I cut deep. The Fox is gutted. Blood pours from his stomach as he looks down, entrails in his hands, he looks up stoic, blunt even in his death.

It doesn't stop, though, the howling continues. Consumes. The blade sings the song of death even as I hold it ahead of me – everything pulls into that one point of madness. My teeth scrape, muscles flatten, anger turns into weakness. Heavy, so heavy. Done.

Master...why is it so empty? The rage against the river, fighting upstream, has destroyed me. Now, I go with the flow, give up. I struggle to bring the wakizashi up to its sheath, falling to my knees. Everything I am starts to flood towards it. As my 'fever abates the pull weakens. I give in. The greyness becomes me, whittles everything into ash – there will be nothing left when it is finished.

Hands grip mine, sheathing the blade. The torment lets go; the claws of dread recede. Sukami's glare thaws me. Someone kneels down beside me. Oboro. I try to fight them. I'm too weak. They're talking, trying to reach me but I'm at the bottom of a pit. Though, his presence somehow fills me with hope. I can do it. I can go further.

He drags me to my feet. My arm over his shoulder, we both face the great man I've felled. Convulsing, hacking, the Fox is an empty husk – blood pours from the sides of his mouth, the colour runs from his face with it. Yet, when I meet his eyes, they're smiling. My heart grips tight. What is it? "WHAT IS FUNNY?"

But it's over. Only the glaze of death looks back now; locked in a smile that fills me with despair, for it is a knowing smile. Knowing something I don't. His head won't be mine after all, I don't have a blade to take it. There's your honour, Master...oozing blood into the earth. Pathetic. Emptiness fills me – I live now without purpose. No longer can I hold it all back, and I fall into the darkness, collapse with the fatigue of a thousand battles on my shoulders.

* * *

"We win, my lady," Oboro's silk tones rouse me. Slowly, I sit. He's not moved, watching over me as the battle turns around us, CrowKiller in his hand. The Fox's body festering nearby. "The Wolfpads broke, gave up. They do not wish to fight against their own, Baraki has rallied those who remain into a frenzy. A turncoat spear aimed at the Taosii." He grips my side, heaves me to my feet, and whispers again, "*We win,*" with less conviction in his voice.

"What is it?" A fit of coughs has me, I dizzy. Almost collapse but he braces me. "And where is Kekkei?"

Heavy, plated footsteps bound through the grass and before Oboro has a chance to answer, the Red Dog of the Okami is upon us. "Tsk, that smell." He puts a gauntleted hand over his mouth, hiding the smile – a thick stench rises from the Fox. As his body sank into death, so did his bowels empty. There is no dignity in defeat. Baraki crouches, his eyes blunt. "The Tanuki wasn't here. We've been had. His..." He gestures to the corpse. "His captain told me as much before I took his head. Simpleton. Kabutomaru left the Okami; a full army of his Wolfpads with him, riding to reinforce the Yokusei. The Samaki won't see it coming. They're doomed." The Sister withheld information? That whore goddess will get...should I have slept with her instead, gods? Nothing but a perverse pantheon. "Don't. You're in no state to try." Even the boy sees through me.

"I led them into this...the Yokusei surrendered though."

Baraki pulls me from Oboro's clutches, gripping me by the scuff as he pulls me in, his breath sweet, stale. "YOU PROMISED!" He shouts in my face. "There's no honour left here! This is why we break them. Don't you see it still? Why change is needed – the north is wretched, a festering pit of dishonour. You're not done, Hawk. If it suits the Yokusei, they'll murder as much of the Samaki as they can, regardless of agreements. What is the brush when the blade makes things more permanent?" Dropping me, I fall into a heap. Hear the thud of his boots as he paces. "We don't stop now, Hawk. I've twice as many Wolfpads at my back now. By common law, they're mine. We will drive the knife into the heart of Orika. The *Gods Senses*, the fuckin' abomination of a government. All of it at once, we will smash the Lord Council to bits. The Taosii exploited cracks that were already here!" The passion of youth...the unbridled ambition of the Lord Council's prized sword. Does he want true change or is he like his father? Will he poison what is left just so he can have his high seat atop Basho sooner? This is mountains more than what I started. In his eyes I see myself, the all-consuming fires that won't stop until you have nothing left. I feel it now, the blaze a candle flame that flickers against a win that'll snuff it out forever. Master, I'm empty.

I want to die. "Kekkei?" I ask.

The wolf sighs. "Come with me."

Chapter 34

Muscles scream with the jolt of each laboured movement; I cannot walk unaided, so Oboro guides me back through the camp. We veer towards the western edge where a much larger tent stands – their command tent. It is bedecked in a vile, ungodly fashion. It spills wickedness in its design; the wooden frame painted gold, figures of animals stand proud atop the stitched hide material that holds the awful thing together; to add to the foreignness of it all, animal bones hang on the sides. Jaws, skulls of horned dread beasts never before seen in Basho, chuckling in the light wind.

We hobble over. Some camp followers or servants, I don't know, gather around the side. It's been ripped open; they worry over mending it. I tell them to leave off, that we're heading for the capital with everything their masters left behind. They don't listen and instead turn more intently towards their task – common folk are animals; they do what they know and don't stop until they're dead or their master says otherwise. Pretend nothing has changed. Get on with it. Maybe there is something to learn from the low births.

There's blood on the dried earth, the smell still has enough bite on it to suggest the fighting spilled all this way. My mouth hangs open as I go to speak to Oboro, touching my tongue to my cheek. A heat worms its way in, suddenly these robes are too thick too hot.

Baraki insists on haste from the doorway.

We enter, and Thousand Hands is not here. There's a bloody mess on the floor; a pain stabs in my chest, my shoulder throbs so much against the wraps I don't think it'll ever be the same. I blink twice and it doesn't register. My vision narrows until there's nothing else in the room but her. No...I. How? "Ropi?" I say but it's futile, wrestling away from Oboro I fall to my feet and crawl over to her. Propped up against the centre-pole, her neck opened from ear to ear. It is savage, a deep cut right to the white bone that gleams between the gore. "You fool. Damn them all...why were you here Ropi?" I d-don't get it. Why are you all dying again?" I bring her cold, rigid body into an embrace, sobbing into her shoulder. My mind races – Kekkei too must be...on my feet, I'm unsteady, my body feels borrowed.

"He isn't here, my lady."

"Another." Baraki's tone is a stabbing pain in my ear. Next to the wind-flapping tear, he marks one that I'd not seen. There are others around her, a woman in grey robes. A set of bloodied tools next to her, a camp doctor busies himself over the body. A servant holds rags to them but from the empty, colourless look on her face, the crimson painted robes, it's no use. "Taos dogs!" He growls and lashes out at a hanging sigil-marked skin, ripping it down. "The Sister. Come, she asks for you."

The armoured wolf sends the help away with an outburst like oil into fire; the doctor pleads in High Bashoan, he can't leave her he has to make it comfortable, but I can see the man fears the bite that might come if Baraki is too hard pressed. Bowing deep, he mutters to the Four.

Oboro grabs me, but I push him away. Stumbling, my breath caught in my throat, towards her. With my arm in a sling, I fall into the doctor, who catches me without thinking. His eyes wide, apologies clamber out all at once. Does he not know I'm not worthy of such inflection? A knot rises in my chest, though I tell him thank you. Not letting me fall, he lowers me to my knees, and I don't notice him leave as I grab the Sister's hand. Bone cold. She already has one arm in the pyre – her eyes are glassy, but as she notices me there's a little spark in them. An ember in a gale. Her body is ravaged, awful; she's bleeding from many wounds. I'm knelt in her blood. Her hand trembling within mine. "Who – did – this?" I say through gritted teeth.

The corner of her mouth tweaks, but nothing.

A gulped down sob, I lean back, my eyes are watery. I can't see straight, the tent walls loom over me; this was meant to be done, we had them trapped, we were meant to end this. The Taosii should be strung up, Kekkei waiting but only death awaits the damned.

Why? Gods, why?

Within, a throb, an ache that should have died. I cannot be quelled. I won't stop. "Did Taos do this?" I ask knowingly, needing reassurance again. Needing reason. And she whispers too low for my ears, a little bit of the life in her eyes fades with the effort. I close mine, swearing to the gods I'll murder them all. Senseless. She hacks, each cough squeezing my hand. When I look at her once more, it pains me all over again. Fucking beasts.

"It's enough."

There's a defiance in her, even now, she says, "I...must. Aibo— set. Free." A slight glow about her that dies instantly. The faint smell of honeysuckle. Gods-fearing idiot wasting her last breaths. Nonsense godspeak until the end. Forcing the words out smooth, calm. Despite the rising lava within, I need to know, "And Kekkei? Was he here?"

I squeeze her hand tighter, she flails, discomfort. "Gone." She fades, her light lost. I hate that I care, but I know I owe it to her; I'd be ash in the winds, Shuji would have executed me if not for her. Regardless of her reasoning. We shared a drink. She came for you, Kekkei, and where are you now? Gods, look at what you have wrought, why do you go without a fight?

The winds of upheaval pull at me, urge me on. I'm sick of it, but it's not enough, still. So, I'll raise a final storm, fan the flames one final time. To bring you back, to put things right for Aibo, to have my family whole again.

Baraki shifts, his face blank. Enduring. He's seen this before, we both have, but the savagery about it, the closeness, hurts.

"We failed!"

"I did."

"What do we do now?" I ask, pulling myself away from her. I can't. I leave the tent, breathing deep as I sway again, not going far before my legs give way. Plate rattles behind me. "What, Baraki?"

He draws his sword, offering it to me as he kneels, "It is my failure. Take my life, I offer it to you. Take my sword, I offer it to you. On my honour and house Akuto. *For the demons that wake, our blades bend.*" His family words wash over me, prickling my skin, as he unclips his cuirass chucking it to the side with a thud. He rips open his under-robes, muscle ripples across his stomach. This is a farce, the farce of a man too caught up in what is right, as far as his Way of the Sword deigns it. A man too dictated to by the blade he holds out; fanatics, it's what makes the Okami so dangerous. Honour is unruly, an iridescent gown worn by my caste. I've gone too far with it. Mine is threadbare, tattered.

A live by the sword, die by the sword attitude that'll take you young gleams from him. "If this is what honour demands, so that you might go further, for those lost, my life is yours to take. Demon, my blood is yours. I thought myself above their plots, that I could invoke their pride. But if you spare me, lord, then I fight to my last breath to end Taos' tyranny."

The way he calls me demon is perverse, the way only one of clan Akuto could make it. Fool! Does he not know what he offers? This is our fault together, a vision too narrowed to see a Taosii plot here. *Take it.* I shudder as the voice, the urge within my blood is clearer than it has ever been. More convincing.

I want to shout nonsense in the boy's face, but I dare not do him the dishonour. Instead, I look him in the eye, turning his blade away with my hand. "Your sword is accepted, but I spare your life; too many have fallen here. Dead, you're worthless to me. I'm just tired of this, boy. Do not mistake exhaustion for a failing spirit." It's a lie for his sake, not mine. "You need not ensure I carry on. My family were destroyed once. There's no way under the Eyes of the Gods that I'll let it happen again, but perhaps you understand that. Baraki. I fear you've more to lose than me, and there's nothing I can do to stop that; my peace can only be found in it."

He stands, pulling his plate back on, sheathing his sword. There's a crackle, a snap of theurgical energy when his armour drops into place again. "I am Okami. We have nothing to lose but honour."

"That is what scares me. One of your kin still has yet to make their move."

His eyebrows squeeze close together, about to speak.

"My lord!" A gruff, harried voice interrupts. The Wolfpad rushing to a kneel next to us. "Jintoka has returned."

Baraki waves it off, his eyes tell me there's more to discuss. "Take me to him."

We find a pack of his men gathered around a downed horse, the poor beast's flanks heave slowly, there's death in its eyes. A man sits on the grass near it, servants dabbing a face that oozes, new burns that'll leave a scar. Even so, he pushes the women tending to him away as Baraki approaches, rolling onto his knee. The man winces, down the same side as his burn, his armour is blackened, stiff. "My lord."

"Out with it!"

"Po and the mercenary take the Lord's Road to Orika."

"Speak plainly, you hesitate. What? Don't look at her!"

Jintoka swallows, pain etches into his face as he does. "The mercenary rides with him, his own horse. A free man, if you ask me." Taos has its ways; I bite my lip as not to rebuff the man. He's earned scars for it already. Kekkei is a prisoner. An invisible hand forces him, just like the Kasuki.

"Soshist magic," Baraki spits. "That is not enough to damn the man. Adami? Why did you leave her to follow?"

"Lost, my lord." He bows his head. "In the flame that caught me."

Baraki wheels on me, his eyes molten black. "How long do you need?"

I don't know if it will work, the gods will damn me to the hells for sure, but I will test his conviction. I lean closer to him and whisper, "With your blood, we can leave now." I know my mouth moves, but it's not me who speaks; while I am weak, the curse is strong, hateful. It remains, it always will. It's here for me, we are strong together. A day's rest could see Kekkei over the border, it says, there's nothing that can reach anyone in Taos – never has a Bashoan crossed into their country, and never shall they, for it is a barren, lifeless hell.

Baraki doesn't flinch as he accepts. The boy is madness incarnate. I don't promise him I know what will become of us both, but I promise him it would be days before I can move without it. He is too trusting. He tells me our paths are entwined; we are guided by the gods. I appeared the day after the Night of the Dragon, so it is a sign. The gods showed themselves real, ever-present. So, he will bind his fate to mine as it is their will. The Will of the Four. I do my best to hide my anguish, which he mistakes for fervour. I nod, knowing it is I who called the dragon, knowing that through my own machinations I've bound a powerful ally. It starts inside a chuckle.

Fear of the divine is powerfully convincing.

Before we leave, he comes to me with my gourd half full of his blood. And I remember the Sister's words as I take the offering, popping the lid nonchalantly. With a bow, I raise it to Aibo. A cackle it ends with. Is this now it feels, goddess?

I sip it. My muscles ease up, the fatigue does not fall away, though I'm gripped with a strength. Refreshed as if I'd slept nights away. A new feeling rushes in, a knowingness. Not like Tetsuya, his spirit was scattered, all for the taking. No. I close my eyes but still see Baraki rooted in this place, readying the horses – know the resolute, undying honour that drives him – there's comfort in his sincerity.

A strange smile is born onto my face, a sickness wells in the pit of my stomach. I retch. Struggle to hold it in. My mind racing. In deeply, I breathe out again, trying to arrest control of myself. There's a flutter in my chest, a tightening. What have I become? This...beyond simply anger. A blood drinker? Fortunate, am I, that I have only a few more steps before I can die.

I'll not have the chance to watch myself become much more of this monster.

Chapter 35

This era will be known as the Rising of the Poppy. The Wicked Devil's Spittle, the histories will say. With war behind me and in front, I still haven't seen anything as disgusting or destructive as that which distilling, consuming the black-flowered demon has wrought. The Lord's Road is littered with those half-dying and dead; black welts ooze yellow puss. The commoner's limbs flail, gripping the Wolfpad escort's leg, muttering, pleading for more, more. A sharp spear-butt to the head sends him sprawling – I turn away, biting my lip. It's a strange time indeed that I've learnt sorrow for a being as despicable as an addict. But they are only caught in the game the lords and ladies play.

Sacrifices for the coffers.

What did Kakihira envision along the Lord's Road when he razed Old Nodo, forging this path through the heartland? Sprawling hills that roll off in either distance, crowned in fog and slithering tendrils of sky and cloud, either side of a road that meant progress, connectivity, trade. But not that of the vile substance that leaves its mark all the way to Orika; vistas of beauty are overshadowed by innumerable, black-pocked victims that litter the great trade route. Perhaps headed to the capital in the hope that their honour, belongings, or a roof over their head can be regained. Barren estates, crumbling walls overwhelmed with vine, great buildings reduced to ghoul hovels can be seen in the distance. The men around me speak of worse deeper in the middle-country. Worse yet, maybe it is the capital they flee.

No one speaks of Orika.

For five days we travel the Lord's Road. We push and push, sleeping as little as we can manage; I burn a light 'fever all the way. It's the only reason I manage. My shoulder heals, but is tight, numbed still. I fear for my use in battle, had it been my sword-arm, I'd have gone to the hells.

Of those poppy-invalid that spoke sense, could be bought for coin, we made sure we followed Soshist Po and his prisoner. The devil-man rides a day ahead, the last had said.

Baraki has long fallen into silence. He is regretful, a blood-feud lays behind him; neither of us wanted to let the Tanuki join his family in the Forest of Souls.

We did not have the choice.

Another trouble nags at us, causes light sleep, drew the black rings around our eyes. It's not something I considered, trifling with the Four Wolves, when I only wanted the head of one. Now I sleep with one eye open for the last. The fourth Okami is yet to make her move; banished from Orika with Baraki, she disappeared, as much as one could with the largest Wolfpad army in the lands. It's befitting of the Slow Bear, Murakami Ainu, that she waits. The household name makes me as uneasy as the look on Baraki's face when I forced the conversation. He shares more with her than the rank of Wolf, it seems.

Of the Murakami house that disappeared in the night, two babes remained. One delivered to the Dattori estate, one delivered to the capital; there, she sat on the Okami seat the longest; bathed in the richness of the Sea Spas; drank in the exquisite plum and flower wines the most; picked the brains of the Learned of the Dying Scrolls and sat at the side of Akuto Takahashi. Advising, killing, conspiring.

Now she has vanished. And we must swallow it.

We rode by with the Tips of Scales in the distance, clan Dorakon's white peaks, and now alongside the forest home to the Kitsutana – word of their lord heir's falling must have reached them. With every league closer, I fall deeper into a depth I cannot swim in and realise how vast Basho is and how foolish I was riding hard to my sentencing, feeling as though I was the only one in the land with the strength to stand up to the godlord.

That my fight was against one man, and it could be solved with another's head.

If I was not sat upon Lonestep's saddle, I would turn away on foot. Though, I doubt Oboro would let me go. We are to finish this together. He rides close to me now, his horse has learned to put up with my gelding's nips, the bad-mannered beast has taken to nuzzling his mare, turning a kind whicker towards her.

We ride up to the first checkpoint the next morning expecting resistance; out this far, there's a low, grey perimeter wall, high enough to give those trying to slip the guard a second guess at climbing it – topped with sword-sharp fragments from the Jagged Sands to stop those still try. I adjust my Wolfpad helm, fidgeting with the clasp but the city guard lets us straight through; recognising Baraki was all it took. Praises, they say, for the godlord has awoken from the bind – calling for his soldiers, his wayward wolves. The gates open. Po welcomes us in? All but the poppy-afflicted who are bludgeoned, beaten with the ends of polearms, hacked at with swords are allowed entrance; it's as though I watch a disease picking at the city itself, who tires, will slowly overwhelm from it. Some are already in, tossed out as we go through.

The road climbs slowly towards Orika – an onyx pathway carved into the stone; the city proper sits encircled by a curtain wall four men high. Still, buildings tower higher, three times again that of the wall, the capital's flowers bloom taller, brighter than those of even my estate, fashioned after them. The city is a moody palette against the bright, starkness of the day. The cold reflected onto the towers painting them navy and black where the shadows lie. The road sparkles in two tones as the pocketed rock Orika sits on shines; from here, beyond the main gate where the road seemingly stops. It snakes off, winding into the capital's hills and finishing where the godlord's inner-complex stands, before the earth cuts off in a dive straight down into the crashing Endless Seas.

There's a fight between commoner, led by black-pocks, met by city guards – red and black plain-plated soldiers. We slip by again unaccosted, with a nod from a kabuto helm.

My gaze darts from one guard to the next, surveying the crowds. Expecting a burst of magic to end it all, an errant dagger – some desperate attempt to stop us, as it was with Ti. Something to say that we've got them on the ropes, we harry them. This...silence is too disconcerting. Too prepared.

"DISMOUNT!" Baraki's shout ripples through our ranks.

"Is it not safer to ride, my lady?"

"Your lady has no choice, islander. Despite our quarry, we follow common law. There's honour in our cause."

Oboro grimaces, his patience unending as he doesn't even go for his blades at the slight. He doesn't have to be spoken to like that, not even by the Okami's captain. I nod to him. Stay safe, he says. It's more of a plead.

We push through the throng, and I'm gladdened to feel him at my back.

My breaths are short, rapid. I've never seen so many people. I can't take this. What if the Soshist can see me now?

A cluster of common folk consumes me. The crowd surges one way and I'm carried with it, grabbing hands go for my sword. CrowKiller is loosened from her sheathe – cannot do anything about it; one arm useless, the other caught in a mesh of people. A rancid, salt-laced smell assaults my nostrils. Wolfpads scatter the group, battering the hands away. I scramble back to Oboro. Chest thudding. "Careful, I said, my lady."

I shrug it off. There're murmurs among the crowd, the same story. They move below to the beach. *The godlord has awoken and promised a spectacle! Watch as new doors open into Basho, they go to speak to the Black Dragons out in the bay! The strangemen become friend.*

There's a ceremony being made from it; the concession is handed candles from guards littered about. They promise progress, but never has the Taka Era seen such. I whisper to my High Captain, "It troubles me. We're on the cusp of ending this, but the Taosii troubles himself with foreign affairs."

"Mhm, it doesn't sit well with me either, my lady," Oboro says, "these... *Whitans* cannot be trusted much more than the Taosii, much less any agreement forged by them. A desperate attempt to reinforce their position, I would say."

"He doesn't see it," I nod to Baraki. "Caught up in family affair. I pray we do the right thing. Kekkei back and home. A retreat for now. Po has to die in the course."

"We will bring Thousand Hands back." I go to say more, to ask if we really should be doing this, but the throng separates us, thickens again. Too unruly and loud.

I've my hand trained on my hilt now; at the first gates I'd sipped a drop of Baraki's blood, keeping my fever low but there. My senses acute from it but strained against the vastness of the crowds, the giant buildings that engulf the skies from where I stand. I pray to Don Yoku for once, that he consumes my fever quickly, so that I do not suffer this longer. It is topped off by the thorny, racing thoughts of Baraki. His presence a pull in this state – as though my existence encircles his. He is troubled.

I push through the crowd, closing in on him with Oboro still at my back, saying, "You mean to barge in there? We were to take stock of the city before we moved."

"Something is happening. We haven't got the time. We are late as it is." His heart races. "This...is eccentric, even for the Taosii."

"The crowds. He should be fortifying the guard, stopping us!" I growl. "My head...this is wrong. We should be harassed, stopped. I'd be pleased more with a sharply thrusted spear."

Baraki falls back to face me, the Wolfpads flowing forward around us. "Tsk, we've little choice, Hawk. Whatever lies in wait, we can handle it. Father doesn't have a force like ours in Orika, the city guard wouldn't stand to us."

"The commotion," Oboro pushes in. "The beach summons should not be ignored! You put us in more danger. We don't have full measure of what is happening!"

The young wolf's arm shoots out to grab Oboro, who catches it, face screwing. "Why doesn't your Dattori man mind his mouth!"

"Stop this!" I widen the gap between them, forcing them back, realising the wicked work now I see it. "These are games. Can you not see it? The ambassadorial gathering, he has the whole city in disarray. The Soshist scum wants us to second guess this, to hang back while he has more time to escape or enact whatever plot he has."

"Then we give him no time, my lady. We must hurry ahead!" The Okami agrees with him. I stand shocked but not for long as I join the last line of Wolfpads. We hurry to the front.

A pulse, before hidden, throbs against my waning 'fever. There it is. Distorted by the crowd. I concentrate. Tendrils of it snake through the city. Bitter, peppery, sulphurous in my nose.

Soshist magic.

There's nothing we can do about it, but Baraki sends a third of our forces, twoscore men, to the Port Beach – if only to have one eye on what unfolds. Even without my connection to the Okami, I feel despair settling in; Wolfpads are not immune to doubt, disarray. The march of the ten and sixty men around is hesitant, careful.

In the upper districts, the crowds lessen but still we push through countless bodies. Close, sweaty. The stench is only marred by the magical tinge. Bit by bit we forge our way towards the castle up on the hill. There's no sign of the poppy here. Even as the city dies back, and the path to the castle is lined with high walls, and towering council buildings behind them, the crowd does not abate entirely. There're eyes darting around me. Something off still. Marching still, I listen. Our soldiers beat irregular, they keep in step as much as possible on the incline, but there's another. In tune. Breaths around us. It's as though the surrounding crowd move in the same beat, breathe the same breath.

BeatBeatBEATBEATbeatbeatBEATBEAT.

I don't hear it at first, not until I separate the erratic huffs, the grunts, and base conversations of the men around me. A low whistling, a singsong murmur. That base, foul tune which carries death where it's spoken, yammering in Monkitan. Still the beat, and then it dawns on me. A chant. A wicked song.

Surrounded by it.

I shout out in alarum too late. Oboro grabs me, jerking me into a dagger-guarded embrace. Baraki up front cannot be warned. Bloodlust blossoms – hoods everywhere. City folk have fallen away. We're now interspersed with the same hood, surrounded. The black cloaks around us chant with magic on their tongues. There's a flash, a strangled cry. My High Captain pushes past me, squeezing between the Wolfpads that surround; there's a hood reaching out to me. He grabs the figure, ripping the hoods from the man. I gasp though I already knew; a childish, stone-smooth face, bald but for a few braided strands. They're here. We're surrounded! "TAOSII!" Oboro cries burying a jewelled dagger in the man's chest before he can so much as shriek out. The crowd surges – surrounding hoods batter our flanks. Bodies pressed up against me, I cannot draw my sword. Panic. My heart flutters, "On me" – Oboro puts himself in front of me, his daggers stabbing as more reach through the crowd – Wolfpads dragged below the human tide. Roaring, shrieking – "Back, my lady! By me. RUN!" I can't. Pinned. All I can do is stay on my feet as there's an uphill surge again.

The Wolfpad line around us bends, breaks, falls. Helpless is the soldier next to me as two hooded Taosii fall on him – strange bone objects in their hands. I'm useless. I watch as they plunge a sharpened animal jaw into his face, another stabbing with what looks like a femur; they pull away, back into the mass. The man screams like the gates of the hells. A spike in the sulphurous scent drives a rancid stake into my nose. I retch, vomit into the crowd. Too familiar is the smell of Meater magic, but this is worse, far worse. The meaty smell is off, rotten by days, like I've been force-fed rotten fish.

The bone-stabbed man erupts into a mass of mutating tissue, throwing Oboro backwards, crashing into me. We're a mesh of bodies on the floor.

Sukami's gaze is blotted out, smeared from existence as a beast from the pit towers two-men high over me; the white Wolfpad now scales on the serpentine, whip-like arms it sends crashing overhead, ripping into those behind me. I hear their cries. Its face a festering amalgamation of skin, teeth, and the bone that started this. Its only resemblance to a man is the memory of the one I saw it born from. The beast is a giant of the flesh creature Jinto became to escape the prison cart months ago.

It cannot be, Don Yoku hasn't crossed the border – the Taosii are messing with magic that doesn't belong to them.

With a sweep of its tendrils, it clears the crowd around me. A whip flicks

THE BLOOD OF OUTCASTS

towards me but Oboro is there again, daggers flashing. The creature moans as the tendril is ripped into bits with precise cuts. There's room, so I draw CrowKiller, running up and slashing the strike he doesn't see. Battered by what I couldn't cut, we're sent crashing into the wall. I grimace. Pain shoots down my side when I breathe. A rib broken. I scramble to my feet, somehow still ahold of my sword. Lesson learnt. Oboro pulls me up as we retreat further uphill, the high castle walls close but unreachable. The buildings around us a stacked tenement like leaves on a tree, or a hedge, trapping us in this insanity. A barrier, or a pit that we should die in.

Baraki's roars split the cacophony, a rallying cry as the Wolfpads are regrouping around us; "DON'T GIVE THEM AN INCH", I hear, "SEND THE FUCKIN' SCUMS TO THE HELLS".

Captain Wanrin flows past me and launches a spear into the dread beast's face; it wails a humanly sound. Taos Cloaks buckle, fall around it as it flails, scattering our men but not catching them. Wolfpads gathering their senses, dodging, avoiding. I look upon the monstrosity, a shred of sorrow thickens my throat. I wonder how much of the man is left to watch his comrades turn on him. Lashing out, he scatters a few but the wolves are working together now, nipping, testing. Packs form, descending upon the broken Taosii. More spears fly, the beast topples. Oboro still dragging me further away. The Red Dog barrels through two robed figures that try to run, cleaving them in two with a swift slash of his sword.

My breaths are erratic, unchecked. I cannot imagine breathing right again, my fever so far gone the weak, hollowness spans from my marrow all the way through muscle. Empty. I look up at the beast, profusely bleeding, and only flashes of what came before that rush by in my mind. The battle is segments of memory around me rather than something happening now. We're up, behind the very back line of our men and I don't remember how I got there. Just trembling.

"We're through, my lady. They're gone. Routed. Baraki's men saw them back. Come on." I take Oboro's hand and get to my feet, and breathe deeply, taking in the cool, crisp air. The magic not gone, but lessened; from up here, the rest of Orika is slopes, spreading into tiled squares that are a patchwork picture of how far Basho has come. Suffering, pain, and conflict. Further down, the white sands of the beach seemingly glisten, a black jewel as the crowds amass, almost consuming the port. "Whore's breath," I say. "Orika is overrun; there must be a small army of them here, hiding amongst our gods-damned city folk. They use magic that they have no business to, Oboro, *Taosii* Greed Shamans."

"A poor imitation of such, but worrying, deadly, indeed, my lady." Oboro shifts, checking over his shoulder before he continues. His confident calm grates on me. "We must finish this and go. Orika is lost. We cannot hope to fight through anymore of this."

First Captain Giju appears through the crowd, Baraki follows – a new long slash from eye to neck; that they touched a hair on him unsettles me. Am I such a leech that I lessen him? "Taos is a disease that only gets stronger as it spreads, more violent as it consumes," he says as if he heard our conversation. "Burn them out, cut them off at the root. Lord Dattori." His eyes bore deep into me, and I worry for a second that our connection goes two ways. He hasn't called me that before. "You've fought worse odds. Were you not the one who faced down the full might of the Lord Council and escaped into the Kirisam? Right, Giju?"

The Captain barks a laugh, "Yer. Taos won't put us down, eh?"

"This is child's play. If they mean to test us, they should've sent more – come, we ready at the Heavenly Gates. *Father* expects us."

"A test!" I say. "You take the enemy too lightly." Boy, I want to call him, but I wouldn't do him the dishonour in front of his captain. "I worry you lose sight of who we face. Taos. Remember what they're capable of before you walk into a knife in the gut."

Baraki turns with *challenge me?* on his lips, but says, "What's become of you? They harried our flanks, put one measly beast at our backs when they could've done more, the cloaked scum fell away with the walls in sight. Get ahold of yourselves. They meant to drive us here. They want us at these gates."

"So, what, then, lies beyond?" Oboro says. The only man who speaks sense, the one I should have listened to long before. Though, Kekkei's head wouldn't stay on long enough for anything else. "Wolf, you spoke of just two Taosii in the capital, now there were over a score more to rebuke that claim. Why're you so fool-headed to believe that more do not prowl in the castle walls. Is that not a position you'd fortify yourself?"

"They'd of killed us then," Giju snaps, pointing downhill and then to the gates. "Not wait till there."

Baraki makes a move towards Oboro but thinks better of it. "*Coward.*"

"There's m–"

"–Listen, Okami!" I interrupt Oboro. "There is cause to rush, yes. There's more amiss here, more at stake if we leave it, but sending all of our men through one gate would be a fatal mistake. We'll spend all of our forces in a vain attempt to break through if a Taosii militia mounts an attack from within." He doesn't speak but I feel him listening, taking in what I say. A flush of agreement through his being. An understanding we have. What we think is commonplace is strange, foreign to the Taos. Why kill us in one place, when they can kill us in the next? It's not something we can risk. Not now. But there is a straight path, he says. The castle is a fortress backed onto the seas, defendable from one gate. There is but one way, a ridge of rock that juts out along the cliff face. The Cook's Path. We can go only as a three, no way to take our entire force. Too dangerous. So, we go first and bring them in when we can.

A forward scouting party, led into the Taosii held depths of our nation's pride, Four Spire Castle, house of the Akuto.

I've never felt like a rat so much in this wretched life.

Chapter 36

The way was barred, of course, but that meant nothing against Okami plate; Baraki hit the sea-facing gate with the force of the storms it was meant to hold at bay. Never did the smith expect that abominable power to hit it all at once.

I'd sooner fight all four of the Okami at once that cross than ridge again. Winds that have travelled the full stretch of the Endless smash against the cliff face with all the might of the last thousand leagues they've travelled; my sure-footed crow-step was not enough to steady me, neither did I see any of the namesake there, only great seabirds that had it in their blood. I tripped, and only Oboro's vice grip saved me. I broke into laughter as he pulled me up, the irony of losing the fight to erroneous footing, and a battered body, after dragging myself from the depths of the hell was not lost on me. It gave me a break, a clear head from the turmoil that was oozing in, vines of hopelessness breaking down all the walls I've built; I'm no longer sure if we can escape this city alive with Kekkei. If I'm buried here with him, it better be after that whoreson, Po, has lost his head. It would seem I never fell into the wrath of Godlord Takahashi, who might have died as pathetically and quietly as the Warrior Godlord.

The gods always have their way.

We enter in through a short tunnel that Baraki leads with a confidence that had been missing from his step, into the kitchens. Cooks, and servants scurry about tending to rice vats big enough to feed the entire household, bubbling like oni cauldrons – fish grilling, fresh vegetables, tofu, kelp, broiled eel, sushi. A feast – pulse quickening, I tense and explode outwards at the already quivering staff, dashing the ingredients onto the floor. Oboro and Baraki watch as I throw one of the pots boiling with rice over, accidently splashing onto the cook tending to it, trying her best to weather what was going on and feed whichever master commanded it. Screaming agony, a swift cut from Baraki ends her. I'm riddled with guilt. The wolf promising the Lord Master's retribution if they speak of this.

My mind is unstable, tumultuous; I cannot contain the lives my curse consumes. A torrent of memories, emotion, thoughts not my own – or are they? Tetsuya or Baraki, I don't know which, or maybe it's all of us. A combined fury that cannot be contained in one body. The memories crash and collide with each other. So much so, I take a moment to myself. Despite the looks, I'm losing grip. My mind is the sum of all the anger-riddled blood I've consumed. I take check of it, wrestle ahold of my breathing, the racing thoughts.

This normality torments me. We tread too carefully, take too much time. It only takes one swift knife and Kekkei will be lost forever, yet we must ascertain whether the cook's staff will squeal? Slit all their throats on the way to the godlord's quarter, drench these gods-damned-halls in blood, I want to say. They deserve it. They deserve it for what they've wrought to Samaki families. But I must care for Baraki, who holds something back. Something locked away.

As we exit the kitchen, Baraki wheels on me, gauntlet connecting to my face in a slap, "Get it together!" He growls between his teeth. Anxious, he fiddles with his plate, he cannot stand still; his hand will wear a hole where it brushes over the hilt of his katana so much. "You'd bring the entire household down on us for what...a tantrum?"

"They mean to feast while they butcher us at the gates! I cannot stand it. The same arrogant disregard that finished my Lord Dattori!"

"My lady." Oboro's eyes quiver. I'm not myself, not here. Not this close. "It is with careful measures and cunning that the cat ensures the mouse is caught. Do not think it a straightforward swipe."

"We will have them, Hawk." Baraki opens the door to the kitchen again. "They've nowhere to run, but through the gates, into our men. Now, stay here." He disappears into the kitchen once more, and I pace like he's been hours. Kekkei is here somewhere, we cannot waste time!

Reappearing, Baraki swears, kicks the wall until it gives way. He says the godlord, his *heavenliness* holds court with a visitor from the south. A traveller so weary a feast has to be prepared – at the behest of the Lord Po; there is no unit awaiting us at the gates, the cook assured him that they've only been cooking meals for the godlord, they couldn't possibly be feeding any more than his *heavenliness* and the staff. So, the young wolf falls silent, glum after the last sentence, for the cook says there's no Akuto here. The estate is abandoned, derelict as if no clan has lived here in years, that's what the servants say. His entire clan gone. I try to console him, but his bite is sharp, harsh. Baraki threatens, second guesses our cause. If my advisor sits with his father – comes not as a prisoner, but as a guest...It all seeming like a plot against his own family. He has little brothers, nephews, and nieces. None remain. There must be a misunderstanding, it cannot be right. A ruse to the end. Taos sow discord in every breath they take. Not to be trusted. Kekkei is prisoner.

There's no one to stop our movement through the estates as we storm the corridors and out into the empty courtyard. No one waits at the gates, not even the household guards. The Akuto family truly are nowhere within the walls. Baraki's wits are at their end; our forces flood into the staging area, and so my body washes with calm. As much as can be had when my only allies are the elites trained to put my sort down, the turncoats who were loyal to my mortal enemy before I spilled his guts. There are a few sideways glances as I walk among their ranks, but these are men passed between the strongest swords of the Lord Council. The respect they have for my sword stops it from becoming anything more. We're warriors in arms now.

The gates are fortified, Wolfpads line the walls, not even an army could take the castle now, but that is no guarantee; the sulphurous tang assures me that the Soshist would bring more than an army. Much more.

"Secure, Milord," Captain Giju says, "but don't trust it. There's things, personal effects up there. Daggers left, and plates. *Vanishing* is right. They've not just up and left, they've smoked into the abyss." Baraki looks between gutting the man and shouting at him. He's all the twitchier. Only, I know of how the Soshists make families disappear, and pray that it's in both mind and body that they're gone, for the bodies left to the disgusting sorceries are worst. "Enough! Father is still here; I'll see to it that he accounts for this."

"I say careful." Giju over-steps. "Take us, full 'Pads n'all."

"NO!" Baraki seethes anger. "This is still the Akuto estate, the Heavenly Towers align in light of the gods. I will not have a militia barge into my father's quarters, common law must be followed. There has to be honour, man! What separates us from the Taos scum if we have leave of that?" The Captain bows, and leaves, shouting orders along the wall, busying himself. We ready to meet the traveller and the godlord. The ease in which we've taken Orika's great castle begs we leave. A nagging in my mind, the base warrior instinct, tells me to run. It's not that I listen to, though. The bubbling, the ceaseless hatred in my blood wants more. Needs to see the Taosii mount a pike, whether it's the end of me or not. Whether Kekkei is dead or not. All these fools sing my tune. *You've done this, Masako*, it says. *This is your might.*

None of the paintings do it justice, nor the stories; the personal estate of the godlord has been barred to the public since Terinda's *assassination*. It had to be the hand of a skilled Man of the Arts, none other could end the fourth godlord's short reign say the Learned.

The towers rise out of the courtyard like four stalks of briar. The thorns meet in a circular canopy that protects each level below from the elements. Central to that, the main Akuto building is a stag beetle sat on its abdomen, wings splayed, mandibles sharp, rising; steps trail down from it, widening until they reach the stone floor on which I stand. It takes my breath away in some terrific way, the blatant lavishness the Godlord Orikaga left behind met by the stark Taka era. The current ruler has done his best to impart his own image on this place. It's a great shame we're here to tear it down. It shall never stand the same, not after I'm done. Gods curse it.

The soldiers wait behind. I lead the way, Okami and Akate at my back – this is never how I dreamt of this moment, not at my wildest. The gods have a sick sense of humour. Each step insurmountable, too far, but I forge ahead, fighting against everything telling me to turn back.

It is stranger still to find red-plated city guard to either side of the door. They bow, letting us in.

Incense. Thick clouds of lavender and orange buffet our entrance to the room. I grit my teeth. Blood rising, bubbling in my chest. Master's incense. They mock me still. We're met with a wall etched in the gold Bashoan symbol of *overwhelm*, the Akuto horns protruding from it, reaching up to join the great beams in support of the building. We spill left around the wall and into the room proper; full plates of armour hang on the walls, vibrantly coloured Saman pots litter the room as though they fashion them here, next to high chairs meant only for lords, unsparingly used. There's hanging silks the likes only still seen in Chisai from the Kakihira period.

A display of power and wealth of no like in Basho.

Beyond it all, cut out of the great cliff face itself, a floor to ceiling opening to the moody skies; the sea winds press into our arrival. Two figures are silhouetted against the seas. My heart falls as we draw closer – the tension in our group heard in the clatter of Baraki's plate. I swallow, my mouth dry.

"K-Kekkei?"

He takes a sip from the cup first and then looks at me with a smile. It reaches his eyes. Sat here as the lands fall apart around us, reclining like some lord; dressed in a strange hide robe – the claws of some beast grip his shoulders, a fur cape falling from them; the red sash of the Akate splits it in some weird amalgamation of identities. At his waist a notched swordbreaker and his double-edged blade. He faces Akuto Takahashi himself, who looks every bit a puppet now dressed in sweeping black silks, the Gods' Senses represented on his ceremonial tiara, but with a vacant, inhuman look in his eyes. "Father? FATHER LOOK AT ME! Where are they? What have you done with our clan?" Baraki cries, but it's no use. The godlord does not see him – only the whites of his eyes visible; but he tries still, kneeling before him, ordering him to sense. I don't see Oboro, but I know he hangs back, know he's there if I need him. Always there.

"Well? I slay the Fox in wake of your capture, drag myself half from death to find you here, sipping tea. What do you say for yourself Genaro Kekkei?

What...what is this?"

Yawning, Kekkei stretches as though he's just woken from a nap. "I'll tell you your problem, shall I, Masako."

"You'll address her as *lord*." Baraki wheels on him, throwing the table aside. He stands over him, breaths heavy. "Or you'll not get a chance to address her at all."

"Whatever it takes, eh, Hawk?" Kekkei ignores the Okami like one would a petulant child. Nose turned slightly, he continues, "It doesn't matter who you step on, nor what means you take to get there, you will have your way. Short-sighted, you don't see those that seek to use that. If you'd have just asked, I would have told you Lord Shuji's plans from the start, but you never did. You assumed I worked in the shadows, encouraged those who would put a knife to your back. I didn't."

My jaw trembles, I go to speak, and it isn't words I speak. Again, I try, "T-then, why? The Lord Council wanted you for what you knew! Were you not brought here on order of execution...the Sister?"

"Was wrong." He takes hold of the flow, as he always does. "Only a bit. Yes, I said that. Thousand Hands truly did believe that. Jinto, too...or did he. That boy scares me. Yes, the Greed Temple fell in Oshima. It was only right for him to believe what he was doing, to run from the Lord Council, to find the Samaki."

"Mad, you've lost your senses, mercenary." Baraki speaks when I don't find the words – drawing his sword. "You talk as if you are not he. I chased you out of the ashes of that temple myself. I know your face, merc!"

Kekkei stands, walking halfway to the opening, where the waves crash into the horizon and turns. "Ah, for a time, I was. As for the charges, somewhere in there, the godlord believes he brought me here to face my family's crimes. You see, he could not live knowing that one of the Fenika line still existed."

My mouth falls agape, the torn-out robes, the way he fought. The Way of the Old Oak; those who move slowly while the rest of the land rushes. Those who wait by the mountains strong, sturdy; the Fenika who were ripped out root by root – on order of the godlord, by – my – own – hand.

"Fenika Dushari."

"Yes. Right. You finally get it," he laughs to himself. "Now...how foolish do you feel? Preaching to me about how wronged your family was. How the Lord Council took everything from you. And what? Because it happened to the great Dattori, everything should fall? The sheer arrogance of it after you happily threw my family into oblivion." He chuckles and waves it off as if I've just offered to pay for his grilled fish.

Wrong. I know who was there...I know the Fenika. We plotted over a table of war for weeks before we executed that order. "You cannot be him. He died a babe, spoils from the mountains as I – except your *father* could not live with the angry little child he stole, so he murdered it!"

"True. You got me." His smirk turns wicked. "Gods know, I don't care about that cunt, nor his family. Do you know what's worse than dying in war and fire? Being sold to Taosii traders. They don't have the same rules about how you should care for a child over there, not a foreign one. I must thank you, though, Hawk. Without your insistence on bringing the Sisters of Aibo into our little campaign, this might have gone on for much longer. I might have stayed *bound* for years before I came across them, no matter. "He waves his hands as if this were a show. Layers upon layers of trust, of strength, that were built up, now fade away. "The *King* was happy as long as I learnt your ways – something is much easier undone from the inside, you see. Oh, of course, you know him, you witch. He wanted you alive. I didn't need to do it personally, Po said it'd be taken care of. But I've waited for this. Long, like the Old Oak." He snickers again, insanity glistening in his eyes.

I draw CrowKiller. I blink hard, not wanting to believe this real but readying myself. The room tenses. Baraki's heart pulses with mine, in step, enormous power welling in his feet.

"Oh, it seems you were both fond of that Aibo girl. A pawn...she bought me the ingredients, save one, to shift the *sleeper's bind*. Takahashi, here!" He calls the godlord like a dog, who happily gets up. Standing by Kekkei with a smile spreading across his face. "Good. This isn't the bind that has him, no. The Soshists are seated in his mind, a parasite, if you will." He taps his chin, some of the man left. "There's a misunderstanding, an old folktale about the way of the bind. My memories were bound. It's not good

349

enough to live amongst the enemy, you see, I had to be the enemy. The blood of one who loved me, yes, Ropi served her purpose." He picks at one of his nails. "Strange how true the stories become. And the tears of gods... wherever Aibo acquired them." I've heard enough. In league with the King of Furs, this bastard. I launch, Crowkiller whistling through the air in a high guard – but it as though time slows, Kekkei moves with an ungodly blur and cries, "Here, you win anyway, cousin!" He grabs the godlord in both hands by face and shoulder and bites a chunk out of his neck, blood spurting everywhere, Kekkei swallows. A realisation comes over me at the same time. I hesitate, pulling out of my sure step too late as he meets me, closing the gap between us in an instant. A quick parry saves me from his first blurred attack, somehow. My stance breaks, I crumple to my knees, the force kindling a fiery pain in my broken rib. I riposte from the kneel. Gods-damn the pain. This whoreson! But he catches Crowkiller in one hand and smashes my beautiful blade with the swordbreaker that I don't even see him draw; black-veined steel...Murakami spell-forge?

Impossible. I'm not running a blood fever.

But he is.

He lashes out in a move that would surely kill me but an armoured high elbow strike is between us, sending his weapon aloft. Baraki forces Kekkei back, dashing into pots, smashing chairs aside, their fight is a blur. Without thinking, I pull out my gourd, sipping the Okami's offering, renewing our connection, igniting the 'fever, working the blood. Immediately gripped by despair, the young wolf is flailing, desperate – he is matched move for move. Only sheer talent saves his sword from meeting the same fate as CrowKiller. But he cannot move on the openings, cannot lay a finger on the man who moves as if he were the embodiment of his sobriquet, Thousand Hands.

The 'fever is loud, unruly. I wince, the injury to my ribs exemplified with it, the pain a white lance.

It looks as though they dance across the sky in the opening. I move to meet them, seeing Kekkei now, his sinewy savagery like my own; muscles fit to burst, eyes black, a wild beast. Mad. All the hells incarnate.

I'm upon him and draw the sidearm; its howl Baraki is ready for as he dashes back, but Kekkei is not. Distracted, his eyes widen, and the grin falls from his face as he catches the blade mid-air, this time my strike biting into his palm, he cries out and says, "A *Bane* sword. Jinto lied!" His blood spills onto the blade, its screaming muffled, then stops completely with his muttering as he runs a slick of blood down its length, throwing my sword aside at the same time. Pain lights up like a flame in my side and I fall to his mercy, not finding the strength to attack; I'm carried in his momentum, his fingers hack, slash. He whittles away at me a woodsman and his tree. The pain flares again and I fall to one knee, but he doesn't get the chance to follow it up as Oboro flies into Kekkei. A force of nature I've not seen in him. Each block springing a riposte and a complimentary block, pushing Kekkei back to the sea window. A strange chill runs down my spine as the mercenary is on his back foot. The relentless, efficiency of my High Captain unreachable. A scorpion so absolute, deadly, and delicate knowing it has its sting; pushing his opponent to the edge, literally – Oboro takes a step back, planting himself and strikes the mercenary into the abyss, who screams, "It is done anyway, demon, you cannot stop us!" as he falls. I rush to the edge but there's nothing, the waters roll in giant waves below. "He's gone."

"No, no, no!" Baraki points to the beach – even from here I can feel the sudden charge, the spike once more in the sulphurous, wicked energies of the Soshist. Po must be down there. Gods-damn-it-all. Along the sands, myriad flashing specks mark the city folk's candles. It all comes together, as I remember Taosii magic well, from the tales, the stories, and our usages of their explosive machinations in theatre and festival. There is but one rule to their filthy pyrotheurgy: *it can only move what is there, child. Do not worry, it is only dangerous when offered a flame.*

The little lights take off, buzzing as glowflies above the crowd. A raucous noise erupts as the peoples panic; the crowd surges away from the shore but it's too late. At once, the smaller fires converge, form a giant, imposing flame; a blasphemous ball in the image of Sukami's glare. It does not wait, it's sent seaward, its target revealed.

I have but a couple of seconds to note the black sea dragons, the boats of the Whitans stand ten beyond the smoking Taosii barges of the sea stockade.

Each one is scaled, carved in the image of a gloomy dragon not unlike the image of the Eyes of the Gods; it must be the jewels in their eyes, but in their last moments, they truly look alive. Until they are engulfed in fire – the giant ball splashes in an arc around all ten boats. It's the next thing that chills me to the bone, that will be burnt into my eyes forever; the flames are parted, lifted off as if a giant hand tossed a blanket aside.

The dragon boats now sit in a bright orb.

Their faces now changed; the carvings angry. Their surrounding bubble starts to move. It glistens, myriad sparkles light the surface. Those sparkles turn into torrents, whirlpools dance upon its surface, faster and faster they spin, turning black, hiding them behind a void veil. With a cataclysmic boom, the bubble spews black, spear-like objects into the air until the sky turns to night.

"GET DOWN!" I turn at the cry, and the Sister stands there as if she hadn't bled out into the earth before my eyes. But she is too late.

The Spear Rain falls.

EPILOGUE

"The rains were slick, coal-black spears from the hells themselves; it was said the Four would return in the end, but not that Metsuku would come before, raining death from the heavens."

Learned Dying Scroll, 105, FT2133

JINTO

ONE MONTH BEFORE THE SPEARS FELL

Cold, close. Working their way, efficient. They've waited a while. I listen again, but don't quite gather what it is he wishes to tell me – why now?

Never mind.

Send the wolves, one and two. They go. The scent of grasses strong, the rains have fallen – I've missed it again. Hm, how we do love the coming of the Cold. It crisps, sharpens. Stuck here, though, with the silly one who doesn't see anymore. He doesn't feel Don Yoku's caring hands any longer. He is lost.

I take his stump anyway; it hurts me so. To not be able to work master's good powers anymore, to be cut from his cord is pain. Massaging them, I work it, work Greed into them, urge them to remember it. For they are not really lost, just forgotten. Now his eyes plead, they lose their shine, watery but not alive.

"Stop this," Hebikawa says. "Boy, it's useless. Without hands, a Shaman is...well, no longer a practitioner of Greed. We've been over this. I may serve Don Yoku, may be a servant but never again will I wield his Will."

"Shh." The old man winces back from me. He is strange, we don't know why he looks at us like that. We won't hurt him. No one hurts family. "You don't believe! Why? Master Hebikawa, there was a great knowing about you, you were Greedy!" A smile tugs at the corners of my mouth and I let it pull. I like it. I get to smile now I live in Hawk's place. The candles are warm, I brought lots in here – master likes them. We speak clearer, but I cleared away the books. They would burn, we don't like burning.

"It is gone. My hands cleaved from me, ruined." He stands, anger is in his eyes. But he is still scared as he looks at me; I know he wants to believe but he is afraid as I'm a bigger believer. "You cannot undo what they've done, boy. It is permanent – mutations of Greed aren't stable, nor nimble enough. *That which is born out of Greed cannot be a master of it.* Did that mercenary take you from the Halls that early?"

"He's not a mercenary!"

"*Master* Genaro, then."

Not that either. He is not that – I thought Hawk would come back, she has to soon, we would take care of it together. Stronger, a family. We have to work it out. He helped me; I help him – but Don Yoku can't touch those with black hearts. So, I might cut it out one day, Kekkei. Greed is Greed but evil will always just be evil.

"Nothing," he spits, mad still. "They send us nothing back. I won't run this household by myself for long...the servants here, they're too spirited. The fieldclans let them slack for too long. Ah, we will teach them again, eh, boy. A present for the lord when she returns." He mutters to himself now; he likes his own words. Not my words. Still angry, they took too many to properly guard this place. Left it open, again. But we're here? Aren't we? I don't say it, he's of a mood again.

"They live. They will come back. They need this army, there's a veil. It's black but she went through it." I smile. "With a knife. She does that."

The old man narrows his eyebrows like I know they do when they don't like the youngers talking too much. "I trust whatever it is you see holds true. We should have gone. Blight on that Lord Shuji, and the rest of them, they need to leave the old ways behind. There's nothing wrong with a Shaman of Greed. She should have taken us, regardless. Won it by force."

"Oh, you believe then?"

"Not so much as you—"

The Cold. No, something colder. I don't mind the Cold but the candles around me die, we're left in smoke scents and the other smell. The one of death.

"—The candles. Boy, what have you done? Light them at once."

We don't like it when our hairs stand on end, each prickling as unfamiliar shivers make me fidgety. Something little steps along my spine, sending the chills with it. This is new — we've never been afraid before.

One gone. No. Two.

I can taste it, their blood. The wolves bit something strange, it fills my mouth with bitter metal. And rage. But they go, my friends. They fall when they've already fallen to Don Yoku. It can't be understood — Greed reaches out to all but now it is blank. A place I can't see, can't reach.

From the mountains, where there was only stone, now I can't see. A blot, a thick unknowing has come.

I spring onto my feet like the beasts do, and run up climbing, climbing. Onto Hawk's balcony, I hope she won't be mad.

Peering out into the darkness, I see it now. Not in the courtyard, under the light of the torches, not in here at all. Out into the deep, vast trees.

A heaving, panting. Hebikawa follows me. It takes him time to get here but it's okay as we have a lot of time now, or we don't have any. I don't yet know.

"B-boy." He can't talk through his laboured breaths yet; an indulgent body has Cat Food. "Y-you'll...leaving me with you. What was she thinking? It'll be the death of me."

"No. Not me. Them."

"What are you talking about, boy?" Worry, riddled with it because he doesn't know, doesn't believe. Master Yoku cannot make him see like that. He is lucky, there's nothing to fear if you can't feel it. The malice, it is not evil, no. It has just waited for so long but there's no sense to it. I don't know why they arrive now. The lord isn't here to greet them, and I don't know if we should. We are just family, not our place. Will we keep our heads, Master Yoku?

"The ones that have hidden in the mountains, they're here."

Acknowledgements

Well, I'll keep this short and say a massive thank you for getting to this page – hopefully, that means you've slogged your way through the entirety of this book. Second, I'd like to apologise for you having made it this far through a book with a protagonist like Masako. She leaves a lot to be desired in the way of likeability, but she's a character that gnaws her way away at things, and that's how she pestered me to write her.

This book, if anything, is my love letter to Rurouni Kenshin, both the manga and the film series are an endless inspiration to me and so very awesome (I'd recommend you watch or read them if you haven't and you're still reading.)

Finally, I'd like to thank the small number who assisted in the beta-reading and in proofreading my work – though, writing is so very personal to me it's hard to share with a lot of people. Which may seem odd having published this now? Ah well, a massive thank you to Shannon, my soon-to-be wife, and to my dear friend, Alex, who put up with a lot of back and forth, were there in the planning, are still here now in the finishing, publishing, and cheering of the work.

Last by not least, a thanks to my FanFiAddict family who inspire me to write, read and review with their endless enthusiasm for everything books, and for the writing community.

And to you, reader, thanks a bunch.

P.s. if you'd like to do an author a favour, and make his day, please leave your review on the book's page on Amazon.

About the Author

I've been writing for as long I can remember, drawing first and adding stories to them, building worlds and places for my characters to belong in, but that wasn't enough. As an avid SFF reader, that consumes way more books than I have shelf space for, I thought it was time I turn my hand to being a novelist.

I wrote my first novel a few years ago, which has yet to see the light of day (nor ever will), and found that writing is in my blood, my passion, so I've stuck to it. Ever since I've been tinkering away with short stories and a few novels that I'm proud of, I've got a few trunked, and one seeking an agent, but I'm very proud of The Blood of Outcasts, it's my love letter to Rurouni Kenshin, the comics I read, and everything SFF.

I'm an English Linguistics and Language graduate working in journal publishing, and this would be my debut; I also review SFF novels for FanFiAddict and my short fiction has appeared in 'Pride: The Worst Sin of All' (Black Hare Press, 2020). I've also had work narrated live on air at Pop-up Submissions. Last but not least, I'm soon to be married and am co-owner of a crazy (go figure) spaniel.

You can connect with me on:

🌐 https://da-smith.co.uk

🐦 https://twitter.com/D_Sauthor

Subscribe to my newsletter:

✉ https://da-smith.co.uk/newsletter-signup

Printed in Great Britain
by Amazon